The Rain Goddess

The Rain Goddess

Peter Stiff

GALAGO

GALAGO BOOKS

Galago Books are published by Galago Publishing (1999) (Pty) Ltd
PO Box 404, Alberton, 1450, Republic of South Africa.
Web address: www.galago.co.za

Galago Books are distributed by Lemur Books (Pty) Ltd
PO Box 1645, Alberton, 1450, Republic South Africa
Tel: (Int +2711 — local 011) 907-2029, Fax: 869-0890
Email: lemur@mweb.co.za

First published in Rhodesia by Jacaranda Press, 1973
First published in Great Britain by New English Library, 1976
Published as a NEL paperback, February 1977
Published in Afrikaans in South Africa as *Die Reëngodin* by Olympos, 1977
First Galago paperback, May 1983
Reprinted, August 1983
This revised edition in trade paperback by Galago, November 2003

Typeset by Galago in 11.4 point Times Roman
Colour correction of cover by Galago
Printed and bound by CTP Book Printers, Cape Town

Front cover designed by Madelain Davies
Cover photograph by unknown photographer

Book by Peter Stiff

Fact
Tommy Goes Home
Selous Scouts: Top Secret War
See You in November
Taming the Landmine
Nine Days of War
The Silent War
Cry Zimbabwe
Warfare by Other Means

Fiction

The Rain Goddess
The Road to Armageddon

Picture Credits

About The Rain Goddess

The Rain Goddess is an explosive novel set in the highly volatile area of Senga on the north-eastern border of Rhodesia (now Zimbabwe) in the mid 1960s and early 1970s. The powerful dram erupts as the British South Africa Police, later joined by the Rhodesian Army and supported by the Air Force, struggle against communist backed guerrillas who use violence and torture to intimidate tribesmen to follow their cause. They fight to restore peace — a peace that is governed as much by force of arms as by the tribesmens' faith in the uncanny predictions of their tribal spirit medium . . . who communes with the spirit of the Rain Goddess.

About the author Peter Stiff and how The Rain Goddess came to be written

In the late 1960s/early 1970s author Peter Stiff was a senior officer in the British South Africa Police, Rhodesia. Internal insurgency combined with major armed guerrilla incursions from Zambia had commenced, but the government played them down to the public at large. In an effort to maintain public morale/ignorance only the police, and latterly regular army soldiers, were deployed on counter-insurgency operations. The government was determined to avoid casualties amongst young national servicemen. Stiff did not subscribe to the view that the public should be kept in the dark. After resigning his commission in 1972 he wrote *The Rain Goddess*, a 'fictional' account of the bush war based on his own experiences and those of his former police comrades. It was impossible to write it as non fiction because this would have carried the sanction of a prosecution under the Official Secrets Act. *The Rain Goddess* served its intended purpose and alerted an amazed Rhodesian public to the undeclared war then raging on its doorstep.

   The Rain Goddess is widely recognised as the classic novel on the Rhodesian Bush War.

Book 1

1

The bushveld on the high escarpment above the Zambezi River Valley was parched and dry in the summer of 1965. It was inhospitable country at the best of times, but before the rains the intense heat reflecting off the rugged ironstone and grey granite kopjes made life miserable for man and beast alike. The spruits and streams that fed the great river were ribbons of dry sand that meandered like long smooth roads through the scorched grass and bush.

A grey Land-Rover with blue inscriptions announcing it to be a vehicle of the District Police, bumped through potholes along the bush road. The heavy-treaded tyres crunched on the gravelled surface and spat out rough fragments of banded ironstone and clear white quartz onto the long, dust-stained grass on the verges. Sometimes along the straights the speed was as high as 50 kilometres per hour, but for most of the time the vehicle merely crawled as the driver manoeuvred it around tight corners between rocky kopjes and through dry stream beds.

'The rain should come soon', grunted Saul Jenkins, casting a glance through the open side window at the cloudless blue sky.

'It is true, *Nkosi*', agreed his black companion. 'By month's end the rains will be here.'

'These bloody flies get me down', said Saul, swatting the squat green maggot fly that had settled on his hairy sun-tanned arm that rested on the window ledge.

'They seem to like the blood of whites better than the blood of blacks', chuckled Ndhlela with a touch of the spontaneous humour that was never far from the surface in his race.

Saul grinned back. 'I don't know why. I suppose it's because there's so many more blacks than whites. I guess they treat my blood as a luxury.'

Sergeant Ndhlela settled back in his seat. He liked Inspector Saul Jenkins, for he was a man he could understand, which was not always the case with the white man. He glanced sideways and studied him for the umpteenth time through half-closed eyes — it would not have been polite by custom to openly stare. His eyes took in the sweat-stained open-necked grey police shirt, which covered powerful shoulders tapered down to a spit-and-polished broad leather Sam Browne belt over the waist of his khaki shorts. Controlling the foot pedals were two muscular, hairy legs which, he knew well from experience, were capable of walking across kilometres of bushland in long loping paces that never seemed to tire their owner.

He had a strong face, thought Ndhlela approvingly. He had stern blue eyes set in strong sun-tanned features. Those were topped by a crop of blond hair that barely showed beneath his cap. He had a compelling personality. To the criminal elements among the tribesmen of Senga, he was a very dangerous man indeed. When he looked at a guilty man it was said that he possessed the power to see right into his soul. Yes, indeed, sighed Ndhlela silently to himself. It was good indeed to serve such a man for the last year of his 35 years' service before he retired. This strange, strong, yet sometimes extrovertly happy young, but old man, of 26 summers, held the position of Inspector-in-Charge of Senga Police. He was responsible for law and order there and in the thousand square kilometres of tribal lands, farms and virgin bush that stretched southwards from the great Zambezi River.

'Are you still retiring to that farm in the purchase area?' Saul interrupted his thoughts.

'Yes, *Nkosi*', nodded Ndhlela. 'It is what I have worked for all my life. For that and my son. The District Commissioner wrote to me two weeks ago and confirmed that the land had been granted to me. It has been surveyed already and the beacons have been put in.' He paused and his light brown, almost Arabic, features lit up. 'My son', he announced with a fierce pride that almost brought a lump to his throat, 'is staying at the farm now. He is on holidays from school and is building a temporary house which we shall live in.'

Saul nodded. He understood Ndhlela well, for he was a Matabele and not from this part of Rhodesia. Matabeleland was where Saul had been born and bred. It was there that he had grown up, learning fluently the dignified slow language of tongue clicks spoken by the proud people who under King Mzilikazi had long ago cut a broad path of blood through less warlike tribes until they settled in that part of Africa that formed the Matabeleland

10

Province of Rhodesia. It was a language he had learned almost simultaneously with his mother tongue. For on the ranch where he was born, there were no white children to play with. Only the black children of his father's farm hands.

'Do you have only one son Ndhlela?'

'Yes, *Nkosi*', Ndhlela replied slowly. 'It is a sadness to me, but my wife died a long time ago during childbirth.'

'You have not married again?' asked Saul.

He looked at the upright man next to him, who showed the stamp of a lifetime of police service by his straight back and the neat black moustache that graced his upper lip.

'No', said Ndhlela shaking his head, 'I have not taken another wife.'

'You have not found the road to do so?' chuckled Saul, laying sly emphasis on the word 'road'. The surname Ndhlela meant just that — road — for Ndlela's people were of the road clan of the old Matabele nation. Not the Royal Matabele — the Kumalo clan who had broken away from the Zulu tyrant Shaka — but one of the warrior factions that was absorbed on the great migration north. 'I suppose', laughed Saul, 'that after you retire you will find yourself one or two young wives with ripe bodies to comfort you in your old age?'

'I will not deny that I have cast my eyes around and been told by some fathers that their daughters won't look unfavourably on the idea of a bride price being negotiated if their suitor owns a farm', replied Ndhlela smugly. 'I may buy a tractor later so that my lands can be ploughed, but the fields will still need weeding. Besides, it is not seemly that a man should live alone. What could I do without wives?'

'So why have you lived alone so long without wives?'

'I am an important man in the black community', said Ndhlela. 'The police law only allows me one wife at a time and having no fields to plough, I felt I could do without.' He shrugged. 'Soon, of course, it will be different. I will not have my uniform to show my standing and who will believe a man's importance and wealth if keeps his money in the bank? The bank, I agree, is a good place to keep one's money, for a thief cannot steal it. But for people to believe in my wealth, they must see young wives at my home and cattle that are more numerous than theirs. If they do not see this for themselves, they will not take me seriously and no one will listen to my counsel.'

'What you say is true. I know your customs', said Saul. 'Haven't things changed somewhat?'

'Yes', said Ndhlela sadly, 'it's true, but it is not as true as many whites believe. You probably believe that young men don't listen to their fathers and with some that is true. There are many young men, and even old men, who listen to the black politicians who say there must be 'one man, one vote' and that we must reclaim our country from the white men. It is such men that cause the trouble, but it is partly your own fault. Don't the teachings of your missionaries tell us to abandon our customs of worshipping our ancestral spirits and that our marriage customs are against the teachings of the Bible?'

'I know this only too well', agreed Saul. 'There have been far too many ignorant men who have tried to get black people to abandon their customs and become black Europeans. It is that sort of teaching that causes men to turn against their chiefs, and daughters to run away from their homes to end up as prostitutes in the towns.'

'I know this, and so do most responsible blacks', said Ndhlela, 'but the politicians make it hard for the people to live in peace.'

'Yes, you and I know that only too well', sighed Saul.

They lapsed into silence, their thoughts almost identical. They remembered the sporadic outbursts of violence in recent years. When many blacks in the towns and country districts had opposed the black nationalist politicians and rabble rousers.

To bring them into line their cattle had been killed or hamstrung and their homes burned, often with the occupants locked inside. Many died although some survived the horrible beatings and mutilations. They learned that in times of unrest it took a brave man to admit that he did not believe in the ways of the radical black nationalists.

So when there was a knock on the door in the middle of the night and a whispered order to attend a secret meeting of the Party, or to contribute to Party funds, few disobeyed although few believed.

For this reason it was usually not long before whispers of renewed nationalist activity came to the ears of the police. Sometimes it was an anonymous letter, sometimes a word in the ear of a black constable on a routine patrol. Then the thugs and trouble-makers were rounded up and gaoled or whisked off to remote restriction areas where they could do no harm to their people.

'The word is that there will be trouble again', said Ndhlela.

'There will be trouble', nodded Saul. 'All the intelligence sources say it will happen and continue until they jam the broadcasts from Zambia that incite violence. Until that happens, the uneducated people will listen.'

*   *   *

Saul noticed a signboard nailed to a creosoted gumpole by the roadside. He slowed down and turned to Ndhlela. 'I would like to inspect this farm of yours. Isn't it down this road?'

Ndhlela smiled and showed his white teeth to best advantage. 'Yes', he said, 'it is about ten kilometres away and I will be honoured to show it to you.'

'Well, let's go then', grinned Saul and turned the Land-Rover onto the side road. 'We're on patrol to see what's going on in the district, so we might just as well start at your place.'

Ndhlela laughed. 'If you are looking for trouble, then my farm will not be the place to find it. My son will see to that. He knows what to do. He keeps a sharp spear behind the door of his sleeping hut.' Ndhlela looked at Saul's big physique. 'He is not as big as you are, *Nkosi*, but he fears no one.'

'I'm glad to hear it', laughed Saul. 'It's nice to know that there is someone I can rely on to see off the troublemakers. What's this boy of yours going to do later — will he work the farm with you?'

Ndhlela shook his grey flecked head, 'No, *Nkosi*, although the farm will be his one day. All men need land of their own to contemplate on. But until his retirement he intends to be a doctor.'

'A doctor!' exclaimed Saul with surprise. 'That's a very worthwhile profession.'

'It is indeed', said Ndhlela simply. 'Of course it will not be for a while yet. He is still at Senga Mission and it will require a lot more study before he qualifies for the university in Salisbury.'

'Good', said Saul. 'The country will need a lot more men like your son in the future.'

Shortly afterwards they came to cultivated lands lying unplanted, waiting for the first summer rains. The great Zambezi River flowed deep in the valley beyond some 90 kilometres away. These were the last human settlements before the river was reached. No man lived in the valley, for it was the home of the stinging tsetses fly, the carrier of the dreaded sleeping sickness. Down there the elephant was king, ruling over the buffalo, lion and the other big game of Africa. Because they were born with the fly, they

13

were immune to its bite. Not that game always remained obediently in the valley. When the fields in the occupied areas were green with succulent new crops, elephants became frequent visitors on the look-out for titbits. If they stayed too long, then a tough ranger of the Rhodesian Game Department would appear with his rifle, shoot one to make the point and drive the rest back into their own wild domain.

Ndhlela pointed to a group of conical pole huts thatched with long veld grass a few hundred metres away. 'My farm', he announced, and hastened to explain. 'The huts you see are only temporary. When I retire, I will mould and burn bricks to construct a proper farmhouse. Meanwhile, those simple structures will have to do.'

Saul nodded and pointed to a figure by the huts. The man was swinging an axe into a pile of felled timber. Stacked next to him was a heap of white wood chopped neatly into firewood. 'Your son?'

'Yes, my son', agreed Ndhlela, leaning out of the vehicle window and waving excitedly. The figure stood up and resting on the long haft of his axe, he gave a return wave. Saul gave the horn two quick hoots to assist Ndhlela's waving. The boy loped down the road towards them. Saul saw what Ndhlela had meant. He stood at least 1.8 metres tall, although his figure, in common with most of his race, was not as heavily built as Saul's, but it was well proportioned and muscular. As he neared Saul saw there was a striking family resemblance. Father and son shared the same coffee-coloured features. The ready grin on the boy's face accented rather than hid the bright intelligent look that gleamed from his dark brown eyes.

Ndhlela alighted as the vehicle stopped. Father and son embraced and conversed excitedly in Sindebele. Saul eased his long legs out of the Land-Rover and stretched his arms to overcome the fatigue of the journey.

Ndhlela, remembering his manners, brought his son around the vehicle and presented him to Saul.

'My son, *Nkosi*', he said proudly.

The young Matabele looked evenly at the white man — a white man who was as African as he. His ancestors had arrived on the continent with the first English settlers in the year 1820. His stock had also proved their fighting qualities in long-forgotten battles that had raged between white men and black men, and white men and white men, over the wide veld of southern Africa and in more recent years, across the green fields of Europe.

The two young men liked what they saw. Saul held out his hand in friendship. 'I see you, son of Ndhlela', he said in the fluent idiomatic speech

14

of the black man's tongue.

'I see you *Nkosi*', replied Kephas, son of Ndhlela. With a broad, friendly grin he took Saul's hand and shook it firmly.

'Your father speaks well of you', grinned Saul. 'He says that one day you will be a successful doctor in Salisbury, but that until then you will defend his farm against any troublemakers who care to come here.'

'My father says a lot of things', agreed Kephas, 'and what he says is the truth, although he sometimes tends to exaggerate his son's capabilities.' He looked fondly at Ndhlela. 'Isn't that true, my father?'

'Fathers don't exaggerate', said Ndhlela evenly. 'They merely see things that the young and less wise are incapable of seeing.'

'Let us hope that's so', replied Kephas cheerfully, reverting to an educated English. 'What brings you here, father?'

Ndhlela nodded at Saul. 'We're spending a few days in the tribal lands to see if any troublemakers have come from Salisbury to stir up strife amongst the people.'

Kephas frowned and looked levelly at Saul. 'There is a lot of talk at the beer drinks about this Declaration of Independence that the government has made. There are whispers of trouble, but I think this is because news has come through of disturbances elsewhere in the country. No one has said anything to me, but that does not mean that nothing is being planned.' He straightened his shoulders. 'I am a Matabele and not of the Mashona tribe, so it's possible that people will not talk to me because they might distrust me.'

Saul looked at Kephas with the trained eye of a policeman. He saw no signs to indicate the boy was lying. He looked away towards the distant hazy hills of the escarpment to the north.

'Your father says you keep a spear ready in case troublemakers come during the night.'

Kephas nodded at one of the huts. 'Yes, I keep it to prick the flesh of anyone who is brave enough to come here and cause trouble. But I am sure they'll not bother me', he said confidently.

Saul chuckled at the brash confidence of youth. He slapped Kephas heartily on the back. 'I hope you will live up to the confidence you display if you are put to the test.'

'He will, *Nkosi*, he will', predicted Ndhlela. 'My son is a man and will not be led astray by the foolishness of others.

Kephas watched the cloud of red dust fade into the distance. It marked the progress of the Land-Rover on its way to the tribal lands adjacent to the block of African-owned farms. The tribal lands were different from the farms because there the land belonged to the tribe, as distinct from the farms where ownership was vested in the individual.

In the tribal areas the chief allocated land to his subjects according to tribal rights vested in him by the tribal spirits — and with the approval of the District Commissioner. The all-powerful spirits manifested themselves when needed through the living bodies of selected individuals. They used those mortals' bodies until their temporary spiritual home died. For death came to all men sooner or later. The tribal spirits controlled the daily life of the tribe. To them, regular offerings were made to ensure that the rains were good and substantial and that the spirits of their forefathers rested easily in the land of the shadows.

He turned away when the truck had disappeared, walked slowly to the hut that served as a kitchen and slowly kindled a fire on which to cook his supper. He frowned thoughtfully as the flames flickered over the kindling and gradually took hold. It was almost dark so he lit a candle and dripped hot wax on to a box and squashed the base of the candle into it. He blinked as the hut filled with smoke from the newly lit fire. When the flames took hold, the smoke gradually diminished as it filtered through the roof thatch and curled up into the sky.

He squatted on the floor and stared moodily at the fire. It was lonely staying on the farm by himself, but it would not be for long as he soon had to return to the mission. His father would have to employ someone to look after the place until his retirement. The night was hot and sticky and there was still no sign of rain. What he had told his father and Saul was only true to a point. When he was not working he frequently went to the tribal lands to sit at the beer drinks and drink with the men. There were indeed signs of trouble in the air. He had heard talk that prosperous men, with the hard light of fanaticism in their eyes, had been visiting the area from Salisbury. At the beer drinks it was said they had come to tell the people what to do. He had not told his father because he knew it might cause trouble for them both.

His father was too old to understand the situation and he had been a policeman too long. Kephas was not so naive as to believe that if people concluded they were government spies, they would not be driven from the area. No, thought Kephas, it was better to say nothing and keep out of the way of both the troublemakers and the police. Perhaps then they would be left alone.

Before he went to bed that night, he checked that a clean shirt was in the cupboard. On Sunday he intended to go to Mandizwidza's village in the tribal lands. The attraction was more than the drums of sour beer that had been brewing for a week and which would have matured to excellence by then. There was also Tandiwe — the loved one — the daughter of Mandizwidza who had taken his fancy when he had first moved to the area. He knew by her shy looks that his interest had not passed unnoticed.

Anyway, he thought cheerfully, he had another good excuse to go there. As his father was leaving, he had pressed money into his hand and instructed him to look out for a good milk cow. Mandizwidza was renowned for his cattle as well as for his beautiful daughter.

2

The house was of a type common in the Rhodesian country districts, and there was little to distinguish it from those on a dozen different farms within a 30-kilometre radius of the mission. It was built for permanence, with thick walls of native granite rising from rough concrete foundations in the red soil. It was not an architect-designed residence and it rambled from the main section that had originally been constructed by long-forgotten missionaries, into a more recent section where one big bedroom led into newer gabled extensions.

There were no ceilings because they were expensive and it was not the custom of the missionaries to spend money unnecessarily on themselves. Their money was put to better use tending to the welfare of the people they were trying to wean, against ancient custom, from the spiritual worship of their ancestors to the teachings of the one true God. Yet, the absence of ceilings did not make the house uncomfortable because the long straight beams of the eucalyptus gum — which crisscrossed the roof and on which thick layers of dry veld grass was matted into thatch — made them unnecessary. Though the ground outside was baking in the heat of the highveld summer, and men sweated out their energy even when they were not occupied with physical work, inside it was cool. It was a coolness that people longed for before the rains, but when the icy winds blew in the winter months of June and July, the coolness disappeared and the house became cosy and warm.

Yet the man who had built the house and the man and woman who lived there, would never have considered the house comfortable, for comfort was not for them. It was an abomination for man to seek worldly comforts, for his life span on earth was but a brief spark in the endless light that was Eternity. This belief was emphasised by the austere furnishings of the house. It appeared to have been provided for the sole purpose of forcing those using them to suffer the discomforts of the flesh. Most of the chairs were wooden, with hard upright backs. Even more uncomfortable were objects that might once have been comfortable easy chairs, but were now old and misshapen. Similarly the beds were boarded and covered with thin straw pallets. The flagged and cemented floors were unsoftened by carpets or rugs.

'Surely, Brother Abraham', protested a visiting dignitary from the home of the Brethren in Pennsylvania, 'it must be right to be pious, but are beds as hard as these a necessary factor when one is seeking salvation?'

Abraham Hale made it quite clear to the abashed elder that even if his Brothers and Sisters in America decided that God would not hold the use of inner-sprung mattresses against them on Judgement Day, only the kind of bedding once used in that manger in the faraway Holy Land was suitable for the Hale household.

Abraham's unbending discipleship had so impressed the committee that they had not bothered to send out another fact-finding mission for almost five years. They merely sent money. Not just a thin trickle of money, but thousands and thousands of dollars worth that had been compulsorily docked from the wage packets of those less dedicated members of the Church who hadn't the courage to venture from the shores of the United States to carry the word of God to Africa's heathen.

What happened to this money? Very little was spent on the persons of Abraham and Mary Hale — only sufficient to keep them from starving and to ensure their appearance was decent enough to impress the less fortunate members of their flock. The rest was used to build school rooms and hostels at the mission and to feed their students' perpetually hungry young bellies. The mission was big business and, as every businessman knows, the overheads of big business swallows up large amounts of capital — particularly since they only demanded fees from the students that they could afford. So the fat dollar cheques from Pennsylvania were absorbed almost as soon as they arrived.

Abraham and Mary sat on a garden bench and sipped tea. The garden was a luxury they both enjoyed. Over the years it had grown like an oasis from the almost magical touch of Mary's green fingers. The rolling green lawns and deep beds of brilliantly coloured summer flowers fell outside the realms of sin. A garden was the work of God, as were the numerous birds that made it their home. The backdrop of song they created sometimes broke into a rackety hubbub of outraged twittering when a silent boomslang invaded their nesting areas in search of a succulent meal of eggs or fledglings.

The Hales were at peace, for the summer holidays had begun and the students had gone home in a banging and hooting caterwaul of young voices. This left the mission deserted until classes re-assembled in January. It seemed strangely silent amongst the rows of deserted classrooms, thatched dormitories that matched the main homestead and the houses of the black teachers who had also departed for their homes in various parts of the country.

Everyone, that is, except for Mr Madziwa, a housemaster who was remaining at the mission for the duration of the holidays.

*   *   *

Abraham sighed and straightened his stringy shoulders that were starting to droop from the intense December heat. Black trousers held up by a thick, worn leather belt bagged loosely over his tight barely protruding buttocks. His shirt was thick and heavy, more suitable to the cold climes of the Atlantic coast of his home continent, but it was a kind he had worn since he was a child.

He didn't wear a 'dog collar', because that wasn't the way of the Brethren, but as a concession to the heat and the fact that the school was empty of pupils, his jacket had been consigned to a hanger in the house. His features, although thin in a way that matched his body, were the sort that men remembered. Perhaps it was the determined set to his mouth and the serious, almost permanent frown below his short, prematurely grey hair which gave his face character. It was clear that Abraham was a man with a purpose.

He looked at Mary kindly. 'Is everything in readiness for our visitor?'

Mary smiled placidly at her husband, and for a moment the click-clacking of her knitting needles ceased for a moment. Mary was still in love with Abraham, although their arranged marriage had taken place 20 years before, when she was just a girl of 18.

'Yes', she said, 'everything is ready for him. I only need to turn down the bedcovers. Supper is ready to serve.'

'Good', said Abraham, with a note of satisfaction in his voice. 'We must make a good impression on this man because the work we will be doing together will be work of God.'

'Is he a man of God himself?'

'No, he's not', said Abraham. He smiled at Mary and for a moment a worried frown flitted across her face. Her husband looked worn out. Although barely 48, his tired features made him appear ten years older.

'No, he is not a man of God. But', he paused reflectively, 'he is a friend of Mr Madziwa who tells me he is a good man.'

'What does he do?' asked Mary, her needles beginning to click out a regular beat again. She was the exact opposite of her husband in appearance. He was tall and thin and almost always on the righteous side of the unforgiving. She was barely a metre and a half tall, with ample proportions and a full bosom that seemed to signal the extreme forgiveness of her gentle nature. That nature almost shone through her fair scrubbed features — free of make-up. The use of cosmetics was a sin and against their religious beliefs.

'Mr Madziwa tells me our visitor has dedicated his life to fighting for the rights of his people.'

'Sounds wonderful', said Mary, 'as long as he is not a troublemaker.' She looked anxiously at her husband. 'Does he work peacefully?'

His face again relaxed into a smile and he shook his head. 'No, I'm sure he is not a troublemaker. Mr Madziwa assures me that Mr Gumede is a man who believes only in peace. That is what we want as well', he said with deep meaning. Violence of any sort was against the belief of the Brethren and they would not raise a hand even in self-defence — even to protect their families. For God looks after the faithful and He always provides.

'Why is he coming to see you?' asked Mary. 'What does he want?' She looked past the green lushness of the garden to the dusty gravel road beyond. Like a strip of brown paper tape, it unwound through the matted bush and the hot rocky hills until it joined the main road to Senga village 32 kilometres away and Salisbury 240 kilometres beyond that.

'Mr Madziwa says money is needed for the cause.'

'Why should he need money?' queried Mary who had always thought intuitively, which she had never disclosed to Abraham, that Mr Madziwa was not to be trusted.

'People always need money', sighed Abraham. 'If we, the Brethren, don't give money to these people who are fighting for their people's rights, then others will, perhaps with more strings attached.' He looked at Mary who listened attentively with her knitting needles poised over her lap. 'The money we give goes with the love of the Lord. That will ensure the money is used to gain men's rights in a peaceful way. Mr Madziwa has assured me that Mr Gumede is a man who would never countenance the use of violence to further his cause. He believes that passive resistance is the only way to confront a government that refuses to recognise the rightful aspirations of its people. He and his comrades will win their country from the white man in the same way as Mahatma Gandhi freed India from the thraldom of the British.'

'I hope you're right', said Mary, her eyes fixing on the wide cloud of dust in the distance that signalled the approach of their expected visitor's car.

*   *   *

It was late in the evening and for a moment while the conversation paused, the only sound to be heard in the missionaries' lounge was the hissing of the pressure lamp hanging from a beam over their heads. The light was uneven because a horde of flying insects brought out by the hot night, buzzed about the glass-enclosed flame creating shadows that danced on the whitewashed walls. Mary had retired to bed long before.

Simon Gumede wriggled his fat soft buttocks on the hard uncomfortable chair and wished the talking would end. His tie was loose at the neck of his expensive silk shirt and although it was late, it was hot enough to cause an almost continuous dribble of sweat to run down his fleshy neck and on to his collar. His nose wrinkled distastefully, for Gumede was not a man who neglected his toiletry and the still air carried the message that neither Abraham nor Madziwa were in the habit of using deodorants.

He smiled politely at Abraham. His smile was open and honest, but it was also carefully cultivated. He would have been surprised to know that Mary had already classified his eyes as 'cruel'. In fact, it was better that Gumede did not know, because he had always firmly believed he had the ability to fool all of the people all of the time — instead of some of the people for just some of the time.

'Can you make $10 000 available to the cause, Reverend?' he asked, licking his lips just at the sound of so much money. From the corner of his eye he noticed the look of greed reflecting on the flat black features of Madziwa. He would certainly never get his hands on any of it. He, Simon Gumede, would make sure of that!

'Yes, I think I can do that', agreed Abraham cautiously. He was troubled by doubts that he knew he could resolve only by prayer. Would the fat and well-kept man in the obviously $100 suit opposite him keep his word? Would the money really be used only to promote freedom by peaceful means?

Abraham saw that the two men who were watching him expectantly. He glanced towards the flickering light of the lamp.

'We must go on our knees and pray to God', he decided, looking for a sign that would give him an insight into their innermost thoughts. But he saw nothing.

He slipped off the chair onto his knees and saw Gumede and Madziwa follow suit. His lips pursed in satisfaction when he took in their pious attitudes. However, in the case of Gumede, it was really a look of dismay at having to kneel on the floor in his immaculately pressed suit trousers.

'God our Father. Give us, your humble servants, guidance . . .' droned Abraham in a prayer that Madziwa knew would last for at least half an hour. He looked through half-closed eyes at Gumede who was kneeling uncomfortably next to him, but he didn't get a return glance. Madziwa could scarcely contain himself. Just think — US$10 000 . . . phew! Who would have thought that old Hale would come across with so much? Sure some of it must come to him as the Party leader at Senga.

Madziwa was still a young man, but he had high ambitions. He was barely 30 and he certainly didn't wish to spend his life teaching at a mission school. He wanted to be someone important like Simon Gumede. He wistfully compared his old jacket hanging on his big muscular body, with the elegant suit that draped the full, fat figure of Gumede. His mouth went dry with excitement. One day, he decided, he would also be a big man in the Party. After all, wasn't it he who had persuaded Gumede to come out to see this old fool in the first place?

Gumede was not listening to the prayer either, although he was too old a campaigner to jeopardise the large sum on offer by showing any sign that he was not as deeply religious as he pretended to be. He lightly clasped his smooth hands in front of his face and silently admired his immaculately manicured nails. He shot a quick glance at Abraham whose eyes were turned to the thatch roof as he earnestly sought guidance. Gumede smiled slyly. The missionary had obviously taken the bait. He was like a fish in the river that was beginning to nibble. It was now the fisherman's job to keep him nibbling until the right time to strike and haul him in. Then, he thought, mentally patting himself on the back, he would land this big fish.

Gumede was a clever man. He had come a long way since that nasty moment some years ago when he had been convicted of theft and sent to prison. He had been working as a wage clerk for a big construction company. Even in those days he had expensive tastes and was extremely ambitious. It had not been easy to live the way he wanted on the money he had been paid — even though he enjoyed a good salary. Girls only looked at men who had money and he found this intolerable. It was good to have plenty of money. With money you could have everything you wanted — good clothes, good food and, of course, the most beautiful women. Poverty had not been to his liking then and it most certainly was not to his liking now.

At first it had been easy. Just the odd fictitious daily paid labourer ghosted on to the wage sheets. Each month that little extra money had come in handy and for the first few months he had not been greedy. But soon that money became a necessity to finance the high life he was enjoying. As the months went by, more fictitious names appeared on the wage sheets and he was living well above his visible means. His fatal mistake was buying that new car. Perhaps the purchase alone would have been all right, but he should never have started coming to work in it. That's why his employer called for an audit. By then, of course, he had become overconfident and had begun to feel that the extra money was rightfully his anyway.

At the time of committing it, the swindle had seemed so sophisticated. Yet, when he was confronted by it in court, the evidence made it appear clumsy and obvious.

The sentence of six months' imprisonment with hard labour had been a hard blow, even though the magistrate had shown extraordinary leniency considering the large sums of money he had stolen. If he had not been a first offender, he would probably have been given a sentence three times as long. But it was this prison sentence that became the turning point in his life.

While in prison he had met a senior member of the Party. He had no job to go to and nowhere to live when he finished his sentence. It had accordingly not taken much persuasion on the part of the Party member to get him to join the Party.

Once out of prison he had found life incredibly easy. You could say whatever you liked at the meetings and promise people anything they wanted. He soon found that people loved being promised things that they thought were unattainable. Naturally, a collection plate was passed around at the end of the meetings. The more fantastic the promises, the more generous were the people — and the Party needed money. Besides that, the speakers had to live on something.

Yes, life had become much more than just comfortable.

There had been a bad moment in 1959 when the government noticed that the cry of 'one man — one vote' had become a serious threat to the security of the country and that they were on the verge of losing control. The black masses in Northern Rhodesia and Nyasaland — as Zambia and Malawi were called in those days — were crying out for majority rule and Rhodesia was caught in the whirlpool.

The Party was declared an unlawful organisation and for a time Gumede found himself in restriction. He was a model restrictee, however, and after a year he was released as rehabilitated.

Once free, he found that the Party had been resuscitated under a new name. It was banned three more times over the next few years, but each time made a return performance under different colours — but with the same old office-bearers.

After 1959 Gumede had been very careful, as he had no desire to lose his freedom again. He had suggested craftily to his superiors that, with his experience, it would be better for the Party if he remained in the background. They recognised his capabilities and readily agreed that he should confine his activities to administrative matters.

Since then he had made certain that he gave the authorities no reason to clamp down on him. The Party kept him well supplied with money and he trod a very careful tightrope.

Party activity became more feverish when Rhodesia unilaterally declared her independence in November 1965. He had been forced to take a more open role or lose his credibility. It was then that he had been allocated the Senga district to act as organiser for the trouble that was to come. Through this he had met the local leader, Madziwa, and through him, this goose.

He glanced at the Reverend Hale who had really warmed up in his address to the heavens. He was sure now that this goose would lay him a US$10 000 golden egg. He experienced a secure, comfortable feeling as he worked out how he would spend the large portion he intended to milk off for himself, either before or after it was given to the Party.

3

Kephas arrived at Mandizwidza's village long after the beer drink had started, even though it was only 8 o'clock in the morning. From more than a kilometre away he had heard the drums beating and the singing as the people danced.

There were about forty people present when he arrived, more than half were women. At this time of the year most of the men were away working in the towns, while their womenfolk stayed at home in the villages to tend to the huts, the crops and watch for the rains. Most of the men there didn't live in the village, but had come from far away on the usual round of Sunday visiting, which was the custom and pleasure of the African people.

He greeted Mandizwidza. He was seated on a large old fallen tree trunk, which had long ago been dragged into the shade of a gnarled mimosa thorn to serve as a seat at beer drinks and for tribal meetings at this, the Dari or meeting place.

Mandizwidza acknowledged the formal greeting with a wave. He had already drunk six mugs of beer and was too engrossed in watching the dancers shuffling to and fro on the sunbaked, hard packed soil in front of him to care much for serious conversation.

Kephas looked distastefully at Mandizwidza, for even though he was attracted to his daughter, he didn't like the man. He was not an old man — perhaps about fifty — yet he was old in his ways and was frequently befuddled by the beer that he swilled at every opportunity. His features were thin and bird-like, as was the rest of his skinny frame. However, what Kephas disliked most was that he smelled. Even the old khaki longs and red shirt that he habitually wore looked as if they were rarely subjected to the indignity of laundering. His wives — two of them— were as dirty as he was, but they were corpulent and bloated in direct contrast to his emaciated figure. They were also just as drunk as he was.

26

Kephas looked around for Tandiwe, but he couldn't see her.

Two youths, about his own age, waved to him from the other side of the circle and he returned their greeting. They were Job, the youngest son of Mandizwidza, and his friend Matavi, the son of Kambula of a nearby village. Kephas threaded his way through the merrymakers and joined them under the eaves of a thatched hut.

'Is it us or my sister you have come to see?' grinned Job, a thin looking boy of about eighteen, who looked a lot like his father but without the ingrained marks of dissipation that showed on the face of his parent.

'I think it's Tandiwe that he's come to see, rather than us', said Matavi. He was a serious looking lad whose face was deeply marked by scald scars caused when a pot of boiling water on a cooking fire had fallen on him when he was an infant.

'You could be right', agreed Kephas cheerfully. He looked around. 'Where is she?'

'I don't know', said Job jocularly. 'Surely women can wait until the men have finished their drinking.'

'I suppose so', said Kephas, squatting down next to Job. He nodded in the direction of Mandizwidza. 'I also need to see your father about buying a cow.'

Job laughed and heaved himself to his feet. 'I'll get you some beer.' He eyed his father who was laughing drunkenly with his cronies. 'As you can see, I don't think it's the right day to discuss the merits of cattle with him.'

'I suppose not', grinned Kephas. 'Are you going to get that beer or shall I go and get it myself?'

*   *   *

The sun was high in the sky and was starting to move gradually west from the 12 o'clock position. Kephas was beginning to feel the effects of drinking for the past four hours. His friends were in a worse state.

'The police are at the rest camp near the village of the chief', announced Job secretively, looking around him before speaking.

'Are they?' retorted Matavi. 'What for?'

Kephas looked silently down and drew patterns in the dust with a twig. It was, of course, his father and Inspector Jenkins camped at the chief's place, but he didn't want to say this because he didn't want it widely known that his father was a policeman.

'Yes', said Job, leaning forward conspiratorially, 'I think they have suspicions about the meeting.'

'Meeting?' asked Kephas in surprise. 'What meeting?'

'The meeting that is to take place tonight in the bush near the hill known as Shumba — the lion', said Job darkly.

'What is all this about?' asked Kephas, a feeling of dread in his stomach. He somehow knew the already.

'I suppose it's a meeting to plan action', replied Matavi knowingly. 'I have heard from boys at school about such meetings happening in other areas. They're usually to tell people what they can do to win our country back from the white man.'

Kephas laughed drunkenly. 'Win our country from the white man?' he sneered. 'That's just so much nonsense. All these men will do is bring you trouble from the police. I have heard that they live with fat whores in big houses in Salisbury and Bulawayo on the cash they collect from the uneducated people in the tribal areas.'

'You laugh', warned Job seriously, looking in alarm at the people nearby to make sure that none had heard Kephas who was speaking over loudly because of the liquor, 'but not everyone who listens to the Party is stupid. They say we must stand together and drive the white men out. Then all their houses and farms will be ours. Maybe we could keep their women', he continued thoughtfully. 'I have often wondered what one of those cool looking white women you see in *Scope* magazine would be like in bed.'

It was Kephas' turn to become alarmed. 'That sort of talk will only bring you trouble', he said firmly. 'Besides, you cannot say that all white men are our enemies. Perhaps some of them have treated people badly at one time or another, but most of them respect us now.'

'But why should they be rich when we blacks are poor?' chipped in Matavi. 'Tell me that, if you like the white man so much.'

'It's not that I like the white man so much', Kephas denied indignantly, 'but I don't see that we should steal what belongs to them. There are a lot of rich blacks as well.'

'Rubbish', muttered Job, a hint of annoyance in his voice. 'They stole the land from us in the first place.'

'They did not steal it', said Kephas, also getting annoyed. 'They won it in battle from Lobengula, the last Matabele king. It was Matabele land and they fought for it.'

'What do you mean the land belonged to the Matabele? This is

Mashonaland, the land of the Mashonas', interjected Matavi. 'Who do you
. . .?'

'What I say is true. The Mashonas might have lived here, but no Mashona
ever moved without the approval of the Matabele.'

Kephas had thrown all caution to the wind and the beer made him forget
himself, but he was sobered by Job's next words which were thrust at him
like a knife.

'So you are a sellout! A traitor to your own people. A man who thinks
more of the white man than he does of his own people. If this gets around
there are people in the area, who will want to deal with you.' The threat was
unmistakable.

Kephas cursed his loose tongue. Why hadn't he shut up? He didn't want
to get involved, yet his mouth had run away with him because of the beer.

Job ignored Kephas and turned to Matavi. 'Are we going to the meeting
tonight or do you think this sellout will run to his police friends and report
us?'

'There is no question of me doing that . . .' protested Kephas. He knew
only too well what the likely consequences would be if the police heard
about the meeting. And the consequences if Job or Matavi reported to the
Party that it was likely he had informed the police?

'If there is no question of what', interrupted Matavi grimly. 'You have to
show us whose side you are on by coming to the meeting.'

'But when we first spoke about it, you did not even intend going
yourselves?' Kephas spoke quietly and reasonably in an attempt to restore
a conversational note to the proceedings. 'You said that the police are
camped near the chief's place. What will happen to us if they come and
break up the meeting?'

'Matavi and I are definitely going', said Job firmly.

Matavi nodded. 'If you wish to be welcome here in the future, you had
better come with us.'

Kephas pondered on his self imposed predicament. The consequences of
refusing could be disastrous. In fact, the least of it would be Job using his
influence to stop him seeing Tandiwe.

Job brightened up and slapped his back in a display of drunken
comradery. 'What are you worried about? It's only a meeting. We don't
have to do what they say. It's not a bad thing to listen to them. There will
be a lot of people there. We are young and can run fast, so if the police
come they will only catch the old men and will not get near us.' He looked

at Kephas expectantly.

'All right', agreed Kephas with reluctance. 'I'll go with you.' He stifled his misgivings.

'Go where?' enquired a soft voice behind him. Kephas turned in confusion and saw the sweet countenance of Tandiwe — the main reason for his visit.

'Nowhere', said Job evasively. 'It's not the place of women to question what men do.' Tandiwe looked suitably abashed.

Job and Matavi looked questioningly at Kephas. 'Tonight then?' asked Job.

'Yes, tonight.'

'Good, then we will leave you to talk to my sister.'

Job grinned at Kephas, but a hint of coolness remained behind the smile.

*   *   *

Tandiwe and Kephas watched Job and Matavi wander off to where the drums were beating. He smiled at Tandiwe.

'What are you doing now?'

'I am going to the stream to fetch water.' She smiled invitingly. 'Would you like to come?'

'Yes', he said glancing quickly at her father, but he was otherwise engaged. 'Leave now and I'll follow you', he breathed.

'Shortly then', she whispered, her voice full of promise.

She moved away through the huts and ten minutes later Kephas found her at the well. She was pumping water into paraffin tins by hand. The carrying of water was the never-ending task of the village women. It was part of a daily round of labour that for them never ceased.

In spite of having just seen him, she shyly greeted him again, curtseying to the superior being who was man — even if he was only a 18-year-old man. He took the pump handle and worked it up and down. She glanced at him but said nothing. She placed the five empty tins at the pump outlet one by one and captured the clear water that bubbled and gurgled from the depths. The well was dug into the bank of a spruit, that only flowed when the rains came. Below the surface, however, there was plenty of water to be pumped up. When the tins were full, she broke leafy twigs from bushes nearby and placed them on top of the water to stop the water from spilling on the way back. The village was about 300 metres away, on higher ground.

He walked beside her while she carried the receptacles one by one back to the huts. They balanced easily on her head. He made no effort to help her for, as a man, it wasn't proper to assist. In fact, Tandiwe would have been astonished had he offered.

Tandiwe was a beautiful girl in the flower of youth. Her skin was a delicate brown, indicating her pure central African ancestry, for none of the tribes in these parts were as black as the men from the north-west coast of the great continent. She barely came up to his shoulder. Her short, curly hair was covered by a pretty floral patterned scarf. Her dress was old and of loose sun bleached cotton. Beneath it, her small virgin breasts were firm and as she walked, her nipples pushed out the thin material. She was shoeless and walked with an upright posture — a posture that would be the envy of her sophisticated white sisters who paid good money to learn how to walk with a couple of books balanced on their heads. She carried the paraffin tins easily, hardly ever finding it necessary to put her hands up to steady the load.

She did not know her birth date age, but she knew she had been born some sixteen seasons before. Her father, if asked, would not have known the year either, but he could say it was the season of the good rains, when the crops had been the best in living memory and his black bull had died.

Similarly, he didn't know the year he had himself come into the world. His father had told him it was several seasons before the year of the influenza. He would not have displayed any interest if he had been told that the year of the great influenza epidemic was in late 1918, about when the Great War ground to a bloody halt. To him dates were unimportant. A girl became a woman when she commenced regular appointments with the moon, and a boy became a man when he gained the capability to break that appointment.

Kephas knew his age. The white corporal in charge of the police camp where Ndhlela was stationed had written it on a piece of paper and stamped it with the station date stamp. Ndhlela had kept this yellowed fragment with its faded ink and had shown it to Kephas once he was old enough to read.

When her water-carrying chores were finished, they wandered away from the beating drums of the beer drink. They walked hand in hand, as young lovers do, before the tenderness of youth is lost to the harsh realities of life, which comes as people grow into mature adults.

'Where are you going with Job?' asked Tandiwe, with the curiosity natural to her sex — a curiosity she had been trying to hide since she had overheard the conversation between the three boys.

31

'Nowhere', said Kephas moodily.

'It must be somewhere', insisted Tandiwe.

Kephas let go of her hand. 'I said nowhere, woman. Didn't you hear your brother well? Not everything that's done concerns women.'

Tandiwe was suitably abashed, but a niggling worry persisted. She soon forgot this when Kephas recovered his cheerfulness and again took her small hand in his.

When they were a distance from the village they sat down and talked. He spoke of his future ambitions and how he intended to go far in the world. She listened quietly, as was the place of a woman, while he talked at length. She had liked Kephas from the day he had first visited her village. She was nevertheless shy. It had been easy once to chase and wrestle with boys, but the thought of Kephas' arms about her now brought a hot flush to her face. She had never made love to a man. Her thoughts were not at all ladylike as she wondered what sort of lover Kephas would be. She could see by the bulge in the tight front of his trousers and by the quick, furtive glances he was giving her that his thoughts were not entirely on the business of his future career. Her eyes remained downcast while he spoke in case he guessed her thoughts. She started once in confusion when she realised that although she was looking down, the direction of her gaze made her far from demure. She redirected her gaze to some scurrying black ants.

She thought perhaps she was showing more leg than she should and observed that this was not lost on Kephas. Tandiwe decided not to adjust her skirt. She had summed him up pretty well, and decided that should he want her, she would not object to becoming his wife. She guessed that with all his talk of the future, he was sounding out her own feelings.

Tribal custom did not demand love as a prerequisite for marriage, but after all it was better if she chose a man who was both acceptable to her father and whom she could love.

Kephas stopped talking and they sat in silence. They stared about them in embarrassed silence, wondering what to say.

The statement, when it came, surprised them both. Certainly Kephas had no inkling he was going to say it when he did.

'I will be leaving school soon and will be going to university. Later I will need a wife. Will you be that wife?'

She felt a cool shock of feminine satisfaction that she hid from him with a deliberately demure and downcast look. She carefully chose her words before replying. She didn't want to appear too eager, but at the same time didn't wish to give the impression that she was unwilling, or that she didn't care for him.

'I would not object if my father told me that I must marry a man like you, Kephas. You know this is true, don't you?'

'Yes, I know', he said tenderly.

'Perhaps though', she said thoughtfully, 'you would not want me later on. It's not that I am uneducated, but I don't know if I have enough education to live in Salisbury in a big house as the wife of a doctor.'

'Of course you have', said Kephas emphatically. 'Anyway, I would be able to teach you anything you didn't know.'

'You wouldn't get tired of me?'

He smiled at her doubts and playfully touched her nose with his finger. 'No, woman, I wouldn't get tired of you. I love you. I suppose I have loved you from the day I first saw you. And you', he said firmly, turning her face with his hand so that she was forced to look into his eyes, 'have loved me since then as well.'

'Have I?' she smiled.

'Yes.'

He slid his arm around her waist and rested his hand below her breast. She felt the warmth of his fingers as they lightly touched her bosom. She shivered slightly as an amazing sensation stole over her body. His hand pressured her in an inexpert but delightful way and after a short pause, stole on to her virgin breast. They both stared wordlessly ahead as his fingers fondled her firm nipple. They were too shy to look at each other.

Kephas felt his maleness rising to the challenge of this woman, who was really still a girl. He moved closer to her.

Her hand wrenched his free, taking him by surprise. In a flash she was on her feet and running barefoot back towards the kraal, laughing and giggling as she went. Momentarily Kephas was stunned, but he recovered and was on his feet and running in pursuit. His long strides were more than a match for hers and within 50 metres he caught her shoulder and slowed her to a halt. Her giggling stopped abruptly and they looked deep into each other's eyes. There was no longer anything to laugh at. She knew that she could not resist this man who had given her his heart.

Her tongue swiftly passed over her lips, moistening them and leaving a thin glistening film. His face came closer and then they were embracing wildly. Now she could not stop him, even if she wanted to. She revelled in his maleness as he crushed her in his arms. She pressed her lips against his and felt the hardness of his masculinity returning the pressure. His hands explored her body, passing down her hips to the skirt of her dress. Then his hands were stroking her smooth legs . . .

4

It had been dark for a long time when Kephas, Job and Matavi arrived at the meeting place deep in the bush. There were at least 80 men standing around in small groups by big blazing fires that had been kindled to provide light.

No one took any notice of them and they stood together, occasionally breaking the silence with a forced joke that prompted no one to laugh.

They had been there about an hour when Matavi looked at his watch. 'Nearly eight o'clock. If the meeting doesn't start soon, then I suppose we'd better go home.'

Kephas said nothing, but he was hoping that Job would agree with the suggestion.

'Yes, I think you're right', said Job yawning. 'It doesn't seem as if anything is going to happen tonight.' He looked at Kephas. 'What do you think?'

'It's getting late', agreed Kephas, trying to sound disinterested. 'I don't mind staying, but I'll do whatever you fellows want to do.'

Job sensed the reason for Kephas' reluctance to take the lead and realised that if they spoke more about it, pride might demand that they stay.

'Let's go then', he said decisively.

They walked slowly out of the light of the fires and into the bush to make their way home. No one seemed to notice their departure.

'Can I stay with you tonight?' asked Kephas. 'I have a long way to go to get home otherwise.'

'Of course', said Job.

'Where are you going?' a rough voice asked.

Kephas drew back startled. His eyes were accustomed to the darkness and he saw three men in front of them. He didn't need to be told that the dark shapes they held in their hands were knobkerries.

'Who exactly are you boys?' asked rough voice. 'Don't you want to go to the meeting?'

'Oh, yes, we do', blurted the youngsters in one voice. It was certainly not the time to argue.

Kephas assumed the task of spokesman while his eyes looked on the ground around him for some sort of weapon with which to defend himself.

'We thought the meeting was cancelled because we have been waiting a long time and nothing has happened,' Kephas said politely,

The owner of the rough voice stepped forward and Kephas saw that he was indeed holding a knobkerrie — a polished club shaped from the hardwood root of a tree — the knob must have weighed at least a kilogram. The bulk of the man holding it, matched the viciousness of the weapon. Yet he somehow seemed strangely familiar.

'We're waiting for the leader to arrive from town.'

He introduced himself. 'I am Madziwa, the leader of the Party Youth League in Senga.'

Kephas felt his throat go dry and heard his friends gasp at the name.

'Mr Madziwa? . . .' he tailed off into silence.

'Who is that?' said Madziwa. He caught Kephas with huge hand and drew him close. Kephas made no move to resist and his hands dropped limply by his sides. He was in a state of shock. Madziwa, his teacher, was here at a Party meeting! If he could have run away, he would , but his feet seemed to be rooted to the ground.

'Kephas Ndhlela!' barked Madziwa with matching surprise. He quickly identified the other two who were also his pupils.

'You are supporters of the cause?' he asked, his eyes flickering back and forth between them.

'We are', chorused the boys miserably.

'Good', said Madziwa making his decision. 'Good.'

He looked the lads over and decided they would be his insurance policy against being arrested. He would make sure that these boys would be involved in everything that was going to happen as deeply as he would be involved himself. That way he could assure his own safety.

'The meeting is not cancelled', he purred. 'All supporters of the cause will attend.'

He pointed at the flickering fires. 'Go over there and wait with the others.' There was no mistaking the dangerous edge in his voice.

'We will', Kephas assured him. He couldn't ignore the iron-hard knobkerrie that was now hanging apparently harmlessly by Madziwa's side.

'Good', repeated Madziwa. He addressed his shadowy companions. 'The boys made a mistake. They thought the meeting had been cancelled, but they now know that it's still on and they are going back to wait.' He sounded strangely friendly now.

There was a burst of unfriendly chuckles from the shadows and without further ado, Kephas and the others turned and returned to the firelit clearing.

They looked at each other dumbly. They were in a real fix.

'Perhaps we can slip away later?' whispered Matavi. He looked a ghastly pale colour by the flickering firelight.

Kephas shrugged and looked accusingly at Job, who looked back in panic.

'We will just have to wait. We have no option now', muttered Kephas.

*   *   *

They were saved from further conjecture by Madziwa who appeared from the darkness, went into the firelight and stood on a log of wood. He shouted for attention. The talking ceased abruptly and those present formed a half circle around him and squatted on the ground expectantly. Kephas saw a man in a smart dark business suit next to Madziwa. He was wearing sunglasses, which seemed out of place considering that it was night time.

Madziwa scowled those still chattering into silence, then introduced his companion. It was Simon Gumede, the Party leader from Salisbury.

Gumede looked over the assembled crowd. He gained pleasure when he saw that some were fidgeting nervously when he looked at them He smiled at Madziwa and nodded approvingly.

'You have done well, comrade.'

Madziwa preened in the praise and murmured modestly: 'It was nothing really, comrade. These boys wanted to help us as much as they could.' He glared at the assembly, daring anyone to defy him. No one did.

Gumede positively beamed. 'We must get down to the business in hand.' He turned to his audience. 'So far none of you know why you are here. But first I would like to tell you how pleased I am to see so many people taking an interest in our great cause.'

Kephas got the impression that he was preparing to make a long speech.

He got into his stride. 'Firstly, I have brought you here because there is no Youth League in Senga. I was surprised to hear this and I knew you would want to help me form one.' He looked at the impassive faces as if expecting applause. None came. 'Our great leader, who has been detained by the government, wants every area to have its own branch of the league. My comrade here' — he indicated a thug standing nearby — 'will take your names. When he has done that you will be a member of our glorious Youth League and entitled to a membership card.'

The taker-of-names went from person to person writing down names and addresses. Kephas was tempted to give a false name, for he was frightened his father would find out, but fear of the men he had become involved with persuaded him otherwise, so he gave his correct name.

Kephas looked around. Very few in the crowd who could be classified as youths. Some were almost middle-aged and he found it puzzling that they should be allowed to join the Youth League. It seemed to make no difference, however, because everyone was enrolled, irrespective of their ages.

When the last name had been noted, Gumede continued. 'Now that you are all full members, I will explain what your first job is. You will have noticed that only about 80 men are present at this meeting. Yet in this area there are more than 30 000 people.' He looked for reaction, but everyone waited patiently for him to make the point.

'Just think, only 80 people out of 30 000. Now I know that we have many more than 80 supporters around here. I am inclined to think that it was laxness on their part. But', he held up his finger in emphasis, 'we cannot allow that to continue. Therefore, you will take action to show them that they had better mend their ways. Naturally', he smiled benignly, 'we will take action only against those people we know don't support us. That's all I have to say tonight. Mr Madziwa will give you the plan you will have to carry out.'

Kephas was even more puzzled. He did not see how people could be compelled to attend meetings.

Gumede held up his hand. 'Farewell comrades, and good luck. May there be 30,000 here at our next meeting.'

Someone clapped and somebody else cheered. Within seconds everyone joined in. Gumede looked nervously around and held up his hands for silence.

'There must be no noise. Do everything silently and in the night. I am returning to Salisbury. It's essential for the Party that it not become known I am involved in any of your actions.' His had a grave expression on his that seemed to imply he had a world of problems on his mind — not just the little problems of Senga. He smiled conspiratorially and held up his clenched fist in salute. 'Good luck, comrades. Remember the Party. We must be willing to die for the Party.'

He gave a final farewell, handed over to Madziwa, and slipped away with the stranger who had taken the names.

*   *   *

Kephas desperately wished that he had not come. It was clear that things were about to follow that he would dread associating himself with. He decided to do the absolute minimum and merely pretend that he was toeing the party line.

It was as if Madziwa had read his thoughts.

'The action we're about to take will teach the sellouts that they cannot be traitors to the people. But I warn you all. Kep an eye on the man next to you. If you do something and he doesn't, or he fails to display the necessary enthusiasm, report it to me. He might be a police informer or a sellout himself. Everyone must play their part. They must not just stand by and watch. That way, no one will dare to run to the police and inform on us.' He glared at his listeners. 'Do you all understand?'

Kephas felt his heart sink. He was too frightened not to join in now. It would be foolish to take the threat lightly. He only hoped that tonight would be the end of it all. No one would persuade him to come on something like this again. Why had he listened to his friends?

'Break branches for yourselves. You need nice thick clubs', Madziwa ordered. The crowd obediently moved into the bush. Kephas heard sounds of snapping wood around him as he fashioned his own weapon. He was in two minds to make a run for it in the dark, but decided against when he realised the very real fear of his friends informing Madziwa. In circumstances like this how could he trust either of them? He glanced at Job and Matavi, but their faces were as impassively miserable as he knew his was.

He walked moodily back to Madziwa, feeling trapped.

Madziwa called for attention once everyone had re-assembled.

'Right, comrades, we are going to deal with the sellouts in the nearby villages. He circled his knobkerrie over his head.

'Let's go, comrades. Let's go.'

In spite of the earlier warning by Gumede, no effort was made to maintain silence. A low hum of voices arose like a growl as the mob made its way to the first village. There was an undefinable throb of excitement. Many drummed their sticks against trees as they ran through the bush. They reached a village. Kraal mongrels, thin and sharp like greyhounds, streaked out and snapped at their heels. These dogs, it was said, could trace their ancestry back to the hunting hounds of the pharaohs of ancient Egypt. There were muttered curses as the intruders kicked the yelping canines aside.

Then they were among the huts.

'Wake them up and ask them why they're sellouts', yelled Madziwa.

There was no stopping the mob. It was aroused by a spirit of violence that lurked in the veins of all men like a sleeping volcano.

They beat on doors and if they were not immediately opened, they kicked them down. Those inside were not given the chance to say whether they supported the Party or not. Men, women and children were dragged outside and battered to their knees with the sticks, while others were kicked and punched into insensibility. The unfortunate victims screamed in terror and begged for mercy from the wraiths of the night. But mercy was in short supply that night.

Excitement gripped Kephas and he was carried away by the emotion of the mob. Suddenly he wanted to join in. In fact, he had to. A compulsion took hold that he could not resist. Someone slipped from a hut and fled into the night. Kephas gave a blood-thirsty animal cry and gave chase. He caught up with the fugitive in a few strides and it gave a violent shove.

His victim fell to the ground. It was an old woman. She pulled herself to her knees and frantically begged him for mercy. The sight gave him a feeling of exultant power that he had never before experienced. With brutal callousness he cracked his stick on her head and she sank back unconscious. He viciously kicked her ribs and felt her shudder against his shoe. He spat on the prone figure and ran off to catch up with the rest, who were leaving the village for the next one. They were like a pack of blood-crazed wild dogs.

They went from village to village, repeating their terrible performance, each time with an escalating enthusiasm. They blended into the form of one enormous thing . . . a thing that had a throbbing pulse of its own. A terrible, unthinking, unseeing and unfeeling thing . . . a monster that wanted blood. The more blood it tasted, the more it wanted.

A woman was dragged from a hut and passed hand over hand over the heads of the mob. Her screams seemed to excite them more. Eventually she was thrown to the ground with terrible force. Her bones cracked as she hit the hard dirt, but no one heard. Nor did anyone hear her cries as they trampled her underfoot. The child in her womb miscarried during the dreadful carnage.

Then on to the next kraal.

'Fire!' someone shouted. 'Burn them!'

The cry was taken up by many voices.

'Fire! Fire! Fire!' they chanted, eyes glazed with a savage excitement. Kephas dragged a handful of thatch from the nearest hut and someone struck a match. He held the blazing torch high and with eyes staring with the madness that had overcome them all, led the chant.

'Burn them! Burn them! Burn them!'

He ran to one hut, then to another, brushing the flaming grass against the dry brittle thatch. The night glowed in showers of flames and sparks.

An old couple, drugged with sleep, were dragged into the open and lost from his sight, as dozens of men surrounded them. For a while Kephas heard hysterical screams, then the voices diminished and became silent. When the circle parted, there were only two motionless shapes there. Kephas observed with suppressed excitement, that the clothing of the woman was pulled up over her face and the lower half of her body was obscenely exposed.

The mob rampaged on. At the next village they were met by a man standing alone. He was armed with a shotgun. A blast split the night air and a pattern of lead hit the ground and spattered dust in front of the racing feet. They blundered to a panicky halt.

'The next one will be you. Get away from here!'

The mob lost its cohesion. They looked for a lead, but no one moved. The excitement was replaced by a realisation of personal danger. They hesitated, which was enough to break the spell.

'Run!' someone yelled.

The mob turned as if one and ran.

A second shotgun blast hastened them on their way. Then they were again covered by the night again. Most were still together, although some had taken off in other directions. Madziwa bawled out for everyone to stop. They gathered around him wide-eyed, frightened, but still excited. He puffed and panted.

'Go to your homes. Say nothing. When I need you again, I will call you.' He cautioned them. 'Tonight traitors have suffered. If anyone speaks, he is also a traitor and will die. Now, go to your villages.'

To Kephas, the message seemed to be addressed personally to him.

They ran off and Kephas found Job and Matavi for the first time since they had joined the rampage. His companions looked at him in awe. It was he who had started the fire and they looked to him for leadership.

The excitement wore off as they walked home. Now that they were away from the mob, the thought of what they had done began to sober them. They discussed the situation quietly. Gone was the blood lust that had possessed them. Replacing it was fear of the consequences when the authorities found out. They began to realise the enormity of their actions.

Kephas displayed bravado in keeping with his new image, but within himself he was deeply ashamed. He saw by the worried faces of the others that they felt much the same way as he did.

Suddenly, overnight, their carefree youth seemed behind them.

5

Saul lay naked on his camp bed, the mosquito net draped loosely over him. The sun was well up above the eastern horizon and it was already hot –– damned hot.

His eyes took in the little whitewashed room that served as a bedroom for government officials visiting the tribal lands on official business. He reached for his shirt that lay on the heap of tumbled kit he had taken from the truck the previous night.

He glanced at his watch. It was 05:15 and time to get up. He was about to swing his legs on to the floor when there was a gentle tap on the door.

'Yes', he shouted irritably. Saul was not a person who woke up in good temper first thing in the morning. 'What the hell do you want?'

He heard the muffled voice of Sergeant Ndhlela through the door.

'It is I, *Nkosi*. There is a problem that needs your attention.'

'All right, I'm coming', he grumbled as he pulled on a pair of khaki shorts. He didn't put his shoes on, but opened the door and padded out to where Ndhlela was waiting on the verandah. An old couple was with him. They must be at least 60 years old, if they're a day, Saul judged. Their clothing was torn and bloodstained. Some parts of their bodies were roughly bandaged. Stiff patches of dried dark blood were visible through the white cotton. The man's face, in particular, was in a terrible state — so badly swollen that it looked like a gigantic puffy pumpkin. Saul looked calmly at Ndhlela. The blood didn't disturb him. Assaults were all part of the day's work for a district policeman.

'Another domestic hoo-ha?' he enquired from Ndhlela who, like himself, was clad only in a pair of shorts.

Ndhlela shook his head. 'No, *Nkosi*, this is not a domestic dispute. These people were attacked by a mob that rampaged through their village during the night.'

'Why?' said Saul bluntly, knowing the answer in advance.

'They say it was the Party. The old man here', Ndhlela said, nodding at the broken features of the old greybeard, 'says that he heard the mob chanting Party slogans before they dragged them from their hut.'

'Bastards!' said Saul with feeling. He walked over to the old couple and gently indicated that they should sit down, which they slowly did. His professional eye took in the nature of their injuries. The little he could do with the modicum of first aid gear he had with him would make little difference. They needed hospital treatment. Still, he told Ndhlela to do what little he could to help them.

'And find out their story', he ordered. Leaving Ndhlela to tend to their injuries and to question them, he went to the Land-Rover and switched on the VHF. radio.

He waited for the set to warm up. When the soft crackle of static came through, he depressed the handset's transmitter button.

'Senga — this is Jenkins. Do you read? Over.'

On the third call, a voice replied.

'Jenkins — this is Senga — go ahead. Over.'

Saul grinned as he picked up the richly accented voice of Constable Elisha, who was on radio duty at Senga police station's charge office.

'Senga, this is Jenkins — call Patrol Officer Roberts to the radio, please. Over.'

'Roger Sah — stahand by.'

Saul put the handset down and decided to make himself some coffee. He knew that it would be some time before Constable Elisha succeeded in waking up Patrol Officer Roberts, who experienced enough difficulty getting up to start work at 06:15, let alone 05:30. He returned to the radio about 15 minutes later and his patience was rewarded. The slightly cockney-accented voice of Bob Roberts acknowledged his call.

'Jenkins — Senga, go ahead.'

Saul gave Roberts a brief run down on the situation. He asked for an ambulance and at least three constables to assist with the investigations to be sent to the rest camp. The Officer Commanding, District was also to be informed immediately.   Bob did not need lengthy instructions.

'Roger—wilco—out', was his terse reply.

Saul turned off the set and returned to the old couple.

'It will take two hours for an ambulance to get out here. Do they feel up to making statements?'

Ndhlela spoke briefly to them in the vernacular and nodded.

'Yes, *Nkosi*, they would like to tell you the full story.'

An hour later, Saul read their completed statements back to them. They agreed with the contents and signed it with 'x' marks, for there had been no opportunity in their young days to get schooling.

Neither the man nor the woman could provide a motive for the attack. They had no enemies that they could think of. They had been asleep when it happened and did not know the time it occurred. This was usual for simple tribesmen who only calculated time when the sun was in the sky. When it was dark, it was merely night time. Very few villagers owned clocks.

There was bedlam when they awakened . What seemed like a hundred voices were chanting and screaming outside their hut. There was a terrible racket as blows from sticks, billets of wood and axes slammed against their locked door. Yes, they knew one of the mobsters had an axe, because the blade had penetrated the wooden door. They clung to each other in terror until the door gave way and what seemed like dozens of men shoved and barged their way inside. They were beaten to the ground and dragged outside.

Two huts nearby were ablaze and sparks crackled from the burning thatch. By the wavering glow of fires they could see men running about the kraal, whooping and shouting. Boots thudded into their bodies, but no one spoke. The woman, bent and white-haired, explained how she was held on the ground while hands invaded her body. The more she screamed, the more she was fondled. She was kicked on her head, face and body until she mercifully lost consciousness. Her husband told the same story, except that he had lost consciousness before they violated his wife.

When they recovered consciousness, the mob had gone and their pole, mud and thatch home was a smouldering heap of red-hot wood ash. Their 11 fowls, heads chopped off, were scattered around in the dirt.

They staggered as best they could through the bush for help, but when they arrived at the next kraal it was to find the villagers there had also been attacked. Four adults and six children had been severely beaten. They had made them as comfortable as possible, but had been unable to do much more because of their own injuries. They walked headed for the rest camp where they had heard the police were camping, avoiding all habitation on the way. They feared for their lives and were terrified they might run straight into more thugs.

At four o'clock in the morning a passing lorry picked them up and brought them to the rest camp. No, they were not politically interested people. They had never been members of the Party and had never wanted to join. They were just elderly people who wanted a quiet life.

6

Saul looked moodily at the glass of beer he held in both hands at the bar counter. He was concentrating on crushing to death a column of black ants coming from a crack in the wall with the base of his glass.

The club was crowded and being the general meeting place for the small community, he knew everyone there. But he was in no mood for small talk. He was tired and fed-up. He mentally sifted through the mound of papers that now comprised the police dockets on the as yet unidentified mob that had swept through the villages the week before. There was no break yet because so far those involved were too scared to talk. He was sure, and so was Ndhlela, that many of the victims knew their attackers, but they stolidly denied it. Fear, like love, exercises tremendous power over the conduct of men.

The culprits would certainly have a lot to answer for when justice finally caught up with them — three dead, including a baby and the old woman he had interviewed at the rest camp. At least another 18 were still hospitalised. It seems that nothing mattered to the bloody savages that had done it. Anyone was fair game, men, women, babies. The tribal area was in a state of chaos.

He thought about other allied cases investigated since the start of the trouble. Three schools had been burned down, a petrol bomb had been thrown into the chief's bedroom, presumably to pull him into line — fortunately while he was away — and just about all the cattle dip tanks had been senselessly smashed and filled with boulders. It was crazy — after all the dip tanks had been put there for the benefit of the tribesmen — not for the whites they professed to hate.

'Hey, Saul', shouted a voice. 'Stop being so bloody unsociable. Come and meet the girls.'

Saul, disturbed from his reverie, looked up to see the grinning face of Jake

Swartz, who farmed on property adjacent to the tribal lands. His farm boasted the name of Swartz Kop — Black Hill. Saul grinned back and his eyes did a double take as he saw the girls who were bracketing his friend very neatly indeed. 'I've just come from town.', said Jake.

'Oh, yeah', replied Saul, eyes were moving admiringly to the girls on his left and right. He was not at all concerned with his thickset friend whose chest was matted with black hair that bushed its way through the top of his open-necked shirt.

On one side was his dream blonde, tall and slim with green eyes and thrusting breasts that threatened to break out of her silky top. She wriggled from Jake's big gnarled arm and slipped on to the bar stool vacated by Saul as he stood up.

'Excuse me', she laughed, in a way that caused Saul to check that his mouth was not gaping open. 'I'm Dawn.'

'She's a Yank', explained Jake.

'Very pleased to meet you', said Saul, taking her hand inside his big knuckles and holding it as delicately as if it was a rare botanical specimen.

'Can I have my hand back?' she asked in a soft drawling American accent, her eyes twinkling.

Saul sheepishly let go.

'Ag man, meet Maria as well', roared Jake, 'and stop behaving as if you have never seen a girl before.'

Saul snapped out of it and directed a friendly grin at the dark-haired girl in the floral dress, who was still snuggling into Jake's shoulder. She smiled primly back with a touch of reserve that warned she considered herself Jake's property, but was still prepared to be friendly with his friends.

Not my type, Saul decided, comparing her slim, elegant, small breasted figure and short black hair to the blonde hair and warmer curves of Dawn. Maria's accent was strictly northern Johannesburg.

'He's really not such a bad bloke for an Englishman', Jake jestingly explained to Dawn. 'It's just that he spends so much time out in the bush that he occasionally goes berserk and rapes the first white girl he sees.'

'Sounds interesting', said Maria in a prim voice designed to pass the message to Jake that he was being disgusting.

Saul smiled. Maria had not yet learned that subtle messages passed right over Jake's head.

'Drink?' asked Saul, changing the subject. He knew Jake only too well and if he was allowed to run on unfettered, the conversation would become completely basic. For once in his life, Saul, who was no prude, did not want this to happen.

'Beer', said Jake cheerfully.

'Gin and tonic', chorused the girls.

'Hey, Joe', shouted Saul to the part-time barman. 'Some service here.'

'Bugger you', muttered the barman, who was otherwise occupied with a game of poker dice at the far end of the counter. But when the girls caught his eye he dropped the elephant hide dice cup on the counter and sidled up with a moon-eyed sloppy leer on his face.

'This is Joe', grinned Saul. 'He's going to get us two beers and two gins and tonics. He farms when he is not slopping up drinks and playing dice.'

'And after he's got the drinks', chuckled Jake, 'Joe's going to go straight back to his dice game.'

'All right, all right', muttered Joe, serving the drinks. 'I know when I'm not wanted.'

'Come on, Joe. Your throw', yelled his boisterous companions.

'Pleased to meet you', he said to the girls and, 'I'm coming — keep your bloody hair on', to his fellow gamblers. He went back up the bar.

'Are all country pubs like this?' Dawn asked looking somewhat perplexed.

'Mostly', said Saul, then changed the subject to something more interesting.

'What are you doing in the wilds of darkest Africa?' asked Saul, finding himself snared by the fascinatingly green eyes of Dawn. She seemed equally fascinated by his penetrating blue ones. They felt a mutual jolt as a mental communication passed between them. It was a chemical reaction that defied description, yet it had happened between man and woman at the least expected times since Adam first set eyes on Eve.

'Phew', said Saul dragging his eyes away.

'The heat?' enquired Dawn innocently, trying to refocus the magic that maddeningly disappeared when Saul took his eyes away from hers.

'Yes, I think so.' His eyes found hers again and this time it was Dawn who involuntarily broke the contact. She cursed herself inwardly as her veneer of sophistication disappeared in a deep, shy blush that made her feel 14 and being eyed by the first spotty adolescent who had taken an interest in her.

Maria hung possessively on to Jake's arm and lifted her eyebrows at Dawn. She gave a knowing bob of the head in the direction of Saul, who was talking to Jake.

'All right?' she whispered.

'More than that', murmured Dawn, keeping her voice low so that Saul couldn't hear.

'Who's all right?' thundered Jake, causing a crimson blush to drop like a curtain over Dawn's face. She grabbed her drink from the bar counter, nearly knocking it over in the process.

'What are you doing here?' asked Saul, returning his undivided attention to Dawn. Are you a tourist?'

'I suppose you could say that I'm an old resident of Senga', said Dawn thoughtfully.

'You're what?' laughed Saul, thinking she was joking.

'An old resident', repeated Dawn, a mischievous look on her face.

Saul couldn't get over how beautiful she was. He shook his head, still believing it was some sort of joke.

'Well, I must be slipping if I haven't noticed you around for the year that I've been stationed here. Funny thing', he added, taking a swig of beer, 'the only Yanks I know around here are that cadaverous old bastard Hale and his wife at Senga Mission. Do you know of any others, Jake? I must say . . .' his voice tailed off as a scowl passed over Dawn's face.

'That cadaverous old bastard and his wife', she said primly and with unconcealed annoyance, 'are my parents.'

'Your parents?' choked Saul, wishing he could bite off his tongue. He gagged on his beer.

'Yes', said Dawn, smiling in spite of herself as Jake beat Saul between his shoulder blades until he didn't know if he was coughing from the beer or from the battering.

'I'm sorry', he gasped, recovering his breath. 'I really am. It's just that I couldn't imagine you being related to them. They're so . . .' He tailed off into silence. 'I mean . . .' He dried up again. 'Look, aren't you one of the Brethren? I mean . . . you're wearing makeup and I know that's against their rules.'

'Their religion', corrected Dawn, 'not their rules. It's true that I'm wearing make-up', she snapped open her bag and took out a small compact. She eyed her lips critically in the mirror. 'Believe me all this comes off before I see my parents. You can bet your sweet life on it.'

Saul shook his head despairingly. 'Well, how do you expect a chap to know that you're one of the Brethren — a sister or whatever you are —

when you don't even behave like one?'

'Well perhaps it is partly my fault', mused Dawn, bringing back a touch of the magic they had felt earlier.

She explained that she had not seen her parents for eight years since they had left the States to come to Africa. The Brethren looked after their own and it was not policy for children to accompany missionaries to Africa unless the parents insisted, she told him. She hadn't questioned her upbringing until she'd been sent to college in the Midwest.

There she had soon discarded the restrictive influences of the Calvinistically-inclined Brethren boarding school she had attended and the humourless homes where she had spent her school holidays. 'Almost everything one did at college, from eating to dating, would have been classified as a sin by the Brethren', she giggled. 'Lots of the students must have thought I came from outer space anyway.'

When she had finished college a month ago, she had decided to surprise her parents by coming to Rhodesia see them.

That night Saul was restless and he didn't sleep well. Jake had left for Salisbury with the girls when the bar closed. Dawn had intended to go to the mission, but had poured down far too many gin and tonics to risk facing her straight-laced parents. Instead, she wisely decided to put the meeting off for another day, return to Salisbury and stay in a hotel for the night. Tomorrow she'd get a lift back, when she was in a more presentable condition.

Saul detected a note of pique when he said he couldn't drive her to Salisbury. When he mentioned it was because he was anticipating trouble in the tribal lands, the pique became more pronounced. That was the trouble with women, he mused. Always expecting a guy to drop everything at a moment's notice. Not that he wouldn't have done in normal circumstances, the warm feel of her hand coming back to him. Dawn was quite some girl.

Saul wondered what the Hales would think when they saw their emancipated daughter. He wished he could be a fly on the wall and see the reaction of those old and up-tight religious maniacs. They will be in for quite a surprise, decided Saul. He wondered when he would see her again.

7

There were 300 people gathered around the dip tank. It was a dark night, but the area was lit by the flames from a blazing shack where stores used in the process of dipping cattle had been kept. Most of the crowd stood around silently and watched, while a small number worked with sledge hammers and crowbars, smashing the brick walls of the tank.

The timbers of the race, through which the cattle were channelled into the arsenical bath, had been ripped out earlier and fed to the hungry fire. Once a month by law cattle in the tribal lands had to be dipped to kill the ticks that carried a myriad of cattle diseases.

The tank itself was overflowing with boulders which had been heaved in, one by each member of the crowd to symbolically show that they had played a part. There was insufficient space for all the rocks and many lay tumbled nearby where they had been tossed.

Kephas wondered where Job was. He spotted Matavi working under Madziwa's direction sledging down walls.

He was sick with worry. Sooner or later, he knew, the police would catch up with him. He had grown up in police camps and knew the form. Eventually someone would talk and progressively everyone would be identified. It amazed him that this had not happened already, because it was clear that 95% of the tribesmen present were unwilling participants.

However, it took a brave man to disregard a midnight call by the Party. In this time of trouble, disobedience could mean death. Now, by their symbolic actions, they were all involved and liable to long prison sentences when the law caught up with them, which was as sure to happen as night follows day. True, the law was sympathetic to those intimidated, but blind justice did not excuse crimes committed by people because they were afraid. The law's view was that they should resist and arrest the wrongdoers. Which just showed how bloody stupid the law could be, thought Kephas bitterly.

'Constable Elisha has a prisoner', announced Sergeant Ndhlela, standing stiffly to attention with his shining brown leather cane under his arm. He nodded his head and Constable Elisha, a shiny young recruit who had only recently arrived from the African Police Training School, ushered a securely handcuffed, miserable looking youth of about 20 into Saul's office.

'What's he done?' asked Saul laconically.

'Tell the *Nkosi*', said Ndhlela, encouraging the nervous young man who was still overawed by authority when it was in the form of a stern white inspector of police.

'I have arrested him for damaging the dip tank two nights ago, sah', announced Elisha nervously.

'Does he admit?' asked Saul. If he did admit his involvement, it would be their first breakthrough.

'No, *Nkosi*, he denies.' He glanced at the prisoner who was staring with resignation at the metal bracelets that kept his wrists together. 'He lives at the village next to the dip tank and when I questioned him, he said he had been away at a beer drink on the night in question.' He pulled out his almost new notebook, studied the pencilled writings on the pages and continued. 'I made enquiries, *Nkosi*, and established that there was no beer drink at the place he said he was at on the night of the crime. So I know he is lying.'

'Good', said Saul. 'Even if he is not guilty himself, it's likely he knows some of those who probably are.' He looked at Ndhlela. 'What do you say, Sergeant?'

'He knows, *Nkosi*', Ndhlela said, firmly fixing a beady eye on the prisoner who shifted uneasily.

Only half hour later, under the determined interrogation of the police officers, the youth broke down and confessed. Some unknown men had turned up at his hut in the night and told him to accompany them. He demurred, but when told that if he refused to go he would be killed, he reluctantly agreed to accompany them. They moved from house to house and village to village gathering recruits, until they had a large body of men. 'We then destroyed the dip', he said simply.

The youth was a mine of information once he started talking. Before he was locked up in the police cells, he had identified 50 others who were involved in the attack. He didn't mention Kephas, Job or Matavi. He knew them by sight, but didn't know their names. He said nothing about the leader, Madziwa, because that could invite retribution, perhaps even death, and he had no wish to die.

For two days the police at Senga hardly stopped to sleep. Many tribesmen were arrested and interrogated. They explained their part and implicated others. The final count was 165, but many more were remained unidentified and avoided arrest. Kephas Ndhlela and his friends, together with Madziwa, remained free. The terror of violent death still held the tribal area in its thrall.

The visiting magistrate paid a special visit to Senga to hold periodical court. Saul conducted the prosecution, as prisoner after prisoner was wheeled into the dock. Some argued, but most accepted their fate and pleaded guilty to all charges. The majority were later removed to Salisbury Prison to begin serving their sentences which, depending on their degree of blameworthiness, ranged from one to three years with labour.

*　　　*　　　*

Abraham Hale opened the front door and eyed Saul, who stood respectfully outside. He knew Saul, but disapproved of him. Abraham was a man of peace. Although he accepted that the keeping of law and order was necessary, he suspected that it was not always done peacefully. He recalled stories that Madziwa had told him about peaceful happening in the tribal lands. The police had moved in, he had told him, arresting people indiscriminately and often brutally beating them. It was for this reason, Madziwa claimed, that the people had ultimately resorted to violence. They felt with despair that if the law did not deal fairly with them, then they had no option but to rebel against the law. The troubles had all stemmed from this.

'Yes, Inspector', hesitated Abraham, hoping it would be unnecessary to invite such a symbol of oppression into his home.

'May I come in, Reverend?' enquired Saul, giving Abraham a casual salute. I wonder what the old sod knows about the goings-on in the tribal lands, mused Saul.

'Of course, Inspector', said Abraham, obeying the laws of hospitality as practised by his Brotherhood. Saul took off his cap and stepped inside. Abraham led the way into the lounge, closely followed by the policeman who dwarfed him. Because his back was to him, Abraham failed to notice that Saul was looking eagerly around as if he were looking for someone.

Abraham turned and gestured him to a chair. 'Excuse me', he said, 'I will arrange for some tea.'

'Thank you', Saul murmured politely, wondering what had happened to the lovely Dawn. His first intention had been to ask to see Dawn, but the frozen attitude of his host made it obvious that this, without doubt at all, would be the wrong first move.

He looked around the frugal room and wondered why people could go to so much trouble to make themselves uncomfortable. He spontaneously smiled, for he couldn't see the fun-loving Dawn putting up with this sort of existence for long. His grin puckered a little as he again wondered where she was. It wouldn't be easy to use another duty call as an excuse to come back a second time and the Reverend Hale was not at the top of his social visiting list.

Five minutes later Abraham returned accompanied by his plump and pretty wife. She gave him a smile of welcome. Saul was only into his second sentence of polite small-talk when a figure walked into his peripheral vision from the passage. It was carrying a tray of tea. His eyes nearly popped from their sockets and he stuttered into silence. It was Dawn — not the sexy, voluptuous Dawn he had met the week before, but a young, scrub-faced girl whose fair hair was tied back a tight bun. Her elegant high heels had gone to be replaced by black lace-up shoes.

Her sexy curves had disappeared into the shapeless folds of a white cotton dress. Gone, too, was the make-up and perfume. Could this be the same girl who had been propping up the bar at the Senga Club sipping gin and tonic only a few days previously?

Abraham frowned when he noticed that Saul was staring at Abigail — for that was the name she had been christened. Dawn was a name unknown to him. It had been chosen by the girl herself as a symbol of her emancipation.

Why did he stare so? Abraham checked her over with critical eyes, but confirmed there was nothing about her except purity. So what could cause a man to gaze at her so? He certainly didn't want his daughter's appearance to stir lechery in the mind of a roughneck like Inspector Saul Jenkins.

Mary Hale noticed the look too, but she was a woman. She concentrated on Saul for only a moment, then switched her gaze to her daughter. She noted that Abigail did not even raise her eyes until she had placed the tea tray on a table. But she knew from the flush on her face that she had met Saul Jenkins before. Womankind, unlike mankind, doesn't require written messages to detect that romance is in the air.

'My daughter, Abigail', introduced Abraham, looking approvingly at the slight curtsey made by his girl. The Brethren at her school had not neglected the finer points of her education, he thought, ignoring Saul's frank stare.

'Abigail?' croaked Saul, and Mary realised with certainty that they had met before. She had no intention of enlightening her stern husband about this, but would wait until her daughter found the right moment to confide in her. That she would confide in her she didn't doubt for a moment.

'How do you do, Inspector', Dawn said, ensuring that was facing Saul so that no one else could see the pleading grimace in her eyes.

She held out her hand and Saul formally shook it — feeling the same quiver of excitement as that first time. So that's the story, he thought. She hasn't told her father about her new way of life. He smiled but quickly regained his composure.

'Abigail has come on a surprise visit to us from America, Inspector', said Mary, looking out sharply for signs and feeling slightly uneasy when she didn't detect any more.

'Really', murmured Saul, on his best behaviour. 'How very nice.' He gave Dawn a deadpan smile and accepted the cup of tea from her. 'Thank you', he said politely. 'No sugar, thanks.'

He watched Dawn's face twitch, and he was concerned that she would start giggling. She managed to control herself without giving the game away, however, but only because she quickly turned away from him.

She sat primly on the edge of a hard chair and concentrated on not looking at Saul. Instead she looked at her mother and smiled, trying to ignore the fluttering in the pit of her stomach — a feeling she had never experienced before. She thought how handsome Saul looked in uniform.

She then determined that some day, whether it upset her parents or not, she would become Mrs Saul Jenkins. A calculating female glint came into her eyes and she glanced at Saul who was making small talk with her parents. She wondered what his reaction would be if he knew what she was thinking.

She had a pretty good idea what her father's reaction would be. She sighed gently to herself. She could also guess what he would say if he ever found out about her lifestyle at college. Not that she was promiscuous, but she was no goody-goody either. She was probably one of the last of her female class-fellows to remain a virgin. She thought back and tried to recall the lean, muscular college boy who had taken it from her, but the incident, although so tender and poignant at the time, now seemed far away. Was that really only six months ago?

His place had been rudely displaced from her mind by this larger-than-life hunk, Saul Jenkins.

8

The village was a small one. There were just 12 huts made from poles, plastered with mud and topped with conical thatched roofs. They nestled amongst the rocky kopjes that framed the top edge of the Zambezi escarpment before the land fell sharply away into the steaming valley below. There were few paths into the village and feet rarely tramped through the wilderness to get there. However, it was not unknown to the white man and was visited occasionally by tough, bronzed men who wore the khaki and grey uniforms of the District Police and the equally bronzed, but civilian clothed officials of the Internal Affairs Department. They were the hands of the government in Salisbury and enforced laws that owed their roots to a long dead prince of Rome called Justinian who had connected his reputation with the honour and interests of a perpetual order of men.

To such men it was merely the village headed by John Magombwe. That was the name inscribed on the registration certificate he carried and in the tax records of the government. To the tribesmen of the Senga district, the village was not referred to by name at all. It was known to many but was only visited by a select few, and then at only certain prescribed times of the year. It had been so since times of antiquity. For this was the home of an aged crone — the *svikiro* — the medium through whom the great *Mhondoro* — the tribal spirit and Rain Goddess — spoke and gave instructions to her people. This was not the *Mudzimu mudiki wapamusha* — the small spirit of a home village that guided their daily lives. Here was manifested the spirit that controlled the destiny of the whole tribe under the overall heavenly umbrella of *Mwari* — God — the creator of all things.

Not that the spirit of the Rain Goddess lived in the village. The spirit spoke only to the people through her medium when it was the time. At all other times she assumed the shape and form of a great black-maned lion that roamed the dense thorn forests of the river valley below. Few people,

58

of course, had seen this lion, although they trembled and hurried on their journeys when it was near sunset and they heard the distant throaty grumbling roar that indicated it was hunting the soft flesh of the myriad impala that browsed in the thickets and grazed in the vleis.

Mandizwidza was an old man and he had left his home village three days ago. He shivered, but it was not cold even though the sun was setting over the hills in the west. He shivered from the mild dose of malarial fever that regularly reoccurred since an anopheles mosquito had first drunk his blood when he was a child.

Not a cloud disturbed the sameness of the darkening sky. It had been like this for a year, without a rain cloud in the sky. The sun had baked the rain clouds away. It shrivelled the grass and cooked the sap out of trees as hardy as even the deep-rooted mimosas. The summer rains should have started long before, but there was still no sign of them coming. There had been some minor showers, but the wetness of that had soon been absorbed by the dry dusty veld. It was a season of drought and famine. People suffered as crops withered and died in the fields. Soon the sparse grazing would be gone and the thin gaunt cattle would begin to die. Even now there was little milk for their calves and even less for the consumption of their human masters.

Mandizwidza looked at his companions — all grey heads like himself. They hailed from the most important villages in the lands of their people. They were amongst the deputation that had been sent by the mediums of their family spirits to see the chief. The minor family spirits did not have the power to break the drought, only the spirit of the Rain Goddess could accomplish that. From those representatives the chief had selected the deputation now waiting for the great spirit to manifest herself. This could take some time. Or perhaps, if the spirit was really angry with the people, she would not appear at all. They all knew this. If there was no rain then, She had been offended, greatly offended.

They had not seen the spirit medium for she did not venture from her hut while visitors were in the village. But their arrival had been reported to her attendant, who would act as the go-between. She would report when the Rain Goddess left the body of the lion and entered the body of the medium to speak to the deputation. The attendant was a beautiful young girl with firm breasts whose lithe virgin body had not yet been defiled by the dark waters of menstruation.

It was two in the morning when the ears of the young acolyte heard the noise from the hut of the medium, heralding the news that the Rain Goddess was about to manifest herself. The attendant slipped quickly from her blankets and pulled on a black dress completely free of ornamentation and hurried out into the warm night air. She scarcely paused at the entrance to the adjoining hut before slipping quickly into the smoke-filled interior. She nodded with satisfaction at the sight of the ancient crone who sat naked and cross-legged on the far side of the smoky fire. The shrivelled form swayed to and fro. Her breasts hung flat against the thin cage formed by her ribs. Her eyes were open, but rolled right back in her head so that only two white orbs could be seen in the sockets. Strange noises bubbled from the toothless mouth of the hag. The sounds quivered in high falsetto, then bubbled into deep throaty roars — the roars of the lion with the black mane. They gradually abated until the only sound disturbing the still smoky air was a breathless sighing that came deep from her throat. The spirit had taken over the ancient's living body.

The attendant squatted opposite and after a respectful pause, addressed the spirit of the Rain Goddess.

'Great spirit', she said, 'the people have sent their delegates from the far corners of our tribal land to complain about the drought. The roasting heat has dried up their crops and the drought will, if not broken by you, cause their cattle to die and their children to waste away from starvation.'

There was a slight pause, then a hollow ghostly voice came from deep in the throat of the medium. Her lips did not move in speech. 'Call them in', commanded the spirit.

The attendant rose swiftly to her feet and left the Presence. She sped from hut to hut, awakening the members of the delegation from their slumbers. She said nothing, for words were unnecessary. Hardly pausing to dress, they threw the blankets from their old bodies and hurried to the hut to hear the oracle speak. They made no noise. No one spoke. They filed into the black interior, each handing a mould of snuff tobacco to the young attendant as a present. They took their places opposite the swaying figure. With legs outstretched towards her, they commenced a slow hand clap that seemed to take possession of them and hypnotise their senses.

The acolyte waited until they were seated and all clapping in unison. She moved over to the frail body from which the words of the great Rain Goddess would be intoned. She tied an apron of skins around the thin naked waist and placed a headdress of black ostrich feathers on the old grey head. A large black shawl was shaken out and draped over the scraggy shoulders.

The medium almost seemed to disappear as the cloak merged with the blackness of the hut's interior. To the delegates it seemed as if her face was suspended in mid-air.

The attendant picked up a narrow steel rod approximately a metre long, and placed it in one of her mistress' hands. In the other she placed an axe. The bony fingers gripped them in a vicelike manner, not at all like the usually shaky grip of an octogenarian. Her assistant picked up a wooden bowl of water and moving to the fire, drew out a burning ember and plunged it sizzling into the liquid. Holding the bowl by its wooden handle fringed with black beads, she brought it to the mouth of the medium who took a long gurgling swallow. The clapping increased to a crescendo as excitement gripped the very souls of her audience. Now was the time when the spirit would speak.

'Why have they come?' asked the Rain Goddess in a rasping tone.

'Why have you come?' the attendant repeated to the old men. No one but she could speak directly to the spirit that had granted the interview.

'We have come', said Mandizwidza, who was the spokesman, 'to ask the great spirit of the Rain Goddess to end the drought.'

The attendant repeated this to the spirit.

'I am patient and long suffering', droned the spirit, 'but the people have committed misdeeds that I cannot forgive. Strangers have come to the area and irresponsible people have listened to their falsehoods and ignored the tribal laws that demand that people should live in peace. Blood has been spilt and only I can wash it away. Until that wickedness ceases, no rain will fall.'

The attendant repeated her words to the deputation, who regarded each other with dismay.

'Can't we make a sacrifice to make amends for this evil?' quavered Mandizwidza.

The delegation waited apprehensively as this was passed on.

'No, that cannot be', said the great Rain Goddess. 'While men do evil and ignore the tribal laws there will be no rain. When the evil stops, the rain will fall. I have spoken.'

Mandizwidza waited impatiently while the attendant passed the words back to the delegation. His heart sank in dismay.

Suddenly, terrible retching noises, punctuated by roars of the black-maned lion, rent the body of the medium. Mandizwidza knew, as did his companions, that the spirit of the Rain Goddess was departing to return to the forests of the valley below. There would be no more words.

It only remained for them to leave, return to their chief and make their report.

The Rain Goddess was angry with the people. Until the trouble stopped the drought would continue. When peace came, the rains would be released from the heavens and bring life back to the sandy loam and red soils of the veld.

9

The situation in which Kephas found himself was like a nightmare without end. He was far too deeply involved for him to use the excuse of intimidation for his involvement. It was not intimidation that drove him to continue his association with Madziwa, his teacher, or that backing down would have lowered his esteem in the eyes of Job or Matavi. They were more frightened than he was and he was scared enough. Not that he would admit this fear to anyone, but it was always in the forefront of his mind. He had a whole jumble of fears. Fear that one day the police would come to arrest him; fear of prison where he could spend many long years; and above all, fear of the deep contempt his father would hold him in if he found out. He was like an alcoholic who wanted to give up drinking, but could not. The Party had given him power over men — the power of life and death — and having tasted it, he could not let go.

'Will you be coming to see me tonight?' asked Tandiwe. They were lying together in the dense bush a few kilometres from her village.

'Not tonight', sighed Kephas. He reached out and stroked the smooth, naked skin of his love.

'Why not?' pouted Tandiwe, taking his hand and flinging it away from her body.

'Tonight I have important business to attend to', he muttered darkly. He glanced at the sun which was low in the sky and stood up. He picked up his trousers and brushed off the leaves and dry grass that adhered to them.

'What is it that is so important for you to attend to?'

'It is man's business and nothing to do with you.'

Tandiwe watched him dress, annoyance clearly written on her pretty features.

'Where is your father?' he asked sharply.

'He's been away for three days', said Tandiwe. Her face clouded. 'It's because he's away that I am able to take you into my bed at night.'

'Yes', said Kephas thoughtfully, 'but where has he gone? Your brother told me that he has gone to the chief on tribal business.'

'Yes, it's tribal business — important tribal business', she said reaching for her underwear. She started to dress. 'He has been selected to go with a deputation to speak with the Mhondoro — the spirit of the great Rain Goddess.'

'The Rain Goddess!' exclaimed Kephas. 'I have heard of this spirit often, but I wasn't aware that this was a time when She was consulted.'

'This is a special time', said Tandiwe. 'The spirit of the Rain Goddess is being asked to break the drought and allow the rains to return.'

'How do you know that?' asked Kephas curiously. 'Surely this is the business of the men. How would you, a mere girl, find out about that?'

'Because', said Tandiwe her eyes twinkling, 'I am a woman — women always find out about things like this.'

'Well, I certainly hope they find out what has upset the great spirit and that She allows the rain to return', said Kephas with feeling. He thought of his father's farm. He had planted seed on three occasions when the chances of rain seemed favourable, but each time it had passed by and the seeds had been cooked by the heat. The onset of the rains was long overdue and it would soon be too late to plant crops. Next week he would be back studying at the mission and he didn't know what his father would do about planting after that.

*   *   *

'But dammit, Dawn', said Saul, leaning through the window of the mission truck standing in front of the charge office. 'Surely I can take you out sometimes.'

'Of course you can and I want you to, but not yet', replied Dawn, brushing her cool hand against his cheek. 'Just try to understand.'

'Understand?', asked Saul stubbornly. 'Of course I understand. It's just that you are living with parents who don't understand you. Look, are you prepared to live the way they want you to?'

'You know I'm not, it's just that . . .'

'I know what it is. It's just that you are afraid of telling them you don't want to be a sister in their bloody Brotherhood for the rest of your life. That you don't want to marry an anaemic son of one of their friends who won't fight to defend themselves.

'That has nothing to do with it. I want to live my life my own way, but I don't want to offend my father and mother.'

'How are you going to do that? You know as well as I do that anything you do will upset them. You'll never be forgiven if you try to live a normal life. Look at you. You look like a bloody pilgrim. No make-up and your hair scragged back like a nun.

'So you don't like me as I am', she asked softly.

'You know I do', grunted Saul, calming down. 'It's just that I want to take my girl out. I don't like pretending when your parents are around that I don't even know you.'

'I'll tell them, my darling. Please just give me more time.' She looked at her watch. 'Kiss me', she ordered, pouting her soft lips. 'I must go.'

Saul shook his head despairingly and ducked it through the window. His lips sought hers and they united in a warm kiss.

'All right', he said, 'I'll give you another week and if you haven't done something by then, I'll do it myself.'

'I promise', said Dawn. 'You won't have to wait another week. I'll find some way of telling them before that.'

*   *   *

At least 200 people were squatted in the forest clearing. Many people who had attended the last Party meeting were in prison, but a summons to attend was not something that could be ignored. Fresh conscripts had soon been persuaded to come along.

After all, when the Party became stronger than the government — when it took over the country — what would happen to those who had refused to join?

Madziwa addressed them, for he had fully taken over the leadership of the Party at Senga. The leaders from Salisbury did not interfere because the police would soon spot a stranger in the tribal area and it was not the place of the leaders to suffer in jail. Kephas stood at Madziwa's right hand. He had become the organising secretary of the local Youth League. Matavi and Job were ordinary members because they hadn't shown the bravery displayed by their friend. But tonight this was their chance to shine, for they were in charge of the pending action. A much more important task awaited Madziwa and Kephas.

'You will follow the orders of our comrades here', instructed Madziwa, indicating Job and Matavi. Kephas smiled as he saw his two friends step forward to face the crowd. 'They will be your leaders tonight and you will obey their instructions', scowled Madziwa. 'If anyone refuses, something will happen to them. I don't say what will happen or when it will happen. It might be when they're walking alone in the forest, or when they're sleeping in their huts. They will know only when the time comes. Remember that death is the lot of cowards and sellouts', he warned. He glowered at the crowd and Kephas followed his example. Wasn't it fitting that people should be afraid of him? After all, he was an important leader nowadays as well?

'We have taken so many actions so far', Madziwa went on. 'Soon the white government will become tired of our resistance and give us our country.' A mumble of approval came from the assembled tribesmen. He held up his hand and restored the silence. 'Tonight', he said, 'you will go with these two brave young comrades and destroy another dip tank so that the people cannot be forced to dip their cattle as the white men want us to. We have destroyed many already as you know, but a few still remain.' He pointed dramatically towards the west. 'Go!' he shouted. 'Go, comrades! Let us win back our country.'

'We are going', responded the roar of 200 voices.

'Follow us', screamed Job, brandishing an axe. The excitement of bloodlust showed clearly on his face. He ran off with Matavi followed by the crowd. Someone began singing a repetitive tune in close harmony that had been passed down from their forefathers.

'Let us kill the white men and toss their bodies into the endless lake.'

Madziwa remained with his hand dramatically pointed to the west until the singing had faded. He relaxed and smiled at Kephas.

'Have you got the stuff?' asked Kephas.

'It's here', said Madziwa. He walked to his cycle and pointed at the sack-covered bundle tied to the carrier. 'I've got a drum off arsenical dip in that.'

'Have you decided on the place we will attack?' asked Kephas.

'Yes, we will attack the farm of the Boer called Swartz.'

So they were going ahead. Kephas had thought he was joking when Madziwa had first mentioned it a few days earlier. Now it was past a joke and he was committed. Anyway, what difference did it make? thought Kephas. He had been involved so much already and he hadn't been caught.

They followed little used footpaths that led from the tribal lands to the farms of the white men. They walked for almost an hour, wheeling Madziwa's bicycle along with its lethal load until they heard the soft lowing of cattle ahead. They moved amongst the herd until the dark oblong of a water trough loomed up in the darkness. They could hear the slopping of water as cattle drank from the trough.

'This is the place', grunted Madziwa and dipped his hand in the water. 'Do you want a drink before we start?'

'Might as well', said Kephas almost in a whisper as if he feared he would be overheard. This was, however, unlikely because Madziwa had told him the white owner's house was at least three kilometres away. It was the same with the compound where the farm labourers lived. He cupped his hands, bent down and took a long swig of the cool liquid.

'If you do that again in ten minutes time, you'll soon be dead', chuckled Madziwa.

Kephas shuddered and wiped his hands dry on his trousers. He felt the mud beneath his feet. 'What about footprints? Won't they show in the mud?'

'Maybe now, but not later. The cattle mill around all the time and they will obliterate them.'

'It seems such a shame', said Kephas, looking at the cattle standing around them. 'I hate to kill cattle. It seems such a pity that we can't just drive them to our homes.'

'Yes,', agreed Madziwa, 'that would be good. But with so many cattle in our possession they would soon arrest us and that would not do the cause much good.'

Kephas watched as Madziwa untied the bundle and removed it from his bike. He shook the sack free from the yellow drum and dropped it on the ground.

'Open the drum', he asked.

Kephas bent down and unscrewed the cap. He picked up the container of liquid death and glanced at Madziwa.

'Pour about half in the trough', Madziwa instructed.

Kephas carried the drum to the trough and tipped it. The liquid arsenic gurgled into the water. He walked slowly up and down the trough, pouring its contents over the surface to ensure an even distribution. Bands of poison showed up in white swirls as it amalgamated with the water. He replaced the cap and put the drum back in the sack. He returned it to Madziwa who tied it back on his carrier.

'Why don't you leave everything here?' Kephas asked. 'You hardly want the police to find you with that sort of stuff.'

'Don't worry, they won't find me with it', said Madziwa. He took hold of his cycle. 'Come on', he said, 'our night's work is not finished yet. This Boer has another watering trough that we must treat. I want all his cattle to die.'

'Isn't it getting somewhat close to first light?' asked Kephas anxiously. 'People will soon be out and about.'

'There is time enough to finish the job', insisted Madziwa.

As they left, cattle began moving towards the trough. They heard gentle slurping sounds as they started to drink.

Shortly afterwards they got to the other trough, but there were no cattle around. They decided it was probably because they were grazing at the far end of the paddock. Kephas poured the remaining arsenical dip into this one. Madziwa discarded the sack but strapped the empty drum back on his carrier.

'Why are you keeping that?' asked Kephas.

'It means nothing. There are plenty of arsenical dip drums around. People use them as buckets to carry water.'

'What about the poison?' asked Kephas. 'Won't it kill you?'

'I'll put the drum on the fire and burn it clean. It'll be fine after that.'

*　　　*　　　*

The three of them stood at the trough. Saul and Ndhlela regarded Jake with sympathy. Unashamed tears of anger and sorrow were running down his cheeks.

'The bastards', he kept saying. 'The bloody bastards. How could anyone do such a terrible thing?'

How could anyone, indeed, thought Saul, looking around. It was an awful sight. Dead and dying cattle were everywhere, with carcases spread in a large circle around the tank. Others were drawing their last breaths. Some lay on the ground, others stood bowlegged, heads hanging in misery and bellowing in agony as their guts were being eaten away by the arsenic they had swallowed. They twitched and trembled as their bowels vented in virtually continuous streams.

Sinister looking vultures were swarming everywhere. God knows where they had come from, for Saul had never seen any at Senga before. They had also been joined by big black and white crows. Both species used their vicious beaks to tear at the carcasses that littered the ground. Some already lay there with the cattle — dead or dying from the same poison that had killed the beasts they were feasting on — devoured along with bloody viscera ripped from the animals' bellies.

'Arsenic. I had a *mombi* accidentally poisoned with it once. You can't mistake the symptoms.' Jake was almost beside himself with rage. 'I've sent for the vet, but there's not much he can do.' He was clenching and unclenching his fists. 'You've got to get them, Saul. Anyone who can do this sort of thing deserves to spend the rest of his life in prison.'

Saul gripped Jake firmly on his shoulder. 'Don't worry. We'll get them. I promise you we'll get them.'

They examined the trough. It even looked abnormal with smoky swirls in the water — the smoky swirls of arsenical dip.

'Take a sample of the water for analysis. We'll need it later', Saul instructed Ndhlela.

Jake walked slowly amongst his dead and dying cattle. A group of black employees who were looking on were absolutely dumbstruck. As was common with cattle herders they had known each animal by name and they were just as upset as their employer, maybe more so.

Where could they start? Saul wondered. The area had been comprehensively trampled by the hooves of drinking cattle. There was no chance of them finding footprints or anything like that. Saul summed up the feelings of both of them. 'What a bloody mess', he said.

Jake returned and Saul spoke to him. 'We must be able to prove the kind of poison used, despite being pretty certain it's arsenic. When the vet comes, get him to take specimens from the stomachs of a selection of the animals so we can have it analysed.' Jake nodded miserably.

'I had 400 head of cattle in this section. At a conservative estimate of $60 a head, that's about $24 000 dollars down the drain.' He shook his head in despair. 'All those years of sweat and toil to build things up, and then some bastards come along and do this.' His face looked as if it was set in iron. It was a hard blow, but men of his line were used to hard blows. They had fought against all comers for centuries — Zulu and other black warriors, British soldiers, disease, drought and floods — for control of the harsh sub-continent of southern Africa. Jake, like his tough, fighting ancestors before him, was not a man who would give up easily.

'I'll start again', he announced quietly. 'I've been virtually wiped out, but

I'll start again. His eyes flamed as he turned to Saul. 'Just get the bastards, Saul.'

'I 'll get them', Saul assured him, looking at the desolation around him and wondering where to begin his investigation. 'Leave it to me, Jake.'

'How about a brandy before you start,' said Jake. 'I know it's early but I certainly need one. He got into the battered Ford that he used around the farm and started the engine. 'I'll see you at the house.'

They didn't get to the house, however, because they were waved down by a farm hand before they could get there.

'There are three dead people over there, *Nkosi*', the man said. He was dressed in old khaki shorts and a shirt as was common with farm labourers. He pointed to their left. 'They are by the watering place.'

Saul looked enquiringly at Jake, who nodded . 'Yes, I have another trough over there.'

Not bothering with further questions, Saul went to the four-strand barbed wire fence that lined the road and climbed through. The others followed. Their guide indicated a place about 30 metres off the road.

They discovered the dead and distorted figures of a young black woman and two children. There was a little girl of about three and a boy they estimated to be about seven or eight. The extensive bloodstains on their clothing told the story of what had happened. Arsenic passes through the guts of a living thing quickly, taking flesh and blood with it in a foul disintegrating torrent. It was doubtful that anyone could have helped them.

'They did not die easily', said Ndhlela grimly.

'They certainly didn't,' agreed Saul, looking at pools of blood and excreta where their bodies had attempted to purge themselves of poison before death. He studied the tortured features of the children and his thoughts were merciless. He would not stop until he had caught the people responsible. People who committed crimes like this deserved to be hunted down and killed like mad dogs.

The water in this trough showed the same smoky cloudiness as the other. A sample of water was corked in a bottle for later analysis. They searched painstakingly for clues to assist the investigation, but found only an old sack in the bushes nearby. It was probably completely irrelevant to the case, but Saul picked up and put it in the back of his truck just in case.

'Is it usual for people to drink from this trough?' asked Saul.

Jake nodded. 'Yes. This is the main route through to the tribal lands and with the drought there is not much water around, so travellers often stop here for a drink.'

'It's true', agreed Ndhlela. 'It is a well-known place for travellers to stop and drink.'

'So those who did this must have known there was a danger of this happening.' Saul took out his notebook and jotted a few notes before slipping it back in his shirt pocket.

10

'So you have returned?' said the Reverend Abraham Hale, his voice lacking a note of welcome. He looked at the tall policeman standing at the door with his daughter. Dawn turned, looked guiltily at her father and blushed. Abraham didn't notice.

'Inspector Jenkins wants to see you, father', she stammered, pushing a wisp of hair back from her forehead and straightening her dress in the way that women do.

'Yes, Reverend, I need to speak to you.'

They looked at each other eye to eye. In her heart Dawn knew that two such very different men would never reconcile their so different ways. Hers was a clear choice. It was her father and the Brethren, or Saul and the ways of the world. Tears welled in her eyes and she turned away so they would not be seen, murmuring that she would prepare tea.

'Come in, Inspector', grunted Abraham with a courtesy he did not feel. He had enough to do without bothering with the police. For a start, everyone was back at school and the work just didn't stop. He glanced at his watch and frowned. In an hour they would be assembling in the main hall for prayers to bring rain. He glanced at the clear blue sky, wishing that clouds would roll up and the heavens would open in answer to his prayers. Perhaps this would cause some of these people to truly believe in the one God, instead of the power of their heathenish tribal spirits. He sighed because he knew in himself that miracles like this would not happen.

They sat opposite each other in the Spartan lounge.

'I am taking away one of your pupils with me', said Saul, coming directly to the point.

'Why is that?' demanded Abraham. 'What do you want him for?'

'I have evidence that along with others he committed politically-inspired crimes in the tribal lands.'

'Crimes?' frowned Abraham. 'What sort of crimes?'

'Many different crimes', said Saul patiently. 'But I won't know properly, or the full details, until I have finished interrogating him.'

'You find it so easy to call these people criminals', said Abraham bitterly. 'Why don't you understand that they're only trying to achieve the human rights that are their due.'

'I have no intention of engaging in a political argument with you', said Saul firmly. 'I'm a policeman and I have sworn to uphold the law. I don't make the laws, I just administer them.'

'But you agree with them?'

'Maybe I do, maybe I don't, but that has nothing to do with this question.'

'So, because a man passively resists your laws, you are content to arrest and imprison him?'

'What do you think has been happening in the tribal lands?' asked Saul coolly.

'I cannot tell a lie', said Abraham, wishing the subject had not come up. 'I know that people have been passively resisting your laws. I know what has been going on, but I cannot tell you anything.'

'I see', said Saul. He really did see. By nature he was not someone who implicitly trusted the work of missionaries, as some did. Sure they did good but they were naive. They just closed their eyes to the evils of black nationalism. 'I must warn you that if you have involved yourself in incitements to commit crimes, you could find yourself in trouble — whether you are a man of the church or not.'

'I have incited no one to commit a crime. I deeply sympathise with their cause.'

'Perhaps you sympathise with the murder of children, Reverend?' asked Saul, challengingly. 'Would you say that was all in a good cause?'

He saw a look of shock pass over Abraham's face. He guessed the missionary had been deceived the troublemakers. Maybe Abraham was involved, but he had also been fooled.

'The murder of children', said Abraham, almost as if he was talking to himself. 'There have been children murdered?'

'Yes, and adults as well.'

Saul glanced at his watch. 'I'm sorry, Reverend, but I can't waste any more time talking. I have work to do. The pupil I want is Job Mandizwidza.'

'Job?' asked Abraham in alarm. 'I know him and he is a good boy — he wouldn't do anything bad. I will have to tell his father first before you can take him. He lives in the tribal lands.'

'His father knows already', said Saul flatly.

'How does he know?' Abraham was panicking. He wondered what he could do to prevent Saul taking his pupil.

'His father knows because he is the one who reported him to us.'

'Reported him to you?'

'Yes.' Saul noted Abraham's hesitation with satisfaction. He guessed that his thoughts were racing and he understood why. He found it impossible to believe ill of people — especially if they were black. Weren't they the children of God?

'He reported him to me because the tribal spirit, the Rain Goddess, has told the people She is displeased with those causing trouble and spilling blood. Until the trouble stops and those responsible are punished, She says there will be no rain. Mandizwidza says his son is one of those responsible and has turned him in.'

'So you are relying on heathen beliefs?' exclaimed Abraham triumphantly. He wagged an excited finger at Saul. 'Those who work with the devil will perish with the devil. God will punish you!'

Saul's face whitened. 'Heathen beliefs or not, his own father is turning him in because he believes he's a criminal. He says that when the other elders do the same, the rain will fall. Frankly, Reverend, I couldn't give a damn what his reasons are, but I want that boy and I'm going to take him.'

'Only God can bring the rain', muttered Abraham in bewilderment. 'How can poor lost sheep believe that heathen gods can do it?'

Giving the missionary a curt goodbye, Saul walked out. He hesitated on finding Dawn in the hall, and gave her a half smile. 'It's up to you', he whispered. 'This has certainly not improved our chances of getting together on terms your father will approve. He now thinks I'm a disciple of the devil!'

*   *   *

'Why have the police arrested Job, Reverend?' asked Madziwa with a truculence that Abraham had not heard before.

'I don't know', muttered Abraham. He waved at Madziwa to take his place with the teachers, so he could begin his prayer. Madziwa opened his mouth to say something, but thought better of it and stumped off to join the

74

rest. He scowled at Abraham who momentarily felt unease, but then turned and looked fondly at his wife and daughter, dressed in plain white dresses and simple hats, who were with the staff. He smiled gently and clasped his hands. He closed his eyes and looked up. 'Let us pray for rain. Almighty God . . .'

*   *   *

'The missionary has betrayed us', said Madziwa. It was late afternoon and the classroom was empty other than himself and Kephas.

'Betrayed us — what do you mean?'

'The police have arrested Job. It was just before the service.'

'They've taken him to the police station?'

'Yes. Once he is there, who knows what he will say?'

Kephas looked thoughtful. 'I wouldn't talk if I were in his position. But what does the missionary know about us? How can he betray us?'

'He knows about me', said Madziwa, his voice faltering. 'I brought one of the leaders to see him — Simon Gumede — he's the one who conducted that meeting before our first action.'

'But he is sympathetic. He will not betray us.'

'He is white', mumbled Madziwa. 'He will side with his white brothers. How do we know that he didn't hear something and tip off his fellow white man — the police inspector — about Job?'

'Perhaps . . .' said Kephas doubtfully.

'We cannot take a chance', urged Madziwa. 'We must make a plan to ensure he does us no harm.' He looked through the open window at the distant hills. 'We will cause the students to riot and while that's going on we will kill him together with his wife and his daughter.'

'Kill them all?' Kephas asked with a sinking feeling. 'Surely that isn't necessary?'

'It's necessary. We must kill them', said Madziwa with finality. He was not going to gaol because of any damn white man. 'It will not be difficult to kill them. He always preaches that stuff about a man turning the other cheek. He will not resist. He'll kneel and pray with his women while we club them to death like sheep. He doesn't have any guns like the farmers do.'

'Do you really think so?' asked Kephas incredulously. 'You mean they'll just allow themselves to be killed? Will we do it ourselves?'

'Yes, you and I together.'

Kephas wondered how he could avoid getting involved in all this.

'We will tell the boys that the Party wants trouble started at the mission because the missionaries are stealing money from the students', Madziwa continued. 'It wants the mission to be removed from the white missionaries and handed over to the people — after which their education will be free. We will incite them to cause trouble over the quality of their food.' His face lit up. 'We will tell them to complain about always being served beans with their meals.'

'Is that sufficient to start a riot?' asked Kephas doubtfully. He was in torment, having heard that a woman and her children had died from poison at the trough. Whether he liked it or not his destiny was tied up with Madziwa. He had to go along with him, because he could not afford to go against him. If he did, he could be signing his own death warrant — either at the hands of the police or at the hands of the Party. He had no choice.

*   *   *

Dawn's thoughts were in turmoil as she bent her head over the supper table as her father said grace.

'Amen', he said and she picked up her knife and fork. No conversation was allowed at the meal table and she picked at her food thoughtfully. She knew that somehow she had to tell her father about Saul.

'Father', she murmured, plucking up courage.

'We don't speak during meal times, child, or have you forgotten?'

'It's important . . .' she broke in mid-sentence as there was a loud roar of voices over in the direction of the school. It was accompanied by a tremendous clattering noise like cymbals being clashed together by a full symphony orchestra.

'What's that?' Dawn asked in alarm.

'What is it, Abraham?' echoed Mary Hale, a disturbed look passing over her normally tranquil features.

Abraham laid down his cutlery and went to the window. He looked towards the school buildings.

'Beans! Beans! Beans! Beans! . . .'

There were many young voices joining in the chant, but what for? The chanting got louder and the banging increased to a crescendo.

There was an urgent rap on the window and Abraham went over, fumbled the catch and opened it.

'Kephas. It's Kephas Ndhlela', he said in surprise. 'What's going on?'

'There is no time for talk, Reverend', said Kephas, looking back. 'Take your wife and daughter and run away and hide in the bush. If you delay, you will be killed.' His eyes flickered nervously back to the school. 'Don't waste time, Reverend. If you don't go immediately, it will be too late. Please!' he implored. 'Just go'. He ducked sight out of sight and vanished from view.

'Kill us?' said Abraham in disbelief. 'He said they're going to kill us?'

'I'll phone Saul', said Dawn, reaching for the telephone.

'Who's Saul?' asked her mother, her face white and her lips set.

'Saul is Inspector Saul Jenkins at the police camp.'

Abraham, with surprising agility, moved across in two quick strides, wrenched the phone from her hand and banged it down on its cradle. 'You will not call the police. We are not fleeing anywhere', he said quietly. 'We have nothing to fear. God will look after us!'

'We will pray', he commanded, dropping to his knees. Mary hesitated, looked at Dawn, then meekly joined her husband's.

'Come', said Abraham to Dawn with unconcealed impatience. 'You will kneel with us and pray.'

'I will not kneel and wait to be slaughtered', said Dawn, defying her father for the first time in her life.

She again picked up the telephone handset and cranked the handle on its side. Abraham began to stand up, but Dawn held up her hand.

'Stay where you are, father. You cannot stop me because I will fight you if necessary. I'm going to phone the police whether you like it or not. If God won't allow you fight to defend yourself, how can you fight your own daughter?'

Abraham collapsed weakly back onto his knees. He wondered how to deal with such an unheard situation. A daughter defying her own father, indeed! He started praying out loud, but his voice was virtually drowned by the clamour at the school.

'Hallo', said Dawn. 'Give me the police.' She spoke with a sob in her voice.

'I want to speak to Inspector Jenkins.'

There was a short pause.

'Saul. Is that you? It's Dawn.'

'Dawn? exclaimed Abraham in horror. He looked at Mary's ashen face.

'Yes', continued Dawn, 'you must come quickly. The students are rioting and we think they intend to murder us. Yes . . . Yes . . . I will.'

She put the phone down and looked defiantly at her parents.

'Saul says he'll be here within half an hour.'

Ignoring them she went and locked every door in the house — using keys that had virtually rusted in the keyholes. They hadn't been turned since they were fitted because the Brethren never locked the doors of their homes. They were men of peace and expected no ills from others. She returned to the dining room.

'Please', she begged her mother, 'please don't just stay here and wait to be attacked. We must do something to help ourselves. Surely that cannot be wrong?'

'God will look after us', said Abraham calmly. 'You are no longer my daughter. I will not have a daughter who associates with the legions of the devil.'

'She is our daughter . . .' interrupted Mary.

'We have no daughter', said Abraham conclusively and glared her into silence.

'But . . .' Mary got no further. A window exploded in a shower of glass, a rock struck her on the forehead and she dropped to the floor as if poleaxed.

There was a hail of rocks and stones while the mindless mob chanted and screamed outside.

'Beans! Beans! Beans! Beans! Beans! Beans! . . .'

Dawn bent over her mother.

'Leave her alone, you woman of the devil!' screamed Abraham. 'Leave my wife alone. Don't you dare touch her.'

Dawn ignored him and cradled her mother's head in her lap. She was unconscious but still breathing.

'Please, father. Do something', she pleaded. ' Otherwise we'll all be killed.'

He ignored her. There was a lull of fully ten minutes, then another shower of rocks hit windows throughout the house. Dawn dragged her mother under the table to get her into shelter. She looked for a weapon with which to defend herself and her eyes lit on the heavy iron bar in the fireplace that served as a poker during the cold winter months of June and July. A rock narrowly missed her as she ducked out to grab it. She saw a sea of mad chanting faces outside the window staring in at her. On seeing her there was another storm of missiles. Abraham dropped when he was hit by one of them. Blood welled from a deep cut on his temple.

'Leave him! Leave him alone!', Dawn screamed in near hysteria.

She abandoned the iron bar and crawled over to her father. Taking him under his armpits, she tried to pull him into shelter. Sobbing and crying she gave three massive jerks and dragged him over next to her mother. Dawn sobbed and put a hand to her face as a sharp stone struck her own cheek. It came away bloody.

There was something different happening at the window and she looked up to see Mr Madziwa starting to clamber inside. His face was contorted with hatred. The billet of wood in his hand was heavy and dangerous and there was no mistaking his motives. He was coming to assault them — perhaps kill them.

'No!' screamed Dawn. 'Go away!'

She picked up the iron bar and threw it weakly at him, but it struck the wall. He smiled cruelly and swung both legs inside the window. He balanced the club in his hand and raised it. Dawn saw by his eyes that she was staring at death.

Crack!

It was a single pistol.

Madziwa staggered and the club dropped. He clutched his shoulder and regarded with astonishment the blood that seeped through his fingers.

Dawn coughed and the scene dissolved as a cloud of tear gas rolled in and burned her eyes. She staggered to the door and fumbled with the lock as the house filled with dense choking chemicals. The door suddenly burst open and she stumbled thankfully into Saul's arms.

11

Saul studied the report and whistled. He frowned as the orderly stamped smartly to attention in front of his desk.

'Yes?'

'An *Nkosi* to see you, Sah.'

He sighed and put the report down.

'Show him in, please.'

A few moments later Jake rolled into the office, for Jake never either walked or ran. He always rolled like a sailor off a corvette, even though he had never sailed on the ocean in his life.

He held out his hand. 'How's it going?' he asked. Saul gripped his hand from a sitting position and waved him to a chair.

'Tea', he shouted to the orderly.

'Sah', came the acknowledgement.

'Any news?' asked Jake.

'As a matter of fact, there is.' Saul picked up the report he had been reading. 'This is from the police forensic science laboratory and it's a report on that sack we found at the trough where the woman and her kids died.'

'What does it say?'

'On the sack itself they found heavy traces of arsenic, indicating it was likely that the container of arsenical dip was carried to the scene in it. There are also soil traces that match the soil at the trough where you lost your cattle. This proves conclusively that the two poisonings were connected.'

'I thought you had deduced that already.'

'I have', said Saul, 'but it still has to be proved in court. Anyway, listen to the rest. There was also a microscopic fragment of yellow paint that matches the colour of the containers used by a commercial supplier of arsenical dip; also, a fragment of dark green paint. The forensic scientist who conducted the examination says that there's a trace of wood on the green paint that indicates it might have come from a painted item of furniture on which the tin had rested.'

'Or', said Jake thoughtfully, giving an obvious alternative, 'it means absolutely sweet bugger all.'

'True, very true', said Saul, 'but you never know your luck and I have a feeling about it. In fact', he said modestly, 'I worked on a hunch and rechecked the house of this chap Madziwa we arrested for the riot at the mission. And guess what?'

'What?' asked Jake.

'I found a wooden cupboard and it's painted dark green. I took it and sent it to Salisbury to see if my prize fragment of green paint originates from it. It's a long shot, I know, but after all, who would have thought that Madziwa would have been the instigator of the riot?'

'Where's he now?'

'In hospital, under guard. He won't get a chance to escape. Besides that things are not going too badly since a father turned his son in. He's admitted involvement all sorts of cases and I have chaps out rounding up the people he has named. It looks like it could be the end of the trail, because no more politically-instigated crimes have been reported for a week. In fact, since the riot at the mission.'

'Hmm', mused Jake, 'and what about Dawn?'

'She's okay. She's got a flat in Salisbury and has got herself a job in a bank.'

'What about her parents?'

'They're still in hospital, but I'm told they're all right, although neither will make statements about what happened. They say that as Brethren they cannot give evidence against any of their flock!'

Saul frowned. 'It's not easy for Dawn. Her father refuses to see her and says he never wants to see her again.'

'That's a bit hard', agreed Jake. 'What about her mother?'

'She has seen her, but without Abraham's knowledge. He's a real miserable sod, as you know.'

'What about the mission? Is it going to remain closed?'

'I shouldn't think so. From what I hear old Abraham is driving the nurses nuts because he wants to get back there and reopen it. Keeps calling the wrath of heaven down on them. Anyway, when he does get to reopen the place, he's going to be about 30 pupils short because we've got them detained for public violence. Another 20 under the age of 19 have been given judicial canings for the part they played. I don't know if Abraham will take them back into his flock. You never know with a chap like him.

'Sergeant Ndhlela's son is also a student there. He had nothing to do with the riot. Dawn says he came to the house when everything started and warned them to flee.'

'It was fortunate he was there', said Jake.

'Very fortunate', agreed Saul. 'If I'd got the call from Dawn only a minute later, I would probably have been too late. I shot Madziwa through the window just as he raised his club to finish off Dawn and her parents.'

*   *   *

Saul studied the khaki drill-clad remand prisoner. He didn't look tough, nor did he look particularly brutal or even dedicated. In fact, he looked just like any other prisoner — nervous and anxious as to what his future would be. It was true that he attempted to hide his anxiety with bravado, but the way his left hand played continually with the cotton sling supporting his bullet-shattered right arm gave him away.

They had been speaking for two hours. At first Madziwa refused to co-operate, but this was only a token resistance and soon the words poured out in a torrent.He did not even try to deny his leadership of the mission riot . How could he, for the nickel-jacketed slug removed from his shoulder by an overworked surgeon gave greater testimony than words alone. Nor did he deny his Party leadership in the area, which gave him much pride. It was true that he at first tried to deny this, but the finger of testimony pointed at him by accused and victims alike made his denials pointless.

Certain things he would not admit, although by his demeanor it was apparent he had guilty knowledge. He was frightened, but he tried hard to conceal his fear from the hard-faced policemen interrogating him. He would not admit he knew anything about the cattle poisonings, for people had died and he could be convicted of murder and hanged — and Madziwa did not want to die.

He did not want to go to prison either, but he was resigned to that. It couldn't be avoided after all that had happened. He had also said nothing about the involvement of Party people from Salisbury. If he supplied any information regarding them, prison would not be a safe place. He would be marked for execution, not by the authorities who administered the law of the country, but at the hands of the thugs who administered the unwritten law of the Party — whether in prison or outside. An example would be made of him to deter others. Perhaps it would be the quick thrust of a home-made knife ground from a spoon while he was in the showers; or it might be the scything swing of an axe while he was out with a wood-cutting gang. There would probably be plenty of witnesses, but none of them would talk and reveal the identity of the Party executioner.

Saul walked to the window and Madziwa followed him with his eyes. 'You are wasting our time, Madziwa', he said flatly. 'You have admitted almost everything we want to know.' He turned around and ticked off what Madziwa had already admitted to on his fingers. 'You admit to the leadership of the Party in the area. You admit to the leadership of the mission riot and you admit involvement in most of the politically inspired cases that have occurred in the tribal lands.'

'I don't deny those things.'

'If you don't deny these things', asked Ndhlela, 'why don't you tell us about the cattle poisoning and name the leaders in Salisbury who gave you instructions?'

Madziwa looked miserably at the floor.

'I can say nothing about such things because I know nothing. I have no idea how the cattle came to be poisoned, or how the woman and her children you have told me about came to die. I have nothing to do with any of the Party leaders in Salisbury, although I am aware of their identities just as you are. What happened here occurred because the people wanted it to happen. I just led them in conformity with their wishes.'

'He lies like his feet stink', said Saul grimly.

Ndhlela nodded his agreement.

'I don't lie', protested Madziwa, looking from one to the other. 'Do you want me to admit to things I know nothing about?'

'You know about it', accused Ndhlela. 'You will admit these things because you were responsible for them.'

'I will continue to deny all knowledge because I know nothing about them.'

'We can prove you were involved in the poisonings. We're certain of it', said Saul grimly.

'I am in your hands', shrugged Madziwa. 'What can I do? You will prove it even if I am innocent. What chance do I stand?' He looked at Saul with a studied indifference, knowing full well that without his admission of wrongdoing he had nothing.

'We have proof', said Saul.

'I don't think so', replied Madziwa uneasily, his mind racing.

Saul picked up a typewritten letter that he had received in the mail from Salisbury the previous afternoon. He studied Madziwa's face for reaction and noted a look of worried confusion. He waved the letter at his prisoner. 'When you were arrested, we searched your house and removed a cupboard. The one painted green.'

'It's true. I know you took the cupboard', agreed Madziwa. 'But how can my cupboard reveal that I am the one who poisoned the cattle?' His worried face did not match his pretended indifference. The cupboard could have nothing to do with the case. What concerned him was a niggling memory of him having once sat naked on the cupboard. This could cause him trouble as intimate parts of his body had come into contact with it. He looked at Saul searchingly, but his face was expressionless. Why had he wanted the cupboard? Were they intending to make some medicine or a potion from the sweat that might have dried on it?

He glanced at Ndhlela and saw distaste. Who knows what that black man might have done. Ndhlela was not of his tribe. He was a Matabele and doubtless he hated Madziwa, whose people were once in the thrall of Ndhlela's warrior ancestors. He was beginning to feel sure that Ndhlela had arranged for spells to be cast to trap him. He remembered his unease when the small twist of rats' claws and forest roots bought from the nganga for four dollars were confiscated by Ndhlela on his arrest. That muti was supposed to protect him from arrest. Madziwa was an educated man and confirmed as a Christian, but he would have been very stupid indeed to have relied on Christian education alone when other things — far more effective things beyond the white man's ken — were available to help him. Suddenly Madziwa lost hope.

'Do you remember the tin we took from your house?' asked Saul grimly. 'It was a tin that once contained arsenical dip.'

'There are a lot of people with such tins. They wash them out and use them to store water', protested Madziwa. ' I have had mine for many years.'

'I know it has been washed and burned out', agreed Saul, 'but there were still traces of arsenic inside. There were also traces of the original yellow paint on the outside.'

'I admit it once contained arsenical dip and that it was painted yellow. I said I have had it for a long time. I told you that.'

Madziwa's confidence returned. How could anybody prove that he had used the tin to carry the arsenic to the troughs? What he couldn't believe was that the police had found traces of arsenic inside. He had cleaned it carefully, burned the tin and scrubbed it for an hour to get rid of any trace of the poison. Anyway, how could a common old tin like that be of evidential value?

Saul continued. 'At the place where we found the dead woman and her two children, we also found a sack. It was just an old sack, but we know from arsenic stains found on the inside that it was used to carry the poison to both troughs. This mis confirmed by soil found on the outside of the sack which matches soil at the trough where the cattle died.'

'Soil is soil', observed Madziwa.

'Not quite', said Saul. 'It's almost identifiable as a fingerprint.'

Madziwa said nothing.

'Also', continued Saul, 'inside the sack we found a speck of green paint. It has been fitted like a piece of jig-saw puzzle into a chipped section of paint on your cupboard. This shows that either the sack or the arsenic tin used in the crimes rested on it. The cupboard belongs to you so that proves you are the man responsible.'

Madziwa blanched.

'You are an educated man — a school teacher — read this letter for yourself.' He handed it to Madziwa who took it with a shaking hand. He studied the contents and read it twice before gingerly handing it back.

'I understand', he said, his face looking as dead as if he were already past the trap in the gallows. Shortly afterwards Madziwa broke down and tears streamed down his cheeks. He collapsed to the floor and grovelled in self-pity. Ndhlela and Saul looked at each other.

'Get him up', said Saul.

Ndhlela gripped Madziwa under his armpits and pulled him to his feet.

'What will happen to me?' quavered Madziwa.

'You will be tried for murder', said Saul evenly.

'And probably hanged like the dog you are', muttered Ndhlela in his own language. Saul frowned at this breach of procedure, but didn't say anything because he knew it was the truth.

'What if I tell you the names of everyone who was involved in all the cases?' bargained Madziwa. His frame seemed to have shrunk. He was a broken man. 'Won't this stop them from hanging me?'

'I don't know', said Saul truthfully. 'Even without the murders you will be going to prison for a very long time. I cannot honestly say that anything you tell me will count in your favour — sufficient to save you from a conviction for murder.'

'But could it help?' begged Madziwa like a wide-eyed child. 'Could it save me?'

Saul shook his head. 'I don't know, but I'll promise to bring it to the court's attention if you help us with our investigations. I cannot promise anything more.'

'I will tell you everything', volunteered Madziwa.

'Warn and caution him', instructed Saul. In spite of himself he felt sorry for Madziwa. No matter what he'd done, his days were numbered.

'Yes, *Nkosi*', said Ndhlela. He formally intoned the words that had been decided upon by judges long ago when they had ruled that man must be protected from the natural human instincts that made him want to confess guilt to clear his conscience.

Saul looked reflectively through the door of the office. It was not yet nine o'clock in the morning, but the heat was building up. The sky was still the same cloudless blue that it had been for months. The rains were still holding off. Sweat was causing his shirt to cling to his back and damp patches stained the cloth in the area of his armpits. He shifted uncomfortably — it must be at least 90° already and it was still three hours to the hottest time of the day. Beyond the door was a lawn of Kikuyu grass, emerald green thanks to the police camp's borehole. Every few seconds a travelling jet of water came into view as the big swinging arm of the sprayer swung backwards and forwards irrigating the grass.

'*Nkosi*!'

Saul's attention returned to the two men. He was puzzled by an expression of alarm on Ndhlela's face.

'What's wrong?'

Ndhlela hesitated and glanced at his prisoner. '*Nkosi* . . .'

He hesitated and looked away.

'Come on, man', Saul encouraged. 'What does he say?'

'*Nkosi*, he says that a boy at the mission helped him to poison the cattle and he shares his blame for the people dying.'

'From the mission, eh?' Saul looked at Madziwa thoughtfully. 'What's the boy's name?'

'He says the boy is Kephas Ndhlela', Sergeant Ndhlela said, his face ashen with disbelief,.

'Your son? He says that your son helped him?'

Ndhlela shook his head. 'No, *Nkosi*, he doesn't say that it's my son. He says only that the person who helped him was Kephas Ndhlela. My son is called Kephas and he is the only boy with the surname Ndhlela.'

'But he would know you', insisted Saul. 'He would know that the boy was your son.'

'No', said Ndhlela. 'He might not. You see, *Nkosi*, I have instructed my son in the past not to tell people that his father is a policeman. In these troubled times it doesn't pay to be completely forthcoming about one's background.'

'Too many people wanting to get their own back, you mean?' said Saul, more as a statement of fact than as a question.

'It is correct what you say', agreed Ndhlela, his face revealed his agony within.

They questioned Madziwa together. Less than an hour later they were convinced — unless Madziwa was deliberately lying. But he was facing a possible death sentence for murder and men in that situation do not usually lie. They said little but each knew the truth. Kephas , the son of Police Sergeant Ndhlela, was probably a killer.

'We'll have to bring your son in', Saul said.

Saul fought the vehicle over the rutted roads. Ndhlela sat slumped in the seat next to him staring moodily out of the window. Saul had almost forbidden him to come, but his heart had softened. He suddenly looked old man. Saul swore that he had aged ten years in the past half hour. He seemed broken in body and spirit. What a terrible thing to happen. Thirty-five years of loyal service to the police and his son turns out to be a murderer.

'He is my son', Ndhlela had said, with quiet dignity. 'If he has committed a crime then I must help the *Nkosi* to arrest him.' They looked each other in the eyes, but Saul's were the first to drop. Did he have the right to deny this of an old man?

*   *   *

Kephas was not at home when they arrived at the farm. 'He's probably away visiting', said Ndhlela.

'I expect so', said Saul as they walked around the deserted buildings. 'He couldn't know that we're looking for him.' He avoided saying what they both knew he meant — that they were there to arrest him.

'Do we wait for him, *Nkosi*?' asked Ndhlela. 'He must be taken back with us.'

'Yes.'

They regarded the other silently, each knowing what the other was thinking. Ndhlela did not ask the question he wanted to ask and Saul's mind was working overtime. He knew logically that he could trust Ndhlela, even though it was his son they were after. But one part of his mind warned him not to be foolish.

'We don't know for sure that your son is guilty.'

'That's right, *Nkosi*', said Ndhlela, 'but we know that it's likely he is.'

'Yes', agreed Saul, wondering if he was about to make a fool of himself. 'He is only a young boy. Even if he is convicted of murder, the judge will not sentence him to death.'

'I know that, *Nkosi*.'

Saul looked at Ndhlela's set features.

'If, in a case like this, the boy gave himself up. Would it count in his favour?'

'It would, indeed', agreed Saul and made his decision. He glanced at his watch and spoke casually. 'Sergeant, I think I should call on the chief and brief him about the arrests. There is no need for me to wait here with you. I will return later. You understand that Madziwa's information is unconfirmed. If you should come up with an admission by your son, I would feel justified in saying that he had surrendered himself. That would mitigate at least some of the more serious aspects of this case. Another mitigating factor is that he warned the missionaries that their lives were in danger. This probably saved them from certain death.'

'You are willing to leave me here alone to wait for him?' Ndhlela's eyes brimmed with tears and Saul looked away.

'As I said', gruffed Saul, 'his involvement in this matter has not been confirmed — and you are his father.'

'What if a father decided to let his son escape?'

'That would not be the father I know.'

Ndhlela gripped Saul's hand firmly.

'You can depend on that, *Nkosi*. I am grateful for what you are doing.'

Saul got back in the driver's seat of the Land-Rover and started the engine.

'I know nothing about that, Sergeant', he grunted. 'I just have some vague information that you may be able to enlighten me on when I return.'

'Sir', said Ndhlela, crashing his boots to attention, 'I will tell you this information when you return.' Saul did not even hear him as he let out the clutch and roared off in a cloud of dust — but he knew what he had said. spoken.

*   *   *

Kephas cycled along the track that led from Mandizwidza's kraal to his home. He had visited Tandiwe and she was pleased to see him. The unease he had felt since the arrest of Job and Madziwa had almost dissipated. It was over a week since the troubles at the mission. So far his name had not been mentioned, so he felt it safe to assume that it would not crop up now. Mandizwidza had welcomed him at the kraal and had even hinted that a visit by his father to discuss the question of bride price would be regarded with favour. This was good news for two reasons — firstly, because he welcomed the prospect of marrying Tandiwe, and secondly, because it was obvious that Mandizwidza did not suspect his involvement in the troubles along with his son. Mandizwidza, in fact, had even told Kephas that he had reported his son to the police.

It was common knowledge that the great *Mhondoro* — the Spirit of the Rain Goddess —had instructed that rain would not fall until the troubles stopped. Mandizwidza had been the spokesman for the delegates who had consulted her. Why else would a father hand over his son to the authorities? This was Kephas' main worry. He was not of the tribe and if the drought continued wouldn't his name be mentioned? Without rain, the land and eventually the tribe would die. No man would remain quiet if he thought Kephas was the reason for the Rain Goddess continuing to exercise her displeasure.

He skidded to a halt by the group of huts that served as home and leant his cycle against a nearby tree.

'You have returned, my son?'

His father's voice took him completely by surprise and he turned in confusion to see his father there in uniform. He looked around the yard but there was no sign of a police truck. He wondered how his father had got there.

'It's good to see you, Father', he said with some unease.

'It's good to see you, my son.' Ndhlela waved to two chairs outside the main living hut. 'Let us sit down.' He placed his hand on Kephas' shoulder, led him to a chair and sat down himself.

Kephas found it difficult to look at his father and he felt a deep sense of shame. It was a shame that threatened to choke him. He nodded at the sunbaked fields that had been ploughed and planted months before, ready for the first rains. By now they should have been heavy with tall waving maize stalks hung with cobs. 'The rains have not come.'

'No', agreed Ndhlela heavily, 'the rains have not come.'

'The people in the tribal lands say the rains have not come because the Rain Goddess is displeased.'

'I have heard this', agreed Ndhlela. 'It's said that she has told the people that the rains will not come until the people stop breaking the law.'

There was a pregnant pause as they stared moodily at the parched fields. A dust devil swirled across the lands, picking up a scattering of dry leaves in its path until it vanished into the long dry grass of the veld.

'I was pleased that you warned the missionaries that their lives were in danger', said Ndhlela. He found it difficult to look his son directly in his eyes. 'It made me very proud of you.'

Kephas felt that this father was making small talk and he had a sense of foreboding. There were other more important things that were about to be said.

'When will the mission be reopening?' asked Kephas, trying to put off the moment.

Ndhlela shook his head. 'I don't know. I have heard disturbing things, my son', he blurted with unaccustomed bluntness. He forced himself to look at Kephas, but his son looked away. 'Very bad things.'

'Very bad things, father?' Kephas tried with little success to show surprise. 'What bad things have you heard?'

Ndhlela took a deep breath. 'We have arrested a man called Madziwa.'

Kephas tried to imagine that it was all a bad dream, that his father was not there, that the conversation was not taking place and that he had never got involved with Madziwa in the first place.

'I know him', said Kephas. 'He's the teacher at the mission who was shot by Inspector Jenkins.'

'We have arrested a man called Madziwa', repeated Ndhlela, as if Kephas had not spoken. 'He says that my son assisted him when he committed crimes. He says that they poisoned the water troughs on the farm of the white man called Swartz together — where a woman and her two children died from drinking poisoned water. What do you have to say about that?'

Kephas opened his mouth to deny it, but it hung open. There was a guilty pause while Kephas gathered his thoughts.

Ndhlela said nothing. There was no need for more words.

'Why have you brought this disgrace on me?' asked Ndhlela. He searched Kephas' for a sign to indicate that Madziwa was lying, but all he saw was guilt. 'Why?' he asked, banging his knee with his fist. 'Why, why, why . . .?' He looked away when no answer was forthcoming. He couldn't face his boy. His eyes brimmed with tears. 'I have given my word that I will arrest you and take you back to Senga for trial. You will go to prison for a long time, but they will not kill you. You are still a boy. One day, when you have paid your debt to society, your wrongs will be forgotten. But you will never be a doctor, as I so dearly wished . . .' The words stopped as emotion choked them off. He paused. 'Get your clothes together. We will wait for Inspector Jenkins to return with the truck.'

'Help me, father', said Kephas tears welling in his eyes. 'I did not mean to get involved — I was forced into it.'

'I wish I could help you, but I can't — even though you are my son. You must give yourself up. I must speak truthfully about what you have done. That's the only way I can help you.'

Kephas saw tears glinting in his father's eyes. A lump welled in his throat and the salty fluid from his own tears rolled down his cheeks. He wanted to throw his arms around his father, embrace him and beg him for forgiveness. But something stopped him. He had grown up in police camps and he knew the routine. He was no stranger to the sight of prisoners being brought in, convicted and sentenced. In prison they worked all day under guard and at night the cell doors were slammed shut until the next morning. This continued for month after month, year after year, until their sentences were completed. He couldn't stand the idea of being locked up like a caged animal for maybe 20 years. He knew he couldn't take it. He had to stay free. He made up his mind. He would run away. Others had gotten away from the police and not every wanted man was arrested. Sure it would desperately hurt his father — but he had already hurt him — it was too late to worry about that now.

Ndhlela touched his wrists in a symbolic gesture of arrest. 'Come on, Kephas, Inspector Jenkins will be here soon.'

Kephas nodded and pretended to comply. Meanwhile, his mind was working overtime, formulating an escape plan.

'Very well, father, I'll get my clothes.'

Ndhlela gruffly told him to hurry. He packed a few clothes into a suitcase and strapped a blanket to the outside while his father looked on. He pulled on his jacket and picked up the suitcase.

'Father, I'm not going to prison. I can't give myself up.'

His father saw the determination on his set features. He was amazed and couldn't believe his ears. Was he dreaming? But this was no dream.

He grabbed Kephas by his arm and shouted: 'You are going. I will take you with me.'

Kephas shook himself free. 'I'm leaving this place now, father and I'm going alone. No one can stop me. Stand aside.'

Ndhlela almost lost control at this uncharacteristic defiance. He grabbed Kephas and they grappled. The older man tried to pin his son's arms to his sides, but although still strong he was no match for the strength of his son. Kephas broke free and threw his father to the ground.

They cried, the father on the ground and the son standing astride him. Kephas spoke through his tears to Ndhlela, who looked up at him, a broken man.

'You stay there, do you hear?' I don't want to hurt you, father, but I will if I have to. I'm not going with you to the police camp and no one, not even you, can make me.'

'I will force you to stay here even if you try to kill me in the process', shouted Ndhlela. He struggled to regain his feet, but Kephas darted nimbly outside and closed the door behind him. Ndhlela tried to wrench it open, but Kephas held it closed and bound wire around the hasp outside, effectively imprisoning his father within.

He picked up his suitcase and ran. His father's shouts and the sounds of him battering at the door to free himself faded as he left the last hut behind. He looked back once with nostalgia, his heart sinking as he realised that he might never see his father again. Then, without further hesitation he set his face to the front, squared his shoulders and made his way deep into the forest.

'*Nkosi*, my son has ran away. It never occurred to me that my own son would defy me. I told him I was taking him to the police camp.' He pointed to a hut. 'He locked me up there and ran away.'

Ndhlela stirred the loose dust with the toe of his boot. '*Nkosi*, I am deeply ashamed. I gave you my word and I have broken it.'

'It's all right, Ndhlela. It's not your fault', said Saul, feeling a deep sympathy for his sergeant. Not only had he gone through hell with the discovery that his son was involved in murders — he now had to live with him being on the run. He might end up later not even knowing if he was dead or alive 'We will get him. He has no place to go. I know that you would have stopped him if you could.'

'Thank you, *Nkosi*', said Ndhlela, and meant it.

'We'll get him eventually', promised Saul. 'He can't hide forever.'

12

Salisbury bewildered Kephas. He was not used to the city. He was tired, hungry and afraid. Last night he had slept in the bush. Early this morning he flagged down a bus that brought him to town. He couldn't stay in Senga. If he did, he knew that sooner or later the police would catch up with him. Perhaps in the city he could lose himself in the crowds and gain the anonymity that wasn't possible at home. Perhaps he could find work, so that he could least buy food to eat and be able to stay in one of the huge hostels in Matapi where single men like himself went and found bed space.

He couldn't turn to his relatives in Highfields Township — how could he trust them not to report his arrival to his father? That would mean prison. There was no turning back now. He had made his decision and would abide by it. His father, family and friends were part of a different life now.

There was only one person likely to help him and he hardly knew him. It was he who had arranged the meeting that had started all the troubles. He didn't know the address, but he knew he lived in one of the townships on the outskirts of the city. An important man like Simon Gumede shouldn't be too difficult to find.

The streets were crowded with whites, blacks, coloureds and Indians who jostled him as they hurried about their business. They took no notice as he stood on the street corner and nervously changed his suitcase from one hand to the next. He felt homesick already.

The buildings around him were very tall. His eyes traversed up and down the huge concrete edifices as he crossed the road. Cars hooted and drivers shouted impatiently and made rude signs as he nervously wove in and out of the traffic.

A policeman strolled casually along the pavement. His eyes rested for a moment on Kephas, who turned in panic and concentrated on the traffic. He felt his flesh cringe as he waited for a tap on the shoulder that would spell the end of his freedom. But it never came.

After a long pause he glanced back and saw the policeman disappearing into the thronging crowd. He relaxed, conscious that his muscles had tensed in anticipation of arrest.

A woman was leaning against a shop window looking at him. He gave her a quick nervous glance, then looked away. When he checked again a few moments later, she was still staring at him. She was unlike any other woman he had ever seen. There was none like her at home. She wore a black wig that reached down to her shoulders. Her brown cheeks had patches of vivid red splashed on them and her mouth was shaped with crimson lipstick. The smart low-cut dress and large expanse of breast excited his senses. Beneath the short dress were two perfectly shaped legs finished off with a neat pair of ankles encased in black high heels. There was a mocking smile on her face. Kephas shifted uncomfortably under her frank gaze. He turned and walked self-consciously away from her. What a woman! He thought of Tandiwe and pictured her in her shapeless cotton dress and bare feet. She was nothing compared to the vision he had just seen.

'Where are you going, stranger?' a low feminine voice came from his side.

He turned nervously and saw that it was the same woman. He gave her an uncertain smile. She moved next to him and took his arm. Unconsciously, or that was what he thought, she brushed her voluptuous body against his.

'Where're you going, good looking?' she repeated.

Kephas looked around uncomfortably and wondered how much attention was being drawn to him. He felt that all eyes were on him. He had to keep moving. He felt a sudden fear that the policeman would return.

'We must walk', he said.

She laughed gently and fell in step beside him. She was really beautiful. Kephas felt her soft body warmth occasionally brushing against his which sexually aroused him in a way that he had never known before.

It was obvious she liked him. Perhaps she could help him.

'I'm looking for Simon Gumede. He's a very important man and lives in Salisbury. Have you heard of him?' he asked anxiously.

She looked at him quizzically. 'Whereabouts in Salisbury does he live?'

'I don't know, but I thought you might have heard of him.' He looked at her glumly.

My God, she thought, what a stupid country bumpkin. A look of triumph flashed over her painted face, but Kephas did not see it.

'Oh, Simon Gumede! Come to think of it, I know him well. I know where he lives. Come, I will take you to him.'

He smiled happily. 'Are you sure it will not be too much trouble? After all, you scarcely know me.'

She gripped his arm tightly and drew her hot little body closer to his, sending further shimmering sensations of passion through Kephas' body.

'No, that's true', she murmured. 'I don't really know you, but we're going to get to know each other better. Much better, aren't we? ' She gave him a sly wink.

Kephas felt shabby. He was dressed in his best clothes and that consisted of a jacket and trousers. Although clean, they were old and patched and his shirt had seen better days. They compared very unfavourably with the smart garb of his new girlfriend. For a fleeting second he wondered why such an attractive woman had tagged on to him. Momentarily he felt a twinge of misgiving, but he dismissed this as nonsense. He was just lucky. She seemed so open, honest and friendly and the way she was gripping his arm in public hardly contradicted this. Passers by seemed to be glancing at them, but he didn't mind. He just felt that, after all, he must be really quite a handsome fellow.

'What's your name, handsome?'

He lied easily. 'Joseph. I'm from Bulawayo. I've been promised a job by Gumede.'

She looked at him mockingly. It should have been clear to Kephas that she did not believe him, but he was so overwhelmed by her charm that he just grinned back. Why should he worry?

'Come', she said impatiently. 'Let me take you to your friend . . .' she paused and he was conscious that her hand was rubbing against the flies of his trousers. 'And later we will make time to get to know each other better.'

She glanced quickly down at the front of his trousers and erupted in giggles. Kephas fidgeted uncomfortably. He was not used to women laughing at him, nor them being so bold.

He wanted this woman. She had virtually offered herself to him and he made up his mind that as soon as he got the opportunity, he would take her. He felt impatient, but first he would find Gumede and then he would attend to the more pleasurable task of satisfying this lovely creature. They strolled down the street, neither of them speaking. There was really nothing to say.

She guided him down streets and around corners until they found themselves in a teeming black township. The white faces had disappeared.

He lost his sense of direction as they walked, and soon had no idea where he was or where he had come from. He was a country boy and unfamiliar with the city layout. But he trusted her and allowed her to guide him. She obviously knew what she was doing. In country areas people would stop and greet each passing stranger, but here they ignored them and hurried by with unseeing and uncaring eyes. The farther they walked, the quieter the streets became. Soon they only saw the odd pedestrian, but still she led him on.

They reached the last of the houses. The blaring notes of a jazzy repetitive tune was coming from one. The music gradually faded as they walked on. They reached an area of widely spread rubbish dumps. Tall grass grew through the rusted remains of motorcar chassis. At some places thin spirals of smoke, where spontaneous combustion had sparked fires, wound up into the sky.

He wondered where she was taking him. The pressure on his arm eased him to a halt. It was as if she had read his thoughts. She smiled reassuringly.

'Wait here', she patted his arm. 'I must go and see if your friend is free to see you.'

'Why here?' he asked in puzzlement. 'Surely I can go to his house?'

'Be patient', she murmured, 'be patient. He's a very busy man and not just anybody can go to his house. I will have to ask him first if he is prepared to see you.' She laughed mockingly. 'It seems that you are not used to the ways of us townspeople.'

Kephas squirmed. He was desperately shy with this woman and she seemed to enjoy poking fun at him.

It was such an odd place to bring him. Wouldn't it have been better to have left him to wait in the street while she made her enquiries? The uneasy feeling he had experienced earlier returned. A half of his mind told him something was wrong, but the other half — influenced by the curves of his companion — felt sure that everything was okay. After all, he had only met Simon Gumede once, but he had seemed important. Wasn't it likely that here in the city he was more important than he had first thought? He glanced at her with half-closed eyes. Anyway, he thought, what harm could come to him by waiting for her here? It was still broad daylight.

'How long will you be?'

'Not long, handsome, not long.' She wagged a playful finger at him. 'Don't go away, do you hear? Don't go away.' She smiled and walked off in the direction they had come from.

Kephas suddenly realised how tired he was. He watched until she was out of sight, then cleared a patch of ground and sat down. He yawned, took off his shoes and rubbed his feet. He yawned again and lay back on the ground, relaxing his muscles. He listened idly with drooping eyelids to two butcher birds calling each other from afar. He was hungry and he hoped he would be able to get food from Simon when he saw him. He had not eaten for a long time. His mind floated between sleep and wakefulness, then gradually, with the sun pleasantly warming his face, he dropped off to sleep.

*   *   *

He was having an amazingly sexual dream about this new woman when his head exploded in pain. His mind reeled as his subconscious tried to weave the pain into his dream. He awoke abruptly and rubbed the sleep from his eyes. He looked up and was astonished to see three men and his recent female companion grouped around him. He sat up and gaped. They were grinning as if in great amusement, but why they were laughing was a complete mystery to him. His left ear felt sore and he rubbed it to ease the pain. It was wet and he withdrew his hand which was wet with blood. He looked around him in alarm.

What's the matter? What's happened to my head?'

The smile left the face of a very black man. Kephas studied his distinctly unfriendly face.

'Well, country boy, have you slept well?' mused Blackface.

Kephas just couldn't understand what was happening.

He felt his heart drop when he saw that Blackface was toying with a wicked-looking Okapi clasp knife. The blade was open and locked in place. He tried to ignore it but he kept seeing it from the corner of his eye. He plucked up courage and decided that boldness was the best way out of the situation. He looked at his erstwhile female companion and asked sharply.

'Did you find Simon Gumede?'

Uproarious laughter greeted his question and he shut up

Blackface stropped the knife back and forth on his hand. 'You see, country boy, our sister doesn't even know this Gumede guy. She thought, however, that you probably have some money to donate to her friends. Of course, we are her friends.' He seemed pleased with himself.

Kephas tried to get back to his feet, but a well placed kick thudded into his chest and sat him back on the ground. He clutched his chest and gasped for breath. He tried reasoning with them.

'I don't have any money. I have nothing. I only have my clothes.' He nodded towards his suitcase.

Blackface gestured to one of his companions. 'Search him.'

A henchmen dug into his pockets and turned them inside-out one at a time. Kephas sat passively until the man announced with chagrin that he couldn't find a cent.

'Well, well, well', said Blackface conversationally, 'that's disappointing'. He again whetted the knife blade on the palm of his hand. 'It looks like our friend here will have to pay for our sister's company in other ways.'

'Please', begged Kephas. 'I have nothing. Please let me go.'

A hand moved down at him like greased lightning. The action was so fast that he had no time to take avoiding action. Kephas raised his arm instinctively and felt a flash of pain as the knife steel slipped into him, deflected on a rib and flayed a large flap of flesh from his chest. He screamed in pain.

He heard a shrill female voice: 'Darling, any time you want to make love to me just say the word.' She was almost beside herself with hysterics, but there was nothing pretty or feminine about her now.

Kephas looked numbly at the blood gushing from his chest. An arm with a half brick in its hand was raised. He noticed a finger was missing and wondered without relevance what had happened to it. He was too shocked to take avoiding action. The world exploded in a brilliant flash of light and he slipped into the dark swirling world of unconsciousness.

*   *   *

He felt as if he was floating on air and waves of pain and nausea swept over him. There was a burning sensation on his chest and his head felt like it had been kicked by a horse.

He struggled back to consciousness. He was cold and his teeth were chattering. He couldn't stop shivering. Why was he so cold?

He experimentally opened an eye and looked around. He was on a stretcher with a blanket loosely covering him. Two policemen, one black and one white, were kneeling and examining a patch of ground. Kephas' hands explored beneath the blanket and he felt dismay on feeling only his naked flesh. Those *tsotsis* had stolen everything and left him naked!

He looked for his suitcase, but it was nowhere to be seen. He tried to move but groaned again as it was so painful. The policemen suddenly realised that he had come round.

'Tell him to keep quiet and we'll soon have him in hospital', gruffed the white man kindly. He bent down and straightened the blanket.

Kephas forgot he was a wanted man and lay on the stretcher in a welter of pain. He tried to relax, not daring to move in case it caused more pain. Tears of self-pity welled in his eyes.

The black policeman coaxed his story out of him. Although Kephas told him truthfully what had happened, he said nothing about his reason for being in town and fortunately they didn't ask.

He glibly gave a false name — the one he had used with the gangsters' girlfriend. They did not expect him to lie, so they wrote down what he said without doubting his word. The white man made a few further entries in his notebook and snapped it shut. 'They certainly gave you a workout, lad. When we first saw you, we thought you were dead.'

Kephas smiled painfully. He felt better now. At least he was alive.

They loaded his stretcher into the rear of a police van and drove him to hospital. In casualty they patched him up and he was admitted to one of the wards.

The police told him that when he had recovered, he was to call at the police station and make a statement.

13

A passerby pointed out a large house with a neatly tended garden on the outskirts of Salisbury.

Kephas paused before the garden gate, looked around and hesitated. He had seen houses like this before on the farms at Senga. They belonged to whites, but this place was supposed to belong to a black man. He had never before realised there were so many rich blacks around. Yet there were lots of fancy houses around here in which blacks were living.

He looked down at his torn khaki shirt and shorts. They were the cast off uniform of a male medical orderly and had been donated to him on his discharged from hospital this morning. He had spent a week there until his injuries had healed. Scars were still livid on his body and he was stiff and wobbly on his feet after being bedridden for so long.

The police hadn't visited him in hospital so he assumed they were still waiting for him to come to them. They would have to wait a long time because a police station was the last place he intended to visit.

He gripped the wrought iron gate and released the catch. It squeaked on its hinges as he swung it open. He walked up the crazy paving path that wandered between cool green watered lawns up to a big door with brass fittings. He squared his shoulders and pressed the bell. No one answered. He looked around the front garden but he saw no one. He decided to explore and moved almost on tiptoe around the house to the back door.

A man in a clean white uniform — indicating that he worked in the house — was in the kitchen meticulously pressing a shirt. He looked up but didn't seem the least bit startled to see Kephas. In fact, he pretended nobody was there until he had finished the shirt he was working on. Finally, he looked up at Kephas who was politely waiting for him to speak.

'What do you want?' he asked, with a haughty indifference.

Kephas shifted uncomfortably as he felt the eyes of the man look over him. The servant made no attempt to hide an expression of disgust.

Kephas looked at the ground and wriggled his toes on the step. He was very conscious of his bare feet.

'I have come here to see Simon Gumede', he muttered, still looking down.

'Sorry, there is no work', the servant warned dismissively. 'Besides Mr Gumede wouldn't employ anyone as ragged and unwashed as you are.' He returned his attention to the ironing in a gesture of dismissal.

Kephas plucked up courage again. 'I'm Kephas Ndhlela, from Senga. I need to see Mr Gumede about a very important matter. I'm not looking for work.'

The man looked him over, searching for something that he might have missed. Whatever it was he didn't find it. He clumped the iron down on its rest in annoyance. It might be political business.

'What did you say your name was?'

'Kephas Ndhlela.'

'All right', sighed the houseboy, 'I will go and see if he will speak to you.' He prodded a finger into Kephas' chest. 'I warn you that he is a very busy man. He cannot afford to waste his time on black trash.'

'It's important', emphasised Kephas stubbornly.

The man closed the door in Kephas' face, clearly implying that he regarded him as a likely criminal who would steal his employer's shirt if he left him alone in the kitchen.

Kephas focussed on a chicken run in the back garden. He watched the stupid birds scratching for food in the dust until he the door behind him opened again.   Framed in the door was Simon Gumede. He was just as Kephas remembered him, except that he was wearing a different suit. It was one of 20, each handmade by the best tailor in Salisbury. Not one of them had cost less than $100. He was of medium height and going to fat. Too much good food and drink and too little exercise was beginning to reflect in his body.

'Yes', said Simon Gumede, 'what do you want?'

He made no effort to invite Kephas inside and it was obvious that he didn't recognise him. This was not surprising as it was doubtful he had even noticed him at Senga. There were a whole crowd of people at the meeting on that day.

Kephas found it difficult to look Gumede in the face. His eyes seemed to be boring into him, exploring his every little secret.

Kephas looked down. 'I'm Kephas Ndhlela. I was at the meeting you held at Senga.'

Simon reached outside the door, caught him by the shoulder and pulled him inside.

'Come in', he said. 'We'll talk.'

Kephas' bare feet sank into the thick pile of the carpets as he followed behind the suited form. Gumede stood aside and let Kephas enter the lounge before him. He followed and closed the door.

He airily indicated a hard-backed chair to Kephas, who perched himself uncomfortably on its edge. Gumede lowered himself into a comfortable easy chair, spread his legs and laid his arms on the armrests.

'What do you want?' Gumede asked tersely. 'It's safe to talk here.' He glanced at his watch. 'I can't spare much my time.'

Kephas started again. 'I am Kephas Ndhlela from Senga. I was at the meeting you held in the tribal lands.'

Gumede nodded impatiently and gestured for Kephas to continue.

'I was one of those whom you ordered to take action along with Madziwa. Some of us went to a kraal as you instructed. Many people were beaten. Later Madziwa and I put poison into two cattle watering troughs and killed many cattle that belonged to a white man. Unfortunately, a woman and her two children drank from one of the water troughs and they also died. The police found out I was involved and came to arrest me. My father actually came to get me. He is a policeman.'

Gumede shook his head incredulously. 'You mean that your own father wanted to arrest you? Well, well, well', he tutted without sincerity. 'That's too bad.'

'It wasn't my father's fault', said Kephas defensively. 'It's just that he's been a policeman for many years and he couldn't accept the idea that his son had committed a crime.' He spoke with an intensity that warned Gumede not to pursue the subject.

'Why have you come to see me?' he asked, changing the subject.

'I need help otherwise I will end up in gaol', replied Kephas. 'I don't know anyone else in Salisbury who can help me. Besides, it was your meeting that created the trouble that I'm now in.'

Gumede was in a quandary. He had no desire to get involved with a youngster wanted by the police. It could be risky and he was not the type who took risks.

'How can I help you?'

Kephas replied with a degree of unsureness that did not escape Gumede. 'I thought that you could find me a job, somewhere to stay. I have nowhere else to go.'

Gumede waved his hand about the elegantly furnished lounge. 'Young man, do you see where I live? I have a reputation of respectability and I cannot possibly jeopardise this just to help you find work. Don't you understand? If they caught me hiding you, I would also be sent to prison and that wouldn't help the cause at all.'

Kephas stuttered as he spoke. 'It's not my fault that I am here. It was you who ordered us to help the Party.'

Gumede grimaced and looked sternly at him.

'If you go around saying things like that, it will land you in trouble. You are a member of the Party Youth League and you must realise sons of the soil have to make sacrifices.'

Kephas wished he hadn't come. It was becoming clear he would get no help from this source.

He made a last attempt. 'I thought . . .' he stopped, then faltered on miserably, 'that maybe you could hide me from the police . . .'

Gumede replied angrily. 'I 'm sorry, but you can hardly expect me to hide everyone who is wanted by the police. How do I know that you're telling the truth. Maybe you are wanted for theft or something like that? Besides, I only have your word that you helped the cause.'

Kephas wondered what would become of him. Perhaps he should give himself up. They would put him in prison for a long time, but that was better than starving to death on the streets. His future seemed bleak.

His reverie was interrupted by Gumede who rubbed his chin thoughtfully. He had changed his mind. 'I'll help you. Perhaps you did fight for the cause and you seem to be a good boy.'

A look of hope appeared on Kephas' face.

'What sort of education have you had, boy?'

'I went to mission school. I was studying for standard six. I can't go back now.' Kephas shrugged fatalistically. 'I hoped that one day I would be able to go to university.'

Gumede nodded to gain time as he thought. He looked at Kephas again. Although little more than a boy, he was still a man.

'You are an intelligent young man', he flattered. It amused him to see Kephas start to preen himself. 'We have a duty to educate our people to get them ready for important jobs after we take over the country.' He paused, giving the impression that he was concentrating deeply, Kephas looked on anxiously.

'I think I have only one educational scholarship left. I believe it will suit you. What would you like to study for?' He got up, went to a desk and leafed through sheafs of papers.

'I have always wanted to be a doctor', Kephas said.

Gumede smiled and waved the papers at Kephas. 'What do you know', he almost shouted, 'it's the only scholarship that I have left. It's for a man to learn to be a doctor.' He wagged his finger. 'Remember, boy, we're going to need plenty of black doctors when we're free. We won't need white doctors then. You are really a very fortunate young man.'

Kephas was overwhelmed. He could hardly credit the evidence of his ears. 'You mean the Party will train me to be a doctor because I helped with the action at Senga?'

'Yes young man, that's exactly what I mean. We'll send you to Zambia where your education will begin. Later, we might even send you to America or somewhere else.' He waved an airy hand. 'By the time you get your degree, this country will be Zimbabwe and not Rhodesia.'

'How will I get to Zambia?' queried Kephas. 'I don't have any money.'

'That's not a problem', answered Gumede confidently. 'You will be smuggled out through our secret escape route.'

Secret escape route?' asked Kephas in astonishment. 'What secret escape route?'

Gumede took in the admiration in the boy's eyes. He was certainly a good listener and it seemed a shame to waste him. He walked to the mantelpiece and leant nonchalantly against it.

'Oh, yes, we have a secret escape route that we use to get our boys out of the country. We use it all the time. Freedom is not far off, but we have not finished the fight yet. There is still a long hard struggle ahead before we free Zimbabwe from the white imperialists.' He rolled the last two words around his tongue. He had always liked how the words 'white imperialists' sounded.

Gumede thought how incredibly stupid these boys were. They believed anything he told them. How, honestly, could this dull boy from the tribal areas possibly believe he has the makings of a doctor? His lip curled in distaste as he took in Kephas' shabby appearance. Well, I suppose where he is going could, at a push, be described as a university. He laughed openly in spite of himself.

Kephas laughed along with him, not understanding the joke. He felt more sure of himself now and he smiled at his benefactor. It was a happy scene, but only Gumede knew their mutual happiness stemmed from entirely different reasons.

'Well, my young friend', he said piously, 'I hope that by the time you return, people will no longer be suffering for the cause.'

Kephas, uncertain what Simon Gumede was talking about, nodded his agreement and looked dutifully serious. It seemed the appropriate thing to do.

He did not know that Gumede's latest responsibility to the Party was to recruit young men to be trained as 'freedom fighters' in the Soviet Union, China, Cuba and Tanzania. He had to show the Party results and that wasn't easy. He knew only too well that if a whisper of his activities reached the authorities, it would be a long time before he again enjoyed home comforts. The thought of returning to prison was enough to give him a feeling of claustrophobia.

To hedge himself against trouble, he had recently offered to act as an informer to the Special Branch on Party activities. He had fed them odd snippets of information, but they had recently begun to pressure him for more. This had made things difficult as the Party hierarchy had also started to make dissatisfied noises about his poor recruiting efforts. It was hard to get recruits. Very few young men were willing to fight and get killed for the cause. It did not help that considerable press publicity was given to the large numbers of 'freedom fighters' that had been killed by soldiers when they infiltrated back into the country from Zambia.

When Kephas showed up with his story, Gumede was tempted to tip off his Special Branch contact. He was not at all concerned with what had happened at Senga and one sacrificial lamb for the authorities would have provided him with a breathing space. After some careful soul-searching, though, he decided the priority was to send him for military training and get the Party off his back.

He couldn't ask Kephas openly if he was willing to be trained as a freedom fighter. He knew from bitter experience with other potential recruits that this approach would probably fail. Instead he used the approach that had worked with his last nine recruits — the offer of an educational scholarship outside the country. Once tricked into leaving, the young recruits were in no position to change their minds. Fortunately, the Zambian

Government helped the Party a lot and always returned any deserters they caught.

He congratulated himself as Kephas regarded him with a benign trust. Someone had to fight so why shouldn't it be a young man like this? In fact, as far as Gumede was concerned, it could be anyone — as long as it wasn't him!

14

Kephas glanced back at the giant Aeroflot Ilyushin jetliner squatting on the apron. It had brought them from Cairo to Moscow. It looked like a great silver bird and he marvelled that he had actually travelled inside it. It seemed incredible. The aircraft on which he had flown from Lusaka to Cairo had seemed big enough, but this was enormous.

The other students caught up with him and they continued towards the airport terminal. It was winter in the Soviet Union and very cold — in fact colder than he had thought possible. The runways and front of the terminal buildings were clear of snow, but elsewhere it was piled in great white mounds. Detouring slightly, he picked up a handful of snow and tasted it. It melted against his tongue but left a burning sensation in his mouth. He tucked the collar of his lightweight jacket around his neck, shivered and bent into the bitterly cold biting wind that had been born weeks before in the polar air masses over Mongolia and central Siberia.

In a few moments he was under cover and out of the cruel elements. A short stocky man with mongoloid features blocked their path. Kephas noted with envy the thick black overcoat and hat with ear muffs made of black shiny fur that he was wearing.

'Excuse me', the man said in English, looking at each other of them as if he were carrying out a quick count, 'are you the comrades from Zimbabwe?'

Kephas, who was nearest, answered. 'Yes, we are the students from Zimbabwe.'

The man looked over his shoulder and spoke a few guttural words in a language that Kephas assumed was Russian and two other men, similarly dressed, approached the group with smiles on their flat faces.

'I am the Interpreter', announced the first man, tapping his chest with two fingers. 'These comrades have come to welcome you.' He indicated the two silent men with an air of respect.

He held out his hand. 'Passports, please.'

Kephas passed his to the Interpreter and the others followed suit. The Interpreter didn't examine them, just handed them to one of the other men, who dropped them into an open briefcase.

Briefcase gave the Interpreter a slip of paper. He looked at it and turned back to the visitors. 'Names please?'

They reeled them off while he studied the paper. When the last had been given, he grunted, spoke briefly to Briefcase and then stood back in respectful silence.

The second member of the trio moved next to the Interpreter and looked directly at Kephas.

'The comrade says', started the Interpreter, clearing his throat, 'that he is very pleased to welcome the socialist heroes of the Zimbabwe revolution to Moscow.'

He paused while more words were said, then continued. 'The socialist peoples of the Soviet Union are always glad to welcome comrades who are engaged in the struggle against the running dogs of imperialism.'

The speech lasted for fully ten minutes. During this time, the speaker never once took his eyes off Kephas' face, so he obviously assumed that Kephas was the group leader. The longer the speech went on, the colder the visitors became. Kephas felt sure that if the man continued for much longer, he would collapse from the cold. His teeth chattered and he was shivering, but the welcoming party appeared not to notice. He gave a sideways glance at his companions and saw that they were suffering in the same way. He was determined, out of politeness, to concentrate on what was being said, but he had never been more relieved when the speaker lapsed into silence.

The two parties stood looking at each other and Kephas became acutely aware that he was expected to make some sort of reply speech on behalf of his group.

'Thank you', he blurted out. And then, with a note of desperation, 'Please could we be given some warm clothes?'

The Interpreter was momentarily startled, then his eyes took in their flimsy summer attire. He looked at the man who had made the welcoming speech and with many gesticulations explained that the honoured guests from Zimbabwe were cold, very cold.

'So', said the speaker nodding vigorously to supplement the only word in his English vocabulary, 'so.' He lapsed back into Russian and poured out a flood of words to the Interpreter.

'We will buy you some warmer clothes', smiled the Interpreter. 'Follow me, please.'

They were ushered through the building to a side entrance, bypassing the formalities of customs and immigration. The Interpreter and Briefcase remained with them, but the other man left after stiffly shaking hands with each of them in turn.

Waiting at the side entrance was a small bus painted drab grey. They clambered aboard and sat down. The Interpreter closed the sliding door and rapped on the window that separated the driver from the passengers.

The engine started and the vehicle ground away through the snow. There was very little talking during the journey and the Rhodesians huddled down in their seats and tried to warm up. How different Russia was to their home country. The bus chugged slowly through the snow-covered streets. People scurried about with their heads down to avoid the biting wind. How drab everyone looked. Not once did Kephas see anybody, man or woman, dressed in a coat of any colour except black or grey. Many wore fur hats like the Interpreter, but even more had scarves wrapped tightly around their heads. A large number of men were dressed in uniforms of some kind or the other.

It was midday and although the streets were crowded with people, Kephas saw only a few motor cars. He could not read the Russian signs on them, but some were obviously taxis. The majority of vehicles around and about were lorries or buses.

The roads they drove along were wide, well-built and imposing and they passed through several flyover complexes. In direct contrast were the buildings that bordered them — the great mass of which were simple and squalid tenements of drab brick or wood in a neglected colour-washed stucco. Interspersed were grey concrete apartment blocks of a dismal sameness that stretched across the skyline. No colour relieved the snow-covered landscape and there was not a flower to be seen.

The trip seemed endless. Several times they passed big open parks dotted with the black figures of people skating on frozen ponds. Others were sliding down hills with what appeared to be wooden planks strapped to their feet. The Interpreter, seeing their interest, explained that the people were skiing.

At last, the bus halted in front of a great brick building that appeared to combine living and business quarters. People hung out of some of the upper floor windows and children played in the streets below. The lower level had a huge department store in the middle of the building on which the sign 'Univermag' appeared in large letters. At the opposite ends of this store were two others with the signs 'Knigtorg' and 'Gastronom', respectively. Kephas concluded that one was a bookshop and the other some kind of grocery store. A long queue of women, heads wrapped in scarves, snaked out of the door of the food store. They looked on impassively as the black Africans alighted and were led into the state-owned department store.

Within a half-hour they had been fitted out with woollen underclothes, thick shirts, heavy drab suits, long overcoats, gloves and fur hats virtually identical to the Interpreter's. When they reboarded the bus, they felt much better and happily clasped the brown paper parcels containing their spare clothing.

Moscow seemed endless to the Africans, who had never dreamed that towns could be so large. Kephas concluded that at least ten Salisburys could be fitted into just that part of Moscow he had already seen.

*   *   *

Kephas felt more talkative now that he was warmer and he tried to start a conversation with the Interpreter.

'Where are we going?'

'To a camp outside town.'

'How far is it? When will I start on my medical studies?'

The Interpreter seemed mystified. 'No one is here to study medicine. You are all here to study political activation.'

'Political activation?' It was Kephas' turn to be mystified. 'What's that? There must be some mistake. I came here to study medicine. The others', he added, 'are here to study economics.'

'You are all here to study political activation', repeated the Interpreter stubbornly.

The others were listening intently.

'I don't even know what political activation is.'

He looked around at his companions. 'At home I was asked what I wanted to do and I chose medicine.'

A chuckle came from the back of the bus and Kephas looked around in annoyance.

'I wondered if you really believed all that rubbish', came from Kumalo, a tall broad-shouldered man of about 25 who, like Kephas, was of the Matabele tribe. 'You want to know what political activation is, do you?' He looked at the concerned expressions on the faces of the others. 'Well I'll tell you. We're here to be trained as "freedom fighters", to free our country from the grip of the white man. I volunteered', he said with contempt, 'but with you sheep the leaders probably thought you might run away if they said you were going to be trained to kill people — even if they are white.'

'They said I was going to be trained as a doctor', said Kephas stubbornly.

'Well, you're not, and that's that. You're all here for the same thing', Kumalo said, looking around at his compatriots. 'I suggest you make the best of it.' He grinned. 'Doctor, indeed. How the hell could you believe that they would ever make a doctor out of a black kaffir like you?'

Kephas laughed in spite of his indignation at his sudden change of career. It was not long before they were all chortling together. The Interpreter, who'd been worried that some of his charges might make trouble for him, relaxed when he saw that they had accepted the situation.

Well, thought Kephas to himself resignedly, at least I'll be someone as a freedom fighter. He had a brief vision of himself in military uniform, rifle slung nonchalantly over his arm, returning in triumph to see his father once the last white man had been driven from Zimbabwe.

Perhaps being a freedom fighter wouldn't be so bad after all.

They started to leave Moscow again. In the suburbs the buildings were less impressive and were little more than wooden shacks. Judging by the way the bus bumped up and down, the road beneath the thick layer of compacted snow was unpaved. Once out of the urban area they drove on through the snow-covered meadowlands and pine and oak forests of the undulating glaciated country to the west of the city.

It was late afternoon when they pulled into a square of barrack-like buildings surrounded by a high security fence. They were shown to their quarters which consisted of rows of rooms, each containing two beds with biscuit-type mattresses and stark wooden lockers.

It was the place they would call home for the next six months.

That evening they started to become acquainted with the 30 or so other blacks there, all of them came from Rhodesia, South West Africa or the Republic of South Africa.

15

It was the 1st March, 1966. Saul stood at the office window with his hands clasped behind his back. Standing slightly behind him in respectful silence was Sergeant Ndhlela.

The drought had broken. This morning at dawn the skies were low and thick with rain. It had thundered all night. At eight o'clock the heavens opened and the life-giving rain came down in torrents. As heavy as it was, the rain soaked into the parched veld as if it was blotting paper for the first half hour. Then puddles formed and tiny rivulets of water gathered in the vleis and trickled down to the river. It showed no signs of abating and had started beating down even harder and was drumming on the Charge Office's corrugated iron roof. The gutters were overflowing and water was streaming over the sides because the down pipes couldn't cope with such volumes. The rivulets were swelling as water rushed from the high ground to get to the rivers on its inexorable journey to the sea 1 000 kilometres away.

The weather report on the radio said the rain was widespread and the whole country was getting a good soaking.

For most of those who lived by the soil, the rains were too late. There was, perhaps, still time to re-plant the mealie crops to replace those that had withered and died from the intense dry heat, but in places like Senga, it was too late for the cattle. Most white farmers had either moved their stock long distances to lusher pastures, or had sold the cattle before their condition worsened and became too poor to sell. But the tribesmen in the Senga tribal lands had refused to sell at any price. They weren't interested in cash and had preferred to keep their herds as a sort of walking bank. They just dug in their heels and refused all blandishments by the authorities to sell, so thousands of cattle died. Ironically, although there would be grazing again within ten days because of the rains, there would be no stock left to graze on it. Even the donkeys and goats, which could live on almost anything, had been seriously depleted.

Saul looked at the beating rain thoughtfully. The rivers and dams would soon fill to capacity. With grass cover virtually gone, there was nothing left to restrict the flow of water and most would run off into the rivers before it had a chance to soak into the ground.

He turned from the window, walked slowly back to his desk and sat down. Ndhlela followed his movements with his eyes, but stayed where he was.

Saul picked up a ballpoint pen and twiddled it in his fingers.

'Are you certain, Ndhlela?'

'Yes, *Nkosi*. When I first received the information I checked it and double-checked it. It was correct.'

Saul looked at the pen thoughtfully. It was certainly odd. They had dealt with at least a hundred politically inspired cases in the area with Party overtones. He had lost count of the arrests. Yet nothing they had done seemed to stem the tide of reports. As soon as they dealt with one and cleared it with arrests, another would be received.

The last report had come in on 15th February when a headman's hut was burned down in the night. He had narrowly escaped with his life. Since then there had been no further reports for a whole two weeks. They had been working close to fever pitch for so long that it seemed strange to go to bed and not be woken by the telephone ringing at midnight or at some other ungodly hour.

'Tell me again and give me all the details', Saul said.

'*Nkosi*', Ndhlela said with a shade of reluctance, 'there are things that are difficult for a white man to understand.'

'I know this, sarge', said Saul encouragingly, 'but you forget that I am of Africa myself — even though I am white. The spirits of my family have been here since the time of Shaka Zulu. So there are things I understand even if they are not of my culture.'

Ndhlela looked carefully for the trace of a smile on Saul's face, because he knew very well that most white men didn't understand the ways of his people. But there was no smile to be seen.

'You understand, *Nkosi*, that we blacks believe in God in the same manner as you white people do?'

Saul nodded. 'I know this.'

'God is not something that was introduced to us from overseas. We have always believed in Him. To the Mashona people the supreme being is

Mwari, or God as you call him in English. He has various spiritual assistants who maintain contact with the people because it's impossible for Him to do it. At family level there is the family spirit, or *mudzimu*, who looks after the day-to-day welfare of the family. At tribal level there is the great spirit or *Mhondoro* who looks after the well-being of the tribe. All these spirits answer directly to *Mwari* or God.'

'I understand', Saul nodded.

'For the spirits to talk to the people, they occasionally inhabit the body of a living person called a *svikiro*.

'We call them mediums', said Saul.

'Yes', said Ndhlela, 'that would be the word in English. You'll understand that certain major matters that affect not just a family alone but the well-being of the tribe as a whole — like rainfall or widespread cattle sickness — are things that only the tribal *Mhondoro* or Great Spirit, can advise on.'

'I understand', agreed Saul.

'Well, there has been a very severe drought, which as you know, ended this morning. The rains should have started at the end of November last year, but they have only started today, the 1st of March. Sure, there have been a few showers, but insufficient to germinate the crops. The people say that this is because the *Mhondoro* — the great Rain Goddess — has been angry with the people. They say She stopped the rain.'

'I knew about this before', said Saul. 'It was for this reason that Mandizwidza told us to arrest his son. I was very pleased about that, but I still thought it was very strange.'

'The Rain Goddess is consulted by tribesmen only three times a year. The times are decreed by custom unless She commands the people to specially attend Her', continued Ndhlela.

'Early December last year was the time of the Rain Goddess and a delegation of elders was sent to consult with Her to ascertain the reason for the drought. She told them there would be no rain because She was angry with the people for listening to strangers and breaking the peace. She said that the rain would start only when the trouble stopped. No rain came and the people refused to listen to the begging of the tribal elders and the troubles continued. When the cattle began to die from starvation, the Rain Goddess again sent for the elders and gave them a final warning. That was two weeks ago. She warned, finally, that if the troubles did not stop there would be no further rain this season. The people offered a sacrifice of a jet black bullock if She would help them, but She refused. Her word before her spirit left the *svikiro* to return to the body of the great black-maned lion, was that all the troubles must stop by the 16th of February. In addition the life of one of the troublemakers had to be sacrificed by the 1st of March. If this happened it would rain on that day and good rains would continue for what remains of the season.'

'A human sacrifice! exclaimed Saul. 'Someone been murdered for medicine to ensure that the rains will come?'

'Yes, but no one has been murdered — someone has died.'

'Who is it?' Saul asked.

'It's Madziwa', said Ndhlela quietly. 'He was hanged for murder in Salisbury Prison at eight o'clock this morning. The people think that the law provided the sacrifice.'

'Well, I'm damned. You honestly believe that if Madziwa had not been hanged this morning, the drought would have continued?'

'Yes. That's what the people say.'

'You believe it also', accused Saul.

'I do, *Nkosi*. 'Look', he gestured at the rain streaming down the office windows, 'the rains have come as She predicted they would. How can I not believe?'

Saul shook his head. 'Thank you, Sergeant.' He dismissed Ndhlela who stamped to attention, did a smart about turn and left the room. The story was unbelievable, yet it was true that the rains had come. This left little room for disbelief. The question that would gnaw at Saul for the rest of his life was a simple one. Would the rains have come if the trouble had not stopped and if Madziwa had not died? Coincidence? Perhaps. But surely there were more things in heaven and on earth . . .

16

The night sky was an expanse of royal blue velvet scattered with the glittering light of diamonds. The moon was rising, but the sky was still smudged with the shimmering of celestial bodies that made up the Southern Cross.

A soft breeze caressed their cheeks. From the country club could be heard the strains of soft romantic guitar music that rose and fell in time with the cool breaths of wind. Occasionally they heard shouts and gusts of laughter as people drank and danced the night away.

They sat in the thatched shelter overlooking the tennis courts. The courts, made from the grey masticated soil of termite heaps, looked dull like lead ingots in the bright moonlight.

Saul glanced at Dawn. She looked really beautiful in the shadow of the shelter, and he felt his heart leap. She was wearing an off-white halter necked terrace gown and her hair, which cascaded on her shoulders, was the colour of burnished gold.

He caught her hand in both of his. She was miles away.

'A penny for your thoughts,' he said softly.

She half inclined towards him and the shadow of a smile ghosted her face. She shrugged and gave a half shiver as a breeze caught her bare shoulders. He slipped off his jacket and hung it over them.

'I'm still waiting', he said.

'For what?'

'For those thoughts I was willing to pay a penny for.'

'I don't know. I suppose I'm not thinking of anything in particular.'

'Are you still going back to the States?'

'I don't know. It depends. I guess I can't stay here. My father seems determined not to have anything further to do with me.'

'You could stay on your own?'

'Maybe. I'll have to see. What about you?'

'I have another month to go before I leave the police.'

'You're still going to leave?'

'Yes, I've made up my mind.'

Dawn looked at the hard, kind and capable man next to her in the moonlight and her recent thoughts were confirmed. She would not return to the States. She would not rush him, but would ensure she would be around when he needed her. Even if her father didn't speak to her again, she'd remain in the country that she'd grown to love. Perhaps when Saul had settled into the farm he had bought, he'd decide that bachelorhood was not the right state for a farmer. When he arrived at that decision — as she was sure he would — she would ensure she was available.

*   *   *

Kephas relaxed in his chair and winked at Kumalo.

'So', said the Interpreter on the lecturer's behalf, 'you'll find that in the Soviet Union we live a free life — not like the oppressed who live in constant fear under the jack-booted heel of American and British imperialism. In the Soviet Union we don't care about the colour of your skin. We don't say that you are inferior just because your face is black — the way the imperialists do. All men are brothers in the brotherhood of international socialism and we live by this principle. If any of you want to find Russian girlfriends, I am sure they will be honoured by your company. We will be delighted to see this too. To our comrades from Zimbabwe, I say this. The oppressed majority is only kept down by the guns of gangster representatives of America and Britain. You will never gain your freedom by trusting such warmongers. They might say that they disapprove of the illegal declaration of so-called independence by the white minority, but I can assure you they all are part of a plot designed to fool the world. But they don't fool us, and I'm sure they don't fool you. In this way the big capitalist mining companies, which feed on the sweat of the poor, can continue to strip Zimbabwe's rich soil of mineral wealth.'

He looked around. 'Can anyone say why they want this mineral wealth?'

A student raised his hand.

'Yes?' said the Interpreter.

'So they can finance the manufacture of H-bombs and missiles to threaten the peaceful communist world', shouted a student who had been in the camp for three months. He was pleased because he had learned his answers by heart.

'Very good', said the Interpreter.

The lecturer was happy that his point had been well taken.

'We'll make sure', he said, 'that a true socialist revolution replaces the mineral wealth they have stolen with the blood of the capitalist robbers.'

*   *   *

'This', said the Interpreter, translating for the stockily built man in the uniform of a Soviet army officer, 'is an Avtomat Kalashnikov assault rifle — more commonly known as the AK47.'

Kephas dropped his eyes from the hammer and sickle badge on the officer's cap, which he had been studying with curiosity, to the short squat weapon in his hands.

'There are two versions. One has a wooden stock like the one you are holding and the other' — he switched weapons with another on the table — 'has a folding metal stock. The one you are holding is most likely the kind which you will be equipped with when you return to your homeland.'

The weapon felt comfortable in Kephas' hands as he balanced it carefully. With this, a man had real power. No one would be able to push him around with this.

'It fires a 7.62mm short cartridge in either ball or tracer ammunition' — the lecturer held up a round of ammunition in his right hand — ' this is ball ammunition, and this' — he held up another round in his left hand — 'is tracer. Tracer is easily distinguishable from ball ammunition because the tip is green.' He tossed both rounds to the nearest student. 'Pass them around and study them. But don't', he cautioned, 'under any circumstances load them in the rifles.'

The instructor turned his attention back to the rifle. 'This weapon is the latest and most advanced rifle in the Soviet Union today. It's the frontline weapon of the great Red Army. All infantry assault units are equipped with it. You will see by this that we consider that our friends in Africa should only be given the best. No obsolete weapons for them.'

There was an appreciative murmur from the class.

'The weapon fires both single shots or automatic.' He turned the weapon in his hands. 'The change lever is on the right-hand side, here.' He indicated its position with his finger. 'To put the weapon on safe, move the change lever up as far as it will go. To fire single shots, push the lever down as far as it will go. To fire fully automatic, place it in the centre position.

He talked on, pointing out the general characteristics of the weapon. The one in Kephas' hands came alive. The pistol grip became warmer as he became used to the feel. He made a quick note in his exercise book that the magazine held 30 rounds of ammunition. What was the other name he had to remember? Oh, yes, the cocking handle. It had to be pulled back before the weapon could be fired. Mustn't forget such things. One day my life might depend on it. When did they say we'll get a chance to try it on the rifle range?

*   *   *

Ndhlela settled easily and quietly into a life of retirement. He had worked loyally for the government for 35 years and he now deserved a rest. Sometimes he looked back with nostalgia on his days as a policeman, but he didn't miss them too much. He certainly missed the early morning drill parades, the sound of marching feet crunching on the gravel of a parade square and the bellowed orders of the sergeant-in-charge.

He led a quiet life as a farmer. Gone was the excitement of police life when each day brought something new — a murder one day and housebreaking and theft the next. Meals were often irregular and sometimes missed. Sleep was something a man frequently did without when working on a case. Times had changed. When he joined the Force boots were not issued to native constables — as they were then called. They walked on patrol barefooted. Week after week, sometimes month after month, they spent on patrol, often leading a pack horse behind a mounted white trooper.

The blacks joining the police now were also different. A higher standard of education was demanded and in his last few years of service he had found it difficult to keep up with the rapidly changing times. The younger men tended to look down on poorly uneducated older men like him with barely concealed scorn. So, in some ways he was glad to retire. He had a good cash gratuity salted away in the Post Office Savings Bank and a regular pension that he collected from the police camp on the last day of each month. Thirty-five years of continuous service was a long time. Now he needed a rest.

His life as a farmer was not such a well-ordered existence as before. He still carried his leather cane under his arm to remind his neighbours that he had achieved high rank in the police force. If he visited the chief, or when he paid his monthly visit to Senga to collect his pension, he took particular care to wear his medals on the left lapel of his jacket.

Otherwise, he stayed at the farm. Most of the time he had very little to do, but there was always a visitor and sometimes beer to be offered in hospitality. But how he missed his son . . .

*　　*　　*

Twelve men were gathered in the room of Kephas and Kumalo. Other than three Zulus from Natal, they were all Matabeles.

The Zulus and the Matabele considered themselves brothers, although their tribal areas were separated by a 1 000 kilometres of land. Indeed they had once been brothers before Mzilikazi had broken away from Shaka Zulu and trekked north to what became Rhodesia. Because they shared the same customs and language, it was natural they should band together in the training camp.

Ndhlovu finished relating the story that had brought them together.

'So you are convinced that Takawira is a witch?' demanded Kumalo.

'I am certain', said Ndhlovu firmly. 'He has been casting spells for the other Mashonas. I have heard it said that he has a set of bones with him.'

'It could be very dangerous if he is a witch', said another. 'There is no one here to protect us from his spells. In addition' — he paused and looked at the others worriedly — 'we're a long way from the spirits of our forefathers and can expect no help from that direction.'

'Do you really think he is a danger to us?' queried one of the Zulus.

Kumalo hawked a wad of phlegm from the back of his throat and spat.

'There is no doubt about it', he said, rubbing his shoe over the wet spot. 'We don't like the Mashonas and they certainly don't like us. Haven't you noticed that they always behave as if they're the most important tribe? Even the Soviet instructors give the impression that when our country is free the Mashonas will take over as the rulers.'

'Yes, it's true', growled Kephas angrily. 'They're arrogant and they look down on us.'

'To think that only 70 years ago, before the white men came, they were the slaves of our forefathers. My grandfather told me before he died, that in those days if they wanted cattle or women, they just sent an expedition into Mashonaland and captured what they wanted. Do you know that when the

Matabele impis raided the Mashonas they could never get them to leave the kopjes and fight out in the open like men? Instead, they used to hide in the caves and throw rocks at our warriors. Just who do they think they are now?' His companions were nodding their agreement. He added: 'They try to behave like men but they have no liver for fighting.'

'I say that if this man Takawira is their leader, then he should die before he can hurt us with his magic', grunted another Zulu in a tone of finality.

'I think so, too', decided Kephas. 'What do the rest of you say?'

'I agree.'

'Me too.'

'Let him die.'

'I also.'

'We're all agreed?' asked Kumalo, looking for dissent.

There was a chorus of 'Yeses'.

'It is decided then', said Kephas taking the lead. 'I will take matches and break the head off one. I will put them in my hat and everyone can draw one. The one who draws the headless match will kill Takawira. He can devise whatever method he prefers.'

Everyone nodded their agreement. Kephas counted 12 matches from a box and snapped off the head of one. He dropped them into his hat, mixed them up without looking, then held the hat above his head with a straight arm.

'The one who draws the broken match should not tell the rest. We need no gossip later about who killed Takawira', Kumalo cautioned.

The men guardedly drew matches. Kephas took the last one. He clenched it in his fist and examined it curiously through his fingers. He breathed a sigh of relief when he discovered that his match still had a head. He looked around trying to guess which one had drawn the match that would make him a killer. But there was no clue on their faces which were blank and expressionless.

Now there was nothing to do but to wait and see.

*   *   *

The camp commandant looked gravely at the Interpreter. 'Last night, as you will all know by now, Comrade Takawira was murdered. Someone stabbed him in the heart with a sharpened kitchen while he slept. I have made enquiries, but so far the culprit remains unidentified.'

Kephas looked at the blank faces around him. One was a murderer, but which one? Kumalo was staring tightlipped to his front. Could he be the one? He was quite capable of it and had disliked Takawira from the beginning. But any one of the eleven could have drawn the headless match.

'I have discussed this matter with my superiors', continued the commandant through the Interpreter, 'and it has been decided that no further enquiries will be pursued. You are here to fight imperialism, not each other. My leaders say that tribalism is a vice which the great leaders of the new African states have tried to stamp out. They have instructed me to warn you that if you don't forget tribalism and stand united against the common enemy — the imperialists — you will never succeed. It's obvious that the man who committed this terrible crime doesn't care about any of this. For his sake and for the sake of international socialism, I hope he will remember it in the future.'

For an instant Kephas noted the trace of a mocking smile on Kumalo's face as the commandant addressed them. That made him almost that he had identified the killer. Well if Kumalo was the killer, he certainly had no intention of saying anything about it. Besides, Takawira had been arrogant and he was a Shona to boot. He had deserved to die.

'The history of the Soviet Union will show you that before the glorious revolution of 1917, we were also subjected to tribalism', the commandant continued. Even now, although the revolution welded us into the mighty people we are today, we're still comprised of 30 or 40 groups or tribes. The majority of us are Great Russians by origin, but there are also Lithuanians, Tarters, Turkmen, Tadzhiks, Armenians, Khakass, Georgians and dozens more. We live together in peace. We don't go around killing each other just because we belong to different tribes. We faithfully serve the cause of socialism, which is what you must do. Remember', the commandant concluded, 'the cause is greater than tribe or nationality. You must live for the cause and forget petty squabbles.'

Kephas was thoughtful afterwards. He wondered if the Russians had truly settled their tribal differences without spilling blood? He doubted it somehow, but it was possible. He promised himself to brush up on his Russian history as soon as he had a chance, and find out. These impassive and humourless people in many ways were like the white Rhodesians. Incredibly, they didn't seem to care about the spirits of their forefathers. He shook his head. It was impossible for a black African to understand the white man, no matter where they originated. The whites were very strange people indeed.

*   *   *

The great ancient walls of the Kremlin with the golden spires of its cathedrals and domes of its palaces peeping over, dominated the huge cobbled expanse of Red Square. From their position in the crowd, they watched with awe the great phalanx of men in uniform marching past Lenin's tomb. Above the tomb, on a red background, was a huge portrait of the occupant of the great mausoleum. Behind its parapet was a line of fur-hatted men who collectively controlled the destiny of the 209 million people who lived in the Union of Soviet Socialist Republics.

From where he stood craning his neck Kephas could see little of this elite, but he could see enough of the parade to leave him open mouthed. The armed might rolling past was almost beyond comprehension. Giant tanks and tracked vehicles mounting enormous guns passed in seemingly unless columns. Huge transporters bearing rockets, taller than a block of flats, rumbled past the tomb in salute, their deadly noses pointed like giant cigars into the dull Moscow sky. Squadron after squadron of supersonic jets, in perfect formation, screamed overhead in the flypast.

With the Soviets on our side, thought Kephas, I can't see how we can fail to drive the white men from our country. Surely no one else has weapons like this?

'What do you think of it?' he whispered to Kumalo.

'I don't know', muttered Kumalo, his eyes on the marching soldiers. 'But I'm glad they're on our side.' He added with unusual perception: 'But I would feel happier if their faces were black!'

*   *   *

'Right', said the Interpreter (they had a different instructor for weapons training today), 'what do you know about the Ruchnoi Pulemet Degtyarev — the RPD light machine gun? You!' He pointed at Kephas who rose slowly to his feet.

124

'It's the standard squad automatic of the Soviet Army.'

'Yes, I know all that', translated the Interpreter testily, 'but what do you know about the gun itself? What do you know about loading it?'

Kephas searched his memory. He had learned about so many weapons now, and although he knew what to do when he was on the range, he often found himself at a loss for words when asked theoretical questions in the lecture room.

He opened his mouth, then closed it again. He had nearly made a fool of himself by describing the loading action of the Shpagin sub-machine gun.

'The weapon is belt fed and each belt takes 25 rounds.'

'Good', said the Interpreter.

'The belts', he continued, 'are joined by inserting a round that locks the sections together. This is only done when you wish to fire the weapon with an ammunition drum on it. Otherwise, the belts can be fed by hand. If you wish to use the weapon with a drum, join four belts together by the means I have described, roll it into a tight circle and carefully fit it into the ammunition drum. The drum is fitted to the left-hand side of the weapon and held in place by a catch.'

'Very good', said the Interpreter, 'but do you think you could do this in the dark in a strange place where revealing a light might mean your discovery?'

'I don't know', said Kephas cautiously. He saw a sardonic smile playing on the instructor's face. He spoke briefly to the Interpreter. Kephas strained his ears because he had begun to pick up the odd Russian word and he wondered uneasily what was in store for him.

'The major says', began the Interpreter, 'that he wants you to do it blindfolded.'

An RPD, wickedly vicious on the stand that supported the front of its barrel, was laid out the floor next to four belts of ammunition and a drum. Kephas quickly refreshed his knowledge of the weapon.

The Interpreter tossed a black scarf over to Kumalo who placed the blindfold over Kephas' eyes and led him to the machine gun.

'Right, start', ordered the Interpreter.

He knelt down and with sure fingers fitted the four belts together. Working fast to show the instructor that he was not the fool he might think, he rolled up the belt and fitted it inside the drum. He quickly ran his fingers over the weapon to locate the holding catch and slipped the drum into place. Hands reached out and pulled the covering off his eyes.

The instructor smiled happily. Even the Interpreter seemed moderately impressed. 'Very good', he murmured, 'very good indeed.'

*   *   *

They were seated in the front of a gilded boxes that rose in tier after tier around the Bolshoi Theatre.

Below them on the stage the Bolshoi Ballet Company was performing Swan Lake. The white garb of the dancers contrasted beautifully with the red plush drapes and furnishings of the old theatre. Kephas looked around and saw the interpreter watching with fascination as the final act built to a climax.

He was really thrilled by this, thought Kephas, and shook his head in wonderment. The music bored him. He had been brought up to appreciate a more lively and rhythmic kind of music that would have been alien to these august surrounds.

Even the women on the stage below didn't really interest him. They were terribly pale and probably, he decided, lacking in passion. Even so, he mused, it had been a long time since he had had a woman. He smiled wryly remembering the first day at the training camp.

'We have no objections to you having Russian girlfriends', they had said. 'It helps the cause of socialism.'

Well that was just so many words. They never got a chance to even talk to Russian girls? Furthermore, they were not allowed out of the camp alone and were always accompanied by the Interpreter who seemed to be their permanent watchdog. It had been obvious how he had kept them well out of the way of Russian women. There were certainly none at the camp — all the cooks and staff were men.

There were times when he would have given anything to hold the young, warm body of Tandiwe in his arms again.

*   *   *

Kephas lay back on his bed and relaxed. Kumalo was asleep on the bed opposite. There was no work today because the course was over. Tomorrow they would split up and go their separate ways.

Book 2

17

It was six years later and 1972 was drawing to a close. The country had been quiet for a number of years.

Saul Jenkins had left the police a long time before. He had remained at Senga and had become a successful farmer. He loved his wife as deeply as she loved him. No one would dare deny her beauty, but then Dawn was not the type of girl to let herself go. Their joint good looks had been passed on to their children. They had three now; Robert, aged six, who was as tough as his father; Molly, who at five looked like a toy doll and baby Joseph, barely six months old.

Abraham and Mary Hale were still at Senga Mission, but Saul saw little of them. Abraham had never become reconciled to the marriage. He saw his daughter, though, because otherwise he would not have seen his grandchildren and he cared for them more than anyone else in the world. But naturally he disapproved of the way they were being brought up outside the Brotherhood. Mary Hale, as women do, was careful to tread the middle road. Unlike her husband, she believed that reconciliation might turn out to be God's will.

*   *   *

Ndhlela lived on his farm with two plump young wives a third of his age. They looked after his needs, planted crops and kept the weeds down in his lands during the growing season. He had not seen his son since that day in 1966 — which still lived as a nightmare in his memory — and he never expected to see him again. He heard of him occasionally, though, as did those who read the newspapers. Kephas was in the military wing of the Party now and had accompanied several delegations to the United Nations in New York to plead for the tightening of sanctions and the overthrow by force of the Rhodesian Government. He had worked at the Party offices in Beijing for a while, but when he last heard of him he was in Zambia.

*   *   *

People on long, solitary journeys through the fastness of the Zambezi Valley still hurried if, around sundown, they heard the savage spine-chilling roar that could only be that huge lion with a black mane. The spirit of the Rain Goddess still looked after the needs of the tribe; but who knew what her needs might be when she was reincarnated in the form of a lion. After all, every lion looked for fresh meat at sundown . . .

*   *   *

There were four groups encamped on the Zambian bank of the Zambezi. Most had been there for several weeks, awaiting the signal to invade Rhodesia — the landmass clearly visible across the river.

Kephas had been the last to arrive. To his surprise, he found Kumalo already there and, like him, a group commander. There was quite a reunion for they had not seen each other since their Moscow days and they greeted each other like long lost brothers. It gave Kephas considerable comfort to find his friend there because most of the foot soldiers were of low calibre. At least they knew the other could be trusted. Not many of the recruits had received the thorough training like they and a few others had got in the Soviet Union. Some, of course, had been well schooled in Cuba and China, but the majority had received only sketchy lessons in guerrilla warfare at camps in Zambia and Tanzania. A few were volunteers. A large number had been press ganged in Zambia — some from secure jobs and others from the ranks of the unemployed — and forced to become members of the Party's military wing because they were Rhodesian born. Consequently, there was little enthusiasm for the move that was due any day now.

Desertion was a problem and at least five slipped away nightly. Some were brought back by the Zambian police who, although it was officially denied, helped the Party as much as they could with the full approval of their government.

The trouble was that the more deserters who succeeded, the more there were who made the attempt. Persistent rumours that circulated in the camp did not assist the problem. It had been whispered around for a long time that the previous groups that had crossed the river had been annihilated by the Rhodesian soldiers and police. No one spoke openly about this because it was in direct contradiction to what the leaders were saying. In lectures, they were told that their predecessors were well established and had captured small towns after killing hundreds of soldiers and policemen. It was dangerous to openly contradict this story — it marked a man as disloyal. Disloyalty could mean a sentence without a trial, followed by a bullet in the back of the head.

Kephas knew the official version was untrue, but he hoped for all their sakes that it would become fact after they crossed.

When the commissar and commander called a meeting of a selected few, Kephas and Kumalo were among them. Kephas looked at the faces of the 30 men present, but except for Kumalo he knew none of them. It appeared that this 30 was the sum total of those who could be trusted. It followed that everyone else was regarded as a potential deserter.

The commissar addressed them.

'The desertions must stop. 'If we lose many more men, we'll reach the stage where we have insufficient forces to make the crossing. We know that you are all dedicated to the cause and to the Party. It has been decided that an example must be made of the next deserter to deter others. From tonight trusted armed guards will be posted secretly around the camp. You will be those guards. Any deserters caught must be brought to me to be dealt with. Any questions?'

He scanned the impassive faces, but there were no questions. He sat down and handed over the meeting to the commander who briefed them in detail on the sectors of the camp they would guard. To his delight, Kephas was partnered with Kumalo. To ensure they remained fresh and awake, each man would do four hours on guard duty while his partner slept and have four hours off.

Kephas was tired and it had been a long night. He leaned against a giant baobab on the edge of the clearing. He glanced at his watch and shifted his carbine to a more comfortable position. It was only six o'clock but the sun had been up for some time. Sweat had begun to run in small rivulets down his arm and on to his hand, making his grip on the weapon slippery. Where was Kumalo? He should be here by now. He was due at six o'clock and he strained his ears for sounds that would signal the approach of his relief.

The bushes along the path that led to the camp rustled. He relaxed for at last Kumalo was coming. He checked the time and noted that he would be on duty for five more minutes than he should be. He made a mental note to be the same amount late when he took over from Kumalo for the next shift. Perhaps that would teach him to be punctual. He listened again, but the rustling had ceased. Kumalo had probably stopped to relieve himself. Trailing his rifle, he walked down the path to meet his friend.

He had only moved a mere 12 metres or so when the bush in front of him parted and a man in olive green uniform began running back towards the camp. He was obviously ensuring he was not recognised, because he was covering his face with his hands.

It was unexpected. For a few vital seconds Kephas could only gape at the running man. By the time he reacted the bushes had closed and the man had gone. However, he could still hear the crashing of bushes as the deserter — for that's obviously what he was — ran desperately back to safety.

'Stop or I shoot!' shouted Kephas, though he knew the call was futile. He had no target but he still slipped off the safety catch and raised his rifle. He lowered it again a second later. It was no use. He hated the idea of reporting failure, but it looked like he had no option.

He slipped on the safety catch and doubled down the path. He heard a shout of pain and came to a halt, cocking his ear to listen.

'Over here!' shouted Kumalo.

Kephas ran over and found Kumalo, his rifle pointed at the ground. At first nothing was visible to Kephas because of the thick undergrowth.

'A deserter has just got away. Have you seen him?' Kephas asked.

'Yes, I've seen him', said Kumalo, grinning broadly. 'I've got him on the ground over here.'

Kephas walked over to him. A man lay \ clasping a deep gash in his head. Blood was pouring down his cheek and staining his shirt. He looked fearfully at Kephas who recognised him as Mambo, a member of his group who had been keeping very much to himself.

'Please', Mambo whined, 'I haven't done anything. Please let me go.'

'You were trying to desert', growled Kumalo, digging the muzzle of his rifle into his ribs.

Mambo winced as the hard metal dug into his flesh. Kephas saw that he was trembling uncontrollably.

'I wasn't trying to desert. I was just going for a walk.'

'Huh', murmured Kephas in disbelief. He turned to Kumalo and explained. 'He came walking along the path towards me and I thought it was you. On seeing me, he covered his face with his hands and ran.'

134

'I know', said Kumalo. 'I heard you shout and he came running towards me. As he ran past I gave him a gentle tap on the head.' He patted the butt of his rifle. 'He stopped running and sat down — or should I say prostrated himself', laughed Kumalo.

'What shall we do with him?' asked Kephas.

'We must take him to the commander, of course', grunted Kumalo.

'I have done nothing. Please let me go', begged Mambo. 'If you tell them I was trying to desert, they'll shoot me.'

'Yes, I suppose they will', said Kumalo unsympathetically. 'I suppose they probably will.' He tut-tutted and wagged a finger at his prisoner. 'At least that will stop you trying to desert again.'

'I wasn't deserting', howled Mambo in denial. 'I keep telling you, I was going for a walk.' He searched their faces for signs of compassion but there was none. He buried his face in his hands and sobs wracked his body.

He struggled in terror as they half carried, half dragged him to the camp. He was crying his eyes out when they dumped him in a shivering heap at the feet of the leaders.

'A deserter', announced Kumalo. 'We have arrested a deserter.' There was another storm of protest from Mambo, but no one bothered to look at him. They spoke over his head and decided his fate.

'Well', said the commissar, a ruthless man of about 40, 'we wanted an example, so we have got one.' He looked with distaste at the shivering wretch clinging to his legs and begging for mercy. He kicked him away and pointed to a big tree. 'Tie him up and shoot him. Keep his uniform — we may need it.'

'No, no, no', screamed Mambo as both Kephas and Kumalo grabbed him.

'Shut up', said Kumalo, and kicked him brutally in the mouth. He fell back with blood streaming from his face. He again tried to sit up but a second kick knocked him senseless.

They methodically stripped off his clothing, leaving him sprawled naked in the centre of the crowd that had assembled to watch the execution.

'Regard him well', shouted the commissar. 'He tried to desert and for this he is sentenced to death. Anyone else who tries to run away will also be killed.' He looked at the sea of faces and was rewarded by sullen and frightened looks. He made a mental note of those who by their expressions seemed to be displaying sympathy. They were obviously disloyal as well. Maybe he would have to execute a few of them later. He returned his attention to the unconscious man who had been roped to the tree. Kumalo slapped his face until he returned blearily to consciousness. He tried to move, but the ropes held him fast.

'What are you going to do now?' he gasped.

'We're going to kill you. Must I keep on telling you?' leered Kumalo. 'You are going to die.'

Mambo opened his mouth to beg for his life, but Kephas anticipating the move, stuffed in a wad of rag and gagged him. Mambo almost vomited as he tried to spit out the gag. His eyes widened and rolled in their sockets. He needed to explain that it would not be fair for him to die. He should never have been a soldier in the first place. He only wanted to continue with his job as a delivery man in Lusaka. The men who had come to his house at night, handcuffed him, dragged him away from his wife and children and taken him to the training camp did it without his consent. He didn't go willingly. He hadn't wanted to leave his children and his pretty young wife who, even now, was with child. How could they kill him? If they did, he would never see his unborn child, or embrace his wife again. Surely they would not kill him until after he had a chance to explain that he had been forced to desert because he was afraid to die? He was not a soldier and would never be one. He didn't even hate anyone, not even the white men.

But none of this was said because he never got the chance to speak again.

He watched with disbelief as Kumalo cocked the action of his rifle and pressed it to his head. He struggled in his bonds, grunting unintelligibly.

'Wait', shouted the commissar.

Kumalo hesitated, disappointment written on his face.

The commissar was smiling broadly at a new idea that had come to him. 'I think that as he has behaved like a woman he should die like one.'

'You mean . . .' started Kumalo.

'Yes', said the commissar.

'My pleasure', said Kumalo, his face creasing in a cruel smile. He carefully laid his rifle on the ground and took a clasp knife from his pocket. He flicked the blade open and ran his thumb along the razor sharp edge.

Crouching low he looked at Mambo who cringed in his bonds as realisation of his fate dawned on him. Sweat poured from his forehead and his skin turned a sickly yellow. Kumalo's hand reached out and caught hold of the condemned man's male parts. He squeezed cruelly and Mambo writhed in agony.

Kumalo brought the sharp blade down, paused for a moment, then slashed through the surprisingly soft flesh. Dreadful noises came from the gagged face as the victim twisted and turned in pain. Kumalo held up the bloody parts in front of his victim's shocked eyes, then threw them down and stamped them into the grass. Mambo slumped in his bonds in a dead faint.

'You're not going to die as easily as that', said Kumalo. He felt cheated and started slapping his victim back to consciousness.

Mambo's eyes opened, but they were glazed from the shock of it all and from loss of blood. Blood poured steadily from his groin and pooled on the ground.

'Kill him', said the commissar, who was visibly shocked at Kumalo's ferocity. The executioner glanced back briefly and nodded. His arm came back and lunged forward as he viciously stabbed his knife deep into Mambo's stomach. He took a more comfortable grip on the knife handle and sawed upwards through the ribs until the point ripped into Mambo's lungs. He stepped back as the dead man's guts spilled onto the ground and he methodically wiped his blade clean on a tuft of grass.

'It saved wasting a bullet,' said Kumalo.

*   *   *

Mambo's body scarcely made a splash as it slipped into the waters of the Zambezi. The corpse floated for nearly 20 kilometres before a crocodile dragged it down to an underwater lair. At the same time, Mambo's widow removed her dress and put her arms around the man she had found to replace him. It wasn't easy for a woman with children to live on her own in a city far from home when her man had gone. Occasionally, while she made love, she thought of him and wondered where he was. Few who were with him when he died would live to tell the story to their grandchildren of that guerrilla incursion into Rhodesia either.

18

The moon traced a broad yellow path over the deep rolling waters of the Zambezi River on the night the crossing began.

Equipment and men were loaded silently into a succession of dugout canoes hired from Zambian fishermen at a high cost, and collapsible canvas canoes supplied to the Party by Czechoslovakia.

One hundred and twenty men were to be ferried over and it was expected to take all night. They dared not do it in daylight in case they were spotted by one of the regular Rhodesian Air Force jet fighter patrols that frequently flew low-level patrols along the winding course of the Zambezi River — ready to blast suspicious craft on the water with cannon and rocket fire.

It would be Kephas' turn when the next boat returned. He crouched low among the reeds with the three who would be accompanying him. No one talked. They concentrated on listening for the slap of returning paddles.

He shifted his pack that lay next to him. It was heavy and contained an enormous quantity of ammunition. He also had spare clothing, tins of food — ironically manufactured in Rhodesia or South Africa — blankets, and a host of other items needed to sustain life. When a man was in the veld with little hope of resupply, he lived or died by what he carried.

His AK47 carbine was strapped securely to his back and was never separated from him even for a moment. He comforted the wooden butt with his hand. Rifles from the same production line had played a major role in almost every recent insurrection since the end of World War II, from Vietnam to Northern Ireland.

He turned his attention to the river and scanned the darkness, but no light relieved the blackness. What would it be like when they got back to Rhodesia? He speculated uneasily about the plans that had been made. No one had been briefed so far and only the commissar and the commander had any idea what they were going to do. He supposed it was because of the

138

danger of deserters. If one in the know escaped on the other side and went to the Rhodesian Police, they would all be finished. At least this way a deserter wouldn't have any concrete information as to their intentions. Anyway, they would be told the plans if and when the need arose.

He knew from his training what the broad aims were. Their first task would be to gain the co-operation and assistance of the local tribesmen. Once this had been achieved, they would recruit soldiers from amongst them and gradually build up their forces until the whole countryside was under their control.

'Ignore the towns', his instructors had said. 'Win the countryside and the towns will fall like rotten oranges.'

They had, he knew, arms for a thousand men and probably more. Once these were seen, tribesmen would flock to join them. The only point that gave him a niggling worry was the previous singular lack of success.

His reverie was interrupted by a low whistle from the river and he instantly switched his attention there. A dugout materialised from the darkness and slid in towards the bank. It bounced into shallower water and grated in the mud and shingle of the beach. Leaning out, he grabbed the prow and guided it in until the craft lay parallel to the bank.

The others stood up and under his direction stepped silently into the rocking boat. The water gurgled and splashed as it sank deeper and took up the weight of its load.

His fellow passengers had their packs strapped to their backs for ease of carrying, but he placed his by his feet. He could scarcely swim and he knew he would sink like a stone if he was weighted down with a pack and the craft sank by some mischance.

The boatman pushed off with his paddle and the dugout was quickly caught by the current.

'Pick up your paddles', he shouted above the roar of the river.

Kephas gripped one that lay wetly on the floor and the others did likewise. There was an a few centimetres of water in the bottom of the boat already and he wondered uneasily if they were sinking.

They dug their paddles into the water and the prow came around. He could not see a thing now they were moving. He just hoped the boatman knew where they were heading. It would be ridiculous for everything to end here out on the river, without him ever having fired a gun in anger. His muscles ached as he battled with the others to master the skill of paddling. He didn't like it one little bit. The water seemed to be at a very dangerous level outside the boat.

There was a sudden splash on the port side. The man in front of him stopped paddling and looked nervously back.

'What's that?' he asked in near panic.

'How the hell should I know', grunted Kephas. He was feeling just as panicky, but was determined not to show it.

'Hippo', called the boatman cheerfully.

'Paddle, you bloody fool', said Kephas, nudging the man in front.

He needed no second bidding and they pulled furiously until the splashing noises faded away to the stern.

Kephas wiped his brow with the back of his hand. It came away soaked with sweat.

The dark shore of Rhodesia loomed and the water became quieter as they left the main current. They grounded and figures jumped out of the dark bush and helped them ashore. As soon as they had disembarked, the boatman pushed off to collect the next load and was soon lost to sight.

Kephas looked back at the outline of the Zambian shoreline. It looked just like Rhodesia had from the other side, but somehow it did not look quite so foreboding. He bent down and picked up a handful of soil. It had been a long time since he had last touched the earth of his homeland.

'Welcome home', he muttered quietly to himself. It was good to be back.

*   *   *

A guide was waiting to take them to a preselected base.

It was a long hard walk and their packs got heavier and heavier. Few avoided cuts and bruises from falls in the darkness. Twice they detoured to avoid elephants which seemed to be all around them. He had never seen an elephant and every new danger seemed worse. First it was the hippos, but they seemed insignificant now. What about lions and other dangerous creatures, they wondered?

It was daylight when they reached base. It was hardly home from home, but was merely a big granite kopje standing gauntly alone. It gave Kephas the impression that giants of a bygone age had once played a crazy game by carelessly piling boulders weighing hundreds of tons on top of each other. The lower reaches were covered with tangled bush with diabolical needle-like thorns that reached out to impale the flesh of the unwary. Trees sprouted at acute angles from cracks in the rocks where rich leaf loam, sufficient to support plant life, had gathered over countless centuries. Dry and brittle grass two metres high grew up to the roots of the trees, making them, and the hill as well, appear lower than they actually were. The top of the kopje was in the shape of a basin, but from ground level the summit appeared to be a ridge. It was an ideal hideout. Once underground bunkers were dug in the rocky virgin soil, without disturbing the trees and the bush, a thousand men would be able to live there without detection from the ground or the air.

There was a stream bed at the base of the hill that appeared to be waterless. However, a hole dug in the sand soon revealed fresh sparkling water from the hidden stream that flowed beneath the sand. Everywhere else, for kilometres in every direction, was densely tangled bush through which there were only the game trails carved out of the wilderness by wild animals. There was no other high ground in the vicinity.

The men who had got there earlier had already started digging the underground bunkers in which they would live. Cadres from Kephas' group were still trickling in as they were the last to make the crossing. With daylight, the digging stopped and the freshly turned earth was covered with branches and grass so that the fresh scars would not be visible from the air. Kephas estimated that it would take two nights of hard work before they were finished. With the sun, the mosquitoes and night flies that made life a misery during the dark hours, disappeared. In their wake came the tsetse flies, bloodsuckers with red-hot bites that would plague them for the rest of their stay.

As far as was possible they left the high standing grass untouched and movement was confined to a few narrow paths. The leaders did not want a general trampled down effect to be seen from the air by reconnaissance aircraft.

A few sharp orders and the new arrivals were deployed to points on the kopje where they could rest and remain out of sight for the remainder of the day. No careless movement was permitted during daylight hours.

Discipline was strict on this point and it had to be. No one moved, lit fires or went to the stream bed well for water. If men were foolish enough not to replenish their water during the night, they relied on friends to supply them. If they had no friends, they went without. There were many men without friends that first day. The tension of the crossing had caused them to drink their water quickly. Humans need to occupy themselves when nervous. If they cannot smoke or talk, they do the next best thing — drink. The agonies of thirst brought on by the intense Zambezi Valley heat paid them back in full for their imprudence. Kephas, Kumalo and an elite few had it somewhat easier. Their training had taught them to never allow their water bottles to drop below the halfway mark unless they were sure of resupply.

The two shared a tree as a communal backrest. That first day, there was little to do but sleep during daylight hours. Luckily, other groups had been detailed to provide the guards and sentries essential to their safety and well-being. Kephas dreamed of home. A vision of his father appeared persistently in his dreams. He seemed to be trying to say something but try as he might his son could not decipher the words. When he awoke, the dream had left him with a chill of apprehension.

The air cooled only slightly as the day drew to a close. Everywhere men began to stir and get themselves ready for the hard manual labour ahead of them throughout the hours of darkness.

Before daylight faded completely, Kephas gathered his group together to organise the night's work. They were a disorderly mob and did not take kindly to his leadership. In fact, there was no doubt in his mind that they did not take kindly to any leadership at all. He had a sinking feeling as he surveyed them. Would they fight when the time came? Would he only discover that when it was too late?

He spoke to each them individually, scowling into their faces to show he meant business and to inflict his will.

'Where did you complete your training?'

'In Lusaka, Comrade.'

'How long were you there?'

'Three weeks.'

'How many rounds have you fired from your rifle?'

'None, Comrade.'

By the time he had finished he found that only two men, other than himself, were properly trained. One had spent a year in Cuba and the other two years in Red China. The others had been only sketchily instructed in the rudiments of bush warfare in Zambia and Tanzania.

Kephas sighed as the realisation came that he might have to face battle-hardened troops with this rabble. At least they had not been committed to action straight away. One thing was hopeful, most showed signs of fearing him. Perhaps he could still put some fire into them if that was so. Perhaps, after all, the lesson of Mambo had been learned? If it had, it should help in the imposition of discipline.

He divided the men into sections of four and allocated them areas on the northern edge of the basin and they started digging.

The idea of digging his own bunker did not appeal to him, so he solved the problem by stabbing two men in the chest with a hard finger and ordering them to do it for him.

19

'What do you think, comrades?'

The commander was an indecisive man who rarely made a decision without help. Kephas grinned sardonically at Kumalo who was seated opposite him in the council of war consisting of the group commanders, the commissar — who was already showing clear signs that he wished he had never left the safety and comfort of Zambia — and, of course, the commander. Neither of them thought much of the commander, who was no fighter. The Party, however, had appointed him to leadership, so that was that. Kumalo grinned back.

'I am worried about the food position', continued the commander, noticing the byplay between Kephas and Kumalo, but choosing to ignore it. He knew they despised him.

'I'm not surprised', drawled Kumalo. 'We seem to be the only army that doesn't march on our stomachs. We just sit on our backsides.'

Kephas giggled quietly . It had become quite a game, this commander-baiting by Kumalo.

'You know we can't go yet, comrades', pleaded the commander. He glanced at the commissar for support and was rewarded with a grudging nod of approval. 'We're expecting important visitors from Zambia and we cannot move inland until they have finished their inspection. They will probably bring photographers with them so that photographs can be given to the world's press.'

'All very well', said Kumalo, 'but we had hundreds of photographs taken in Zambia for the press. I must have seen a dozen or so in magazines, with captions about freedom fighters slaughtering white soldiers somewhere in Rhodesia. Surely we have enough photographs already?'

'We should strike inland and attack the soldiers and police. What do you think comrades?' asked Kephas. 'That would give the press a good story.'

'You know the instructions as well as I do', muttered the commissar, interrupting for the first time. 'We're going inland to attack weak spots like white-owned farms and isolated homesteads. Our purpose is to terrorise the white men into leaving the land and win the tribesmen over to the cause.' He visibly shuddered. 'We're certainly not going to directly attack soldiers and policemen. That would be asking for trouble. We will only lay mines in the roads where their vehicles travel.'

'Ridiculous', said Kumalo emphatically. 'Comrades, this is ridiculous. We have been here for a week and we have hidden arms and supplies all over this part of the Zambezi Valley. We're ready to move. Yet we have to sit here for another week eating supplies. Soon we'll have to abandon the expedition and return to Zambia for food.'

Kephas looked around and saw they were getting nowhere. But he knew that if the instructions from Lusaka had said they were not to move until after the visit, then they would not move. There was insufficient democracy in the Party to give them that much freedom of decision. He frowned at Kumalo who was about to make another comment. But he saw Kephas and stopped.

'We have insufficient food for a long stay', Kephas pondered. 'We have rice for one week only. Look, I am familiar with the Zambezi Valley. No one lives between the river and the escarpment because of tsetses fly. There are no villages or kraals'

'I can understand that', said the commander ruefully. The others laughed because it was common knowledge that he had become a favourite target for the lazy flies with the red-hot bites.

'There is plenty of game around here', continued Kephas. 'Why can't we shoot some for our present needs and dry the surplus meat for future requirements?' He saw by their faces that everyone approved his suggestion.

'I told you so', said the commander, smiling at the commissar. He slapped Kephas on the back. 'I knew Kephas would come up with the answer. There is no habitation for kilometres around and there are animals aplenty for the taking.' He rubbed his chin thoughtfully. 'There are only fishing camps along the river, but they are kilometres away. Maybe we should be careful, though, in case the police find and arrest us for hunting without a licence', he added, his eyes twinkling.

There was a roar of laughter from the others and the commander seemed pleased that his joke was appreciated. He looked warmly at Kephas.

The idea of fresh meat made Kephas' mouth water. They had not tasted it for over a week. He wondered what elephant tasted like. There would certainly be plenty of it. He laughed out aloud. The others seemed mystified. He smiled: 'I was just wondering what an elephant steak would look like on a plate.'

The conversation quickly turned to the various kinds of meat they had eaten in their lives. It was quite surprising really, because although most of them had grown up in the bush, only a minority had ever seen an elephant — to say nothing of buffalo, rhinoceros, or hippo. This was because virtually all the big game had been shot out years before in many areas of Rhodesia.. Kephas was familiar with the ways of the smaller game which he had trapped as a young boy, but he was not up on the larger species of wild animals because, although Senga was near the valley, he had before never set foot in it.

It was arranged that the hunting would start immediately. There would be two hunting parties. Kephas would lead one that would hunt to the north of the camp and the other would hunt to the south to minimise the danger of shooting accidents. Kumalo asked to go with Kephas. He was left to choose the other two men needed. It would be a daytime hunt. Other than by aircraft, they had little fear of discovery. It was only when they moved into the more inhabited areas as they advanced that danger would come from man. Other than the occasional game ranger, no one moved in this part of the valley which was inaccessible due to the absence of roads. Tsetses flies, the carriers of the dreaded sleeping sickness with their animal hosts in the valley, ruled as kings.

Kumalo found two men. Only one had any kind of hunting experience. He was an alert little man called Watura, who came from the lowveld country. He had poached big game and scouted for white hunters since he was a boy.

The other was Dzingani, a quiet man, but one whose depth of purpose impressed Kephas. Like Kephas he was a volunteer and absolutely devoted to the cause.

*   *   *

They set off before dawn the next day.

They found game within a kilometre of the base. A herd of some 50 impala were grazing by a vlei. Shoulder to shoulder with them was a herd of zebra — the wild horses of the bushveld.

They were grazing quietly and there was no hint that danger threatened. In this area they didn't know the hunter's gun and weren't skittish about the proximity of man.

Watura took charge of hunting operations. He motioned his companions to circle round the herd until they were directly downwind.

There was no hurry. They had all the time in the world. Kephas suppressed his rising excitement. He could see by the faces of the others that they were also experiencing the thrill of the hunt — everyone except Watura whose intense concentration was professionally focussed. He was the perfect hunter. He moved slowly and surely through the bush without making a sound. His feet, although Kephas did not see him look down once, trod surely, missing dry twigs and leaves — even clumps of grass whose swish might alert the quarry. His eye never moved from the herd.

Kephas and the others had difficulty keeping up. Nobody wanted to be the one who made a noise that disturbed the unwitting herd. Kephas quickened his pace and waved to Watura to slow down. Watura was startled by the gesture because he was concentrating so deeply. He nodded gravely, then continued the encircling movement at the same pace as before.

They reached a large tree on the far side of the vlei and he signalled them to a halt. The stragglers on the edge of the herd were less than 70 metres away, but they continued to graze undisturbed.

Kephas was fascinated by the sight of so much game. He had seen impala and zebra before, but never without fear like this. Normally in areas where game was continually hunted, it was difficult, if not impossible to get within 200 metres of a herd.

Kephas gently slipped off the safety catch and raised the rifle to his shoulder. He aimed at the large doe grazing nearest to him.

Watura touched him on the shoulder in admonition. He lowered his weapon, and looked at him quizzically.

Watura indicated with his hand that they should form a line about three paces apart. Kephas nodded and watched for further instructions in sign language. They were to move forward closer to the herd. Watura tapped his safety catch and moved it to the fire position. Everybody else did the same. The hunter tapped his chest to indicate that no one should shoot until he did.

They moved forward from cover. They had gone about 18 metres before an old zebra stallion, obviously the leader of the herd, sensed them, turned and looked them full in the face. Other zebra followed suit and faced the human intruders. The impala moved nervously, but did not flee. Watura began a high-pitched whistle. The animals prickled up their ears, but stayed where they were.

Kephas glanced at Watura from the corner of his eye. He was still moving slowly forward. They must shoot, he thought, otherwise the animals would stampede at any moment. But Watura continued to lead them forward. When he finally stopped Kephas almost missed the signal. They were only 40 metres from the herd. He felt he could almost reach out and touch an animal.

The impala shifted nervously and began sniffing the breeze. Watura raised his carbine and aimed. The others also brought their rifles up and squinted down the sights. Kephas again zeroed in on the large doe.

Why did his rifle shake? He found difficulty keeping his sights on target. Must hit the buck in the chest. A shot there would drop it. Don't aim at the head. Too small a target. He was still steadying himself when the others opened fire. He squeezed the trigger and the weapon jumped as it fired, the sharp crack snapping in his ears. He had missed. The herd exploded into movement. He knew there would be no second chance. The animals thundered across the vlei into the distant bush with Kephas and his fellow hunters firing wildly into the rear of the herd. Before he realised it, his magazine was empty. He couldn't believe that he had fired 30 shots. He pressed the trigger again. Nothing happened. He could only remember firing three times, yet he had emptied the whole magazine! The herd was gone. Even the haze of dust beaten up by the drumming hooves had almost disappeared. All that remained were three carcasses — a zebra and two impalas — where the herd had been. They were all on Watura's flank. The others looked shamefacedly at each other. They had all missed. The herd had been so close, yet except for Watura, they had all missed. They hadn't hit a thing.

'Let's go.'

Watura didn't comment on their incompetence, but started towards the fallen animals. The zebra was still kicking. Blood stained the naked earth and air bubbled from its windpipe as it breathed its last. He drew his knife and cut the throats of all three animals.

Now came the hard work. Kephas sent Dzingani back to base to call men to carry the meat. The others drew knives and helped Watura butcher the carcasses. First they flayed the tough hides from the flesh. They didn't need the hides, just the meat. The stomachs were slit open and the entrails flopped on to the wet skins.

The impala carcasses were quartered and the yellowy meat of the zebra was cut into large chunks to make for easy carrying. Later, when they got back to base, the meat would be cut into strips and hung from the trees to dry.

Kephas hoped the other party were better shots. Three animals wouldn't provide nearly enough meat for the number they had to feed.

Kephas felt tired. The excitement of the hunt had worn off, draining him of strength. The tsetses were biting and he pulled the sleeves of his shirt down as far as he could, leaving only his hands and face unprotected. Even so, they provided big enough landing areas for the flies. The others were having the same trouble.

It was stinking hot and the back of his shirt was wet with sweat. The summer sun blazed down. He took a pull from his water bottle and the others followed suit.

The entrails of the slaughtered animals were soon black with flies. They hummed and buzzed in the fierce sun, drawn seemingly from nowhere to the feast.

A vulture settled on the ground some 45 metres away, waiting for the chance for some pickings. It wouldn't come close as long as the men were there. It was soon joined by more that came swooping from the sky. It was uncanny how they found the dead. Kephas had heard they cruised in the sky at the height of a Boeing, drifting with the wind until they saw or maybe scented death far below. It was beyond his comprehension how they could see or smell anything from that height. Yet a vulture was rarely seen until something died. They were never spotted roosting or flying low in the sky. They came seemingly from nowhere.

'Here they come.'

Kumalo shaded his eyes with his hand. 'About time, too.'

Kephas looked and saw ten men in single file making their way towards them.

He stood up. They were men from his platoon led by Dzingani.

He greeted them. 'We have meat for you, brothers.'

They were delighted when they saw the kills. It had been very monotonous living on dry tack and tinned food and morale had been badly affected. A good meal of meat would work wonders. If a man's belly was full, he was happy.

They quickly packed the meat into dripping bundles, carrying them on their heads they started for home. They sang as they walked. The harmonising helped them to forget the heat and the uncertainty of their situation.

'We have meat today', they sang in close harmony, 'tomorrow we will have beer.'

The other hunting party bagged only a couple of animals. But that night the fires burned brightly below ground in the bunkers where they were safe from prying eyes in passing aircraft. Everyone slept contentedly with full stomachs. For today they were okay. And who cared about tomorrow?

After that they hunted every day with an increasing degree of success. The second day there were two buffalo, of which Kephas killed one. The next day three kudu, four impalas and a buffalo. The fourth was the day of the elephant. He was working with the same team who had all become good shots by now.

It was Dzingani who spotted the herd.

There were about 20 of them browsing in a thick clump of trees about 200 metres away. Their grey bulky outlines could be seen moving about, swaying to and fro among the trees. Saplings cracked as they were wrenched up by the roots and stripped of bark, a succulent delicacy for the great creatures.

They stood and watched the huge beasts for ten minutes, overawed by their size. They were upwind of the herd, so their presence remained undetected.

'Are our guns powerful enough?' Kephas asked Watura in a whisper.

'Perhaps. I think they will be all right, but we will have to get very close. Shall we try?'

Kephas looked at the others. They were all willing to have a go at killing the largest of all land animals.

Watura took charge. 'You must do exactly as I do. We will approach them slowly and carefully and select an isolated animal. We will try for the heart shot as I am not sure if these rifles will be powerful enough to penetrate the head and hit the brain. It is important that we approach the animal on its left-hand side. The heart is protected by its front leg when it stands normally. We must wait until it lifts up its leg to walk forward, then we must all fire as many shots as possible into the folds of skin to the rear of the leg, about halfway up the body. Do you get the idea?'

He looked at his companions who nodded.

Rifles were checked to ensure magazines were full and actions cocked.

'A final word', Watura cautioned. 'If we fail to drop it and the elephant

150

charges, whatever you do, don't run. If you do, it will surely catch you. An elephant can run faster than any man. You'll never escape by running. Find a tree and step behind it and stay still. If you do otherwise, you will probably be killed.'

It took an hour of careful manoeuvring to get to the spot Watura had in mind.

Kephas felt like his heart was in his mouth. Surely they were getting too close, he thought nervously. The elephants seemed to loom over them. What chance will we stand if they charge? They were less than 20 metres from the one selected as a target. It was a big cow, gently swaying to and fro on her feet. He could see little of her legs as they were all but concealed by the long dry grass that covered the area.

Kephas moistened his lips with his tongue. He glanced at Watura, who was standing like a statue to his left. The others were on his right.

Watura didn't move. His eyes never left the elephant which was picking shoots from a nearby tree with its trunk and dropping them into its mouth.

The other elephants were farther on, the nearest about 40 metres away.

Why didn't they get on with it? Kephas had never felt so exposed in his life.

Although he couldn't see the feet, he sensed rather than saw the beast move its leg to walk forward. He didn't need Watura to tell him.

He raised his rifle and poured automatic fire into the general area of the defined target. The others fired on automatic too. Watura placed his shots carefully so they would all count. The others just emptied their magazines in the general excitement.

The great animal's lungs were punctured. She was going to die and she knew it, but a savage instinct demanded that her attackers accompany her in death. She raised her trunk and bellowed in mortal agony. She scented the air and caught the sweet-sour smell of man. She turned and faced them. A bellow of rage rent the air and she charged. They were nicely grouped in the path of the charge.

Kephas broke left and made for a large tree that he had previously sized up. He didn't climb — he almost ran up the trunk!

Safe in the thick foliage he looked down in time to see the drama play out.

Watura and Kumalo had broken right and were standing stock still by another tree.

Dzingani had run blindly, not knowing where he was going, but only knowing he had to escape. Terror drove him on. His carbine lay on the ground at the spot where they had fired the shots. Gone was Watura's advice.

The elephant lumbered after the man focussed in her dying eyes. In passing a giant foot crunched Dzingani's weapon into the ground, bending the stock from the barrel at an acute angle. Kephas watched as the beast inevitably gained on Dzingani. There was nothing anyone could do. It was true what Watura had said, Kephas thought. A man cannot outrun an elephant.

Dzingani let out a terrible scream when he realised he could not escape. The wounded animal towered over him, casting a huge shadow on the ground. Her trunk flashed out and almost in slow motion, wound around Dzingani and lifted him bodily from the ground.

Kephas went cold as the raging animal dashed Dzingani to the ground. As soon as he struck the ground the elephant leant down and knelt on him, crushing any life that might have remained.

The beast's mortal wounds had taken their toll. It bellowed and tried to get back on its feet, but it could not. It seemed to be frozen in the kneeling position.

Kephas' thoughts switched to himself as a new danger loomed. While he had been concentrating on the unfolding drama, he had forgotten about the rest of the herd. They were coming to the aid of the wounded cow. They bellowed and trumpeted and thundered to the rescue. The herd moved fluidly past the tree in which Kephas was hidden. One brushed it with a huge flank, rocking and swayed it, causing Kephas to hang on for dear life.

Before they were blocked from view he caught a glimpse of Kumalo and Watura still crouching by the tree they had chosen for shelter.

Then the herd was trumpeting and milling around the wounded cow. The dangerous young bulls were scenting the wind for more humans.

Two big bulls approached the cow and stood on either side of her. They supported her with their bodies and tried to push her back to her feet. But it was to no avail. Her legs finally crumpled and the huge body crashed to the ground in a cloud of dust. Forty-six bullets were leeching the life from her.

The herd stayed there for an hour moping protectively around its late member. Then they wandered off slowly and disconsolately, leaving the hunters in possession of their spoils.

At what price? thought Kephas, as he shinnied down the tree and rejoined his remaining hunting partners. They walked wordlessly over to what remained of Dzingani. There was little left that was recognisable. His own mother would not have known him. His flesh and bone had been mangled into bloody pulp and this was mixed with leaves, dirt and dried grass. The blazing sun was already bringing out a repulsive smell. Big green flies buzzed over the pitiful remains.

Dzingani's shattered corpse was buried in a shallow grave scraped in the ground where he had died. No one had the time or interest to dig a deeper one.

The hyenas came that night and with their big paws cleared away the soil and devoured what they found. Only the crickets chirruping at the moon witnessed the final desecration of Dzingani, but the crunching of human bones did not concern them. In their world only the fortunate survived anyway. What was so different about the man creature?

None of the hunters could bring themselves to eat the flesh of the elephant killed.

20

Kephas was tired of waiting. They had been there for a month. The bunkers had been improved until they were almost luxurious.

There were daily conferences. A lot was said, but little was done. The accent was on more and more supplies. Tons of supplies were being paddled across the Zambezi River every night. Gangs of men manhandled it to the hilltop lair and returned to the safety of Zambia for more while darkness cloaked their activities.

Rifles still packed in grease, RPG7 hand-held rocket launchers and the rockets that went with them, ammunition and still more ammunition, landmines, medical supplies, clothing, food and still more food. Surely they would be ready to go soon, Kephas thought. Surely by now they had enough supplies to fight a major war?

Time passed. It was taken up with hunting trips and long lectures by the commissar on the thoughts of Chairman Mao. To Kephas' deep concern very little time was being spent on matters he deemed essential — like weapons training and military tactics.

He had several times suggested that he take a section to the nearest tribal lands over the escarpment — some 100 kilometres away — and make contact with the tribesmen. This was what they were here for. If they did not start finding local recruits and training them, they would never get anywhere. The commander cautioned patience. The commissar cautioned caution. No one, except for Kephas, Kumalo and a few others were eager to start. They behaved as if they had achieved a major success already. Getting in supplies had become the be-all and end-all of the exercise.

In the Soviet Union it had been drummed into Kephas that a guerrilla fighter had to be mobile. It is essential he carries his needs and lives off the land. If he is bogged down by supplies, he will be smashed by conventional forces which have greater firepower. As far as he was concerned they would bog themselves down if they continued like this. The supplies could be the death of them all.   They had escaped observation so far, but how long would their luck last?

Quantities of arms, ammunition, mines and grenades had been hidden in various caches within a 35-kilometre radius of the main base. Hollow baobab trees, caves and underground diggings had all been utilised.

The morning conference revealed another pointless exercise. The leadership hierarchy in Zambia was at last coming on an inspection. It was said they were pleased with the progress made so far. What progress, he thought, and spat on the ground in annoyance. When the hell would they wake up?

*   *   *

Solomon Pingurayi, a game scout working for the government, was a puzzled man. He had found the bones of an elephant. Poachers were not unknown in a wildlife reserve as large as this, but he didn't believe they were responsible. If they were, why hadn't they taken the ivory? No poacher would shoot an animal like this for the meat alone. Besides, no one was living within 100 kilometres of the place.

He thoughtfully tossed the torn and twisted metal into the air and caught it. It was all that was left of the bullet he had dug from a sun-whitened bone with his clasp knife.

He glanced with an experienced eye at the ground surrounding the bones. The grass was trampled and it had been like that for some time. There was no sign of the spoor of man, but it was obvious that many animals — mostly hyenas and jackals — had been tracking back and forth over the area. That was to say nothing of the vultures and crows. Between them they would make short work of a carcase and leave little if any trace of spoor. He looked again at some saplings within 90 metres or so of the remains. They had been stripped of their stringy bark. Only man, who used the tough bark to tie up bundles, would have done that. There was no need for animals to make bundles.

The tusks of the dead animal pointed whitely from their sockets. He shook his head. No, this was the work of man. But what type of man he couldn't decide. He also wondered why he had seen so little game. Usually the area was alive with all kinds of animals. They had nothing to fear as there were no men in the area. Yet it looked as if the herds had moved on. Game only moved on when it was extensively shot at.

He glanced around uneasily as if expecting someone to appear from out of the bush. He had to find out more before he returned to the base and reported his discovery. He needed to investigate further. He shifted his uniform cork helmet with its legionnaire's neck protector to the back of his head and cast around the area for spoor.

There seemed to be several game trails going through the thick Jesse thorn bush, but one looked more used then the rest. He moved his old Lee Enfield .303 to a more comfortable position and set out along the track.

A half hour later he was even more concerned. He had found tracks leading to the interior from the Zambezi River. This was no ordinary trail. Game trails were normally very narrow because animals of the veld almost step in each other's footprints. This was trampled as wide as a motor car.

All game scouts had been lectured time and again on the threat posed by terrorists infiltrating from Zambia. Many scouts had been responsible in the past for the capture of guerrillas who had crossed the international boundary. He had studied photographs of the standard spoor patterns of their boots many times. He had even studied the actual boots of captured terrorists. Yes, he well knew what to look for.

The whole track was patterned with a familiar spoor — some fresh, some recent, some old. He couldn't believe his eyes. He had been taught to expect the isolated track or two, but here the imprints had been made by what looked like a thousand pairs of boots. They had been marching backwards and forwards to the river for weeks. This was no small group. This was an army. They were careless because no effort had been made to brush it out or cover it.

He had to get away before he was spotted. With apprehension he looked up, then down the trail, and darted into the cover of the surrounding bush. It took two hours of walking at a careful and painstaking rate through the gauntlet of clinging thorns before he traced the trail to its inland source. He didn't dare walk on the track itself, but crept through the thick bush on a parallel course. Much of the time he crawled on his belly, tunnelling agonisingly through low hanging branches.

It materialised over his head at last. It was a low rocky kopje. He knew the place well. It was a landmark because the Zambezi Valley is generally flat and featureless. High ground was like their own back yard to people like Solomon who earn their living in that inhospitable terrain.

He lay flat on his belly for an hour, completely motionless and peering with his binoculars through the branches at the lower slopes. Eventually his vigilance was rewarded. Two men appeared on the skyline. He saw them clearly through the glasses and shook with excitement. Their olive green trousers and shirts were unmistakable. The fact that they weren't carrying arms wasn't important. Those men were terrorists. They must be encamped in the basin on top.

He lay still until the sun had gone down. Then, slowly and carefully, he worked his way out to safety. It took him a day and a half of forced marching to get back to the game camp. He stopped to rest only when his tired body refused to continue and he frequently fell asleep on his feet.

The warden heard a knock on his door very late, just as he was about to retire for the night. He opened the door and Solomon collapsed at his feet. He found it difficult to understand, let alone believe, the garbled story that the exhausted ranger told him.

He bundled the exhausted man into his Land-Rover and they set off. All night the vehicle bumped over the rough tracks of the Zambezi Valley floor, while Solomon slept in the passenger seat as if he were dead.

He was shaken from his sleep at the police camp. It was only dawn on the third day that he reported his story to the police.

21

Saul patiently sat in his big armchair watching television. He was dressed in an immaculate although unfashionable white dinner jacket that he put on very rarely. It had taken considerable persuasion by Dawn to get him into it. He glanced at his watch. It was nearly seven o'clock. He sighed impatiently.

'Come on Dawn', he groaned. 'Surely it doesn't take an hour to get ready?'

'What's she doing, what's she doing?' squeaked Molly, jumping up and down on the carpet where she was sitting with her nursemaid Sarah — a fat and comfortable middle-aged woman who was married to Saul's farm foreman.

'She's getting ready to go to the dance', explained Robert with an air of superiority. He paused for a moment in his repairs of the toy motor car, which Saul knew from experience would leave it more wrecked than before.

'What's a dance?' asked Molly, who always had an inexhaustible supply of questions.

'A dance, silly', said Robert, 'is somewhere big people go to when they want to get drunk.'

'Enough of that', laughed Saul, sweeping both of them up onto his knees. 'A dance, my children, is a place where grownups go to get away from inquisitive children.'

'What's quiztive, Daddy?' asked Molly, then forgot the question and clapped her hands. 'Look at Mummy! Look at Mummy!'

Saul smiled and looked up to see Dawn pirouetting in a gorgeous dress with a low neckline.

'Mmmmmm', said Saul appreciatively. 'Mmmmmm.'

'Do you like it?' his wife asked anxiously. She looked critically down at herself. 'Perhaps I should have bought the pink.'

Saul chuckled and stood up, his son tucked under his right arm and his daughter under the other. They squealed with delight as he swung them around and deposited them back on the carpet next to Sarah. He turned back to Dawn.

'What do you mean you should have bought the pink? I said Mmm, didn't I?'

Dawn pouted her pretty lips and struck a pose that she knew showed off her slim figure to best advantage. 'Well, I think a girl should get a little more than just an "mmmm" from her husband.' Saul moved over and before she knew it he had a hand on her bottom. She gave a muffled shriek and spun out of his way. 'I was only adding to my appreciation', he said grinning lasciviously. 'To let me show my appreciation properly, let's cancel the dance and we can stay home for the evening.'

'No, you don't, my boy', giggled Dawn. 'You've been working so hard on this farm for so long without a break, I was beginning to think you were married to it instead of to me. You're not getting out of taking me to a dance as easily as all that.'

'Right then', said Saul. 'Let's go.'

'You know what to do, Sarah', said Dawn. 'You have the telephone number of the club and there are bottles in the fridge for the baby if he wakes up.'

'Yes Madam', smiled Sarah.

'And Sarah', she added, 'the children can watch TV until the end of the programme and then to bed without any arguments.'

'Oh, Mummy', bawled Robert and Molly in unison.

'Bed, I said', repeated Dawn firmly. 'Bed when the programme is finished and no arguments. Goodnight, darlings.' She bent and kissed each in turn and gave them quick hugs.

'Remember what your mother says.' Saul wagged a semi-stern finger at both of them and turned to the door. 'No nonsense, otherwise I will personally spank you when I come home.'

Saul helped Dawn on with her cape and led her to the door.

'Are you sure you know what to do, Sarah . . .?'

'She does, she does', muttered Saul. 'Please, if we don't leave now, we'll never get away.'

'All right then', said Dawn, taking a last look around. 'Sarah, the bottles are in the fridge if the baby wakes up. Don't forget.'

'Yes Madam', said the baby sitter.

'Enough's enough', said Saul firmly. 'God bless you, kids.'

The car was parked in front of the verandah, he opened the door and helped Dawn to get in. He was about to go to the driver's side when the telephone rang within the house.

'Damn. Just as I thought we were getting away. I expect it's Jake trying to find out what time we're leaving.'

'Leave it then. We'll see him at the club.'

Saul's hand hesitated on the door. 'No, I'd better and see who it is. I won't take a moment.' He left the car door open and hurried into the house. The phone was fitted to the wall on the stoep.

'Hello', he said, 'Saul Jenkins here.'

'Hello, Senga Police Camp. Inspector Smythe.'

'Hello Inspector', said Saul. 'I have been meaning to look you up and welcome you to the area, but I guess I've been too busy to get around to it . . . you know, planting the tobacco seed beds and all that. Is it anything important because we are just leaving for the New Year's Eve dance at the club. I expect I will see you there. You are coming, aren't you?'

'No, I'm afraid not. Not tonight. I'm sorry Mr Jenkins, but all police reservists are required to report to the police camp as soon as possible.'

Saul felt a chill pass through his body. 'Trouble?'

'Sorry. I can't discuss anything on the phone. Can you get here as soon as possible?'

'Of course.' Saul glanced at his watch. 'Do I need to bring my kit along?'

'Yes, I'm afraid so. I must ring off, I've got a lot to do.'

'I see. Goodbye.'

He replaced the phone and looked thoughtfully at the car.

'Who was it, dear? Was it Jake?'

'No', said Saul, 'it was the police camp. They want me there as soon as possible. Some sort of flap, although it's probably a false alarm.'

He helped an anxious Dawn out of the car and they went back inside. She looked at him with big serious eyes. 'I wish you weren't in PATU', she said referring to the Police Anti Terrorist Unit. 'Surely you've done enough?'

Saul shook his head. 'No, I had to join. My experience makes me more useful than most of the other chaps. They're all in the Police Reserve. What would they have thought if I hadn't joined?'

'What about the children and me?'

Saul sighed. 'We've been through this before', he said quietly, taking her in his arms. 'Everyone has a wife and children, but you can't just stand back

160

from life because of it. It affects me in the same way as it affects everybody else. We all have our duty to do.'

'Is it safe for us to stay at the farm?'

'I think so at the moment. I'm sure I would have been told if there was any immediate danger.' He led her into the lounge. She smiled bravely at him and ran her hands wistfully down her dress. 'I had a feeling I wouldn't get a chance to show it off.'

'We'll fix an evening in town when I get back. Lock the doors', he cautioned, 'and send Sarah to the compound, just to be sure. You've got the rifle?' She nodded. 'Keep it loaded by your bed.'

'Where's Daddy going?' asked Molly.

Dawn picked her up. 'Daddy's got to go to the police camp.' She smiled bravely at Saul.

'I'll get my kit', he muttered and left the room.

*   *   *

A half hour later he drove into the Senga police camp. The open space behind the charge office was packed with army and police vehicles. To the side, a field kitchen was in operation and black troops of the Rhodesia African Rifles, dressed in camouflage uniforms, common to all units of the security forces, were queueing up with mess tins. Handing out plates of steaming hot stew was a shining black army cook with a very corpulent stomach.

Saul grinned to himself. It was strange how food in the field was always stew at base and hard tack on patrol. Never seemed to change anywhere in the world. In front of the office being briefed were the white officers and the black NCOs. A map sheet was spread out over a trestle table that had been scrubbed white.

A troop of white troopers of the crack Rhodesia Light Infantry relaxed by their vehicles. They were among the most proficient and toughest jungle fighting troops in the world and they were ready for action. Some were stripped to the waist with heavy bandoliers of ammunition slung casually over brawny shoulders and grenades hooked to their belts. They were superbly fit and ready to fight — then to follow up and fight again no matter what the odds or how rough the terrain might be. Some smoked, while others had last minute meals of bully beef from their ration packs — 'rat packs' as they were universally known.

Formidable fighters indeed were these men with names like Du Plessis, Smith, Bezuidenhout and Brown, whose ancestors had fought together and against each other over thousands of kilometres of trackless veld while the turbulent southern African history of the past 150 years was written. But these were the professionals, not the direct successors to the citizen commandos of southern African tradition who were always ready with their horses, guns and provisions to fight for their rights or for their country.

Their successors were today's police reservists like Saul, men who farmed, dug for gold on the mines or worked in banks or offices. They were always ready at a moment's notice to don their jungle camouflage, take their FN rifles from the bedroom gun cabinets and mount the air force choppers that had replaced the wiry Basuto ponies of the last century.

He joined a group of 12 men on the office verandah who were helping themselves to mugs of hot sweet tea from an urn balanced precariously on a chair.

'Hallo Saul', came greetings from among the group.

'Hallo Dave. How's it Van? Ja you bastard, I see everyone's here.'

There was muffled laughter. He picked up a tin mug and helped himself to tea. The muscular bulk of Jake appeared at his side.

'Missed out on the dance, hey?' Saul grinned.

'Ja, the girls aren't too happy, I'll bet.'

'My wife thinks I arranged it', chuckled one man.

'Didn't you?' queried another voice, followed by a roar of laughter.

'No sign of rain yet?'

'How's your tobacco?'

'Just about dried out of the lands, but luckily I've still got plenty of plants in the seed beds.'

The talk turned to shop — the shop of farming because most of them lived by the soil. They were more concerned with the lack of rain than the threat of terrorists, but the talk soon switched again to the business in hand.

'We should send over a few Canberras and bomb Lusaka to the ground. Wouldn't take more long.'

'At least the SAS could go cross the river and attack the terr bases.'

'Don't you know, old boy, that there are no bases there!'

'How can you speak with such authority, man?'

'Read it in the newspaper. The Zambians told the United Nations only last week.'

'Section leaders!' came a shout.

'That's you, my boy', said Jake, banging Saul between his shoulders, almost causing him to choke on his tea.

Saul grinned and put his mug down.

'Come on, Van', he said to a blond giant of about his own age who was already moving to the door. 'And you, Pete', he nodded to a stringy little ex-Cockney who still smelled strongly of the particularly powerful aftershave lotion he'd sprayed when getting ready for the dance.

'Bloody fine way to spend New Year, eh mate?'

'Right', grinned Saul.

He blinked to get his eyes accustomed to the light in the office and held out his hand to the dark-haired angular man of about 28 who was obviously the new Inspector-in-Charge, Jim Smythe.

'Saul Jenkins', he said.

'Pleased to meet you', nodded the Inspector, taking his hand in a firm grip. He waved at some chairs and the section leaders sat down.

He wasted no time on preliminaries.

'Gentleman', he said, picking up a pointer and pointing to a 1:50 000 wall map. 'We have trouble.' He indicated a series of contours indicating high ground.

Saul's mind raced ahead as he scanned the familiar map. He knew what was coming. He took in the picture and his mind's eye filled in the thick bush and rolling country of the escarpment. The place indicated was in the valley, about 30 kilometres from the river. Another 60 kilometres inland to the south, the mountains of the escarpment rose to the plateau on which most of Rhodesia was situated. Above the escarpment were the Senga tribal lands and the African Purchase Area. Another 20 kilometres inland were the farms. There was the Senga Mission. His eyes shifted. There was his farm, and there was Jake's. The straight survey lines showed where they bounded each other.

'We have confirmed information', continued Inspector Smythe, 'that a group of terrorists has infiltrated over the river and based up in this high ground.'

I know it well, thought Saul. He had often used it as a landmark when patrolling the valley while a policeman. Most of the valley floor was flat and the hills really stood out. An image of the thick Jesse bush that covered the area came to him. It was a hell of an area to conduct an operation in.

'The plan is for groups of security forces to be choppered into the area at first light tomorrow', continued Smythe. 'He nodded towards Saul. 'You know this area and it will be your section's job to act as guide for the main group to get close in. Then you'll base up for the night. You'll be under army command while doing this job.' He glanced at his watch. 'At exactly 06:00, the day after tomorrow, air force strike jets will soften up their defences with rockets and bombs. They expect to catch them with their pants down. After that, it's over to the ground forces.' He looked expectantly at the three section leaders. 'Any questions?'

'What about our section?' asked Van, nodding at Pete who for once had lost his cheerful grin.

'Initially, you chaps will be kept in reserve until the main contact has been made. After that, you'll be used to best advantage.'

*   *   *

The shirt-sleeved pilot relaxed in his seat. The rotors were already turning and the scream of turbines deafened their ears. Saul took his seat and strapped himself in. He looked around to check that everyone was ready and gave the pilot a thumbs up sign. The engines wound up to full throttle and the aircraft lifted jerkily from the ground. Its rotors created a miniature dust storm and the clothing of those below was blown tightly against their bodies as they protected their eyes with their hands. Saul looked around and saw two other helicopters rising to join them in formation. He gripped his rifle tightly. It was laid across his lap and the muzzle pointed through the open side.

Until now the excitement had stopped him from thinking too much about the situation, but now he was airborne and committed to action, he felt a queasy nervousness in the pit of his stomach. It was a feeling he had experienced before. He looked out of the open side to the north and saw the Zambezi River snaking through the bush. A shimmering heat haze dulled the glint of the distant water.

He thought of Dawn and wondered when he would see her again. Would he be dead by this time tomorrow? He looked over his shoulder at his friends. Jake caught his eye and gave him the thumbs up. Jim Wilkie was preoccupied with his own thoughts and was staring pensively towards the middle distance. He was only 22, but he looked younger with his pale girlish features and thin boyish figure. The army had rejected him as unfit, but he had volunteered for PATU and had soon shown he had the necessary endurance and stamina. But like the rest of them, he had never seen combat before. He felt a tap on his shoulder and looked back at the grizzled features of Jon du Toit. Like Saul and Jake he was also a farmer, but he was closer to 50 years of age than 40. Much too old for this type of game really, but he still had the endurance of a horse when it came to marching through the veld. Jon pointed down and Saul looked in the direction he was indicating and nodded. It was the rugged escarpment and it looked like a plasticine model from this height.

The choppers zoomed down the escarpment in a crazy type of follow-my-leader formation and fell in at treetop level. Game below scattered in panic.

Saul watched as the trees flashed by beneath the squat belly of the machine. He was quite startled when they slowed down, lost height over a clearing, dropped down to ground level and landed. He looked at the pilot, who nodded. Saul signalled for his section to deplane and snapped open his safety belt. He jumped through the open side, ducked down to avoid the whirling rotors, dashed for the side of the clearing and took cover in a thicket. He was closely followed by the rest. The pilot had scarcely cut power and he opened the throttle again and thundered off brushing the tops of the stubby trees fringing the drop zone.

The remaining helicopters roared in low and disgorged their cargoes of tough fighting men. A grim-faced army captain of no more than 24, took command and formed a defensive perimeter around the clearing. The heat was like a furnace as they settled down to patiently wait out the day.

For the next six hours helicopters dropped in and out of the landing zone, bringing in men until there was almost two companies of regular soldiers, both black and white, as well as regular police and reserve forces deployed. The army officers and police section leaders got together for a final strategy briefing and they studied maps of the area. Afterwards they briefed their own men. In operations like this it was essential that everyone knew the part they were to play. There was no room for mistakes.

Saul gathered his men around him. He explained what the position was and detailed the plan of attack. Their unit would scout ahead with Solomon, the Game Department ranger who had found the base. He would guide them to the enemy. It was still unknown how many enemy there were. Units would follow at specified intervals behind them. Once at their predetermined position 500 metres from the hill, they would be joined by a troop of the Rhodesia Light Infantry and the captain in charge would take command of the attack. Units of the Rhodesia African Rifles would take the right flank and another troop of the RLI would occupy the left flank.

Stopper units of police and army at section strength had been dropped to the rear of the enemy positions to cut escape routes.

They had eight kilometres to go to get into position before nightfall. They would spend the night there, unseen and unheard (they hoped) by the terrorists. At 06:00, the Rhodesian Air Force would mount an aerial bombardment of the terrorist positions. The soldiers and police would then move in. There were no questions. Saul looked at his watch and indicated it was time to move.

They got to their feet and adjusted their webbing and equipment. Saul, who had drunk hardly anything since leaving Senga, took a quick swig from his water bottle to moisten his mouth. He looked up at the sun. If only it wasn't so hot.

He waved at a group of army officers. They waved back and moved quietly about readying their men for the move.

With Solomon in the lead, Saul's unit set off in single file formation ready for instant action. Once on the move, they soon lost sight of the following units because of the thick bush, although they were rarely more than 50 metres away.

It was a long, cruel walk, and thirst hit them badly. They couldn't drink much because what they had had to last until the next day. They had no idea how long they would be fighting once they were in contact with the enemy.

They marched in silence. Voices carried a long way in the bush and enemy watchers could be anywhere. Not once did they relax vigilance. They behaved and looked like the feared fighters they were.

The sun was low in the sky when Solomon finally raised his hand in a signal to halt. The section took up defensive positions while Saul squatted on the ground and discussed the geography of the area with their guide. He pointed and indicated in a hoarse whisper that the target hill lay directly ahead of them. In the thick bush visibility was strictly limited.

Shortly afterwards the rest arrived and deployed silently on a front of about 70 metres. Saul could not see the flank units, but he was told they had taken up their positions.

*   *   *

Kephas could scarcely credit the evidence of his eyes.

He had been called along with the other group commanders to the commander's bunker late into the night. It was big, roomy and comfortable.

An oil lamp hung from the roof.

The bigwigs from Lusaka had finally arrived to inspect them. He had expected Amon Matenga, the Regional Party Secretary for Lusaka, but it was the man with him who surprised Kephas.

He was dressed in garb similar to them — olive green shirt, trousers and jungle boots — but there the resemblance ended because this man's uniform was tailored at the waist and shoulders, while theirs were baggy and ill-fitting. But then Simon Gumede wouldn't allow himself anything but the best. He had fled Rhodesia for Zambia two years before. He had been most reluctant to leave his comfortable home in Salisbury, but the eyes of the authorities had focussed on him and he had only just managed to escape the country one step ahead of a restriction order.

He was no longer unhappy. Being part of the hierarchy of an expatriate nationalist organisation in Zambia had given him more power and money than he had ever dreamed of at home. Now he wouldn't return to Salisbury even if he was ordered to. He had access to fantastic sums of money donated by all manner of foreign sympathisers and he cut a most dashing figure with the girls. His uniform had been tailored not to make it more suitable for military action — which he intended to avoid at all costs — but to ensure his heroic appearance in Lusaka society.

He had certainly not wanted to cross the river on this damn inspection tour, but Matenga had insisted. He had pointed out his backlog of work at the Party offices, but Matenga was adamant. After all, he was a general on the military committee of the Party. Surely he wanted to see his troops before they went into action? Finally he had run out of excuses, so here he was.

He hated everything about the trip. First there was the hair-raising crossing of the river, then the long night's walk to the base. He had been absolutely terrified by the elephants and ever since he had stepped foot back in Rhodesia, he had been expecting to be cut down by a sudden hail of enemy bullets. Yet despite all that, the trip had so far been uneventful and everything at the base seemed to be quiet and safe.

The commander explained how far they were from the nearest habitation and how they had not so far tried to move farther inland. Gumede nodded knowledgeably for outward appearances, but inwardly he heaved a deep sigh of relief that they hadn't.

Introductions were made by the commissar who couldn't hide his delight at the visitors' arrival.

'Comrades, this is Comrade Matenga and General Gumede from Party Headquarters.'

He introduced his own men, who saluted with clenched fist salutes and then shook hands.

Matenga and Gumede beamed at the assembled men. The man introduced as Kephas seemed oddly familiar. He was sure he had met him before, but he couldn't place where or when despite racking his brains. He noticed that Kephas was also glancing at him strangely.

'You don't remember me, do you?' Kephas asked, the tinge of a smile crossing his face.

'I'm sorry', Gumede hesitated. 'You look very familiar but I just can't place you. Have we met in Lusaka?'

'No', said Kephas shaking his head gravely.

Kephas made an immediate impression on Gumede. He looked hard, tough and confident in his own ability and he did not usually forget men like that.

'We met in Salisbury', said Kephas. 'I went to you for help after I escaped from the police at Senga. You arranged for me to leave the country to study for a medical degree. But it turned out that the scholarship was not all what it was cracked up to be!'

A look of recognition passed over Gumede's face, and with it a shadow of fear. Kephas laughed spontaneously. It was clear that the general with the nice clean uniform was frightened of him.

'The university was not quite what you led me to expect, but I liked it anyway. Of course the education I received didn't do much to qualify me as a doctor.' He nudged Gumede slyly and laughed uproariously. The others caught on to the merriment at Gumede's expense.

The general looked visibly relieved and joined in the merriment. It wouldn't have been right for an important guy like himself to hold a grudge. He sized Kephas up and decided it would be better to have him as a friend than as an enemy.

He placed his arm round Kephas' shoulders. 'I certainly made a good choice, didn't I? I wish all the lads I selected for training had turned out the same way as you have.'

Their discussions continued until the early hours of the morning. Matenga spoke first and he was followed by Gumede. They assured the assembled men that they still had contact with the earlier parties who had all achieved their objectives. They had indeed fought in many battles and defeated

Smith's soldiers time and time again. Karoi and Sinoia had been captured and they were awaiting reinforcements so they could advance on Salisbury.

Soon the freedom fighters would spread out from this base and help to win the cause. Every man who took part would be given a farm taken from a white farmer.

'You can even have one of their skinny white wives if you want one', Gumede promised extravagantly.

Maybe some believed him, but Kephas felt sure their idle boasting served only to conceal the singularly unsuccessful military actions the Party had engaged in so far.

22

It was a long night. They kept watch in shifts to allow some sleep. Saul, who was used to roughing it, curled up on the ground as if he were at home in bed, but excitement and the cool sober thoughts of possible death on the morrow kept him awake.

There was no smoking and no talking. Sometimes they heard the sounds of animals crashing through the bush around them. The area was infested with elephants and their trumpeting came at frequent intervals. Luckily none came too close.

He was relieved when the sky lightened in the east.

The sky brightened quickly. Saul checked his rifle and ensured the magazine was firmly in place and the action cocked. He patted the pouches on his belt and satisfied himself that extra magazines were easily available. He looked around and saw some men nibbling at biscuits — a bush breakfast. He glanced at the pack containing his own rations that lay on the ground nearby. He was not hungry and he was not going to carry the extra weight into action. His water bottle was strapped to his belt alongside the ammunition pouches. He needed nothing else. Water and ammunition were essential, but everything else would be an encumbrance.

Saul looked at his watch. It was 05:59. The aircraft would arrive overhead any second now. He glanced at Jake who grinned and gave him the thumbs up sign. He squinted through the trees trying to see the hill they would soon be attacking, but he couldn't see anything.

There was a sudden startling howling scream as a flight of Hunter strike jets passed overhead at treetop level. Saul actually saw the bombs release and he involuntarily ducked and clutched at the ground. Dear God, they were aiming at him.

It felt like an earthquake as the hot, gusty wind of the bomb blasts struck his face. The noise was tremendous. God, oh God, what was happening?

Somewhere ahead of him he heard the screams of men in torment. Men were dying. He lifted his head and looked at Jake, but his friend's face was looking straight to his front.

Farther down the line, the captain was kneeling with his rifle held in front of him. He was staring un-movingly at the sky. He noticed Saul and waved for him to get down. He ducked his head and lay flat again. The earth felt cool against his cheek.

The thundering of the jet engines returned as the murderous birds came in for their second attack. This time they strafed with an explosive hail of cannon fire that deafened the ears. Then they were gone again. Surely there could be no one left alive after this?

Saul glanced at a pale-faced Jim Wilkie and gave him a smile of encouragement. He got a weak grin in return.

Each moment seemed like eternity. When would the order be given to attack? His stomach muscles felt as if they were knotted in a tight ball and his bowels felt weak. He was scared. In fact, he had never been so afraid. For the first time in years he lay on the ground and prayed. He prayed that he would have the strength to move forward when the time came — and prayed that his bowels would not dissolve into liquid when he did.

He did not hear the Hunters arrive on their final run, but merely saw a flash overhead followed by a deep crump, crump, crump followed by a whooshing and crackling. A pall of black smoke billowed into a cloud about 30 metres above the trees. Mixed with the cloud were tongues of flame that seemed disconnected to anything on the ground. Tinder dry bush and grass on the hillside erupted into flame, fanned by the explosive force of the blast.

Saul stared in horror at the terrible fires. He felt a wave of heat as they boiled up. Surely no one could live through that?

*   *   *

Kephas was surprised at how light it was when he stepped outside the command bunker. He glanced at his watch. It was two minutes to six. It looked like a lovely morning, but he was certain it was going to be hot as hell again.

It had been decided that the visiting VIPs would address the men a little later.

Kephas took in the morning scene. The sentries were coming in for breakfast and the reliefs trailed their rifles and yawned as they made their way out to their posts for another four-hour stint of boring duty.

There was a low murmur in the sky and Kephas looked up. The murmur increased to a screaming roar as aircraft tore towards their positions at half the speed of sound.

'Aircraft!' someone shouted.

'Take cover or they will see us.'

For a few seconds nobody moved. They just looked at each other. Then men desperately threw themselves into cover.

The jets came in low. Few saw the bombs fall. It seemed amazing that the enemy had discovered where they were.

Kephas heard the whistle of bombs, but he had never been under an air attack before and did not recognise the sound for what it was.

The hill vibrated in a gigantic tremor as a pattern of fragmentation bombs struck home and exploded, sending torn metal slivers in every direction like a hailstorm from hell. They whined off rocks and ripped through human flesh.

The commander and the commissar died at exactly six o'clock without knowing what had hit them. A jagged piece of white-hot metal ripped off the commissar's head, leaving his body jerking and convulsing like a decapitated chicken. His shirt pocket gaped open and a wad Rhodesian dollars fell to the ground.

Kephas leaned over, grabbed the bloody bundle and slipped it in his pocket. It would probably come in useful later. He thought at first that the commander was asleep. His features were composed and serene and his eyes were closed. But he had gone to sleep forever. A tiny bomb fragment had entered the back of his skull and lacerated his brain. A massive cerebral haemorrhage had instantly snuffed out his life.

Kephas looked about him but he was alone except for his dead leaders. He didn't know it, but 20 others had died when the first bombs exploded.

The aircraft will be back. Must organise the men.

He didn't hear the aircraft coming in on the second run and awoke to their presence only when they followed each other in a strafing cannon run that churned up the top of the hill in a line of explosions. Kephas could feel the wind from the hammering hell as he dived back in the command bunker for cover.

Moments later the planes were past and screaming into the sky to start the tight turns that would bring them in for another merciless assault.

A man in the command bunker clutched his rifle and stared out with glazed eyes. He mumbled incoherently, but at least he was alive and unharmed. Kephas grabbed a rifle leaning against the wall and checked it. It was loaded.

'We must shoot at them when they return.'

He shook the shoulder of the bomb-shocked man impatiently. He looked back at him with lacklustre eyes with little comprehension.

'Come on, you bastard.' He slapped the man viciously with the back of his hand. 'Get on your feet.'

The man stood up unsteadily and gave Kephas a hurt look. 'Why did you hit me?'

Kephas ignored him.

'Get to the entrance and when they return, direct your rifle at the sky and squeeze the trigger. With any luck we may hit one. At least we can try.'

Kephas shoved him to the entrance. He moved as if he was an automaton. The two crouched down and pointed their rifles at the sky.

The first jet was past before they realised it.

'Fire! Fire! Fire!' Kephas yelled.

He directed a long burst into space. Within what seemed like seconds the magazine was empty. He looked around for his companion, but he was back cowering in the bunker. He re-loaded.

He didn't know how many more planes screeched overhead, dispensing their cargoes of death. Bombs exploded everywhere and a direct hit on an ammunition dump sent great sheets of black and red fire searing through grass, trees and men.

Another dump blew with a tremendous roar, but he hardly heard it.

A fragment of burning wood stuck to Kephas' shoulder like a blob of red hot tar. He dropped his rifle and beat at the searing pain, hollering his agony.

Men died in the holocaust without uttering a word, their speech and life burned out of their lungs by the tremendous heat.

Others died noisily with their terrified screams rending the air above the crackle of burning trees. No man could be brave when facing death like this.

'Mother!'

'No, no, no, no . . .'

'God, oh God!'

'Mother, help me!'

'I am dead.'

There was no time to waste with the dying. Who could still fight? Kephas glanced at his cowering bunker mate who, like him, had survived the terrible battering.

'Reload', snarled Kephas.

The cowering wretch made no move until Kephas pointed his rifle at him. Then he hastily grabbed handfuls of ammunition from an ammunition box and stuffed them in his pockets.

'I told you to reload', shouted Kephas angrily.

'I don't need to', the man replied. 'I haven't fired anything yet.'

Kephas' finger tightened on the trigger and he shot him.

Kephas stuffed his pockets full of ammunition. There were fewer screams now. Something had changed and there was silence. He poked from the bunker and tried to make out what had happened. Suddenly he realised there were no screaming jet engines and no bombs were falling. This meant troops must be nearby readying to attack.

Must get things organised. Blood pounded in his head. He scrambled from the bunker, clutching his rifle.

One side of the hill was a smoking mass of burnt vegetation. The blackened and burning bodies of men were everywhere. Some were frizzled into cinders with claw-like hands and arms reaching for the sky. The acrid smell of explosives mixed subtly with the odour of roasting flesh.

Kephas retched and puked on the ground.

He ran over to where his group was dug in. Their area was not as hard hit as others and the bush was not on fire. Men were standing around paralysed into inactivity by the inexplicable disaster that had overtaken them.

'Get your rifles and take up defensive positions. There will be a ground attack next.'

Kephas became a rallying point and men from all over the kopje began making their way towards him in ones and twos.

He could see no other group or platoon leaders.

* * *

There were shouts and Saul looked around in surprise. Troops and police had got to their feet and were advancing with rifles at the ready at a strange stumbling double, equipment bouncing on their hips and against their buttocks. The captain led the way, shouting for them to advance. Saul dragged himself up and joined the rest.

The bombs had seemed so close that he expected to burst through the trees and find the hill right in front of them. Instead it seemed an age before the hill loomed up through the trees. He looked up and could see no signs of life. Large patches of grass and bush were burning fiercely.

Rifle fire began to crackle on either side of him and bullets were whipping through the trees. From somewhere above them fire was being returned. No one stopped or took cover. Saul found he was involuntarily screaming abuse at the unseen enemy to his front.

A guerrilla in green denims broke from behind a large boulder. He was so close that Saul could see a darned patch on the seat of his pants. He was clutching a rifle and screaming hysterically as he made for the summit. Jim Wilkie fired from the shoulder. The man took two giant steps forward, then fell flat on his face. When they stepped over him, he was dead. More men broke cover in front of the advance and ran for their lives, throwing away their rifles as they did. The deadly accurate fire of the attackers hunted them down amongst the rocks. Two fell as Saul's carbine chattered a message of death.

Grenades blasted other escaping guerrillas to a standstill.

Saul's section reached the top of the hill and saw the devastation in the rocky basin. Fires were burning and mutilated bodies were sprawled in grotesque positions. A few soldiers were targeting a man who was sprinting desperately for the opposite lip, ducking and weaving as he ran. Automatic fire whipped up the dust at his feet, but his life must have been charmed as he got over the edge and disappeared. Soldiers raced over and fired after him but he had gone.

Saul stood next to the troopers who were looking dejectedly at the silent bush below.

'The bastard got away', muttered one of them.

The sounds of battle began to subside. Desultory firing occurred at various parts of the hill as the enemy were hunted down and prised from their underground bunkers. They were killed if they did not immediately surrender.

Then it was all over.

The various units that had taken part gradually coalesced. Men wearily leaned on their weapons, lit cigarettes and looked about them.

There were seven prisoners, but four were badly wounded and lay stretched out on the ground groaning in pain. The remaining three squatted on the ground under the watchful guns of two privates of the Rhodesian African Rifles. There was no fight left in them and they wouldn't have tried to escape even if they had been given the opportunity.

The security forces' casualties lay nearby. A black private of the RAR and a white trooper of the RLI lay side by side, camouflage smocks covering their dead faces. Some soldiers were wounded, but only a few of them seriously. While waiting for a helicopter to lift them out, they joked and swopped war stories in the true comradeship that only occurs when men have faced death together. An overworked medic beavered away doing what he could for them.

The enemy dead were dragged by the feet to a central point and left sprawled on the ground. Their numbers seemed endless.

There was a roar of turbo jets overhead and the casevac helicopters landed in a clearing that had been hacked out of the virgin bush. The wounded, both friends and foe, were loaded aboard.

Follow-up groups of soldiers and policemen set off to track down escaping guerrillas. They gave casual waves to their comrades as they moved out. These were tough, resilient men who could live in the bush better than those who were born there. They wouldn't stop until they could report with confidence that the area had been cleared of the enemy.

A team of Special Branch and CID policemen who had arrived in the helicopters got to work interrogating the prisoners and photographing the enemy dead for later identification. Saul and his section rested on their rifles and watched as the twisted corpses were searched for documents and papers that might reveal valuable intelligence. It was a horrible, gruesome task, but it was a job that had to be done. A large number of the dead were terribly mutilated or burned to cinders. The sour odour of death, aggravated by the heat of the sun pervaded the area.

The bodies were numbered in the order they were photographed. Any letters and papers found were placed in plastic bags marked with the same numbers. A few little red booklets of The Thoughts of Mao tse-Tung were taken from the pockets of the torn and bloody uniforms. Their former owners would not be needing them again.

It was almost midday when they were done with the final count. The enemy had suffered an immense defeat and 83 of their dead were laid out in rows in the rocky basin.

In addition to manpower losses, many tons of arms, ammunition and equipment of all kinds were recovered from the bunkers. Sufficient supplies had been cached to equip a small army. There were Soviet and Chinese manufactured AK47s, RPD machine guns, Tokarev pistols, 40mm rocket launchers, plastic explosives, land mines, grenades, booby traps, ammunition of all kinds, medical stores, radios and countless other military items.

*   *   *

After running about a kilometre Kephas rested in the bush to recover his breath. He checked himself, but by some miracle he was unharmed except for the burn on his shoulder and some scratches picked up while running through the bush.

He still didn't know how he had managed to escape. The spirits of his forefathers must have come to his aid. The ground attack, when it came, had taken them by surprise. A burst of machine-gun fire from the foot of the hill heralded the start. Three of his men dropped. Two died immediately and the third lay screaming in agony. A bullet had severed his spinal column. The rest ducked into cover and awaited the onslaught. At first he saw nothing, but bullets hunting for targets whined and ricocheted off the rocks.

He saw a movement in the trees and fired blindly. Then the attack was on. Soldiers in camouflage appeared from below and charged up the hill yelling like demons, shooting as they went. He was astonished that they got so close before he saw them.

He returned fire, shooting short bursts on automatic. He saw a soldier fall, but suddenly realised he was the only one returning fire. He looked behind him and saw his men were abandoning their weapons and fleeing in panic.

'Come back here, you bloody cowards!' he yelled, but no one paid any heed.

Their cowardice did them no good whatsoever as one after the other they were shot down by the soldiers.

With a sense of shock he suddenly realised his own danger and clutching his AK he fled up the slope. A fusillade of shots followed but by a miracle he wasn't hit. Then he was in the basin and running for the far side.

When almost there, he again felt the air disturbance of near misses and heard the zinging ricochets of bullet striking nearby. He glanced back and saw that soldiers were in hot pursuit, firing as they ran. He careened down the far slope, and headed for the relative safety of the thick bush below. He jumped from rock to rock with the agility of a goat, never once losing his footing. Rifle fire pursued him, but it was wide and he reached safety.

Now was the time to make plans. Having escaped death by millimetres and seconds, he had no wish to run into an ambush. He checked his AK, slipping off the magazine and pressing the cartridges inside down with his thumb. There were only few rounds left. He felt his pocket and discovered another six or seven rounds. He loaded them into the curved magazine and slotted it back into place on the carbine.

The obvious course of action was to make for one of the supply caches he had helped to establish. There would be ammunition, tinned food aplenty and water. That was the most important, for without water he would die quickly.

Nobody had planned for such a contingency. It was likely that some of the others had got away, but they would probably be wandering around alone, not knowing where to go because no plans had been made for rendezvous points. He thought of the commissar's legs twitching their last dance of death. He at least would not need to rendezvous!

A distant burst of small arms fire crackled from the direction of the hill he had just evacuated. Someone there must still be resisting. He quickened his pace, knowing he had to get away before the enemy started their follow-up.

He cut a branch from a tree, slung his rifle over his shoulder and began walking backwards, backtracking and brushing out his spoor as he went.

He continued for an hour before some animal instinct told him he was no longer alone. He stopped, eyes darting around, but he couldn't see anything. A bird was twittering in the trees as he dropped into cover and silently leopard-crawled about ten metres through the long grass to confuse the enemy in case they were watching him.

He lay unmoving for some minutes

The voice came so suddenly, so unexpectedly, that it unnerved him.

'We must get water.'

He fixed the source immediately. It was nearby — no more than 15 metres away by a huge baobab. Its base was obscured by thick Jesse bush. He wondered if he could ease himself away from the voice, but decided he was too close. It would be better to dash forward and shoot whoever was there before they shot him.

He wished he had a grenade.

178

How many of them were there? Would he have the time to shoot them before they shot him?

He eased himself into a crouching position, then charged the tree, AK at the ready. It took a few seconds to cover the distance and at any moment he expected a hail of nickel-plated lead to rip him apart.

How he had stopped himself from firing, he would never know. He found himself staring into the startled eyes of Watura who was crouched down, holding his hands in front of him as if to ward off the expected bullets.

'Kephas!'

Watura's startled cry caused him to hesitate. It was enough to keep Watura alive.

There were others there besides Watura. He had caught them in stages between sitting and standing up. Their faces reflected their helplessness and fear.

'Kephas! I thought you were dead!'

Kumalo mopped his brow with the back of a shaking hand.

Quivering on the ground and unable to get to his feet because of a violent panic attack that he had suffered and which had almost choked him, was Simon Gumede. His uniform was no longer impeccable. It was filthy with dirt and dried blood. The knife edge creases in his trousers were gone. He looked as if he had been screwed up and rubbed in the dust.

Watura leant down, grasped him by the shoulder and yanked him to his feet.

'Come on, general. Get up.'

He laid sarcastic emphasis on the word 'general'. There was not much respect there for Gumede.

Taziva from Kumalo's platoon was another survivor, but Kephas didn't know him.

They looked at each other almost speechless. Kephas noted that he was the only one armed.

'Where are your AKs?'

They looked sheepish. Kumalo drew a Tokarev pistol from the waistband of his trousers.

'I've got this.'

He looked at the rest with contempt. 'They obviously decided they could run faster if they threw away their guns.'

Kephas tapped his own rifle.

'Perhaps it would have been better if you had kept your rifle instead of that thing', he said coldly. He changed the subject. 'We'll head for one of our caches and rearm ourselves. That way we might stand a chance of getting back to Zambia.'

No one disputed his assumption of leadership.

They were demoralised and it wouldn't take much to get them running again. But Kephas was sure of Kumalo. He didn't think he would run, in spite of him having abandoned his AK.

He smiled wryly. He could hardly talk, because he had also done a runner. He glanced up at the sun. It was almost midday. If they left now there was a danger of them running into an ambush. He decided it would be wiser if they hid until nightfall and then moved out.

'Get some sleep while I will stand guard. We will move out at nightfall.'

Kephas eased his rifle on to his lap. Although he was as tired as anyone else, he had no intention of entrusting his AK to anyone. That would stay with him.

23

Saul and his section lay in ambush on the game trail that led down to the river. Except that at this time of the year it could hardly be called a river. There were a few isolated pools of stinking algae-covered water. Otherwise, the river bed consisted of a long stretch of golden sand pockmarked by the spoor of game that snaked through the bush. It would only become a river again when the belated summer rains commenced.

His section had been choppered out of the main battle area along with other police and army sections that had been dropped at predetermined map reference points in the bush. The escaping guerrillas had to go somewhere and various trails had been selected for ambush. The security forces couldn't cover them all, because the bush was vast, but educated guesses by experienced men scanning battle maps more often than not were proved correct. It was the ability to put oneself in the enemy's shoes and guess what his next move would be.

Saul lay over his automatic rifle and stared down the trail. Next to him was Jon du Toit chewing a stick of biltong. Jake was resting at the rear with Jim Wilkie. After the excitement and strain of the battle this morning, they were all exhausted.

An hour ago they had heard a distant rattle of machine gun fire, followed by a series of hollow thuds which they recognised as grenades exploding. So far no one had wandered into their killing zone.

Saul glanced at his watch. It was 18:00 and it would soon be dark. He glanced at Jon who grimaced and cut off a segment of biltong for him. Saul nodded his thanks, popped it in his mouth and chewed thoughtfully.

'A half hour to dark', he whispered.

'Ja', muttered Jon. 'If we don't make contact soon, it'll be too dark to follow up.'

Right, thought Saul. If darkness fell and the enemy stumbled into their ambush, they would indeed be unable to follow up. It was too dangerous to move at night in an area where friendly forces might be laying up. No one had the time to ask if you were friend or foe if you stumbled into their ambush position. They just shot you. The others would be returning to their positions soon. It was important they be settled in before nightfall. He and Jon had eaten earlier, quietly gouging cold braised steak from cans they had opened with their clasp knives. There would be no hot food tonight. The enemy would smell a whiff of wood smoke from a kilometre away. The basic senses of people became acute when they had been living in the bush for weeks on end.

The grass rustled lightly and Jake wriggled back into the firing line, followed by Jim. It was fantastic how quiet a man could be when he was trained for it.

They smiled the look of close comradeship at each other and felt warmer for it. They had carried out a good job earlier in the day and they knew it. This was something they would one day be able to tell their grandchildren about — Jon, in fact, when he got home.

The sun touched the horizon to the west and a few wispy clouds glowed red in the rich sunset. It was almost like they were reflecting the bloody carnage from earlier in the day. The sun sank rapidly and darkness came like a curtain being drawn. Frogs in the few stagnant pools at the river commenced a croaking chorus. At least they were free to advertise their presence.

Then a disturbance. Something was coming along the path. Saul glanced sideways at his companions, but they were all staring steadily down their sights seeking the source of the commotion.

A herd of impalas appeared and Saul relaxed. The old buck in the lead halted nervously and sniffed the wind. He couldn't smell the men because they were downwind, but he clearly sensed danger. The herd shifted nervously. Eventually, deciding that it was safe, he led his charges through the killing ground of the ambush to drink at the river. Their brown shapes and white tails could be seen clearly, as they milled around and drank in the darkness.

A lion coughed in the distance and the herd, catching its scent, bounded off into the bush in great running leaps. Within seconds they were gone.

Saul wondered if other lions were close by waiting to pounce on the herd. It was usual for the old male of a pride to go upwind and roar to stampede a herd down into the untender care of his savage spouse. The men would never know. A lion killed silently and an impala scarcely whimpered as its living entrails were torn out. Cries for help were not recognised in the bush. By the law of the jungle, death was always silent and lonely.

They lay there and strained their eyes at ground level in their quest for a human silhouette framed against the night sky to target. The ground is always darker than the sky, he thought. I should have carrots in my packs, like it was pretended the Battle of Britain pilots relied on. He smiled to himself as he recalled his mother's blind faith in the vegetable's abilities to improve her children's eyesight.

* * *

Saul and his men were not the only ones who heard the king of the jungle roar his challenge. About two kilometres away other men had been encamped in a clump of thick bush since midday.

Kephas snatched up his AK. He glanced at his companions who were still asleep, exhausted mentally and physically from the disastrous events earlier. He still could not really believe his luck in escaping.

They would have to get arms for the rest, but most important of all, they had to get water.

He glanced contemptuously at 'General' Simon Gumede in his rumpled uniform. His mouth was open and he was breathing noisily in his sleep. The sight cheered up Kephas. I bet the bastard never thought his inspection tour would end like this. He pondered on the idea of abandoning the lot of them and just taking Kumalo with him. They had no weapons and more importantly, no water bottles. Still, he pondered, they would probably prove useful later.

What had happened to the rest? He guessed that most had been killed or captured. Some had probably got away like his little group, but he doubted if an effective fighting force remained.

What had been planned? Where could they go? He cursed the commissar and the commander for keeping everything close to their chests. This had been fine when they had been grouped together, but what about now? He began to doubt that they had had any plans at all. Perhaps they had just intended to sit in the safety of the valley for a few weeks, then return to Zambia to boast of their 'victories'! He hawked phlegm from his throat and spat on the ground. Nothing would surprise him.

It would have been very different if Simon Gumede and the rest had got off their fat backsides and fought, instead of enjoying the good life in Lusaka. His experiences of today made it obvious that the white men were far from defeated.

'Time to go', he grunted unsympathetically digging his toe into Gumede's ribs. The general groaned and sat up, his eyes wide with fear.

'Time to go', Kephas repeated with unconcealed contempt. 'No, the Boers aren't here.'

He was clearly yellow — not the big fighting general of yesterday. Kephas turned his back in disgust and wakened the rest.

They regarded him with trust as they awaited his orders.

'Once we have rearmed, we will head for the river', he told them. There was relief on their faces. 'With any luck we should be able to locate dugout canoes along the shore and paddle over to Zambia. If we march hard we should be able to rearm and reach the river tomorrow morning. We will hide up during the day and make our attempt to get across when night falls.'

He regarded them contemptuously. There was little doubt that they had lost the will to fight. The humiliating battering they had gotten had been just too much. Now all they wanted to do was remain alive.

'Move out in a single file'. He nodded curtly at Gumede. 'You will take the point and you', he gestured at Kumalo, ' take the second position.'

Kumalo patted his pistol.

'But I'm unarmed', whispered Simon, his face an ugly grey colour. 'I'll get killed if you put me out in front.'

'How can you get killed, General? You're a general and generals don't get killed. They normally sit on their arses in Lusaka and do nothing', Kephas said sarcastically. 'Besides, don't you remember telling us that the war has practically been won? That we already have Karoi and Sinoia in the bag and soon we'll capture Salisbury.'

Gumede nervously licked his dry lips. 'I didn't know what was happening', he whined.

'I didn't know what was happening', mimicked Kephas. 'You seemed very knowledgeable before.'

He nonchalantly sprang open the bayonet on his rifle and clipped it in place. He moved menacingly towards Gumede.

The general stood rooted to the spot, looking fearfully at Kephas.

'I . . . I . . .' Gumede tried to speak but the saliva dried in his mouth. He was sure his last moments had arrived.

Carelessly, as it swatting a fly, Kephas carefully dug his bayonet point into Gumede's throat just enough to draw blood.

Gumede went faint as cold steel cut his flesh. His skin crawled.

'You might be a general, but if you don't obey my orders, I'll kill you', Kephas told him. 'Do you understand? I'm not leaving anyone here to surrender who can say where we've gone. If you stay, it will be as a very dead corpse. What is it to be?'

'Please, please, I will go with you. I don't want to surrender.' Gumede whimpered like a kicked dog acknowledging a new master. He held on to a tree to prevent his tottering legs from collapsing beneath him. No one moved to help him.

'Any questions by anyone else?' growled Kephas.

The rest, except for Kumalo who was expressionless, looked down, afraid to meet his eyes. Hatred for Kephas simmered inside Gumede, but his fear was greater that his hate. He knew that Kephas would show him no mercy.

Kephas caught his shoulder and gave him a violent shove.

'Get to the front, you fat ox.'

They formed into a single file with Gumede in the lead, followed by Kumalo and the unarmed men.

Kephas brought up the rear.

*   *   *

Saul strained his ears. Occasionally an animal crashed about in the darkness, but no sounds that seemed to be manmade were heard.

His eyes stared into the gloom of the trail. He consciously blinked to refocus concentration. He was tired, but sleep must not come. He licked his finger and wetted his eyes with the spit.

He was beginning to doubt they would make contact tonight.

A twig cracked like a pistol shot which alerted him instantly. He touched the dark shape of Jake next to him, who nodded.

They lay with rifles at the ready with charged magazines and a round up the spout. They couldn't afford the sound made by a sliding breech block. Such a sound would be magnified a thousandfold in the silent night What's more the enemy would be straining their senses for the slightest warning.

Saul cuddled his carbine and stared down the barrel out into the darkness. No one would fire until he did. He heard Jake take a deep breath next to him and at the same time an upright shape appeared in his vision. The shape gradually assumed the proportions of a human being.

Peep sights were no use in the dark. Stare down the barrel in the general direction and fire . . . aim low . . . a ricochet from the ground is better than a bullet lost in the sky . . . 70 metres approximately . . . wait for 35 metres . . . make sure they couldn't miss.

*   *   *

Gumede stumbled. He couldn't see a thing. A stick snapped underfoot and momentarily he froze. Damn, that could be heard for kilometres.

His face was clammy and his stomach a knot of tight muscles. He felt sick with fear. A hand touched his shoulder, commanding him to continue.

He took some more stumbling paces. There must be a river ahead. The ground was dropping and the shimmer of sand, much lighter than the bush, could be seen in front. He rubbed his tongue around his dry mouth. It felt like sandpaper. Tears came to his eyes. He'd do anything for a drink. Even a sip. Where was the river?

Even that bastard Kephas would surely allow them to stop for a drink and a rest. He would appeal to his reason. He would beg him if necessary. How he hated that arrogant youngster. When they got back to Zambia he would have him shot. The pleasure of seeing Kephas dead in his mind's eye gave him new strength. He would sure be there to see this happen. He straightened up and stepped out with renewed vigour.

The bush exploded in a hell of rifle shots.

A 7.62mm bullet travelling at plus 600 metres per second tore into his right kneecap, smashing muscle and bone. His lower leg was all but amputated except for a few vague pieces of connecting skin and flesh. He felt no pain as his body was twisted by the velocity of the bullet into a falling turn.

As he fell Jon squeezed his trigger again and a fraction of a second later a round ripped into Gumede's shoulder, causing irreparable damage.

He fell on his face pressing it close to the cool earth. The control centre of his brain shouted for his muscles to move, but they wouldn't obey the commands. Nothing would move. He still felt no pain and didn't realise what had happened. It was as if it had happened to someone else. He saw the cover of a large rock in front. Bullets ricocheted and whirred like angry hornets off into the darkness.

The firing stopped with shocking suddenness. Silence boomed in his ears, louder than the cacophony of shooting.

He was gripped by terror, his chest felt cold and his hand wouldn't move. He tried the other one and there was movement. He groped his shoulder and touched a sticky mess. His heart felt as if it would stop when his clutching fingers touched the jaggedness of a protruding bone. Why couldn't he move his legs? Suddenly he understood. He rolled over on to his stomach and fierce pains shot through his body. Using his one good arm, he levered himself into a sitting position. His leg was splayed sideways at an impossible angle. Even before he reached down and felt the damage, he had realised it was scarcely attached to his body.

Something in his mind snapped and he screamed a piercing howl that almost curdled the blood of the men laying silently in ambush.

Automatic fire searched the ground. Shots hit the rock that sheltered him and buzzed off like angry bees into the darkness.

The firing stopped as suddenly as it had started. Saul and his men were afraid of giving away their position.

A cricket chirruped in the grass near Gumede. What had happened to Kephas and the rest? He squinted back through the gloom straining his eyes for anything that might resemble human shapes. If somebody else had been hit, he would surely see the body. There was nothing — they must have got away. He took no comfort from that. The full realisation that he was alone struck home. He sobbed softly in self pity. Why me, he thought?

He would surrender. If he didn't, he would die before morning. It was better to face the Boers than die alone in the bush.

What could he say? He could tell them he was a Special Branch informer and that he had intended to desert with information about the guerrilla's escape routes. They would probably believe him.

'I want to surrender. Please help me.' His voice echoed in the lonely bush. 'I'm badly wounded and I need help. I'm unarmed. Please don't shoot. I'm badly wounded and I cannot walk. I am alone.'

He sobbed and his cries for help became more intense.

'I'm a Special Branch informer. Don't shoot me! Don't let me die!'

No one answered his cries. The crickets continued their chirruping and ignored the human intruder.

*   *   *

Saul gripped his carbine tensely and searched for the source of the voice. It seemed to be coming from behind that big rock.

Jim Wilkie raised his head, but Saul put a finger to his lips. It could be a trap. If they responded, they would away give their position. The guerrillas could easily be waiting for that sort of movement preparatory to opening fire.

He shuddered at the thought of that first horrifying scream. They had probably hit someone, but it was impossible to investigate while it was dark. There might be a terr out there with the pin removed from a grenade. Just waiting there to take someone with him in death.

*   *   *

Gumede's thirst accentuated his delirium. His mind wandered between pain and thirst. He saw water bubbling in the spring at his home village. He was drinking, crouched between the goats he had herded as a boy. The water was cool and thirst quenching. Then he was turning on the tap in his Lusaka home. Water came rushing out in a cold torrent and swirled wastefully down the sink. There was so much water, yet he couldn't reach it. Why couldn't he reach it? Somehow he had to get to that water.

His mind returned to the present. There was sure to be water in the river close by. Could he get to it? He no longer cared if he was shot in the attempt because he must have water.

He again experimentally attempted to move. His body had stiffened from the ghastly wounds, but his exploratory fingers told him the bleeding had slackened.

Blood — perhaps that could quench his thirst. He slid a sticky mass from his shoulder. Funny, it didn't hurt. He eased a congealed mess into his mouth. It was salty and he recoiled at what he was doing.

He could move an arm and a leg, but try as he might he couldn't move his torso which remained stubbornly in a sitting position against the rock. His senses again slipped away into a coma.

He awoke with a start an hour later. What was it that had awakened him? The moon had risen and was casting a ghostly light on the surrounding bush and the trees. His vision blurred as he glanced around him.

What was that? Surely, it couldn't be? His body quivered in terror.

Facing him only five metres away was a huge dog hyena. It was the largest he could ever have imagined. It sat on its haunches and stared impassively at him. Its mouth was open and it panted as saliva drooled from its lips. A strangled cry burbled through Gumede' clenched teeth.

His primitive past took over. In spite of his education and his white manner of living, he was still a child of Africa — as much a son of Africa as his forefathers had been before him.

Everyone was aware that hyenas are witches . . . witches that are human during the hours of daylight, but who assume the form of a hyena when the sun goes to sleep. No African sleeps with his windows open at night and he always makes sure his doors are closed. If he doesn't, the witches will surely enter.

Why had this witch picked on him? Why hadn't it chosen somebody else? He looked tearfully at the horrible beast.

The baleful unmoving eyes were fixed on him.

'Please go away. I have done nothing wrong', he whimpered. 'Whoever you are, I will give you money . . . I will give you cattle . . . I will give you everything I own . . . just go away.'

The great brute ignored his pleas and continued to mesmerise him with its eyes.

It got up from its haunches and took an experimental step towards him. The stink of the animal filled his nostrils. He desperately groped on the ground with his good hand. His fingers closed around a rotten branch. Fear summoned his reserve of strength and he waved the branch wildly at the awful beast.

It backed off in alarm, then stopped and its lips slavered when the man did not follow up. While it is big and frightening, a hyena is still a coward and an eater of the dead. It depends on carrion to stay alive and will not attack the living unless they're clearly helpless. In spite of that strong tempting smell of blood, it had still not decided whether the man creature could defend himself.

Its stomach was hollow with hunger and it was dragging a leg that had been caught in a wire snare a week before. No food had come its way since then. The injured leg was agonising because of a deep-seated inflammation and a saturation of pus. A continual gnawing at the seat of the pain had made it worse. This combination of hunger and pain had made the animal far less timid than it normally would have been. It watched the man unblinkingly.

Drained by the sickening pain and loss of blood brought on by his panic-stricken movements, Gumede sank into a stupor.

For ten minutes the noxious beast kept watch, but it detected no sign of life. It experimented with a cautious step forward and still the man didn't

189

move. It took another step forward. Then with its great jaws slavering, it rushed forward and clamped its jaws on the almost detached leg. The limb's owner awakened to the full horror of what was happening. The terrifying brute pulled and worried at its prize in an attempt to break the limited bonds of flesh and skin that was keeping it attached. It became more excited as the taste of fresh blood stimulated its senses.

Gumede's bowels and bladder evacuated as he was dragged along the ground from his sitting position. His terrified screams pierced the night, again and again, chilling the blood of the men who had shot him.

With a final wrench the leg loosened and came away and the beast retreated with its spoils.

Simon Gumede struggled back to a sitting position. He was demented with mortal fear. He heard the bones that had come from the womb of his mother being crunched in most powerful jaws in the wild. While the dog hyena masticated, its greedy eyes remained fixed on its prey.

'Help me, for God's sake, help me', Gumede screamed in a high-pitched falsetto. 'For God's sake . . . no . . . no . . .no . . .'

He watched his attacker finish his leg with a final gulp and he knew it would be back for more.

It took a few exploratory steps towards him, by now emboldened by its first attack.

'No . . . no . . . no . . .' Gumede screamed, feebly waving his hand at the monster. His stick had been lost in the darkness.

The animal hesitated, puzzled by the movements. It then began to circle slowly. Its greedy eyes reflecting sufficient light from the rising moon seemed to glow red.

Gumede gesticulated madly with his good hand madly and his tormentor lay down again with its head on its paws and patiently watched him. He clearly heard its stomach rumble.

'Go away! Go away!' His screams echoed in the night air.

Why me? Why me? his mind asked. Let me die in peace. He couldn't face being eaten alive. Let me die! Let me die!

*   *   *

The cries were too much for Jim, who whispered hoarsely to his companions.

'What's going on? Shouldn't we go out there and see?'

190

He was motioned into silence by Jake.

Saul was himself upset by the horrifying noises coming from the darkness. He had almost decided to risk a move to see what was going on. But his training came back and Jim, by expressing his own thoughts out loud, brought him back to his senses.

'It's only a terrorist', he whispered to himself. 'It's only a terrorist. A wounded terrorist, but still the enemy.'

He would wait for daylight. He couldn't risk the lives of his men for the sake of curiosity.

In spite of the conversation between himself and his conscience, another little voice in the back of his mind kept whispering quietly. It's a man. A man like you. Help him. No man should die like this.

Still he wouldn't move and he mustn't move. His hands gripped his rifle tighter until he realised what he was doing and consciously loosened his fingers, forcing himself to relax. You'll crack up, old boy, if you don't stop. He gave himself mental orders. Wait until morning. Wait for daylight to come.

He concentrated on the ground out in front.

He could clearly see that big rock in the moonlight. The screaming was coming from behind that. He touched Jon's shoulder and pointed at it. Jon nodded his agreement. He looked quizzically for an order but Saul shook his head in the negative. The responsibility was his. They would wait until morning.

*   *   *

Meanwhile, Gumede felt hysteria rising in him. He cackled wildly with uncontrollable laughter. His situation was as unfunny as it was ever likely to be, but he could not stop. He knew he was on the verge of losing his sanity.

The hyena, uncertain of what was happening, bayed to the moon — that wild blood-chilling cackle that caused romantics to call it the laughing hyena. But this was no laugh. There was no humour in this terrible breed. Hyenas don't laugh. Neither are they romantic.

Nevertheless, the dying man and the predatory beast lay there and laughed at each another.

The man-hunters went cold as they listened. A hyena and a human, each crying out with sinister laughter that sounded as if it came from within the gates of hell. But there was nothing they could do. Who else could be waiting out there in the darkness? Waiting for them to show themselves.

*   *   *

The stinking animal approached again, bolder now. The anticipation of more fresh meat caused it to slaver and drove away any fear of man that remained.

Gumede feebly tried to push it away, but it took no notice. Its great jaws opened and huge incisor teeth showed white by the light of the moon.He pushed at the furry head with his hand, but it was beyond his strength to defend himself. It tossed its head and brushed his hand aside. The terrible teeth fastened on his bunched up stomach and emphatically worried it. A strangled moan escaped his lips as his stomach burst open like an overripe melon. His entrails, a gunmetal blue in the moonlight and shining with mucus and blood, were dragged from his belly. They hung like great tubes of macaroni around the hyena's jaws. It retreated slowly, pulling the slithering delicacy from the stomach cavity. The man's working hand clutched weakly at his belly, but pain and terror had sapped any remaining strength. The slimy guts slid wetly through his fingers.

The hyena gulped quickly and worked its way back towards its victim. Simon Gumede was still conscious and he watched death approach with dull clouding eyes. The hyena nuzzled its muzzle deeper into his open body, its teeth chopping and tearing at the man's pulsating living organs. Gumede's terrible pain left him as the spark of life snuffed out in his body.

*   *   *

Silence descended on the veld, except for the sound of bones being crunched for the marrow. The jackals followed the hyena. The men in ambush waited tensely until the sky lightened and took away the ghosts of darkness. With their rifles at the ready, they investigated the night's happenings.

The ground was stained with blood and faeces, but other than this the only sign that a man had lived and died there was a tiny blood-stained rag of clothing with a solitary shirt button sewn to it. Even Gumede's boots had been eaten.

In the cold light of day, it seemed unbelievable that a man had vanished

192

so completely. The men who had heard Simon Gumede die knew about it. So did the big blue flies buzzing around the boulder.

They took that bloodstained rag back with them in the helicopter as evidence of a kill when they were relieved. Those in charge of the operation refused to confirm the kill of another communist terrorist. There was no real evidence that this one had died. Perhaps he was wounded and had got away. Blood on the ground and that small fragment of cloth indicated that was a good probability. Besides, who had ever heard of a single hyena devouring the body of a man whole. There was no such thing as a hyena that big.

24

They were four now — Kephas, Kumalo, Watura and Taziva. They had escaped the ambush and had ran back down the game track. It was a miracle none of them had been hit. They stopped about 400 metres away from the ambush point. They waited for ten minutes, but Gumede did not show up.

'We must assume he's been shot, or that he ran off in another direction, or was captured One thing's for certain, we're not going back to look for him', Kephas said. He looked at his companions for dissent, but none were willing to take the risk of returning to look for Gumede.

'Let him took out for himself', grunted Kumalo.

'What will we do now?' Watura ventured.

'Well', murmured Kephas thoughtfully, 'we will keep to the plan. We must get food, water and arms from a cache. Then we'll try to get across the river. We must take the risk of returning past the ambush site to get to the cache. It is the nearest one. We should be able to detour around the ambush in the dark and get past the soldiers. In future', he said to Watura, 'you'll go in front. You're the best in the bush of all of us. If you can't get us through, nobody can.'

Watura smiled modestly. The others couldn't see how pleased he was that he had been chosen to lead. He had thought it was asking for trouble when Kephas had put Gumede at point. Still, Gumede had suffered for his incompetence and was probably dead.

They set off again. They first dog-legged 400 metres off the track into the bush, then walking by the stars which by now had come out, they found their way around the ambush position. It was slow progress through the tangled Jesse. By the time they had covered 300 metres, they were all covered in thorn-inflicted cuts and scratches on their faces, hands and arms. Blood dried in caked patches on their skins, and the night flies stung their flesh until their bodies throbbed from the discomfort.

Nevertheless, they pushed on as fast as they could, for there was no time to dawdle or rest. If they did not get well away from the ambush site by dawn, they would be dead from either thirst or gunshots.

Once they heard a high-pitched scream in the distance. It sounded like a man, but Kephas couldn't be sure. He wondered if it was Gumede or another fugitive who the soldier had caught. Maybe they were torturing him? But screaming wouldn't do him any good nor bring him help. Perhaps that idiot Gumede, finding himself alone in the darkness, had cracked up. That wouldn't do him any good. It would only give the soldiers an idea where to shoot. Fortunately, Gumede had no idea where the arms caches were located, so he posed no danger to them — even if he was caught and interrogated. The real threat lay in the possibility that others had been captured who had been there when the stuff was cached. If they talked, the soldiers would be in ambush awaiting their arrival. But it was a chance they had to take. He could only hope that they were too busy hunting fugitives at the moment to have the time to worry about arms caches. That no doubt would come later.

Once again they saw the sand of the river bed shimmering in the moonlight. This time they would not be caught. Watura dropped down low in the shrubs on the river bank. Kephas crawled up to him.

'Do you think it's safe to cross?'

'I don't know. We won't know until someone has crossed.'

Kephas looked at the expanse of sand. It was about 30 metres wide and once on it someone would be completely exposed. A watcher on the far bank couldn't fail to see someone crossing. Crawling across would be worse than walking or running, because a man would not only stand out like a fly on a white sheet, he would lose the benefit of speed. The crossing would have to be done quickly. He decided to go last, so he could cover the others with his rifle. He glanced at his companions. He scarcely knew Taziva so there was no emotional attachment. He could go first. If he was killed, it would just be bad luck, but he could be spared more than the others. He crawled over to Taziva.

'Okay, run for the opposite bank. I'll cover you.'

Taziva looked resentful, but said nothing.

Kephas tapped his rifle and signalled to Kumalo that he should also cover Taziva with his pistol.

Kumalo did not require involved explanations. He immediately crawled to the edge of the river bank and held his pistol at the ready. Kephas joined him, then waved his arm in a bowling motion.

Taziva got to his feet, scrambled down the bank and ran on to the sand. He ran as fast as the thick sand would allow, desperately trying to reach the other side before somebody spotted him. Kephas was expecting a machine gun to open up at any moment, but nothing happened. Then Taziva was clambering up the far bank and moments later he disappeared into the cover. They waited for five minutes just in case, but nothing happened.

Kephas nodded to Kumalo who stood up and ran down on to the sand. He also ploughed his way to safety. Watura followed also without a shot being fired.

Kephas was the last. He broke a fresh branch from a tree. He spat on his fingers, dipped them in the dirt and rubbed a mud paste on the fresh scar from where he had torn the branch. When satisfied it was unlikely to be noticed, he moved backwards down the bank smoothing out tracks with his homemade broom. It took him at least five minutes to cross, but when he looked back he was satisfied. There were no telltale traces left in the sand that would indicate to a tracker that men had crossed there.

After that it was relatively easy. They reached the arms cache in another hour, with about an hour of darkness left to cover them. The enemy had not beaten them to it.

They rearmed themselves with pistols and AK47s. Packs were filled with food, ammunition, extra magazines and grenades. The water bottles, full of cool clear water, provided the most welcome relief. They quenched their thirst, then packed three extra full bottles into each of their packs.

25

Eight days later the fugitives climbed the escarpment and made their way out of the Zambezi Valley. There had been another close brush with death three days before when they had again walked into an ambush. But thanks to Watura who had spotted it in time, they miraculously escaped without loss. They had spent the first night after reequipping themselves fruitlessly trying to locate a boat on the Zambezi River. Without one, they couldn't cross the river and get back to the safety of Zambia.

Kephas decided on the alternative plan of making their way over the escarpment and hiding themselves in the Senga area where he was familiar with the terrain. They could perhaps get help from villages where he had friends. After all, Kephas reasoned, this was why they had come — to make contact with the villagers and win them over to the side of the Party. No one objected, although by then none of them believed that any of the previous groups had achieved the successes that had been attributed to them. It wasn't said out loud, but they had tacitly accepted that the previous groups of comrades had been killed or captured.

Kephas looked at his companions. Whereas eight days before they had been in shining good health and at the peak of physical fitness, they were now emaciated and almost starving.

They had not eaten for two days.

Their clothing was filthy and in tatters and their boots had the soles tied on with bark rope to stop them from falling apart.

They had soon run short of water, for once they left the Zambezi River there had been no water to be found. The rationing that Kephas imposed almost killed them, but it kept them alive. It got them through, but only just. They didn't swallow a drop of liquid for 24 hours. Their tongues dried up and lay in their mouths like rawhide.

The cocks were crowing in the dawn as they stealthily approached the village. Kephas wondered whether they would be able to get help from there or not. They had to drink, eat and get some rest somewhere. None of them was in a fit state to continue.

They took cover in a patch of trees about 300 metres from the edge of the village. They did not have to wait long. Women and children progressively appeared from the huts. They saw only one old man. Kephas supposed, correctly, that most of the men were away working in the towns. The tempo of movement increased as the morning progressed.

Two young boys collected the cattle from the stockades, the goats and sheep from their pens, and drove them into the veld to graze and browse away the day. They knew they would not be returning until evening.

The women attended to their household chores, babies strapped to their backs, and gossiped together. It was the usual scene of African village life. There was food to be cooked, lands to be tilled, beer to be brewed and mealies to be ground into meal. They laughed and joked as they worked, their voices carrying on the fresh morning breeze to the watchers in the wood. The old man, who they assumed was the kraal head, dozed in the shade of a large tree in the centre of the kraal, oblivious to the giggling of his women.

They had to take a chance. Taziva was a Shona and he was from Salisbury. The villagers would be more inclined to help someone from their own tribe, than men of alien tribes.

'Go and speak to the kraal head. Find out if he will help us', Kephas instructed. 'Leave your rifle and pack and take your pistol. Hide it in your trousers. If he is friendly and willing to help us, call us over. If he is hostile return here immediately. We will cover you while you talk. Be as friendly as possible, but don't let him know how many of us there are. If you decide he is more likely to help us out of fear, suggest to him your part of a large force camped out in the hills.'

Taziva didn't protest but it was clear he didn't relish the task. He reluctantly unbuckled his pack straps and slipped it to the ground. He handed his rifle to Watura.

'Go and circle around the village.' Kephas pointed across the cleared area. 'Don't let them see where you've come from.'

Taziva crawled to the rear through the trees and was lost from view. It was 20 minutes before they saw him walking into the village from the other direction. Kephas nodded approvingly. Taziva had done well.

The women stopped working at the appearance of the stranger. They greeted him in the courteous manner common to people who live a life almost untouched by western culture. Even the little girls clapped their hands in greeting and curtsied to him.

Taziva conversed with them and a woman pointed to the old man who was still sitting under his tree. He had not moved and was clearly waiting for the stranger to approach him.

Taziva strolled over and greeted him.

The old man returned the greeting.

Formalities were exchanged and Taziva squatted on the ground opposite him. His elder wife appeared with two large mugs of native beer which she handed to each of them.

Kephas watched Taziva take a long pull from the mug and envied him. His mouth would have watered if there was any moisture left in him to do so. He glanced at his companions and saw that their eyes were also rivetted on the mugs which were being rapidly drained.

Taziva could not get to the point immediately. This would have been an unheard of breach of etiquette. They first had to talk about their health, then the weather, then the crops, the cattle and all the other mundane subjects peculiar to village life.

Neither showed impatience to discuss Taziva's visit. They were both aware that this would be fully explored in the fullness of time.

After half an hour and two more mugs of beer, the formalities were deemed to have been completed. A plate of sadza with various relishes in enamel communal dishes were brought and the old man and his visitor helped themselves.The headman opened the business proceedings.

'Where have you come from, friend?' he enquired.

There was a pause while Taziva finished masticating the food in his mouth. He waved vaguely in the general direction of the Zambezi River.

'I come from over there, comrade.'

He did not explain further.

The old man mulled this over in silence.

'We have seen people come from over the river before.' He looked enquiringly at Taziva. 'None of them seemed to have been as hungry as you.' He looked away. 'I have often fed these people.' He enquired politely: 'Are you alone?'

Taziva digested the question. There was no need to rush his answer. It was better to let the old man drag the story out of him little by little.

'No, I am not alone. Many of us came across the river. We came here to fight the white man.' He looked the old man straight in the eye.

The headman returned his look and nodded sagely. 'It's good that you do this.' He wiped a rheumy eye with the back of his hand. 'It's said that these people that come from across the Zambezi call themselves "sons of the soil". Is that what you call yourselves?'

'Yes, we do call ourselves as such. Mostly we call ourselves freedom fighters.'

His voice rose as he lied proudly: 'We have killed many soldiers in the valley. We also shot down two of their aeroplanes with our rifles.'

The old man looked duly impressed and nodded thoughtfully.

'Where is your gun?'

'It's with my friends who are waiting not far from here.'

The old man looked round the outskirts of the kraal until his glance steadied on the patch of trees where Kephas and the others were in hiding. They saw him looking and involuntarily ducked lower in the undergrowth, although it would have been impossible for him to have seen them.

The kraal head again spoke. 'How many of you need food and rest?'

'There are four of us here, with another hundred in the hills about 20 kilometres away', Taziva lied blandly.

'It's good. Tell your friends to enter the village and we will give them food.' He clapped his hands and gave instructions to the women hovering nearby.

'Cook more food and bring more beer.'

Taziva stood up, raised his arms and gesticulated towards the trees. His comrades stood up, picked up their things and walked into the kraal. The old man and the village women regarded their weapons and packs with interest.

Greetings were exchanged. The headman fussed around his visitors, treating them as honoured guests.

They were ushered into the main hut and seated comfortably on a clay bench that lined the complete inside circumference. They took off their packs and stacked them in a heap by the door along with their rifles.

It was a very ordinary hut. In the centre was a clay hearth. Several boxes containing possessions were stacked against the wall. The one thing out of the ordinary was a massive french-polished battery-operated radiogram. Kephas and his men looked at it admiringly. It was magnificent.

The owner smiled at their wonder. He told them that without doubt it was his most cherished possession.

'It's beautiful', mumbled Watura, 'quite beautiful.'

Kephas was delighted with their reception. Later he would have many questions to ask. How did the people in the area feel about the Party? Which areas did they hold? Where were the police and army detachments?

But all that would have to wait. Food, drink and small talk came first.

The sorghum beer was delicious. Kephas didn't think he had ever tasted beer so good. They drank thirstily, savouring the thick sour beer to the full. Their host was delighted at their obvious pleasure.

So much kindness and good cheer after the privations they had suffered weakened their guard and blunted their alertness. They would not have felt so safe and comfortable if they had they intercepted the intense glance that the kraal head gave to his youngest wife. She acknowledged it with a slight inclination of her head. If their senses had been less blunted, they might have noticed that she left the celebrations and did not reappear. Kephas would only remember this later.

They were plied with food and drink until they were sated. Kephas had intended to question the old man, but he felt too drowsy by then.

'We must get some sleep,' mumbled Kephas.

The others were also nodding off.

'We must get some sleep, old man. We have been walking for many days without proper sleep. We have been living like animals in the bush', Kephas explained. 'Can we sleep here?'

'Of course. How impolite of me. You are safe here.'

Nevertheless, Kephas had a feeling of unease. He focussed on the radiogram pushed against the wall. He didn't know why but it signalled something ominous. In a big house in Bulawayo or Lusaka it would have been nothing peculiar, but in a hut built of mud, poles and thatch it was somewhat incongruous. However, he was too sleepy to work it out and he dismissed the thought.

They had to sleep. Could he trust his host?

'Thank you, old man.' Kephas said to the kraal head.

He decided he had little option but to trust him. Kumalo was already asleep and Taziva and Watura were not far from it. No one could stand guard. They were all too tired. Kephas knew he would be asleep as soon as his head touched the ground.

He could see that the kraal head was well aware of this.

'When you have gone', said Kephas politely, 'I will remain awake and guard my friends while they sleep. I will, of course, fasten the door from the inside.'

The kraal head murmured that he had no objections. He stood up.

'Sleep well, freedom fighters. I will see you when you wake up.' He opened the door and left.

Kephas fastened the door from the inside with wire as best he could. Then he lay thankfully on the floor and within minutes he was asleep.

Even if they had been less soundly asleep, they might not have heard the slight scratching sounds made by the kraal head as he bound the outside staple and hasp securely together with tough fence wire.

Kephas' sleep was troubled. White men in camouflage uniform were chasing him. No matter how fast he ran, he couldn't get away. They threw bombs that exploded in front of him. He ran through the smoke and debris but his feet were becoming heavier. He couldn't keep going. A hand gripped his shoulder and he screamed and struggled to escape.

'Wake up! Wake up, Kephas!' The words penetrated his subconscious and he awoke to reality.

Kumalo was shaking him by the shoulder. 'Wake up! You've been screaming like a madman.'

Kephas rubbed his eyes as he awoke from his nightmare. He was still exhausted from lack of sleep.

'Sorry', he grunted wryly to Kumalo, 'I was having a nightmare.'

Watura and Taziva were watching him. It was almost nightfall and only glimmers of light came through the door cracks. He scrambled to his feet.

'We have slept all day. Where's the old man?'

Kumalo shrugged. 'I've only just woken up.'

'Open the door. Let's see where he is', Kephas snapped.

Kumalo went to the door and removed the fastening. He pushed but the door didn't budge. It appeared to be jammed from the outside. He gave it a shove with his shoulder, but it still didn't move. He shook it roughly backwards and forwards, but that didn't help either.

'That old jackal must have fastened it on the outside.' Kumalo sounded unusually panicky.

'Let me try', Kephas said, his cool voice in no way reflecting the cold feeling in his chest. He tried but the door obstinately remained shut.

'Listen!'

Kephas cocked his head to one side and the others listened.

'There's nothing. I can't hear anything', Watura said.

'There may be a simple explanation for this', Kephas said thoughtfully. 'But it could also mean that he has betrayed us.' He touched the thatched roof. 'If it comes to a push, we should be able to get out through the thatch.'

'Before we try the roof I think we should try the obvious', said Taziva. He had shown no sign of panic and he had gone up considerably in Kephas' estimation.

'Open this damn door', yelled Taziva. If you don't I will shoot it open'

There was soon a hurried movement outside the hut.

'Are you awake?' It was the kraal head.

'Open this bloody door or we'll shoot it down', shouted Taziva in reply.

There was fumbling outside and moments later the door opened.

Kephas rushed out with his pistol. He grabbed the old man by the scruff of his neck and thrust the cocked weapon into the small of his back. The man stiffened in terror.

'Please, please', he whined, 'I was not trying to lock you in. I was afraid that children might try to get inside and disturb your sleep. I also thought they might play with your guns and cause an accident. You were sleeping so soundly', he explained.

It made sense, Kephas thought. Why would he want to lock them in? He would know they could escape through the thatch. He looked about him and the darkening village gave an appearance of normality. Children were playing in the fading light and the glow of cooking fires indicated that the women were preparing evening meals. There was no one around posing a threat to them.

He stuck the pistol in his waistband.

'I am sorry, old man. It's just that we don't know who to trust. We have been hunted for too long.'

His erstwhile prisoner recovered his composure, but was still breathing heavily.

'It's all right, my friends. I understand.' He adjusted his clothing. 'Your food will be ready soon. I have slaughtered a goat in your honour. Can you smell it cooking?'

Kephas sniffed the air. Indeed he could smell it cooking and his mouth watered at the delicious aroma.

The headman clucked happily. He caught Kephas' arm. 'Come, my friends, you must eat. There is plenty of beer.'

They felt safe in the security of the dark and warm summer night. There was no need to sit inside. They squatted outside in a semicircle around the fire. On Kephas' instructions their packs and rifles lay beside them. Their host protested and said they should leave them in the hut, but Kephas insisted that where they went their guns and equipment also went.

'You see', he explained, 'we have no relatives to look after us in this part of the country, so we treat our weapons as our relatives.'

The old man chuckled.

The food and drink arrived and they were soon eating and drinking merrily. This was the life. At first they thought they would easily demolish the goat, between them but their stomachs had shrunk and there was plenty of meat left over at the end.

When they were sated, they lay back on the ground and talked to their host. He answered their questions easily. It was true that no other men were staying in the village at the moment. They were away working in the towns. Their wives stayed home to tend the crops and look after the flocks. Soldiers and policemen seldom came by, so they were quite safe here. Yes, the people in the area were sympathetic to the Party. Yes, it was true that Sinoia was in the hands of the freedom fighters. No, they could not say where the other groups were, but he was sure there would be no difficulty finding them. Yes, there would be many young men in the surrounding villages who wanted to be trained as fighters. No one would betray them to the authorities. Kephas became more content the longer they talked. He felt much surer of the old man and gave him his best smile while he carefully rolled rough, untreated, home-grown tobacco into newspaper provided by the kraal head. It was coarse, but he exulted as the rough smoke burned deep into his lungs. It was deeply satisfying and he had not smoked for a long time.

The old man stood up. 'My friends, it's time for you to sleep and recover your strength. We can talk more on the morrow.'

His words brought home to Kephas the realisation of how much punishment his body had taken. Yes, he could certainly do with more sleep.

'Right boys, sleep it is. I'll take the first guard.'

Kephas picked up his carbine and stretched his arms.

The others collected their kit and wandered back to the hut.

Kephas sat and talked to the old man for the next few hours. He was relaxed. It was the first real moment of peace he had experienced in a long time.

The embers of the fire died and were rekindled. Finally the old man retired to bed and left him alone.

Four hours he awoke Taziva who was snoring like a wounded buffalo. He grunted and woke up, grabbed his carbine and went outside to take over the guard.

Kephas lay down. But sleep eluded him. He was overtired, but his senses stubbornly refused to succumb to the blandishments of sleep. He could see the shape of the radiogram standing against the wall. It still worried him, but he couldn't think why. He gave up trying to sleep, sat up and rolled a cigarette from the course makings provided by the kraal head. He struck a match and realised that Kumalo was also awake.

'Can't you sleep either?' Kephas asked.

Kumalo sat up and yawned. 'I woke up when you changed over with Taziva. I haven't been able to sleep since.' He yawned again. 'Give me some of that tobacco and paper.'

They sat there without talking while Kumalo fashioned himself a smoke and lit up.

'I'm worried', Kumalo confessed. He didn't want to disturb Watura who was truly fast asleep. His snores sawed gently through the darkness.

'I cannot explain it, but something is wrong.' Kumalo lapsed into silence.

'I'm worried, too. There's something that makes me uneasy and I don't know what it is', Kephas confessed. 'It's stupid, I know. The old man has been helpful and is friendly, but I am note sure that we should trust him too much. I am just wondering if he isn't a little too friendly.'

'You might be right', agreed Kumalo, 'but you could be very wrong. And we need people to help us'

They sat quietly in the dark mulling over their thoughts. A comforting glow came from the tips of their cigarettes.

'I can't sleep. I'll go outside and join Taziva.'

Kephas stood up, yawned and picked up his rifle and pack. Kumalo did the same.

' I know it's stupid, but I guess we'll both feel happier outside.'

'What about Watura?' asked Kumalo nodding at the man.

'Leave him to sleep. He seems happy and it would be a shame to disturb him', grinned Kephas.

They found Taziva sitting by the fire. His head had drooped to his chest and his rifle lay on the ground. He was out cold to the world.

Kumalo shook him roughly. 'Wake up, you son of a hundred fathers', he snarled. 'Your incestuous slumbers could get us shot while we sleep.' He scowled threateningly. 'Next time you do that I'll kill you.'

'Come on', said Kephas impatiently. 'We'll wait in those trees till dawn.'

He walked to the trees where they had hidden when they first arrived. Kumalo continued to snarl reprimands at Taziva.

Kephas glanced at his watch. The luminous hands were creeping towards three o'clock.

They settled down to await the sun.

Kephas debated with himself whether he should go back and call Watura. Perhaps it would be safer if they left the village now. Staying in one place for too long was risky. On the other hand they couldn't stay in the bush and live like animals forever. Sooner or later they would have to rely on the locals. On the other hand if they went to another village for succour, they might easily be betrayed there. Maybe he was just getting the jitters.

Kumalo gripped his shoulder and nodded towards the village. Kephas blinked, wondering if he was seeing things. Then he was certain. Shadowy figures were moving in a single file towards the village. They reached the huts and for a moment he lost sight of them. When next he saw them they were darting from hut to hut, using them as cover.

They were armed with rifles. Kephas felt a chill of apprehension. He measured the distance between the figures and the hut where Watura was sleeping. He was beyond help. They would be seen if they attempted to warn him.

'We will stay here', he growled to Kumalo and Taziva who were watching the scene unfold in front of them.

The figures deployed around the hut where Watura was asleep. They apparently weren't making a move and Kephas concluded they had settled down to await first light. What chance of success would they have if they opened fire and attacked in an attempt to save Watura? He peered through the darkness to estimate the strength of the enemy. The odds weren't good. There were too many of them to wipe out in a sudden surprise attack. When dawn came the survivors would call for reinforcements with helicopter backup. They wouldn't stand much chance in a follow-up like that. It was also doubtful they would succeed in freeing Watura.

He made up his mind. Watura would have to be sacrificed. He whispered his order. 'Come, we're going. Watura will have to take his chances.'

Taziva looked as if he was about to rebel, but he obviously changed his mind for he said nothing. Kumalo didn't hesitate. He swung his pack on his back and began to crawl snakelike away from the village. Kephas gesticulated for Taziva to follow and crawled after him.

In his waking dreams Watura reached out to brush away something cold from his throat.. He sat up with a start and found himself looking into the hard and unsmiling eyes of two policemen who were covering him with sub-machine guns. He froze. He could see by their eyes — one the eyes of a white man and the other of a black man like himself — that if he resisted they would shoot him without compunction.

They pulled him to his feet, threw him against the wall, forcibly splayed his feet and raised his hands so that the palms were touching the wall. Expert hands searched him and removed the pistol from his waistband. His hands were wrenched behind his back and handcuffs were slipped on his wrists.

Moments later he was outside blinking his eyes in the growing dawn. Two other armed policemen were searching the rest of the kraal.

The kraal head watched from nearby with his women and children. He was smiling as the females giggled and ogled the captive. Children were running around in front of Watura jeering. 'Animal!' they teased. 'Animal!'

It dawned on Watura that he had been sold out. Where were the others? He looked around, but they were nowhere to be seen. They had deserted him. He felt the bitter taste of despair.

The white man with the silver stars of a police inspector on his epaulettes who had caught him in the hut was in charge.

'*Nkosi*, the others were here', the kraal head said. 'I don't know where they have gone. They told me they were part of a large group that is camped out in the hills.'

'You have done good work, old man', the Inspector said. 'You mustn't be afraid. They can't have gone far. We'll soon find them.'

The old man spat on the ground. 'I am not frightened of those swine — I hate them.'

Watura shuddered at the vehemence in his voice.

The kraal head nodded at the hut his guests had used. 'You will find a radiogram in there that belonged to my brother. He was murdered by members of the Party Youth League in Salisbury seven years ago.'

The white policeman looked grim. 'I remember the case. It was in the early days of the troubles. He was refused to go on strike when the Party ordered it.'

'That's right, *Nkosi*', agreed the headman bitterly. 'The Party said there must be a strike and my brother refused to join. They caught him outside the factory gates and doused him in petrol. It was said that a policeman heard his screams from nearly half a kilometre away as he burned, but by the time he reached him the fire had burned the flesh from his bones.' He wiped tears from his eyes with the back of a shaking hand.

Watura felt despair. He knew he had nothing to look forward to. If they could prove he had killed someone, they would hang him. If they couldn't prove it, he would get life imprisonment. He decided to be as helpful as possible. Perhaps this would save his life.

He coughed politely to draw the attention of the black policeman standing guard. 'Tell your *Nkosi* that I wish to make a full confession . . .'

26

They moved fast and avoided all traces of habitation.

Their objective was to put as much distance between the village and them and as soon as possible. They had no inclination to trust strangers again.

Perhaps they had been unlucky, but Kephas was beginning to wonder if most people they came across would be against them. He had no idea how they would be able to survive without the help of locals.

They had no food, but at least they had plenty of water. Their stay at the village had refreshed them and that was a blessing.

Watura was of the past — a closed episode. Perhaps if he had listened to his innermost feelings, Watura would still be here. He dismissed the thought. There was little point dwelling on what might have been.

Little mention was made of Watura after that. It gave them feelings of guilt and brought out into the open the question that was uppermost in their minds.

Would they be abandoned if their turn came, or would the others fight to rescue them?

Helicopters had flown overhead on several occasions, causing them to take cover. Sometimes they flew so low they could identify the weapons clutched in the hands of the camouflage uniformed passengers.

Their recent experiences in the valley had taught them a healthy respect for military aircraft. If they had been spotted from the air, they wouldn't have stood a chance.

Where possible they followed routes over rocky ground. Where they couldn't, they carefully obliterated their tracks. The hunt was clearly still on, but their luck continued to hold.

It took Kephas an hour and a half to reach Matavi's village by a circuitous route. He was careful to avoid two other villages that lay on the same footpath. He dared not openly walk straight into the place, so he hid on the outskirts in the hope of spotting him.

There was a lot of movement but no sign of Matavi. Women went about their chores, talking and laughing. Naked children played with toy cars ingeniously fashioned from wire. He felt nostalgic as he looked at the peaceful village scene and nostalgically thought of home. On a roaring wood fire in the centre of the kraal an old 44-gallon petrol drum was propped up on rocks. Steam was lazily rising from the top. Women were brewing beer for the weekend and Matavi would probably be drinking some of it later.

The cattle kraal was empty, so it was likely that Matavi was out herding them in the veld. If that was so he would not return home until sundown. Kephas pondered what to do. He could scarcely remain in hiding the whole day. He had no water with him and the heat was already boiling up. He swore silently, wishing he had got there earlier and caught Matavi before he left. His eyes looked around the nearby veld. Which way had he gone? He decided to search for him instead of just sit there waiting. If he couldn't find him, he would return to the village before dawn tomorrow and get him then.

He eased himself from his hide and staying in cover, moved carefully away from the huts. He put his hand behind his back to check that his pistol was still tucked safely away in his trousers.

It was midday before he heard the lowing of cattle. They were grazing on the open veld. The herdsman was asleep with his head resting against a tree. From his position Kephas couldn't see if it was his friend or not. He daren't make an approach without being certain. If it wasn't Matavi whoever it was might recognise him as a wanted man, because he was well known around here. He waited for an hour until eventually the herder woke up. He watched as he saw him stretch his arms and legs. Kephas willed him to stand up, but in the event the man didn't get to his feet for another half hour. He began to check that his cattle hadn't strayed and suddenly Kephas saw his face. It was Matavi.

Kephas conducted a final check to see that no one else was around. There wasn't, but despite this he felt somewhat exposed as he trudged across the open ground. Matavi watched his approach curiously, but as he got nearer he suddenly realised who it was.

'Kephas!' he shouted and ran forward. 'Is that really you?'

'Yes, it is me indeed', called Kephas with a broad grin.

They embraced and danced around, thumping each other on the back until they were breathless. When they had calmed down, they sat in the shade of a tree and talked.

Matavi brought him up to date with what had happened while he was away. There had been big changes since he had left home. Almost every local Party member had been rounded up and sentenced to long prison terms for their activities. Kephas listened uneasily while he heard how Madziwa had been sentenced to death for murder and later executed. Job was serving a long sentence and would probably be an old man when he came out of prison.

'My family spirit must have been looking after me', said Matavi. 'Every day I expected them to come and arrest me, but the police never came. Like you, I was thinking of running away, but I had no place to go to.'

'Why made the people stop the struggle?' asked Kephas. 'Surely they could have continued.'

'It has not been easy', said Matavi, shaking his head. 'Those people who were against the Party were easily intimidated in the beginning, but once the police had arrested hundreds of our people and put them in prison, they lost their fear of us. The Party members did not stand a chance. Everyone wanted to be on the winning side and they clamoured to give evidence in court against our activists. It became very dangerous to engage in Party activities.'

He looked around as if he was afraid of being overhead. 'The spirit of the Rain Goddess in the hills was consulted and said that if the people did not live in peace, there would be no rain. Meetings were held for the chief to address the people. When we discovered the spirit was against us and that we had offended Her . . .' He shrugged. 'The tribe cannot live without rain. So what could we do? We had no option but to halt out actions.'

'This is strange story indeed', said Kephas. 'Why would the spirit of our people demand we stop fighting the white man to get our country back?'

'I don't know, I just don't know', answered Matavi. 'We would have stopped anyway, because soon there would have been no Party members left. You have no idea how we suffered.'

'Perhaps', said Kephas, reaching to the back of his trousers, 'the spirit of the Rain Goddess was waiting for something like this.' He produced the Tokarev pistol with a flourish.

Matavi's eyes bulged as he examined the weapon.

'Where'd you get this?'

'It was given to me in Zambia.'

'Zambia?' exclaimed Matavi in astonishment. 'You have been to Zambia?'

'Yes, I have been to Russia, Egypt, England and sorts of places. I have just come from Zambia.'

'Are you a terrorist?' asked Matavi in awe.

'A freedom fighter', corrected Kephas. 'It is only the white men who call us terrorists. They call us terrorists because they become terror-struck when they think of us.' He boasted: 'They know that just one of us can kill many of their soldiers.'

Matavi was hugely impressed. He gestured at Kephas's pistol.

'Have you many more of those?' he asked edging closer.

'Many, many more in caches out in the bush', murmured Kephas. 'How many do you want? We have come with weapons to fight the white man and win our country back.'

'We?' queried Matavi. Are there others with you?'

'Sure', said Kephas, 'there are two others. We're the first, but many more will follow. That's why we have brought guns so as to train you boys how to fight.'

'If we have guns we can at last fight and beat the white men', said Matavi excitedly 'The last time we had only our hands and minds to fight with. If we have guns, we can drive them from Senga. Once they're out of Senga thousands of people will join us. We can then drive them from the country — just like our brothers elsewhere in Africa have done.' There was the fervour of fanaticism in his voice.

'Steady on', Kephas laughed. 'It won't be quite as easy as all that.' He felt an uneasy twinge of doubt returning. He had also thought like Matavi before they crossed the Zambezi to get back to Rhodesia. That terrible air strike and the ferociousness of the government soldiers in combat had damaged any illusions he might have had about the fight for freedom being an easy one. It wasn't only the white soldiers who had fought like leopards — the black troops had been just as committed. If blacks were willing to fight and die for the white man, was it likely that thousands of black people would actually flock to the freedom banner? These were doubts he dared not share with Matavi.

'It's premature to talk about thousands of people fighting for us', said

Kephas backtracking somewhat. 'We have only got six guns with us. We have three like this' — he indicated the pistol — 'and three rifles, although we have many more cached in the valley. What we require at the moment is two or three good men who are committed to the struggle, willing to be taught by us and who can be trusted. With them we can carry out attacks on the whites and bide our time until more comrades join us from Zambia. It's better to start this way, then go from strength to strength. No, we will not go out and confront soldiers and policeman. We will fight like the mosquito. We will creep up with stealth and bite them while they sleep. Until we're stronger, we cannot hope to beat the soldiers in open battle. The white farmers and people who live alone in the bush must be our targets. If we can drive them from their farms, the policemen and soldiers will also leave.'

'What do I have to do?' Matavi asked with enthusiasm.

'I will be camping out in the hills with my comrades', replied Kephas. 'We have plenty of money, but we need someone to but food and supplies from the stores. We can't do this ourselves because obviously we cannot afford anyone to get to know that we are here. During the hours of daylight we will train you to be soldiers. When you are sufficiently ready, I will decide how you will be deployed and what you will do. We need to recruit men willing to join us and who can be trusted. Can you think of anyone?'

Matavi's brow creased in concentration.

'They must be trustworthy', emphasised Kephas.

'There is Dingani', said Matavi thoughtfully. 'I trust him and he is as keen a Party supporter as I am.'

Kephas frowned. 'Is that the Dingani who was at school with us?'

Matavi nodded.

'You are certain he is trustworthy?'

'I trust him as much as I trust you', breathed Matavi.

'It's agreed then', said Kephas. 'I had hoped that along with you my friend Job would be our first recruit, but now he is suffering for the Party in gaol. We will have to use others until we get strong enough to break him from prison.'

'Do you really think we will be able to free him from prison one day?' asked Matavi in awe.

'Later, perhaps. Who knows what we will be able to do by then.'

He gave Matavi detailed instructions as to where the camp lay and instructed him to report there with Dingani as soon as possible. He gave him money and a shopping list of supplies needed.

'Until tomorrow then', said Matavi happily.

'Until tomorrow', reciprocated Kephas. He added a final warning. 'Remember, you must not mention us anyone but Dingani. If you do and it causes us trouble, we will kill you, even though you are my friend.'

*   *   *

They settled into their hideout. Bunkers similar to those they had dug in the Zambezi Valley served as shelters. Matavi and Dingani proved themselves good recruits. They were eager to learn and were soon handling their weapons like veterans. Unfortunately, they could not practise live firing. They dared not risk this because of the danger that shots might be heard. Each night the recruits returned to their homes to keep up an appearance of normality. With proper rest and adequate food Kephas and the other two regained some of the flesh that they had lost during their punishing escape from the valley.

On most days Kephas pumped Matavi for news of home. He soon began to feel that he had never been away. His father was in good health, but was ageing rapidly. Tandiwe was no longer there. She had got married soon after he had left and was now living with her husband in town. Kephas, who had been without a woman for a long time sometimes yearned for her lithesome body, but he knew that he had missed his chance and it was not to be. He frowned when Matavi told him that regular police patrols still made enquiries in the area for his whereabouts. The police, he knew, had long memories. They would continue searching for him until he was found, or until they had confirmation that he was dead. It seemed amusing to think that they were searching the country far and wide for him, when here he was practically right under their noses.

27

'I want you to take the kids and go and live in Salisbury for a while', said Saul. 'I'll rent a flat there. The border is no place for a woman while this terrorist nonsense is continuing.'

It was late evening, which was the same time almost every day that Saul brought up the subject. Dawn sighed and put down her magazine. Her voice had an edge of irritability. 'Please Saul, we've been through this before. I'm just an old-fashioned girl who believes a wife's place is with her husband. I'm not going to stay in Salisbury. I'll stay right here on the farm.'

Saul looked at her and saw that strain was beginning to show on her face. He wondered glumly when and if she would agree to go. It was not as if it would be unusual — a large number of his neighbours had already sent their families to live in town and to stay there until the troubles subsided. But the men weren't going. Most farmers had no intention of being driven from their land. Saul was prepared to fight for his land, and that's exactly what he was doing. The Police Reserve, previously small in the Senga area, had burgeoned into a fairly large fighting force since the troubles began. It was now a force to be reckoned with. Almost everyone who lived in the district belonged to it, no matter what their ages. Housewives, working in shifts, manned the main control room at the police camp for 24 hours a day and looked after their homes in their spare time. The older men and those who were unfit, also played their part by manning mobile patrols that patrolled the populated areas by day and night in case of trouble. The younger men like Saul were bound up in various anti-terrorists units that had already killed almost as many terrorists as the regular soldiers and police.

'Be reasonable, darling' — Saul had another try — 'I'm out on Police Reserve duties almost every other night. I hate leaving you alone.'

'I'm all right', smiled Dawn tiredly. 'I guess you can get used to almost anything if you have to live with it for long enough.'

It had indeed become almost anything, for the past few months had not been easy. People living in the border areas had contended with the terrorist threat for many years now, but this particular set of troubles had been far worse than anything experienced before. Troops had been operating in strength along the north-eastern border since the terrorist threat had suddenly escalated at Christmas 1972. Since then the terrorists had suffered an incredibly high number of casualties, but it had not been exacted without cost to the other side. Although armed with top-class equipment supplied by the Communist Bloc, they went out of their way to avoid engaging their well-armed counterparts. Their targets of preference were isolated homesteads occupied by unarmed civilians. They didn't care whom they killed as long as they were white. It was celebrated as a victory, even when the victims were women and children.

Not that they restricted their attacks purely to property belonging to whites. Almost any soft target was fair game, as the tribesmen in the villages had learned to their cost. If they did not co-operate, feed the invaders and keep them posted on information about security force patrols, they were shot out-of-hand, or sometimes made to suffer the most horrible deaths as an example to their neighbours.

But after the initial attacks that had taken the unready by surprise, the days of easy successes for the terrorists were soon over. People took precautions. They fixed steel shutters over their windows to guard against machine gun or grenade attacks. They illuminated the area outside their homesteads with security lights. They installed a farm radio network. They gave themselves every chance of fighting off attacks with guns that the men and their wives kept with them at all times. White and black Rhodesians were fighting back. They had no intention of handing over to a bunch of people who had revealed themselves as murderous gangsters. Because they were defending their homes, Saul and others like him were completely confident the terrorists would not, and could not, win.

'How long do you think this will go on?' asked Dawn. 'Surely we won't always have to live like this?'

'You can be sure of that', said Saul grimly. 'It may get a lot worse before it gets better, but I'm sure we'll win in the end.'

'But are we getting anywhere?' she asked despondently.

'I'm not sure. Jim Smythe at the police station says that a lot more tribesman are coming forward to give information about where the terrorists are hiding out. Very few are joining them as willing recruits. The ones I feel

216

sorry for are the poor bastards they're press-ganging for military training and hustling over the border to Zambia. Not that that helps the Party overmuch because a hell of a lot of them desert once they're back in Rhodesia. Did you see your parents today?' asked Saul, deftly changing the subject.

'I did but it didn't do much good', Dawn answered with concern. They still refuse to take even the most elementary precautions, like locking their front door.'

'I saw them as well', confessed Saul. 'I knew you were worried and I thought that perhaps I could make them see sense. But they're adamant and still say that because they're here to help black people, the terrorists won't harm them.'

'That's what they told me', said Dawn worriedly biting her lip. 'You know them. They believe that God will look after them.'

He glanced at his watch. 'Yes, but God helps them who help themselves.'

Dawn stood up. 'Patrol tonight?'

'Yep', sighed Saul. 'I'd better get my uniform. In a way, I suppose we're lucky there's a drought. With little to do on the farm we can devote most of our time to the Police Reserve.' He gave a short tired laugh. 'It looks as if that lady old Sergeant Ndhlela once told me about is displeased with everyone — just like in the 1965-66 season.'

'What are you talking about?' asked Dawn.

'The locals call her the Spirit of the Rain Goddess. She's the one who decides whether the tribe is behaving sufficiently well to merit good rains each season.' He gave a wry smile. 'But we don't need a census to conclude that they haven't behaved themselves this year.'

'Superstitious nonsense', said his wife dismissively.

'I expect so', said Saul and laughed. 'But you never really know, do you? There are more things . . .'

The hut was smoky and dark and the deputation from the chief sat silently in front of the black-clad figure and her attendant.

'The great Spirit of the Rain Goddess', the young girl who had not yet menstruated spoke in a monotone, 'says that until the blood of the leader of the men who call themselves freedom fighters has turned rotten with death, there will be no rain.'

28

The old man carefully excavated the wood ash that lay in a deep, fluffy pile on the hearthstone in his kitchen hut. He reached for the spear propped against the wall and eased the blade into a crack at the side of the fire-blackened rock. He grunted as the rock came free. He grasped the smooth edges with his bony hands and moved it to the side. A tin nestled in the hollow beneath. He carefully picked it up and blew off the dust. He opened the lid, brought his treasure closer to his face and squinted at the fat wad of dollar bills that lay like a golden egg in a nest of silver coins.

He looked up in consternation at the sudden commotion outside the door. He tried to replace the lid and fumbled to return the tin to its hiding place. The door burst open behind him. He tried desperately to conceal his portable bank with his thin body. He realised it was futile when he saw the grim expression on the face of the man who blocked the doorway. He held a Russian carbine.

The kraal head's lips moved to speak, but then he recognised the face. He went cold and his mouth snapped shut. His hands shook and he even forgot his money. The tin drooped from his nerveless fingers and the contents spilled out on the polished black surface of the cow dung floor.

'Yes', snarled Kephas, looking at the frightened face. 'It's me. The man you were so anxious to help last time.' He jabbed the muzzle of his carbine into the old man's ribs and twisted it. His victim stumbled and fell over. An involuntary tight scream escaped his lips.

'You're just lucky I do not have a bayonet on.' Kephas looked over his shoulder. 'Get him outside', he ordered.

Kumalo bent down, gripped the kraal head by his ankles and twisted him over so that he lay helplessly with his face in the dirt. He dragged him outside like a sack of mealies. His face grazed raw on the hard stony ground, for he was too old and too shocked to resist. Kumalo dumped him in a heap and watched sardonically while he struggled shakily to his feet.

Kephas noted that the village's entire current population — 11 women and children and a man, who was on leave from his work in Salisbury — had been herded into a group and made to squat down under Matavi's gun. The headman was looking with terror at the ten armed men who now made up the group.

Kephas had found a fair number of local recruits and another ten had been sent from Zambia to join him. However, many had been killed or captured in running engagements with the police and army, who always seemed to be breathing down their necks nowadays.

Kumalo, of course, was still there to answer the roll call, as were Matavi and Dingani. But Taziva had gone — he had been ripped apart up by machine gun fire when they walked into an ambush. Two others had died in the same hail of bullets.

They were not short of equipment, for when the main hunt in the valley had subsided, they had retraced their footsteps and re-supplied themselves from an arms cache that the security forces had failed to find. They had moved the stuff into the hills using sullen tribesmen who they had forced to help as porters. A few had refused, but after they were shot by the self-proclaimed fighters for freedom, there was no more open defiance.

This was another occasion when tribesmen would be shown that it did not pay to refuse to cooperate with their liberators. Kephas intended to exact revenge on the village and its inhabitants for the part they had played in the betrayal of Watura and his arrest.

'You sent a messenger to tell the police we were at your village.' Kephas said harshly.'Who was it?'

The headman glanced nervously at the villagers, then looked back at Kephas. He shrugged in a gesture of helplessness. 'I beg you to believe me. I didn't send anyone for the police. They just came by themselves. Why should I have done such a terrible thing? You must remember that I helped you. I fed you.'

Kephas smashed the back of his hand against the old man's face. He rocked sharply backwards, blood streaming from a split nose.

'You didn't help us, old man. You betrayed us.' He nodded to Kumalo. "Where's the money he was counting?'

Kumalo gave a humourless grin and tossed over the tin. Kephas caught it with one hand and examined the contents. He whistled when he saw the big bundle of dollar notes.

'Where did you get this?'

The old man looked down at the dust where a small pool of blood was forming. 'It's mine', he stuttered. 'It's from the sale of my cattle.'

'An unlikely story', sneered Kumalo. He caught the old man by his ear and jerked him painfully to his feet. 'An unlikely story indeed.'

'It's just another donation to the cause', said Kephas, handing the tin back to Kumalo.

'Of course, of course', said the old man desperately. 'I would like the freedom fighters to have it. You are the people who will win our country back for us. Please let the women prepare you food and beer.'

Kephas smiled but his eyes were ice cold. 'The last time we accepted your hospitality, old man, it cost the life of one of my men. This time you will entertain us, but not by plying us with food and beer.'

'Bring that young wife of his,' he said to Kumalo. I remember that she left the village just after we arrived last time. I'm sure she's the one who went for the police.'

'She had nothing to do with it', shouted the old man. 'She did nothing.'

His tormentors ignored him and paid no heed to his near hysterical protests.

'We'll see', said Kumalo. He swaggered across to the group of villagers. The women screamed, the children cried and clung to their mothers' skirts as he menaced them with his rifle. 'That's the one', he said, indicating a pretty girl of about 20 — the youngest wife of the kraal head.

She recoiled in terror, but Matavi grabbed her by her neck, propelled her forward and threw her flat on her face at Kumalo's feet.

'Stand up', Kumalo ordered. The sobbing girl struggled to her feet. 'Come here', he snapped, crooking a finger. She looked around desperately for help, but it was not a day for that. Trembling with fear she stumbled towards Kumalo. He shot out his hand, gripped her dress at the neck and ripped down. She screamed and tried to cover her nakedness with her hands. The raucous laughter and hot searching eyes of the terrorists followed her every movement.

'Let our entertainment begin', jeered Kumalo to the kraal head.

He shoved her violently towards the men, who caught her with clammy hands and dragged her to the nearest hut. For the next few hours screams and moans rent the air as one terrorist after another took turns at going into the hut and raping her. Some went in two or sometimes three times. Often when they had had their pleasure, some found it amusing to burn her with glowing cigarettes or to slap or punch her — sometimes into unconsciousness. Her screams eventually died to a whimper.

Finally, she was dragged from the hut by her feet and dumped naked and bleeding at her husband's feet. Gone was any sense of shame or modesty — she was too far gone for that. She lay there, her legs spread obscenely, low moans coming from her lips.

Kumalo made a move towards her, but Kephas stayed him. 'Leave her now. We have no more time for play.'

'Old man', said Kephas, addressing the quivering kraal head, 'around here people will think twice before they betray us again. In future when someone mentions the name of your village, people will tremble and remember the price paid by those who sell out to the white men. We're going to hang you', Kephas continued coldly. 'Why are we doing that? It is because the man you sold out to the Boers will probably end up being hanged. His name was Watura. I want you to remember his name well, because the way he will die will be the way you will die.'

Kephas snapped his fingers and the condemned man was pulled unresisting to his feet. His hands were bound behind him, but they did not tie his feet. Two men went into the hut where Kephas and his companions had slept. They dragged out the radiogram and put it beneath the overhanging bough of a big tree. It was to be the platform for their makeshift gallows. A length of rope was found — not too thick but it was thick enough to serve the purpose.

'It is now your turn to dance', said Kumalo. 'I'm sorry we can't find some music to play on your radiogram.

But his victim wasn't listening. He made no move to resist as two men lifted his frail frame on to the polished item of furniture.

Kumalo deftly threw the rope up and watched it coil through the air and drop over a projecting bough. Two men took one end watched Kumalo. He climbed up on the radiogram and stood next to his victim. He whistled while he fashioned a crude noose from the loose end. He dropped it over the grey head and adjusted it loosely around the scrawny neck. He gave a breezy wave of his hand to the two men below. They gripped the rope and pulled. The noose tightened and a strangled gasp gurgled from the old man's lips.

The women and children wailed pitifully in the background.

'Pull some more', laughed Kumalo.

The men holding the rope walked away from the tree jerking the headman completely upright until only the tips of his toes touching the radiogram stood between him and everlasting oblivion.

It looked like this dance of death would be a ballet.

'Tie up the rope', shouted Kumalo, making circles with his finger. The men wound the rope around a tree stump and knotted it to keep the dancer perfectly poised.

'Please!' gasped the headman as Kumalo jumped to the ground causing the radiogram to wobble. The toes scrabbled desperately on the polished surface to maintain the body's tenuous support.

After a while of watching this balancing act, Kumalo became impatient. It was losing its entertainment value.

'Remove the furniture', he instructed.

Someone kicked the radiogram away from the dangling feet.

A choking gurgle emerged from the old man's lips.

There was a howl of delight from Kephas' men and a chorus of screams, sobbing and shouts of dismay from the villagers.

The rope took up the full weight of the body. This execution would not be quickly or cleanly ended by the snapping of the neck. Slow strangulation was far more satisfying for the visitors.

Kephas was fascinated by the sight of the lynching. He couldn't take his eyes away from the dangling figure as the kraal head began his last macabre dance.

His face started to swell and darken horribly. His shoulders worked spasmodically backwards and forwards as torturing pain tormented his flesh and the air in his lungs was used up. This caused him dance from side to side like a puppet on a string. The muscles on his arms stood out like cords as they used the last desperate reserves of strength in an effort to break loose from their bonds and reach up to release his neck from its stranglehold. His legs threshed wildly, trying to locate a firm platform that was no longer there.

Kumalo laughed until the tears ran down his cheeks.

It seemed like an hour, yet it was actually only ten minutes that the old headman took to complete his lunatic jog. His neck muscles bulged in a final effort as they tried to force the loop of the tightening rope outwards. His eyeballs almost burst from their sockets. Suddenly he relaxed, and his mouth gaped open. His eyeballs protruded until they seemed about to drop onto his cheeks. His tongue slid wetly out between his lips and slipped down his chin.

Kephas relaxed and nodded at Kumalo. Sentence of death had been carried out.

A sudden shock hit the kraal head's system and the body again jerked in a spasm, while the feet again kicked wildly. The rope resumed swinging, then just as suddenly, the kicking stopped. The rope gradually stopped its swing and the corpse spun slowly on the end while goggling eyes leered sightlessly at the now silent spectators in a slow and grisly merry-go-round of death.

Kumalo took his knife to cut the body down and the tension broke. Kephas gestured irritably for him to leave it hanging.

The crying of the villagers had subsided into a chorus of low moans and crying. The youngest wife of the kraal head lay sprawled where they had left her. She had mercifully fainted before the life was finally choked out of her husband.

'Lock them in the huts', Kephas ordered.

He watched as his men drove the villagers, women, children and the man, into the two largest huts at bayonet point. Kumalo closed the doors and bound the outside padlock hasps shut with wire.

He pointed the toe of his boot at the ravished woman. 'What about her?'

Kephas shook his head. 'Someone must tell the story.'

'Do we burn them then?' asked Kumalo flatly.

'Yes', replied Kephas. 'Let's get it over with.'

Kumalo pulled a bundle of long thatching grass from the roof of a hut and went over to an open cooking fire. He dipped the grass into it and it came away a blazing torch. Holding it high he walked from hut to hut, whether they had people in or not, and stroked fire onto the tinder dry roofs.

Terrified screams came from within the two huts holding the villagers as they smelt smoke and heard the crackle of flames taking hold. There were terrible panic-filled screams as they realised they were about to die a horrible death. The screaming subsided into choking, coughing and retching as dense smoke filled the interiors. The flames crept up to the conical roofs and began to envelop the complete structures. From the inferno the head and upper torso of a man emerged through the blazing thatch of one hut in an attempt to escape. His flesh was on fire and in his arms was a little girl, no more than five years old, whose hair and clothes were ablaze. Two shots rang out and they dropped abruptly back into the flames. Kephas glanced back and saw Kumalo lower his AK.

There was a soft whoosh and the roof of one hut collapsed in a shower of sparks and flames onto the by then dead victims. The roof of the second occupied hut also fell in. Soon all the huts in the village were only burning shells. The only sounds were the spluttering of timbers as the fierce heat bit into the heart of the wood.

The kraal head's young wife came to and squatted silently, mesmerised by the horrifying scene. Then suddenly she came to realise what had happened.

'My babies! My babies!' she screamed.

She leaped up and tried to throw herself into the flames. Kumalo grabbed her by the shoulder and cuffed her back to the ground.

When they left the village a half hour later, her mind had snapped. She babbled wildly and her head swung like a pendulum between the dying fires of the village and the grotesque swaying form that had been her husband.

29

There was the occasional clatter of dishes from the kitchen as Lot washed up the dinner things. They had made an occasion of the dinner tonight — a kind of Thanksgiving. Later they would say some special prayers for which Lot would be asked to join them. They were celebrating the first time their daughter had allowed their baby grandson to stay with them overnight. It would not have happened normally, they knew, because Saul did not approve. Not that his approval would have been withheld for any reason other than the security situation, because in the last two weeks there had been considerable reconciliation between Abraham and Saul. After all these years Abraham had at last decided — for the sake of his daughter and his wife — to agree to disagree. He could never bring himself to condone killing, no matter what the circumstances. Nor were the duties that Saul carried out as a police reservist ever mentioned in the Hale household . . . except in their prayers.

Abraham got up, drew the curtains and looked out into the night. The sky was clear and starlit. 'All we need to make the evening perfect would be rain.'

'Yes', said Mary. 'The people are wretched enough without them having to suffer another drought.'

'They've suffered it already, I'm afraid. Even if the rains come now, it will be too late for the crops. But if it fills the dams, perhaps there will be enough grazing for the stock to last the winter. God knows I have prayed enough for rain, but for reasons best known to the Almighty, He has not granted our prayers.'

Mary looked at her husband. He was beginning to look old.

He had always been thin, but recently he had lost more weight and his hair was almost snow white. She felt her own cheek. The lines there were becoming more pronounced. The years of living under the harsh African sun had taken their toll. She sighed. At 50 she could hardly expect to still look like a young girl of 18. Perhaps the Brethren would soon decide to recall them from Africa to continue their work at home in Pennsylvania. Perhaps her husband could enjoy some well earned rest before overwork cut too many years off his life. Yet, if they were recalled, would they ever see their daughter or grandchildren again? She studied the tired, worried face of her husband, and she knew that he would resist with all his being any move to recall him. The people at the mission were his children. What would they do without him to see to their spiritual needs? In fact, he felt that he had failed already in the light of the killing and the ongoing troubles in the area. It was a situation that had got beyond him. He just couldn't handle it.

'Is the baby asleep?' he asked anxiously, cocking an ear for the sound of crying.

'Yes, dear', smiled Mary. 'He's asleep and God is looking after him.'

'Let us hope that God will always look after him', murmured Abraham with deep feeling. 'Now we can do very little, but when he's old enough to understand, perhaps he may wish to follow our way of life. With God's will', he said with sad emphasis.

'Ah, Lot', said Abraham as the wizened little man with grey curly hair came hesitantly into the lounge. He was dressed in a white shirt and white shorts held up by a drawstring and he had a white kitchen cap on his head. He wore no shoes, for he had grown up in a time when such things were a luxury bestowed on only a few. He believed that even when a man was lucky enough to own shoes, and he owned several pairs, they should be worn only on Sunday to church. 'Come in', said Abraham, beckoning the old black with a kindly smile. 'We would like you to join us for prayers, to thank God for allowing us to have our grandson with us this night.'

A smile passed over Lot's features. It seemed to light up his face. He had served the mission for so long now that his early days there were difficult to recall with clarity. His father had come here long ago from the lake area of Malawi to work on the gold mines. He had never returned and Lot, along with his brothers and sisters, had been born in Rhodesia. A member of the Brethren serving at the mission had taken Lot in, taught him to read and write and told him of the splendours of Christianity. He had never left in all these years, except for very brief holidays. When still a small boy, his job had been to keep the weeds down in the garden, but later he had graduated to the house and became 'the cooker' — as he described himself to his cronies. Now he would certainly never leave. He had no other place to go anyway and where would he retire to? He would die in the service of the American missionaries who served God at Senga Mission.

They knelt together quietly, Abraham, Mary and Lot, and found peace. Peace was what they all desired. Wasn't this what all men wanted?

Their peace was shattered by a piercing scream from over at the school.

'What's that?' asked Mary in alarm.

'I don't know', said Abraham. 'It sounded like a scream. Did you hear it, Lot?'

'Yes, Reverend,' concern showed on his face.

You never knew what might happen in these troubled days. He stood up.

'I will go and see, Reverend.' He walked to the door, opened it and disappeared into the darkness.

'Come back and tell me when you find out', Abraham called after him. He stood at the door with Mary and looked towards the dark shapes of the school buildings, but there seemed to be nothing untoward. Then they heard a murmur of voices from the direction of the school dormitories. Lights started flickering on one by one in various buildings. Abraham looked at Mary. 'I had better go and see for myself what is happening.' A puzzled frown creased his face.

'Wait!' said Mary. 'Someone is coming. It's probably Lot.' Footsteps could be heard moving in their direction.

'It seems like several people', Abraham said peering into the darkness.

'Who is it?' called Mary. 'Is that you, Lot?'

She gasped as Lot appeared from the darkness, but it was not he who had frightened her. It was the two grim men, armed to the teeth and wearing olive green military-style uniforms, who flanked him that did.

'What do you want?' asked Abraham sternly, recovering from his initial shock. 'This is a place of peace. No guns are allowed here. Go your way in peace, and leave us alone . . .'

His words ended in a sharp grunt as Kumalo punched him in the solar plexus. It doubled him over and sent him reeling back into the house.

'Inside', ordered Kumalo, shoving Mary ahead of him.

Kephas kept his AK covering the missionaries.

'You must not assault the Reverend', said Lot indignantly. 'He's a man of God.'

His words were cut off abruptly as Kephas smashed him in the mouth with his rifle butt, knocking him to the floor. He sat there with astonishment on his face, spitting out teeth and blood pouring onto his white shirt.

'Move', snarled Kumalo without a trace of pity.

He lined the three of them up against a wall inside the house. 'If you try anything, we will shoot you.'

'We are people of peace . . .' protested Abraham, but his words were cut off as the point of Kumalo's bayonet stabbed viciously and raked flesh from his cheek.

'I told you to shut up', purred Kumalo.

Mary moved to help her husband, but she stopped when the bayonet moved in her direction. She covered her eyes with her hands and sobbed uncontrollably.

There was a commotion at the door and another armed man walked into the house. 'Is everything going according to plan?' Kephas asked him.

'Everything is fine', acknowledged the other. 'We have rounded up the whole lot. At first count we have two hundred and fifty.'

'Two hundred and fifty what?' asked Abraham, slurring because of the wound to his jaw. He risked a touch of Kumalo's bayonet by speaking, but no move was made towards him.

'Two hundred and fifty children and teachers', jeered Kephas, with a hard smile. 'Two hundred and fifty recruits for the Party's cause.'

'What are you talking about?' asked Abraham in horror. 'What do you mean two hundred and fifty recruits for the Party's cause?'

'What we're saying is that our work is nearly finished here, but others will be coming to take our place. We have suffered greatly for the cause of freedom and many of us have been killed.'

'So why do you want the children? They have done you no harm. How can they help your cause?'

'We're taking them back to Zambia', said Kephas matter-of-factly, as if the children were going on an outing to a game park. 'When we have them there, they will be sent on our friends in the Soviet Union and China to be trained to be soldiers. You might not think so, but they are old enough for that. When they have learned to use arms, they will be brought back to fight the white imperialists to win back our country.'

'But how can you do that?' Mary gasped in horror. 'What about their mothers? They're just children. How can you take them away from their parents?'

'Everyone must suffer for the cause', hissed Kephas. 'I haven't seen my own father for seven years and I will probably never see him again. Yet I don't complain because I know that we must all suffer for the cause.'

'Do you really think this is the way to win?' asked Abraham, overawed by the enormity of what the guerrillas were planning.

'The white government finds its soldiers by compulsory national service. This is compulsory black national service,' said Kephas.

'The soldiers will catch you and hang you', Abraham continued, for once in his life feeling that death for people such as these could well be God's vengeance.

'So you would like us to die?' asked Kumalo, fingering his AK.

'If you decide to kill me, I will not resist', said Abraham. He resignedly closed his eyes in a silent prayer to the Almighty asking Him not to take his life at a moment when his presence on Earth was needed so desperately by so many people.

'Report to me when you have the kids ready', Kephas said curtly, dismissing the other cadre.

The man gave a clenched fist salute and left.

'What should we do with them?' asked Kumalo, nodding at the three prisoners. 'We'll take the men with us', said Kephas. They can carry things and besides, they'll make useful hostages if the soldiers catch up with us.'

Mary glanced at Abraham in desperation. An unspoken message passed between them and their eyes closed in a prayer. A prayer that asked the Lord to spare their baby grandson who was sleeping peacefully in an adjacent room. They were not concerned about themselves.

'What about the woman?' asked Kumalo, eyeing Mary in a way that made her flesh crawl.

'We don't need her', said Kephas. 'She would never be capable of making the journey back through the valley. Besides, she is useless to us.' He paused thoughtfully. 'We can't just leave her behind either. She would alert the authorities.'

Mary sat ashen faced, hands clasped tightly, knuckles showing white through her skin. Her husband was close to panic.

'You can have her as a present from your commander', said Kephas. Kumalo licked his lips and reached out, grabbed Mary by the arm and dragged her to her feet. She gave a terrified scream, then her throat froze.

'Pray', said Abraham, looking at her with wild eyes. 'For God's sake, pray.'

He tried to get to his feet, but Kephas slammed his rifle butt against his head and he crashed to the floor unconscious.

Lot tried to protest, but subsided into silence as Kephas made a threatening gesture. Mary tried to pull herself from Kumalo's grasp to go to her husband's aid, but she was no match for his brutal strength.

'Come, little white bird', he leered, dragging her into the passage that led to the bedrooms.

Kephas lit a cigarette. He stood contentedly inhaling and exhaling while desperate high-pitched screams came from the bedroom.

'Please . . . please . . . no . . . no . . .'

A short period of silence was followed by a scream which cut off abruptly as the dull thudding noise of a fist striking flesh came clearly through to them. Lot vomited on the floor, then took Abraham in his arms and cuddled him like a baby.

Minutes later Kumalo strolled in, put his rifle down and used both hands to adjust his clothing.

'What about the woman?' enquired Kephas.

'Fine', said Kumalo casually. He did not elaborate.'

'You have killed the missus', gasped Lot, tears pouring down his cheeks. 'You have killed the missus.'

Kumalo shrugged. 'She was white and she had to die.'

'But why?' asked Lot. 'Why? These whites have always helped black people. They have never harmed them and they are good people.'

Kumalo shrugged again. 'She was white. Death was her due. Africa is for the Africans. It's not for the white man.' He nudged Kephas. 'Anyway, you can believe me that she was not much good when compared to one of her black sisters.' He made an obscene sign with his fingers.

They doubled up with laughter while Lot regarded them with wide eyes.

Kephas took a lamp, walked into the last bedroom and looked around. To his astonishment there was a white baby in a cot. It was smiling and gurgling happily. Little Joseph was used to black faces and his mind associated them with the friendly people who spent much of their time being nice to him. Kephas looked at the child thoughtfully, then reached down and moved its napkin aside. So it was a boy child. Well, he thought, this is one white boy who will not grow up to fight us later. He grabbed the baby by his legs and pulled him upside down from the cot. Joseph gurgled happily. He was used to his father swinging him upside down. It was a game they played regularly.

Kephas looked pensively at the wall. One swing would be enough to crack the child's skull. Joseph chuckled below him. The man then put his hand down and gently brought the baby up into his arms. He looked at the fat face thoughtfully. Perhaps there was another way. He looked down and made his decision. A smile creased his face. He gently returned the child to the cot and covered him up. He watched for a few minutes until Joseph dropped off to sleep, then tiptoed from the room and silently closed the door.

He didn't mention the child to the others. He knew Kumalo would have killed the white child without a qualm. To him it would have been like squashing a fly.

*　　*　　*

The children were crowded tightly together in the centre of the football field. Armed men lounged around on guard. Some were as young as ten, but others — the secondary school students — were as old as 18. The school staff were sitting amongst them — male and female teachers, nurses and matrons. Lot sat amongst them, cradling Abraham's head in his lap. The missionary was semiconscious.

Lot whispered to those around him, telling them about the terrible happenings at the house. The story circulated around the crowd like a wildfire. They had been frightened enough before, but now that they knew what had happened to Mary Hale some were close to hysterics.

No one made a move to escape, knowing that if they did they would most likely be shot down like dogs. Later perhaps, an opportunity might come once they were in the Zambezi Valley. They looked with compassion at Abraham. His lips moved in silent prayer, but no one dared to make a move to lend him comfort. Who could tell what would happen to them if they showed solidarity with a white man.

'We need food and water for s the captives', said Kephas. 'We have to get them to Zambia alive and it's a long march.'

'Some will die on route anyway', said Kumalo callously. 'It will be a tough forced march because it will not be long once the news gets out, before the soldiers set off after us in hut pursuit.'

'We still want as many as possible to get to Zambia alive. If we lose some on the march, it's just tough.'

He beckoned to a junior pupil and the boy got up and approached Kephas hesitantly. Kephas administered a friendly pat on the child's shoulder, frowning when the child recoiled in fear. 'We need food to take with us', he said. 'Where can we get it?'

'There's mealie meal and meat in the school kitchen', answered the child.

'Uncooked food is no good. We can't stop to cook. I want tinned food. Food that can be carried. Is the store next to the school still open?'

'Yes', said the child. 'It's still there, but it is not open at night.'

Kephas and Kumalo guffawed. Kephas winked and turned back to the child. 'I don't think we'll wait until morning when it opens. Does the storekeeper still live in a house next door to the store?'

The pupil nodded.

'Okay then', said Kephas. He detailed Matavi to remain in charge of the prisoners and told Kumalo to get ten of the children to accompany them. They approached the store slowly, menacing the children into silence. It was the usual one-roomed country store with a few thatched huts at the back where the storekeeper lived. The surrounds were littered with general old junk, papers, tins, bottles and weather-stained corrugated cardboard cartons. The front double doors on the verandah were fastened with heavy padlocks. The windows were protected with heavy burglar bars.

'Get the storekeeper', Kephas ordered.

A few minutes later Kumalo returned, pushing a little man, naked except for underpants. He was protesting volubly. Kumalo threw him to the ground and jangled a bunch of keys. 'He refused to give them to me at first but I persuaded him', he told Kephas.

Kephas noticed a bloody swelling above his left eye.

'Why don't you want to help the freedom fighters?'

'You are criminals, that's why', said the little man bravely. 'You are thieves and you want to steal my property.'

'Get over there with the children', ordered Kephas and cocked the action of his AK with a dull click. The man looked at him with contempt, but obediently did what he was told. Somehow he retained his dignity in spite of his near-naked state.

Kumalo tried the keys and unlocked the padlocks one at a time. He swung open the doors which squeaked noisily on their rusted hinges. To the half-starved guerrillas the interior was like an Aladdin's cave. There were ample supplies of foodstuffs on the shelves — tinned meat, fish, baked beans, biscuits and so on — as well as blankets and clothing. Dresses and suits on hangers were suspended from hooks in the roof beams.

They knew what they wanted. They left the clothing, but all the tinned food and biscuits were bundled up in blankets to carry it away.

When the loot was back at the mission, Kumalo drew Kephas aside and surreptitiously indicated the storekeeper. 'What do we do with that gentleman?'

'He's more trouble than he's worth', mused Kephas. 'He is certainly no friend of ours and is a disruptive influence. If we take him with us, I'm sure he'll be encouraging people to escape. If we leave him behind, he will be off to the authorities as soon as we are out of here. I think we'd better kill him.'

Kumalo nodded and cocked his rifle.

'Just a moment', muttered Kephas, keeping his voice low so he couldn't be overheard by the prisoners. 'We can't shoot him here. It will frighten the kids and probably prompt some of them to rum away the moment they get the chance. Besides, someone might hear the shots. We need to get rid of him quietly. What about that abandoned mine shaft we passed en route to the store?' He looked at Kumalo knowingly. 'Let's dump him in that. You'd better find some rope to tie him up.'

Leaving the rest, they marched their brave little prisoner back towards the store.

'What are you going to do with me?' he asked anxiously. He was a worried man. 'Are you going to kill me?'

'No', said Kumalo soothingly, 'of course not. Why would we do that? You are black like us. We only kill whites.'

The storekeeper let out an audible sigh of relief. Eventually they stopped. The storekeeper was feeling so relieved that he was not going to die, that he didn't particularly notice of where they were. 'What are you going to do with me then?' he asked. 'I won't say anything about you. I was just angry before. I'm all right now. Do you understand me?'

'We understand', nodded Kephas solemnly. 'We understand that you were just angry.' Kumalo nudged Kephas.

'We're going to tie you up and leave you here. Someone will find you in the morning and let you go', said Kephas. 'By then we'll be a long, long way away.'

'Are you certain?' their anxious prisoner asked.

'Of course', said Kumalo. 'Come, we cannot waste any more time.' He held out the rope and the storekeeper stood passively while they securely bound his hands, knees and feet until he was incapable of moving.

Kumalo suddenly felled him with a hard clout to the ear. He landed heavily because he couldn't break his fall. Without further ado, Kephas grabbed his bound feet, Kumalo took his shoulders, and together they carried him off the pathway.

'What are you doing?' the helpless bundle asked in terror. 'Where are you taking me?'

They didn't answer him. The mine shaft had been disused for many years and was surrounded by a protective rock wall that had been built to stop cattle falling down the shaft. They lifted the storekeeper and placed him on top of the rock wall.

'Don't kill me! You mustn't joke about things like this', said the man not believing what was happening to him.

'We're not joking', grunted Kumalo. 'Goodbye', he said. 'I hope they find you in the morning.'

They gave the trussed storekeeper bundle a gentle push. There was no way he could resist and he felt himself rolling off the wall and dropping into the abyss. Dislodged stones rattled against the rocky sides and accompanied him on his last journey. He screamed a long scream as he fell, bouncing against the rock sides on the way down

It was several seconds before they heard the splash, but it was a long drop.

The underground water closed around the storekeeper like cold hands and drew him down into its depths. His limbs strained against his bonds and his body convulsed with fright. He had been badly injured during the fall, but he managed to gasp for air. Instead of that he gasped in water and his lungs filled. He died quickly. His body sank slowly into the murky depths and was never found.

30

The column wound slowly through the bush. Some children were crying, but most had been comforted into silence by the teachers. They were fearful that the guards would kill those who hindered or delayed them or who gave them trouble. The terrorists had made it clear that those who did not keep up would be killed. There were over a hundred kilometres to go before they got to the border. The longer it took before for the authorities heard what had happened, the greater would be the delay before the search started. Their guards attempted to keep the prisoners four abreast in the column to maintain supervision. But 60 or 70 ranks, even marching closely behind the other, made it a very long column. Eventually, though, the bush thickened and the footpaths became narrower, so it became impossible for the marchers to keep any formation except a single file. They were strung out over two kilometres, with stragglers even further back. The supervision of so many people by only ten guards became impossible, particularly in the dark.

Inevitably, many took the chance to escape when the guards were out of sight, They slipped quietly away and hid in the thick undergrowth. Some remained in hiding until dawn, then made their way back to the mission. Others attempted to get back in the dark. Some took the wrong footpaths and got lost in the wilderness. A few eventually died of starvation or fell prey to hyenas and wild dogs. But most trickled back to the mission and safety in small groups or in ones and twos.

They didn't know it but the trail they had followed had once been the main route to the interior of Arab slavers for hundreds of years before. Now the slave drivers were not Arabs in long flowing robes, but Africans in olive drab uniforms and bearing communist weapons.

It was close to midnight when Lot and four children slipped away. They ran blindly into the darkness, and although they were spotted by a guard they were pursued only by his shouts. No shots were fired for fear of it attracting an army or police patrol which by then might have been in hot pursuit. Lot sat his exhausted young charges down at the foot a huge tree and told them to stay there and not to move. He knew he would have no difficulty finding that tree again in daylight. He stumbled as fast as his thin old legs would carry him, looking for the nearest habitation.

It was two hours before the dark shapes of the outlying buildings on Ndhlela's farm appeared in view. He forced his aching legs over the furrows of the ploughed land, slipping and falling several times. His heart thumped painfully in his chest and his panting caused the night air to rasp through his lungs.

Dogs, disturbed by the sounds of strangers, came racing out to meet him, snapping and snarling about his feet. He was much too far gone to care and he just ignored them. They seemed to sense that he presented no danger and drew back, although their yapping and snarling continued without abatement. There was a flicker of light and an oil lamp illuminated a figure in a doorway.

'Who is it?' came the stern voice of Ndhlela. 'Stay exactly where you are. I must warn you that I have a gun.'

'It's me, Lot, from the mission', gasped the old man, falling on his knees.

'Lot?' queried Ndhlela. He warily walked several paces forward until he was satisfied that it was really Lot. Then he ran forward, shotgun in hand. He helped Lot to his feet and was clearly concerned at his condition. 'What are you doing here at a time like this, Lot? What's the matter with you? Don't you know that terrorists are about? I might have shot you.'

Lot could hardly gasp out his words he was so exhausted. He pointed weakly to the north.

'Terrorists . . .' he panted. 'Terrorists . . . Missus dead . . . Reverend Hale . . . they've taken the children . . . the children . . .'

'Terrorists have killed Mrs Hale!' exclaimed Ndhlela in disbelief. 'She is dead? What about Reverend Hale?'

'Yes, yes . . .' Lot nodded his head vigorously. 'They took Reverend Hale . . . they've got him . . .'

'They've kidnapped the Reverend? The children? What about the children?'

'They took them . . .'

'Speak up man, speak up', said Ndhlela urgently. 'Pull yourself together. How many children did they take?'

Lot looked at Ndhlela wide-eyed.

'All of them. They have taken all of them away. They've got all the teachers and they are taking them to Zambia. . . all of them . . .' He collapsed in a dead faint.

'Women! Women!'

Ndhlela clapped his hands with urgency and his two wives appeared. They stood there attentively.

'Hurry up', he said, 'lay him down in the bedroom.' Under his direction they took hold of Lot, put his arms around their shoulders and pulled him to his feet.

'No, wait', said Ndhela, changing his mind. 'I must report this to the police and they will need to talk to him.' He pointed to his car. 'Put him in the back. Get a blanket.' He opened the door of his old sedan and helped them lay the semi-conscious man on the back seat. Ndhlela placed his shotgun on the front passenger seat. 'Stay at the house until I return', he told his wives. 'Don't open the door for anyone.'

The first light of day was beginning to creep over the eastern skyline when he drove into the yard of the Jenkins' homestead. He had intended to go to the mission and phone from there, but concern that the terrorists might have laid mines in the road prompted him to change his mind. There were phones nearer than the Jenkins' farm, but he knew that Saul would listen and was also a man of action.

Lot had recovered from his state of shock, but he was sleeping soundly on the back seat, completely exhausted. Ndhlela stopped in front of the verandah and started to get out, but he changed his mind and hit the hooter with the heel of his hand, sounding several long blasts.

There was an almost immediate commotion within the house and he heard the babbling of young voices. Shortly afterwards he heard Saul asking from behind the front door who it was.

Ndhlela got out of his car. 'It is I, *Nkosi*, Ndhlela.'

'Ndhlela?' asked Saul in surprise. There was a rattling of bolts as he unfastened the door from the inside while he talked. He did not stop talking. 'What's it Ndhlela? What's the matter?'

He came out to the car, glanced into the back seat and saw Lot's prone figure.

'That's Lot, isn't it — the mission cook? What's the matter with him?'

'You must hear what he has to say, *Nkosi*. There is very little time.'

Saul nodded and noticed Dawn framed in the doorway in her dressing gown. She had his FN rifle in her hands and looked quietly capable of using it.

'Lot came to my farm a few hours ago. He says terrorists have attacked the mission and have taken away all the children and the teachers. They're marching them through the valley to Zambia.'

'The mission?' asked Saul, his face blanching. 'They've attacked the mission?'

He looked at Dawn, but she had heard enough and was running to the car.

'My baby, my baby', she cried, her face paling. 'They've taken my baby.'

'Shush my girl', said Saul grimly. He put his arm around her and turned to Ndhlela. 'Our baby is staying the night at the mission with the Hales', he explained chokingly.

'I haven't been there', said Ndhlela gravely, 'but Lot says they've killed Mrs Hale and taken Reverend Hale with them. He said nothing about a baby.'

'My mother is dead?' asked Dawn, as if to herself.

'We must try to stay calm', said Saul.

He led Dawn inside and returned to help Ndhlela carry Lot. By the time Lot was on the sofa, Dawn had forced herself into a state of desperate composure.

'Phone the police', Saul told her. 'Tell them everything we know. I'm not going to waste time waiting for Lot to wake up.' He turned to Nhdlela. 'Will you come to the mission with me? They may have laid mines on the road, so it could be dangerous.'

'I'll come', answered Ndhlela simply.

'Good', snapped Saul. 'Let's go.'

He grabbed his rifle, took spare magazines from the gun cabinet and ran out to his car. Ndhlela fetched his shotgun from his own vehicle and got into the front passenger seat. Saul drove off at top speed towards the mission. He took the narrow bush roads like the expert driver he was, accelerated down the straights, slowing at the corners and accelerating out of them again. A thick pall of dust billowed behind them, rolling up in a cloud and obscuring their view to the rear. They hardly exchanged a word as Saul drove with dread in his heart — dread that they had killed his baby son. Murdered him as they had killed the gentle Mary Hale and probably old Abraham as well. The minutes seemed to tick by like they were hours. Two kilometres or so from the mission he braked and pulled off the road.

'Ndhlela', he said, 'I think you should walk from here. There is a danger the terrorists have mined the entrance road. 'I cannot waste time', said Saul. 'I'm going on ahead in the car. I've got to get there as my baby may be dead.'

'What about you?' asked Ndhlela. 'You have decided not to walk because you do not want to waste time? But what good will it do if you are killed in an explosion? If you intend to carry on in the car, then I will come with you but.' he looked thoughtfully at the bush by the road side. 'It might damage your car to get to the mission by driving off-road through the bush, but it is not far to go and at least there will be no mines. Don't you think this is the most sensible solution?'

'You're right', said Saul coming to his senses. He took a pair of wire cutters — from the glove compartment, got out of the car and went to the fence that lined the road. Several snips later he had cleared a passage. He got back in the car, revved the engine and drove into the bush. Twenty minutes later they stopped by the mission homestead.

The front door was swung wide open and there was a puddle of blood in the hall. Throwing caution to the wind, they ran inside.

They found the mortal remains of Mary Hale sprawled on the double bed in the main bedroom. She was naked and her legs were obscenely splayed. He skin was a ghastly chalky white, set off by several vivid red gashes. She was barely recognisable in the grisly horror of death. Her throat had been slashed, almost severing her head from her trunk. A large patch of blackish blood had soaked into the bed cover and congealed in a sticky pool. Big shiny green flies were buzzing about. His service in the police had ensured that Saul was used to the sight of death, but this time he turned away and his stomach heaved.

When he touched the door handle of the next bedroom, Saul heard a cry from within and his heart leapt. He threw open the door and confirmed it was baby Joseph. He was gurgling and kicking his tiny legs and sucking his little fingers in hunger. His face grimaced into a howl when he saw his father. Why was he being neglected? A quarter full baby bottle was on the dressing table and it was soon in the baby's mouth. With wobbly legs Saul lowered himself into a chair. He looked at Ndhlela with open-mouthed relief.

'They haven't harmed him. He's alive.' His eyes were wet with tears.

'Yes', said Ndhlela, sharing Saul's relief. 'He's safe and sound. 'I think your family spirits have looked after him. Terrorists show no mercy to whites and if they had found him, I am sure they would have killed him.

They have murdered plenty of white babies. I think, *Nkosi*, they did not suspect a child was here, so they did not bother to search.'

*   *   *

By seven o'clock in the morning the mission was a hive of activity. Police and army follow-up units with trackers had set off after the terrorists and their captives. A search of the mission revealed that they had taken everyone with them. Everyone, except for poor Mary Hale and the baby.

Helicopters flew in with batches of grim fighting men. Engineers checked the roads with mine detectors. They found four big, squat mines painted olive green and bearing Russian markings. Any one of them would have blown Saul and Ndhlela to eternity if they hadn't taken to the bush.

*   *   *

'Keep moving', snarled Kephas, lashing out with a switch at the crocodile of humanity as it filed past.

'Half of them have run away', he ranted to Kumalo. 'What's the use of risking our lives to get recruits if half of them escape?'

The captives, both pupils and teachers, were exhausted, filthy, and suffering from the heat. They stumbled along slowly as they wound down 300 tumbled rocky metres of escarpment that led to the floor of the Zambezi Valley below.

'Move! Move!' shouted Kephas.

Kumalo waved his rifle at the laggards. 'I'll start shooting if you don't move faster.'

The children regarded them with big, frightened, sobbing eyes. The teachers carried some of the weaker children.

'They can't move faster', protested a young male teacher who had only recently qualified from university. He was rewarded with a rifle butt that smacked into his kidneys.

'Where are our rear guards?' asked Kephas.

Kumalo shrugged. 'I guess they are back there backtracking.'

240

Kephas grunted, wondering if they would be able to get across the Zambezi River alive before the soldiers caught up with them. 'We must be leaving a track like a herd of elephants for them to follow. How many prisoners have we got left?' he asked.

'About one hundred and fifty, I would think', estimated Kumalo.

'Damn it', muttered Kephas, in chagrin. 'Over a hundred gone.'

'True', said Kumalo, 'but not all escaped. Some just dropped from exhaustion and couldn't carry on.'

'Well, they must continue', screamed Kephas furiously. 'They must all carry on.'

He lashed out and cut an exhausted teenage girl across her face with his switch. She put her hand to her face but did not otherwise react or break her ragged step. Her sensations had been deadened and she was like an automaton.

'No one has spotted us so far', said Kephas. We've been lucky.'

He looked up at the sky but everything was quiet and peaceful. They had heard planes and helicopters in the distance earlier, but none had come near.

They stood there until the rear guards caught up. Abraham Hale was with them, his hands bound tightly behind him. His guards had their carbines slung and were brushing away the tracks of those who had passed. It was a hopeless task.

'If they attack us make the white man stand in front of you. They won't shoot if they see him', shouted Kephas.

'Don't worry about him', retorted one of the men. 'He'll die before they get us. He's still praying and just won't stop.'

'God will punish you', said Abraham. His eyes were strangely calm and they seemed to bore into the eyes of the two leaders.

'Don't you know that we killed your wife, old man', Kumalo jeered. When you've served your purpose, you'll die as well.'

'Yes, you have taken my wife's life', murmured Abraham, a look of tortured sadness in his eyes. And I may die, but that doesn't matter. We have both done our work on Earth. It's not for us to punish man for his wrongs. That's for God. But unless you let these children go and pray for His forgiveness, an awful retribution will fall on you. Release them and pray, I beg you.'

It was developing into a situation beyond Kumalo's capabilities to handle. He couldn't understand a reaction like this from a man whose woman he had defiled and butchered.

'I think I'll kill him', he muttered to Kephas, but made no move to do it.

'Leave him alone', said Kephas who also felt the influence of this strange man. He grinned weakly and shrugged. 'Come on', he said, 'we must get a move on.'

31

The radio crackled to life in the temporary control room established in the mission's cookery classroom.

The men grouped around a wooden table were instantly alert. Mugs of tea that had been moving to mouths stopped in mid-air as they focussed their attention.

'Mission control, this is chopper two zero, do you read me, over?'

The corporal signaller depressed the transmitter button. The static ceased abruptly.

'Chopper two zero, this is mission control — go ahead, over.'

Saul felt an adrenalin shock surge through his body. He glanced sideways at Ndhlela who like himself was dressed in the camouflage combat kit of the Police Reserve. Their eyes met and a feeling of comradeship flashed between them. This was it. It looked like contact had been made. They could scarcely wait for the rest of the helicopter's transmission . . .

'Mission control, this is chopper two zero', drawled the firm and sure voice from the single sideband radio. 'We have located the enemy. Captain Fitzgerald's unit is engaging.'

'Got the bastards', yelled a young lieutenant, slapping Saul on the back. 'We've got the bloody bastards.'

'Shut up', snapped the thickset major in control of the operation. He grabbed the handset from the radio operator.

'Chopper two zero— give me a situation report. I say again — give me a sitrep.'

'Mission Control — chopper two zero', sang back the voice. 'Roger. Will let you know as soon as the situation stabilises. I can't bring my machine guns to bear in support because I can't identify the terrs, our guys or the kidnapped kids. They're all mixed up together down there.'

'Keep them together', snarled Kephas, his heart jumping in his chest. He gripped Abraham's arm and roughly pushed him forward. 'Blast', he said, biting his lower lip as he surveyed the frightened pupils clustered in front of him. 'No more than twenty left.'

'If that', agreed Kumalo.

'What do we do now?' asked Matavi. He had blanched to the colour of a mushroom and was shivering despite the intense heat. He still had his rifle, but he held it limply as if he'd forgotten it was there.

Kephas felt an intense hatred for Matavi. It was his fault. The fault of him and the other weak and useless men who called themselves freedom fighters. Kumalo, Matavi and the others had escaped the battle along with himself. Except for Kumalo they stolidly gazed at him with fear and uncertainty. What did they have to worry about? At least they were still alive — not dead like the rest back there.

Kephas pointed the muzzle of his AK at Matavi's chest. He grinned dangerously as Matavi backed off nervously, then traversed his weapon across the cluster of wide-eyed pupils. Some started to cry again, but most were too tired to even do that. They just stood there and looked numbly at the man who had the control of life or death over them .

'They're just like sheep', he sneered to Kumalo. 'But when they've been in the training camp for six months, they'll be like lions. We're still going to Zambia', he said to comrade and captive alike. 'Anyone who doesn't want to go with me, step out and you can die right now.'

He licked his lips and stared from one to the next. There was a hollow silence disturbed only by the occasional bird call. This was rudely broken by the sudden distinctive rattle of automatic fire, but it came from some distance away.

'They are going to find us,' moaned Matavi, swaying gently from side to side. 'I know they are going to find us and kill all of us.' He had lost all heart for fighting.

'They've already found us', said Kumalo, simpering sarcastically at the beaten man, 'because they have helicopters and we don't. I knew they'd catch up with us. Did you really think we would all get back to Zambia without casualties? But stop worrying? You can only die once.'

*   *   *

Saul froze as Ndhlela raised his arm in a signal to stop. He scanned the thickly-bushed terrain through which the game track twisted and turned. For

244

a moment he noticed nothing untoward, then he gasped as he saw it — the biggest lion he had ever seen — a great tawny muscular beast with a black mane. It stood in the track about twenty paces ahead of Ndhlela.

Saul carefully eased his rifle into a firing position. He saw Ndhlela do the same and other safety catches clicked off behind him. A fly landed on his nose, but he ignored it.

A great coughing roar came from the huge beast. It rolled its head and snarled angrily at the intruders.

Ndhlela began to back off, inch by inch, his legs moving stiffly like a puppet.

Slowly, thought Saul, slowly. A sudden movement would send the great cat into a pounding charge that would flatten Ndhlela before they could get off sufficient shots to stop it.

Beads of sweat formed on Saul's forehead and ran coldly into the corners of his eyes. He marvelled at the muscles rippling beneath the loose hide and the great brush of black mane that framed its wide flat face with its drooling fangs. This truly was the king of the jungle.

It seemed like an eternity that they stood there in that face-to-face confrontation. The creature broke the impasse. It gave a dignified roar, looked behind it at the men and ambled off into the bush by the side of the track. There was a slight rustling of bushes then all was silence. It had gone.

'Phew', Jake said. 'I wouldn't like to go through that again.'

'That's for sure', said Saul, letting his tension out in a deep exhalation of breath. 'I would have laughed at anybody who tried to tell me they'd seen a lion that size. I'm not even sure I believe my own eyes.'

Ndhlela bent down and examined the ground where the lion had made its exit. Saul looked over his shoulder at the huge pad marks pressed into the dust at the edge of the path.

'I have never seen one like that, Ndhlela', he said in awe.

'It's true, *Nkosi*', said Ndhlela. 'That one is more like a god than an animal.' He was studying the ground as he spoke. He paused thoughtfully, 'but it is not only the lion that has passed this way.'

'What do you mean?' Saul said kneeling down.

'Look at that', said Ndhlela. He pointed between the great pad marks where there was a clear impression of a child's foot print, partially covered by the part impression of an army boot. There were unmistakable signs that someone had been backtracking. Looking around it was clear that a lot of people had recently passed this way.

'How many of them are there?' Saul asked Ndhlela.

'I think there are about twenty of them', said the ex-sergeant. His eyes moved methodically along the ground. 'Five of them are men, probably the terrorists, the rest are children.'

'Well what do you know,' said Jake from over Saul's shoulder. 'If that lion hadn't been there, we would probably have missed those tracks. You begin to suspect that it wanted us to see them. Do we call for reinforcements?'

There was a dull rumble of thunder.

'The rain is coming, *Nkosi*', said Ndhlela.' He pointed at the sky where dark clouds were collecting. 'The rain will be with us in two hours. We can cover a lot of ground in that time. If we stand around and wait for reinforcements, the enemy will probably get away. Even a slight shower of rain could wash out their spoor. I think we should carry on.'

'What do you think?' asked Saul, looking from Jake to Jim to Jon.

'You're the boss', said Jim Wilkie easily. Saul looked at his determined face. Surely this was not the same pensive youngster who'd first seen action only a few short months ago. He was a man now — a real professional.

Jake gave a short nod. 'I'm in.'

'So am I', grunted Jon du Toit. 'I would never forgive myself if we allowed those bastards to get away.'

'I'll still be walking when the rest of you have dropped', grinned Jon. Saul looked searchingly into his wrinkled features and his face creased into a smile too.

'You're probably right at that', he agreed.

Ndhlela ranged ahead, crisscrossing the spoor that for most of the time was only visible to him. Saul and the others followed, rifles ready for instant action.

They were amazed at how Ndhlela found the signs. A slight depression in a patch of grass, or a broken twig told their tracker a story. Sometimes it was only slightly scuffed soil or a turned leaf. And the speed he moved at was amazing. He barely paused, loping along with his eyes either to the ground or looking in the middle distance, like a hunting dog scenting an antelope. After an hour Saul thanked his lucky stars that he was so fit. He could tell by Jake's posture that he was beginning to feel the strain. Sweat poured from their bodies.

The rain continued to hold off, although the sky was more threatening. Thunder growled throatily in the distance.

Once Ndhlela lost the spoor and they paused for ten minutes while he cast about until he found it again. The others thankfully sat and rested. They marvelled at Ndhlela's energy, considering his age.

Ndhlela pointed out that the fugitives were taking more care with their backtracking. There were just the occasional faint scuff marks to follow. But this care was probably slowing them down.

They tramped through bush, forest and open vlei. Sometimes the tracks led over wide flat rocky outcrops where Ndhlela battled to regain the spoor. But never once was he stumped. The white men were continually amazed by his skills.

The ground became broken and rocky as the tracks led to higher ground. They wended their way between rocky kopjes that stood like silent sentinels in the veld. They clambered through deep dongas eroded by the rush of waters in long-forgotten rainy seasons. They slogged along dried-up sandy spruits and through valleys choked with thorn bush. Their eyes never ceased searching the terrain for a movement that could spell their bloody deaths in bursts of automatic fire.

The veld was starkly beautiful although they weren't appreciating the scenery. It was a mixture of browns and oranges with the greys and fawns of the kopjes blending in. If one looked at the rocks closely, they were a kaleidoscope of colour. The darker hues were overlaid with patches of white and orange from fungus and other growths. By June or July a profusion of red, yellow and orange aloes, growing in pockets of humus in the nooks and crannies of the weathered granite, would be poking spikily towards the sky.

Ndhlela stopped and raised his arm for them to halt. He listened intently, satisfying himself that they were still alone. He pointed to the clear imprint of a boot in the loose sand.

'We're close now', he announced in a whisper. 'They are getting careless again.' He indicated a trail of crushed vegetation that even the untrained eye couldn't miss. 'They're in a hurry to get home and obviously believe they're safe from immediate pursuit.'

Saul looked thoughtfully at the marks. The need for a tracker was past.

'Thank you, Ndhlela, you have come far enough. We can continue without you. You are no longer a regular policeman and the days of risking your life should be over. It's said that when a man is old he should be left to live out his autumn years in peace.'

Ndhela was hurt and he drew his shoulders into the position of attention

247

he had learned all those years ago as a police recruit.

'*Nkosi*', he said proudly, 'those terrorists are enemies of my people as well as yours. The Reverend Hale and his wife were also my friends. And what about those children? Where you go, I'll go', he added simply.

Saul spoke gruffly to cover his inner feelings. 'So be it, Ndhela. If you want to carry on, I'll be proud to have you.'

He quickly outlined his plan. 'We will advance cautiously. When someone sights the enemy, break and go to ground. If you realised we've been sighted, don't wait for me, just open fire. Be careful and watch for the children — only target those in combat gear. There are teachers with them. We don't want to kill anyone but the terrorists.'

His men indicated that they understood.

Without another word they carried on down the trail, but more carefully. If they blundered into an ambush, they wouldn't stand a chance because there were only a few of them. In the veld warfare was brutal and death came at point-blank range. It was not often that one got a second chance. Mistakes meant almost certain death.

They examined every tree and bush critically as they advanced, leapfrogging from cover to cover, with Ndhlela and Saul in the lead. They paused frequently to allow Nhdlela to check the ground and for Saul to indicate their next move.

There was absolute silence as they glided from bush to bush and from tree to tree, their senses acutely tuned to their surroundings. They were armed predators stalking their prey.

Saul's heart thumped beneath his shirt. For a ridiculous moment he was worried the noise would give their position away. Adrenalin coursed through his veins as his excitement mounted.

Ndhlela dropped into cover like he'd been shot and the rest followed suit a split second later. Saul wriggled up to him on his elbows.

Ndhlela indicated the beginnings of a kopje no more than 30 metres away. It inclined sharply upwards for about 100 metres. Ragged patches of thorn bush covered its slopes.

Saul strained his eyes but it took him a while to focus. Halfway up the slope was a large rocky outcrop. Next to it, clustered in a group he could see the heads of children. They were just visible through the long grass. They were sitting or squatting and they were not making a sound. There was no immediate sign of the enemy.

'Have they abandoned them?' he asked, without taking his eyes away.

248

'No', Ndhlela pointed. 'Look — beside that rock!'

Saul spotted him immediately. His olive green uniform blended with the terrain. He was supposed to be guarding the children, but his rifle was slung casually over his shoulder. Saul wondered if there were more amongst the prisoners.

He fingered the trigger. The guard could be got easily. But what if the remaining terrorists used the children as cover? Where was Abraham? Was he with another group?

There was laughter behind the rock. He heard the distinct sound of a hand slapping bare flesh. The guard glanced behind the rock and grinned.

'God will forgive you.' It was the unmistakable voice of Abraham Hale.

Without realising it, Saul surveyed the rest of the scene through the backsight of his rifle. So they had him behind the rock!

A terrorist armed with an AK47 appeared from behind the outcrop and linked up with the guard. Oblivious to the presence of the hunters, one took a packet of cigarettes and offered one to his companion. They were so close that Saul had no difficulty in identifying the brand from the colour of the pack. The other took a box of matches from his pocket and struck a light. They both lit up and inhaled.

A cold rage enveloped Saul at the idea of the brutal killers, chatting away so happily and enjoying life. They were behaving as if they were in their local shebeen, secure from retaliation. A mental picture of Mary Hale's ravaged and brutalised body appeared. These same men had probably violated her poor body time and time again, until she must have screamed for the release of death. And they had her husband as prisoner — Dawn's father. A man who wouldn't raise a hostile finger — even to defend himself. Well, someone had to defend him.

A blood haze of hatred clouded his eyes which narrowed into slits. He shook off Jake's restraining hand. The background of trees and rocks faded from his vision as the laughing men became the only reality. His lips curled back from his teeth and he snarled like a leopard that had cornered its prey. Superhuman strength flowed into his body as he sprang to his feet. Six men could not have held him down.

The laughter died in their throats, as Kumalo and Matavi saw the terrifying white apparition rise from the ground. Kumalo screamed and tried to bring his AK into play, but it was too late. He tried to turn and run, but his feet seemed rooted to the spot. Matavi did nothing either. He stood as if hypnotised. The executioner casually brought his rifle to bear as if he were shooting paper-covered targets on the rifle range. His finger tightened on the trigger. The weapon jumped in his hands as a long burst of fire spat from the barrel, cutting down first Matavi and then Kumalo. They were dead before they hit the ground, their vital organs ripped to shreds. Saul continued to pour shots into the bodies which jumped and wriggled under the concussion.

A pandemonium of terrified screams and shouts arose from the children. Some remained where they were, others stood up and looked around them in bewilderment, ignoring the flying bullets. Some ran downhill towards their saviours, while others ran uphill to get away.

'Lay down! Lay down!', yelled Ndhlela, but few took any notice.

Abraham Hale appeared as if from nowhere. His hands were roped behind his back and he ran down the slope. Saul regarded his unexpected appearance with astonishment.

'Get down', he shouted.

'Don't shoot', sobbed Abraham, stumbling and tripping on loose stones and clumps of grass. 'For God's sake don't taint your hands with more blood.'

Saul lowered his weapon and stood looking at the missionary and the scattering captives. Perhaps there had only been two terrorists . . . and they were both accounted for.

His eyes were on Abraham, so he didn't notice the other armed men who appeared ready for battle.

Jon screamed for him to take cover and change his magazine, but this failed to register. A burst of fire that cut through the body of Abraham and threw him face down like a rag doll brought him back to reality. He heard bullets whining against the rocks at his feet. He threw himself flat in a twisting roll, changing his magazine almost in mid-air. He hit the ground and the rattle of automatic fire crashed around him as his stick opened fire.

A terrorist yanked a young boy of about ten from the grass to use as a human shield. Before he could complete his purpose, a crimson patch appeared on his uniform as the heavy impact of a bullet kicked him to the ground. Saul watched fascinated as he dropped the lad and clutched his chest with both hands. Blood spurted through his fingers.

The remaining two took advantage of the diversion created by their companion being shot. One broke left, and the other right and they escaped up the hill, throwing away their weapons as they scrambled for safety.

Saul struggled to his feet.

'You all right?' asked Jim Wilkie anxiously.

Saul grinned crookedly. 'Never felt better.'

'You take the bastard on the left', Jake muttered through closed lips. 'The one on the right is mine.'

Without waiting for Saul to answer, he ran after his quarry, his rifle held out as if it had a fixed bayonet. The man tried to get away, but the more he tried to run the less his legs obeyed him. Jake was within ten metres when the man raised his fist in a throwing motion.

'Grenade!' yelled Saul.

Jake fired a long scything burst from the shoulder.

A bullet happened to slice through a tendon in the terrorist's wrist, springing open his hand. The grenade fell from his nerveless fingers and dropped at his feet. He gripped his shattered wrist and tried to kick the grenade away.

'I can't die . . . ' he screamed.

The delay on the fuse expired and the grenade exploded, throwing him a metre into the air along with a host of debris. The body hit the ground, mutilated and lifeless.

The blast caught Jake and slapped him back onto the ground and he passed out.

Saul turned his attention to the man escaping to the left. He was scrambling frantically to reach the safety of the summit. He seemed to have a charmed life as bullets spattered around him, missing him by hair-breadths. He reached the top and for a brief moment the top of his body was silhouetted against the sky.

'This time I'll get you', murmured Saul.

His rifle recoiled and the terrorist threw up his arms and fell backwards.

Silence settled over the battlefield and Saul looked around anxiously. Jon was there and so was Jim. They both seemed okay . He saw a movement to his left and Ndhlela emerged from behind the tree where he had taken cover.

Saul was drained of strength and his knees were wobbling as delayed-action shock set in.

'It's all over, Ndhlela. It's all over', he sighed.

They walked to where Jake lay unconscious Saul checked him for injuries, but except for scratches and lacerations caused by rock splinters — and a lump the size of a hen's egg on his head — he seemed okay. His pulse thumped steadily under the tips of Saul's fingers. He would need a casevac.

Saul looked at the men awaiting his orders.

'Round up the kids', he said tiredly. 'We have a long way to go. And while you are about it, check to make sure that all the bad guys are dead.'

From all over the hill the hesitant figures of children appeared from cover, chattering excitedly as they made their way towards their rescuers.

32

Ndhlela used his foot to turn over the body of the man killed by the grenade. He was certainly dead. His head had been split like a melon and chunks of brain lay spattered on the ground.

Suddenly he saw a movement at the top of the hill. It was the terrorist with the charmed life and he was back on his hands and knees trying to drag himself over the summit. He realised that Ndhlela had noticed him and clawed at the ground in a desperate effort to inch himself to safety.

Ndhlela started after him, rifle cradled in his arms. The guerrilla knew he could not escape. It was too late. He dragged himself into a position where he was half sitting. He was quaking with fear as he watched his pursuer inexorably close the distance.

He cupped his hand to his mouth and shouted, panic apparent in his voice.

'I surrender. I am a soldier. Don't shoot me. I am your prisoner. I have rights under the Geneva Convention. Don't kill me . . .'

His voice trailed off. Surely it couldn't be? That walk. He would recognise it anywhere. He felt relief as recognition came.

'Father! Father! It's me — Kephas — your son.'

Ndhlela stopped several paces away. He held his rifle loosely at the trail as his eyes searched the face of the wounded man. His eyes narrowed in disbelief as realisation struck him. But his face did not soften.

'So my son is a terrorist — a murderer?' he said heavily.

'I am not a murderer. I am a freedom fighter. I have been fighting to overthrow the white imperialist oppressors. Help me. Help your son.' Kephas looked at his father with wide eyes, searching for some small sign of compassion, but there was none there.

'Father, I am wounded and bleeding. Help me.'

Ndhlela turned and looked around the hill at the bodies sprawled in death. He saw Saul tending to Jake's injuries. No one had noticed the drama being played out at the top of the hill — not even the excited children.

He looked back at his son. 'You say you have been fighting to overthrow the white imperialist oppressors. I understand that Africans want to be ruled by Africans one day, but I think this can be achieved by peaceful means. But why did you murder the white missionary Hale and his wife? Were they oppressors? Why was it necessary to violate and murder the Hale woman? Like Reverend Hale she had spent most of her life working for the upliftment of oppressed Africans? You know that as much as I do. Was it for this to happen that I sired you ?'

'You don't understand', said Kephas, trying to convince his father. 'They were white and the whites — all of them just by being here — have oppressed us. They introduced a religion alien to our culture — Christianity — to make us meek while they stole our land. So they have to die. If we don't fight the white men and drive them from the country we will never be free.'

He lapsed into silence and waited for his father to understand and help him. He had to help him. No matter what he had done, no matter what his father believed, a father couldn't reject his own flesh and blood.

He felt a chill as he saw the cold and pitiless look on Ndhlela's face. There were contempt and revulsion written there. And horror that the fruit of his loins had turned into a bloody murderer.

'Father, just let me escape. No one will know. They will hang me if you take me in. Do you understand that, the white men will hang me? Can you allow that to happen to your own son?' Sweat beaded his brow as the pain of his wounds made him breathless and sent stabbing pains deep into his guts.

Ndhlela looked at Kephas anew as if he were a stranger. Surely such a man couldn't be his son? He wondered what his late wife, Kephas' mother would have said. He searched Kephas' face for signs of the son he had been thinking of for so long during his absence. The boy he had nurtured so much hope for. But it was true what he had said, he could not allow them to hang his son. Kephas was still his son.

He slowly brought up the barrel of his rifle and pointed it at Kephas' chest. He hooked his finger around the trigger and looked down the sights. His face was wooden.

'You are wrong . . . I have no son . . . my son is dead . . . he ran away many years ago', he whispered.

Kephas look at him disbelievingly. He held up his hands to shield himself from the bullets and hysterically screamed for mercy — a mercy so many of his victims had futilely begged him for.

'You cannot kill your own . . . oh, now you've . . .'

A short burst of fire punched a line of red holes in his chest.

His face showed hurt astonishment. He tried to speak, but as he opened his mouth blood welled up his throat and spilled through his lips. He toppled slowly over and convulsed.

Ndhlela glanced mutely at his dead son, then at his rifle. It dropped from his fingers and clattered to the ground. He held out his hands in front of his face and stared at them in disbelief. What had he done? With a muffled sob he threw himself on Kephas and hugged him close. He kissed the bloodied face as if he were trying to bring back the spark of life. The dead eyes stared at him accusingly. He raised his head and cried out in anguish to the darkening skies for his son to be brought back.

He looked up to see Saul with wet eyes standing over him. His strong arms separated him gently from his dead son and led him away. They might have been men of different colour, but no brothers could have been closer. Explanations were unnecessary. Saul knew that Ndhlela had been through an experience more terrible than death itself.

A clap of thunder resounded as a bolt of lightning struck a tree at the foot of the kopje. It was so close that they ducked in fright and the concussion rang in their ears. The tree caught fire and burned through, glowing red as the intense searing heat dried its sap and turned it into charcoal. It toppled to the ground in a cloud of twigs, leaves, dust, glowing embers and sparks.

The silence was sudden and absolute.

A strong wind sprung up seemingly from nowhere and miniature whirlwinds vacuumed up the dust and leaves at their feet. A glistening raindrop exploded on the ground. More followed. Then the heavens opened. The rain fell in a drenching intensity, washing away the scars of ricocheting bullets and diluting the spilled blood.

*   *   *

A small wizened woman sat in her hut in the hills and peered into the dense blue smoke of the crackling wood fire. A group of men bearing gifts sat in fascinated silence as she stared at the swirling smoke, seeing things that no ordinary being could see.

She cackled softly. Her virgin attendant quietly signalled to the deputation that they should leave the gifts they had brought.

The spirit of the Rain Goddess had got its sacrifice of blood and was satisfied. The rain had been released from the heavens.

*   *   *

There were more than five hundred people at the funeral of Abraham and Mary Hale — four hundred were black tribesmen from Senga. They had come by car, bus, on foot and by bicycle from afar to pay their last respects to the missionaries who had dedicated their lives to them. They watched in sombre silence as two plain, unostentatious wooden coffins were lowered simultaneously into the double grave.

Dawn, baby Joseph clutched tightly in her arms, stood with Saul's arm around her in comfort. Since the attack she could not bear to let her son out of her sight.

Ndhlela stood next to Saul, head bowed.

The shovelfuls of earth rattled on the lids of the coffins.

Saul whispered softly, his voice quiet and washed with emotion. 'Why, Ndhlela? Why did it have to happen?'

Ndhlela shook his head and struggled to find the right words. '*Nkosi*, I don't know. My son and his followers claimed they were bringing freedom to the people. But is it freedom to bring the wholesale of innocents to the land? Is it freedom when children are stolen from their parents to aid a political cause? Is it freedom when men are killed only because their skins are white? Is it freedom when blacks are killed because they disagree with their political leaders? Are all men mad? We must respect each other and not hate. The killing must ultimately end and when it does we must live together in peace. But until that happens, the killing will go on.'

They left the grave side together — two men, a woman and her baby.

Baby Joseph gurgled happily. He had come closer to death than he would ever know, but he was too young to know — too young to know that men found it hard to live together in peace.

256